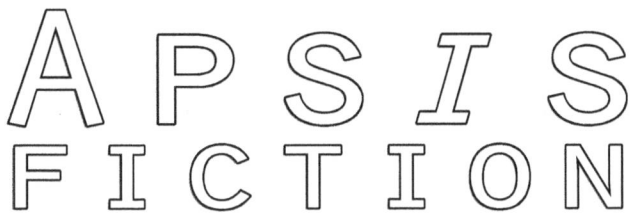

APSIS FICTION

The Semi-Annual Anthology of Goldeen Ogawa

Volume 5, Issue 1 • Perihelion 2017

CONTENTS

I0526187

author • *illustrator* • *editor* • *book designer*

GOLDEEN OGAWA

a HELIOPAUSE PRODUCTION

Apsis Fiction: The Semi-Annual Anthology of Goldeen Ogawa
Volume No. 5, Issue 1, Whole No. 8 (Perihelion 2017).
Published semi-annually by Heliopause Productions.

FICTION/Science Fiction/Short Stories

FICTION/Fantasy/General

First Edition 2017

ISBN: 978-1-945781-03-2

STATE OF THE ORBIT

THOUGH I AM RESTRICTED by circumstance when it comes to assembling these collections, I do try to keep to at least a vague theme for every volume. In this case, one could say the theme is trees. Both the Bouragner Felpz novella *The Wolves of Riddlemoor* and the *Driving Arcana* episode "The Earth it Weeps" feature trees and their attendant spirits prominently. I have also included as a primer for "The Earth it Weeps" the short story "Abandon All ____" which though written as a standalone, is tied to *Arcana* through its characters. I am happy to say, after dutifully examining them, that they deal with different aspects of treeness, and complement each other without feeling repetitious.

With this in mind, this year's perihelion *Professor Odd* episode is (suitably enough) the odd one out. It deals less with trees, and more with the delicate relationship between celebrities and their fans. Also aliens. Still, it is outnumbered three to one, and so even though it is the lead story, I have chosen for the cover a painting that is more evocative of the themes of *Riddlemoor* and "The Earth it Weeps."

"Death in the Forest" is a large watercolor that I painted with little thought to the events of *Riddlemoor* yet illustrates one of its core concepts well. Readers would be well advised to take another look at the cover after they finish *The Wolves of Riddlemoor*.

Happy Perihelion (that is January 4th, 2017), and happy reading, wherever and whenever you are.

—GOLDEEN OGAWA
Oregon
December 2016

The tenth Professor Odd *story, "The Thousand Songs" follows "Star Walkers"* (Aphelion 2016) *and is the fourth episode in* Professor Odd: Season Two. *Though all the* Odd *stories can be read individually, this one offers an exceptionally good entry point for new readers. Previous episodes are available as singles from* Heliopause, *and an omnibus volume of* Season One *will be coming soon. Originally written in the Spring of 2014, "The Thousand Songs" will be followed by "Davebot," coming in* Apsis Fiction's Aphelion 2017 *issue.*

THE THOUSAND SONGS

Prologue

IT ALL BEGAN when Professor Odd came storming into the Oddity, up the stairs and past the cockpit, to stand at the head of the table. Alister and Elo had carved spaces out of the perpetual clutter on it in order to eat breakfast there, and they regarded her curiously as she raised her fist triumphantly into the air and declared:

"I *got* them!"

Alister and Elo stared at her. She was wearing her most colorful wig to date: a rainbow of orange and pink with streaks of sky blue. It should have clashed horribly with the rest of her clothes, but the royal blue trousers seemed to complement it, and her shirt, Alister noticed, was a matching light blue with pink buttons. He couldn't see much of it, however, because she was wearing a shiny orange coat over it. The only thing that didn't fit was the lime green scarf, but this was tucked mostly under her collar—leaving the tentacle that sprouted from the base of her skull to coil excitedly over one shoulder.

Alister swallowed a mouthful of porridge and asked: "Got what?"

"*Tickets!*" Professor Odd said, grinning hugely, her jaguar eyes gleaming.

"Tickets . . . for what?" Elo prodded, cautiously.

"The *show*, of course," said Professor Odd, doing a giggling dance at the head of the table. "You'll like it, I promise!"

"That's what you said about that planet with the Italian aliens," Alister pointed out. "And the beach with dinosaurs. And the nebula."

Professor Odd deflated a little. "Didn't you like them?" she asked, concerned.

"Well, yes," Alister admitted. "But the first time, we were attacked by robots from outer space. The second time, we got plopped in the middle of a political *and* natural disaster, and when we went to look at the nebula the spaceship we were on turned out to be lost in the wrong universe, and you were nearly killed!"

Professor Odd made a sound like *"Pffft,"* and flapped her hands at him. "That wasn't *on purpose,*" she insisted. "Those things *happen.* Sometimes. Not always. And it *shouldn't* happen this time. This world is quite stable—I made sure of it. And I've got *friends* there. And you won't have to pretend to be my guide dog," she added to Elo. "It's a borderline unconventional world, and they've seen stranger stuff in the last few years. Dave can come too, if he doesn't mind being mistaken for a robot, as usual."

"WHY WOULD I WISH TO GO, THEN?" Dave asked from the catwalk above them. Looking up, Alister saw him lounging on the railing, three bright green, yellow-tipped octopus arms wound securely around the beam. There was a flash of orange and gold as his single, huge eye blinked down at them. Tucked in amongst the fine, anemone-like filaments that covered his underside was a square gray box with some cables and a speaker. This was Dave's slime-to-audio translator, which he had to carry everywhere because his native language consisted of chemical changes in the psychoactive slime he oozed from every pore. It was a much more efficient way of communicating, especially if you lived in a liquid environment (which Dave preferred), but short of clamping himself physically over someone's head, the mechanical translator was the only way for Dave to "speak." It made him sound like an angry computer, and combined with the fact that his panvironment suit resembled a barrel with gears and a glass dome, decked with sensors, anti-grav plates, and flashing lights, it was understandable that people multiversally mistook him for a robot.

Since Dave was *actually* a bright green creature roughly the size and shape of a pie pan with ten arms, one large eye, countless underbelly tentacles and no recognizable brain, the misconception was something of a sore point with him.

"*Because,*" Professor Odd answered, her grin growing, if possible, even wider. "It's a *Princess Die* concert! She's got a new album out, and everything. It's going to be *marvelous!*"

"I'm sorry," said Alister, shaking his head a little. "*Who?*"

"Princess Die," said Professor Odd. "Dee, ai, eee, like 'to die.' But she hasn't yet, which is good, because it means we can go watch her perform. Her shows are great fun, *and . . .* " here Professor Odd actually clapped her hands to her cheeks and bounced up and down, her voice becoming an impossibly high squeal. " *. . . Extrascape* is opening for her! They've come back, just for this tour! You *have* to see them!"

Alister and Elo blinked at each other in confusion.

"You're certainly excited," the wolf said. "Are they very special then?"

Professor Odd dropped her hands like they had suddenly turned to lead bricks. "Didn't I *tell* you about Extrascape? The mad god? The thousand songs?"

Very slowly, her canine face blank, Elo shook her head.

Professor Odd let out a sound like "*Gh-huh!*" and flopped into the nearest chair. This brought the upper half of her figure in front of one of the Oddity's windows, which looked out on the void between universes, and gave her a surreal, multihued backdrop. She looked almost like a colorful tropical fish against the night beyond.

Heaving a sigh she kicked her feet up onto the table, and knitting her fingers together, she said, "Well, we do have time. I suppose I should tell you about them. Care to listen, Dave? You might find this rather interesting!"

There was some squelching, and then the reply came:

"I HAVE SATISFACTORY AUDIO RECEPTION FROM MY CURRENT LOCATION, THANK YOU."

Professor Odd shrugged.

"Right then," she said. "Since you haven't even heard of Princess Die—she must have gone by a different name in your world, Alister—I'd better start a little before the beginning and tell you about her. Because she's very important. Right. So you know how some performing artists won't use their real names? She's one of those. Only Princess Die has sort of *become* her real name, and that's what I've always called her. I first heard her music, my, my . . . a long time ago now, and quite by accident. That doesn't really matter though. What matters is that I liked her songs so much that I took the Oddity and snuck in to one of her concerts. I didn't know it then, but that concert was rather a big deal: she'd been having problems, and her managers were trying to give her one of those 'reboots' they do with artists. As if you could fix them by turning them off and on again, like a computer." Professor Odd snorted disdainfully. "Anyway, it was a big to-do at a famous club in a large city—but because one of Princess Die's trademarks was her wild costumes, most of the attendees were *also* dressed a little . . . well . . . a little *oddly*. So for once I fit right in without trying."

Professor Odd grinned in an inward sort of way, clearly relishing the memory. "I remember it was hot, and stuffy, and they'd set up a laser light show to go along with the music. It *should* have been tacky and annoying, but combined with everything else—with the music and the costumes and the audience all clapping and cheering . . . well, it was really quite marvelous. And then, right in the middle of it all—just as she was getting to the end of one of her best songs—she vanished. Poof. Gone. There was a puff of smoke and everything, and all the lights went out."

Alister blinked. "You mean, she disappeared as part of her act?"

"*Noooooo . . .*" said Professor Odd, her eyes wide and earnest. "Not at *all* part of her act! I mean, people thought it was for about five minutes, but then they got bored and started asking questions. Someone turned on the house lights, and her security—big people in black clothes—went up on stage and started looking around, and her dancers all sort of shuffled off to the side and stood there, looking confused and helpless. And they couldn't find her *anywhere*."

"And what did *you* do?" Elo asked.

Professor Odd grinned at them. "What do you *think* I did?"

Part One

"I RAN AS FAST AS I COULD for the Oddity, of course. Had to wrestle my way through the crowd and into the hallway. Good thing I'd left the portal so close, really. Everyone was confused and some people were panicking. Once I got back, I immediately ran a sweep for other transdimensional activity. It was a bit of a long shot, since this universe was fairly conventional back then, but it paid off! I'd barely started the sweep when the Oddity went agog with lights: she'd found a *rift*. A major rift in the fabric of the universe. Dangerous things, they are, but this one had been stitched shut again almost immediately, so there had been no excess damage.

"I disconnected the Oddity and did a search of nearby universes for one containing an alien—er, that is, a person from a different universe. And not only did I find one . . . I found one containing *multiple* aliens, all from *different universes* from *each other*. There was this little island where a whole bunch of people from different universes were all crowded together. Tightly. It looked suspicious even from that distance, and when I brought the Oddity in closer I saw that universe was *riddled* with stitched rifts.

"I'd like to say I took a break at this point and examined the situation more closely, but you have to understand that I was younger then—this was before I even met Elo!—and I was still getting to know the Oddity. So I simply opened the door nearest to where Princess Die was and went running out, not knowing what I would find on the other side.

"I came through into a place that felt like a *furnace*. I was on this narrow metal walkway with thin, cable railings, and the floor was a grate through which I could see more walkways crisscrossing beneath me, down and down, until they were lost in a haze of steam. The whole place was monstrously hot, and the lights were all orange or red. It looked a little like being suspended over the mouth of a volcano, but not *that* hot—obviously.

"Anyway, the whole thing was roughly tube-shaped, with little doors set at intervals along the wall, and a big column up the center that looked like a track for some sort of elevator car. I turned right around again and found that the Oddity had used one of those doors as an anchor. The doors on either side were locked, so I banged on both, trying to get a response. There was none from either, and I was just considering how I would go about picking the lock when the elevator car turned up, hissing to a stop on my level, and a couple people got out.

"I say they were people, but that doesn't mean they were *human*, you understand. These folks looked a bit more like praying mantises . . . with thin, sticky legs and fat abdomens. They also had a third set of appendages behind their shoulders that sort of zigzagged into these huge, single-digit pincers. Like, if you hold your hand up so it's level with your shoulder and bend it down, and pretend that your fingers are fused together and reach *back* down to your elbow—that's sort of what these arms looked like. I think they were what put me in mind of praying mantises, really, because they were the same shape as a mantis claw.

"They were wearing dark uniforms and helmets, so I couldn't see their faces, and each one carried a set of chains with clasps on the end, like collars. I decided I didn't want them to see me, so I hurried along the catwalk to a little crevice between some pipes and squeezed in between them. From there I heard the mantis people walk over to one of the doors I'd been banging on—*clickity-clack*, just like giant insects—and they opened the door, which creaked. One of them went inside, and I heard the collars snap onto something, and then there was more clicking as they walked back to the elevator, and when I leaned around to look I saw they were leading someone between them. Someone tall and slender with long, lavender hair, who they'd apparently dressed in a white paper slip—like a stiff hospital gown.

"It was Princess Die, of course, but she didn't look like herself. Not the lavender hair, mind you—that was the same as when I'd last seen her—but she walked kind of blindly, and when she had to turn onto the catwalk to the elevator it was this sharp right-angle, not natural. It was like something else was making her move.

"I knew I couldn't just barge in and rescue her—the mantis people were bigger than me, and besides, they had extra collars. I had my sword-cane with me, but I also didn't want to *hurt* anyone. Not unless I had to. So I waited until they were safely in the elevator, and then I skipped back to the Oddity and brought up a schematic of the whole place—which was what I should have done in the first place.

"It turned out the tube where I'd come through was just one of a dozen towers, all connected at their base by a network of underground tunnels, which converged in the form of a giant, underground ring consisting of a lot of rooms with electrical generators, a structure that looked like a sort of hospital, and one big, spherical room with a single chair in the middle. All this was under an arena of sorts, with a huge circular grandstand and *something* suspended over it. I say *something* because even the Oddity couldn't make out what it was, and at the time I was more interested in the spherical room, because that was where they'd taken Princess Die.

"Now, I wish I could tell you I'd done something *clever*, like figured out how she was likely to exit that room, and then put the Oddity on standby so that the portal would activate the moment she passed through . . . but this was a long time ago, and I didn't know the Oddity so well back then. So I opened the door onto a ventilation duct—just big enough for me to peer through—and listened in on what was happening.

"The mantis people had sat her in a chair like the kind you find at the dentist's. It was on a hydraulic lift and held Princess Die at about head height. From my vantage point I could see her collar, which was a thin strip of silver metal with little bulbs of glass on either side. These were blinking, slowly, with purple light. A cord led out from the back of the collar, trailing over the chair to a plug in the floor. Over to one side, in a little cube of glass, was a mantis person dressed like a medical technician: all stiff, white folds. They were also wearing a helmet with a visor, but from what I could see their face looked surprisingly humanoid—only gray-blue, not pink-brown. They were typing away with their stick-like hands, with their shoulder arms folded tightly at their sides.

"Then, all at once, a jumble of mechanized arms descended from the ceiling and spread out over Princess Die. There was a whirring, and green lasers shot from the tips. These passed back and forth over her body, side-to-side, like the toner head of an inkjet printer, and with each swipe her clothes changed. Line by line, the outfit she'd been wearing in the club was erased, and behind it was printed a sheer, black garment like a bathing suit, with big, triangular mirrors decorating the left shoulder.

"It reminded me very much of an outfit she'd worn in one of her early videos, right around the time she became really famous. It was puzzling, but what was even more distressing was that she didn't seem to be restrained in any way—except for the collar. I kept trying to get her attention—I knew I was in her line of sight, because I could see her eyes—but she just stared past me at the ceiling.

"After a while, when the lasers finished printing her new clothes, the chair changed shape so she was in an upright sitting position, then descended until her feet touched the ground. Then more arms appeared out of hidden holes in the floor and printed shoes—really amazing shoes, like crystal, with immensely tall heels—onto her feet. More lasers restyled her hair, and some specialized arms sprayed her face with a fine powder that formed into eye shadow and mascara and lipstick. They'd changed her hair color to turquoise, like it had been in the video, with matching lipstick and warm, red eye shadow. Finally the tech came over and unplugged her collar, and Princess Die sat up and looked around.

"I kept hoping she'd panic, or show some sign that she realized what was happening to her, but she didn't. She looked right at the mantis person's humanoid-but-not-human face and didn't react at all. She let them help her out of the chair, and followed them out of the room.

"As soon as they were gone I recalibrated the Oddity's door to let into the little cubicle. I wanted to see if I could figure out what they'd done to her, but the controls were labeled in a language I didn't recognize. It didn't look like mind control, though, so I assumed that must have something to do with the collar she was wearing. Then I looked out into the room, and up at the ceiling—and finally saw what Princess Die had been staring at the whole time.

"Directly above the chair where Princess Die had lain there was a video screen, and on it was a series of images depicting various musicians performing in front of huge, cheering crowds. I couldn't make sense of it, which bothered me. Now it's so obvious I don't understand why I didn't see the reason, but that's experience for you.

"You'll laugh, but this was when I began to get *really* curious about what was going on. Before, I just wanted to get my favorite musician back. Now I wanted to *understand* what was happening. Because, just from looking at the whole setup the mantis people had built, and the way they all seemed to be going about their business like this was something they did *every day*, it was obvious that Princess Die was not the first person they'd kidnapped . . . and she wouldn't be the last, either, if I didn't do something about it.

"I fetched a multiversal translator from the Oddity, and while it was working on the controls inside the cubicle I carefully locked all the doors, so I wouldn't be interrupted. I had that much sense, at least. I remember everything was very clean and smooth and well maintained, and there were lots of little cameras, now I looked, which I belatedly went around and switched off.

"By the time I'd finished, so was the translator, and when I went back into the cubicle I found that the controls mostly had to do with the lasers that disintegrated and reintegrated Die's clothes. I left them alone, and went for the little computer terminal that had access to the building's mainframe. From there I was able, with some careful fiddling, to gain access to the network of cameras that fairly blanketed the place. And what I found . . . well . . . it wasn't at all *nice*.

"The tubular silos where Die had originally been kept were only about half full . . . but they were filled with *people*. And not just any people. *Multiples* of the same person from different universes! Some of them I didn't recognize, but a few names I did. There were two David Joneses and *four* George O'Dowds *and* a Robyn Fenty and almost a dozen Rose Seberts. Which, by the way, are all notable musicians and singers—though you might not know them by those names. Going through the list, I found enough of them that I guessed the rest were probably kidnapped musicians as well.

"And then I found a directory labeled *'Discontinued Series.'* That's right, *'Discontinued Series,'* like these people were a toy or motor car that the company had stopped producing. And those names . . . *those* names gave me pause.

"The first on the list was *Amy Jade Winehouse*. Then there was Roger Barrett, Dana Haughton, Kurt Donald Kobain, and a long list of others. Farrokh Bulsara, who is better known in most of his universes as *Freddie Mercury*, was about halfway down. And then, right at the bottom, were three names very close together, and then one more. These were Janis Lyn Joplin, James Marshall Hendrix, Alan Christie Wilson, and finally Lewis Brian Hopkins Jones. Which won't mean anything to you unless you are familiar with popular North American musicians of the third quarter of the twentieth century A.D. Which, as it happened, I *was*.

"It made me forget almost entirely about Princess Die. Because the first thing I can tell you about all the people listed under *'Discontinued Series'* is that they were, in the vast majority of their universes, *dead*. In the case of Joplin, Hendrix, Wilson and Jones, they had died over the course of about a year relative to each other. They were all twenty-seven, too, which doesn't mean anything, really, except that some people seem to think it does. Which it *did*, but not what they thought.

"It *meant* something *was* killing these people. Maybe it looked like drugs or disease or even murder to the natives of their home universes, but I was convinced all their deaths were linked to whatever was going on here, in this distant world.

"Then my line of reasoning jumped forward, and I remembered universes where certain musicians died earlier, or later, or not at all. And I realized that wasn't just because of randomness and differences between worldtracks—it was because not all of those people had been kidnapped yet! And, what was perhaps worst, they now had my favorite musician of them all.

"It made me sick. It made me *furious*. But under all that, I still wondered *why?* To run a transuniversal kidnapping operation would require a *huge* amount of energy and resources. So these mantis folk—or whoever was in charge—*must* have a good reason.

"And that's when I went back to the blueprints of the building and figured out what it was. It only took a little bit of turning about, and then the image was, like I mentioned before, *obvious.*

"It was a *stadium.* The kind with a grandstand all the way around, and we were under the ground beneath it, and there were elevator shafts leading up and down, and the silos were linked by underground rail lines. Above it ... well, the schematics didn't show anything above the grandstands, but there was an illustration for the thing that had confused the Oddity.

"It was as if two giant arches had been built over the stadium, so they crossed in the center, and from these arches hung a net that covered the center of the stadium. From the junction of the arches hung a kind of ... well ... I suppose you could call it a *gun.* It was only a gun in that it shot things, however. I don't think it was ever meant to be a weapon. I recognized lasers, and some things that looked like proton accelerators but probably weren't. They were meant for shooting very small, very dense particles, I could tell that much.

"This whole contraption was pointed down at the net, which looked a little odd from the blueprints, but without seeing it in person I couldn't tell what it was.

"It was around then I began hearing things—pounding feet outside the door, clicking voices—and decided it was time to move on. I hopped back into the Oddity, disconnected, and reconnected at an out-of-the-way maintenance hatch at the base of the grandstand.

"I stepped out and got hit by the noise. That's what it felt like, anyway. Roars and cheers and a high buzzing sound. Underneath all that was a steady, heavy beat of a bass that vibrated the air and the concrete walls around me, and through it all were faint wisps of music, but I could barely make them out.

"Looking around, I found I was in a small tunnel that led under a block of seats and out onto the field—which was built up with a stage on lots of stilts with lights and fog machines underneath. Behind me was a sort of thoroughfare, but access was blocked by a fence made of silver wire, which suited me just fine. I went the other way, toward the stage, and climbed up next to one of the lights—a big thing, wider than my arms could reach—and looked around.

"I could barely see the roaring crowd, but from the few I glimpsed, peeking over a high parapet and far in the distance, up near the canopy, they looked more human than anyone else I'd seen in the world, save Princess Die herself. They were all dressed in exciting outfits with lots of face paint, but they were unmistakably *human.*

"This really confused me for a moment, but then I caught a flicker—almost unnoticeable unless you looked closely—and suddenly all the little wrong things about the crowd stood out glaringly. The fact that *all* the members that I could see were more or less the same ideal shape. At the real concert I had seen fat people, thin people, tall people, short people, old, young, and all sorts of combinations. *These* people were more or less the same size and shape, with only minimal effort given to making them appear male or female, and all had a plasticky agelessness that was a little creepy. And—and this was something that had struck me as wrong from the very beginning—the crowd had a strange look to it like there were patches of more green or blue or black. Not like blocks of color, you understand, just like a group of people who were wearing *mostly* black—or green or blue. And I realized the reason I was noticing these collections was because they were arranged in a perfect, repeating *pattern.* Like the pattern on a carpet or a tablecloth. That is to say, the *crowd* was made up of maybe fifty or so unique individuals, which had just been copied until they filled the stadium. Combined with the flicker I'd seen earlier, this made me realize they weren't real people at all, and I looked around for something that might be projecting the image.

"That's when I looked up and saw the gun for the first time in person. It looked a lot smaller than on the blueprint, being suspended hundreds of feet in the air, and it was further hidden by the colored lasers that were shooting down onto the stage, but I guessed that was where they'd put the projectors.

"Projectors to create the visual illusion of a packed house of excited fans, with speakers hidden in the grandstand to make the cheering, the entire thing was . . .

"Well, it was a *show*. But not a show for any audience. There *was no* audience.

"Then I caught movement under the stage, and a trapdoor opened, and the noise from the stands tripled as Princess Die was raised into view.

"She was wearing the same outfit I'd seen them print onto her, a headset microphone, and the silver collar with flashing purple bulbs. She swelled up at the sight of the crowd, coming alive for the first time, and I saw her inhale deeply.

"That's when I realized the whole thing was back to front. The fake audience was the show *for her. She* was its audience. Which made no sense at all. Unless there was *another* audience. A hidden audience. Something watching her being watched. So why did they need the fake audience in the first place? For the same reason they needed the giant stadium and the powerful sound system and the lights and the lasers and the smoke. To make her *feel* like it really was a stage, so she would give a real performance.

"It's a well known fact that performers—actors, singers, musicians, anyone who gets up on a stage to entertain people, really—draw energy from their audience. All that enthusiasm pouring out from people buoys them up, makes them give bigger, better performances. *That's* what the audience was for. I just didn't know what *Princess Die's* performance was for . . .

"I didn't have time to think all this, in order, just then. It sort of happened at the back of my head while I was watching Princess Die look around, square her shoulders, and march down the stage to where a grand piano, covered in mirrors, had been set up. As she went she began to speak, welcoming the audience (which wasn't actually there) and telling them how excited she was to sing for them.

"It was the exact same speech she'd given at the beginning of her last performance . . . back in the club . . . the one she had been abducted in the middle of.

"It was—and you know I don't use this term lightly—one of the *oddest* things I'd ever seen. I stood there, holding onto the side of the light, and just stared as she threw a leg over the piano bench, sat down, and began to play.

"She played quite well. You'd never have guessed she had been abducted, drugged, and brainwashed. The song she played was one of her ballads, all slow and throaty. Not my favorite, but she performed it well. I had to tear my eyes away from her to look up, though, because something was happening with the gun hanging above her.

"I really didn't like the look of it. I didn't like that I couldn't tell what some of the barrels were for, and I didn't like how it was pointed directly at the stage. I also didn't like how the biggest barrel, the one ringed by lasers, was beginning to belch a kind of steam. I say a *kind* of steam, because it *kind* of looked like steam, but wasn't. It was too . . . too *stringy*. And it fell in waves that stretched and formed into gossamer fine strands, like spider-webs floating on wind.

"These strands slowly sank, until they pillowed on the net below the gun, and collected there, growing denser and denser. Their color kept changing, from purple to blue and then black and back to purple again. At first I thought it was the lights making them change. I was wrong, but I didn't find out until later.

"Staring upward, I finally noticed the little screen attached to the side of the gun. It had a digital readout that said 'Sac-rifice of Song' in the native's language, and under that the nu-meral '1', followed by a slash, then another '1', a comma, and three '0's. One out of one thousand . . . somethings. Songs, I guessed, when Princess Die finished her first song and moved on to the next. Then the first numeral flickered, and became a two. Two out of one thousand. I wondered what would happen when she reached a thousand songs . . . assuming she could even perform that many in one sitting. Unless it didn't have to be in one sit-ting.

"I decided I didn't want to wait around to find out. The Odd-ity was nearby, and so was Princess Die. I had my trusty sword-cane, and I couldn't see any mantis people. So I hopped down off the huge light, climbed up onto the stage, and ran across it toward the woman sitting at the piano.

"I made it . . . *oooh,* about halfway, before a few guards showed up. Several, actually. They came swarming over the edge of the stage, all dressed in black, with their third appendages snapping like wings.

"Princess Die didn't seem to notice them. She noticed me, because I managed to reach her and take hold of her collar by one purple bulb. It zapped me. As I swore and shook my hand she stood up, turned around and glared at me. It's funny to think of it now, but she was absolutely *furious*.

"'*Excuse me,*' she said. 'This is very *rude* of you!'

"I'd never had to apologize to the person I was rescuing before. It struck me dumb. Also, I was standing *right next* to Princess Die, of all people, and my heart was pounding from nerves. I couldn't think what to say, and I was so embarrassed I just cackled, and said the first thing that came into my head:

"'You've got to get the collar off. That's what's keeping you from remembering—I think!'

"She just stared at me, her eyes wide. I could really see the makeup around them. From a distance it all blended into her face and made her look like some supernatural creature, but up close she was just a woman with a lot of paint on. It made her even more amazing, in a way. She was suddenly, urgently *real* in a way that helped calm my nerves a bit. Princess Die was an awful lot of things to me, but at that moment she was mainly a human being, in over her head in trouble, and she needed my help. Whether she knew it or not.

"'Come *on*,' I said, reaching for her arm. 'I'll explain on the way home!'

"But she stood there like a rock, staring at me in disbelief, and the mantis people closed in around us.

"They seemed not to want to touch Princess Die, which bought me a little more time. I leaned in close and whispered to her: 'There is a collar around your neck, you *need* to take it off. Also, there is a *gun* pointed at this stage and I don't like what's coming out of it.'

"This seemed to get through to her. She looked up for the first time, saw the mouth of the largest barrel, now almost entirely obscured by the thick tendrils of purple, blue, and black smoke, then looked back down again and saw the mantis people. I think it was the first time she noticed them. She frowned and wrinkled her nose and said, '*What . . . ?*' and took a step back.

"Then the mantis people were on me, and I was kicking and lashing out with my cane and trying to keep ahold of Princess Die . . . but she was surrounded by mantis people in seconds, and I was forced backward, off the stage.

"Someone caught the end of my cane and nearly unsheathed the sword. I yanked it back, and began looking for an escape. There was no way of getting through the crowd, but I knew there were trapdoors under the stage, if only I could find one. The floor was smooth, but by stamping and listening I was able to find one—still beating back guards as I shuffled around the stage—and by sheer luck there was a little recessed switch in the floor next to it which opened it. Right out from under my feet.

"I dropped, landed *hard* on the concrete beneath the stage, and found myself in a maze of huge pipes. One of them was marked with a pictogram of a mantis person throwing something that looked like crumpled paper into a chute. Garbage disposal, I presumed, so I went over and opened the hatch in the side. It smelled tangy, but not bad. And it was big enough for me to fit. And it led *away* from the huge swarm of mantis people.

"I didn't think. I jumped. Vaulted into the pipe, and began to slide. Then the pipe turned, and I went into free fall. And that, my friends, is when things began to get *interesting.*"

The Oddity made a chirping noise, not unlike a bird, making Alister start. He had become so absorbed in Professor Odd's story that he found he was gripping the table in his anxiety.

"And *then* what?" Elo yelped.

"I just realized something," Professor Odd said, a worried frown growing over her brow.

"What?" asked Alister.

Professor Odd looked up at him. "I'm *hungry.*"

"I think we have some leftover meatloaf," Elo offered, but Professor Odd shook her head.

"*Meatloaf* before Princess Die? No, no, no, that will not *do.* The show is in San Jose this time, we are *not* eating *meatloaf!*" She was rummaging in the pockets of her coat as she spoke, and now produced a small, blue card—it looked a bit like a credit card to Alister, but it was longer and narrower. She tapped it on the table, rubbed it on her sleeve, and squinted at it critically. Then her expression cleared, and she smiled.

"Oh, this is *more* than enough. *Bless* Jill. Do either of you feel like a nice dinner before the concert? There is a *wonderful* little bar where they serve sushi instead of alcohol. It's extra friendly, so you can come as you are."

"Sorry?" said Elo. "What does *extra* friendly mean? Are they so friendly they won't mind a talking dog and a tentacle monster in a barrel?"

Professor Odd waved her hand. "It's native slang. *Extra-ordinaries*, is what they call creatures like . . . well, creatures like *you*. This universe is rather special that way. So . . . would you like to come? Though we could always order out I suppose . . . "

She trailed off, looking woebegone. Elo rolled her eyes. "Of *course* we'll come," she said.

Professor Odd grinned expansively, and five minutes later they were tramping down the steps of the Oddity and out onto a cement walkway beside a wide road. It was evening, and tall buildings were just lighting up against the dim purple sky. There was an immediate sound of car engines and the distant blare of a train, and for one moment it was so bone-achingly ordinary Alister thought he was back in his home universe.

Then something loomed past them that was *not* a car. It had long legs, and moved rather like a horse, and there was a shining horn on its head. It glowed orange and yellow, a strand of light like a flowing tail trailing behind it.

"What was *that*?" Alister gasped.

"What?" said Professor Odd. "Oh, that was a unicorn. They like using the roads around here. Harmless, as long as *you* don't hurt *them*. Akairyu Sushi is this way, come on. I'll tell you the next bit while we walk. It's good, you'll like it."

They had barely gotten five yards, however, before the door to the Oddity (which was currently the chain-link gate to a junkyard's back lot) flew open again and Dave trundled out, sloshing rather as his suit adjusted to the sidewalk.

"I WILL ACCOMPANY YOU," he stated, his antigravity plates giving out a small blast that sent him sailing sedately toward them.

"So you *were* listening," Elo said.

Dave didn't answer, but rolled patiently behind them while Professor Odd led the way down the street, under a raised freeway (cars, unseen, roared by overhead, rendering all conversation pointless). Once they were clear, and had passed onto quieter streets, Professor Odd continued her story.

"Yes, I fell. Plummeted, really. Down the tube. Not pleasant. I lost track of my cane, and heard it clattering away below me. That was distressing. That cane was *important* to me, you understand. But I couldn't very well let myself continue falling. Who *knew* what was at the bottom! Actually, I could guess. Excrement. Biological or otherwise. Either way I didn't want to hit it at speed. I didn't want to hit it *period*. So I stuck out both my legs and my hands . . . which of course just tipped me backward. Luckily the shaft was narrow enough my shoulders caught on the wall and, braced three ways, first I slowed, then skidded, and finally came to a complete stop.

"I hung there, listening to my heart pound, and the clattering of my cane growing more and more distant, until it disappeared into a faint splash.

"Considering the probable velocity of a tumbling cane down a vertical chute I calculated that I was maybe one hundred meters above the liquid into which my cane had fallen—and as I had no idea how deep or of what consistency it was, I judged it best to let myself down slowly, inch by inch.

"This took a long time, as you can imagine, and my back got quite sore and every part of me that touched the sides of the shaft got rather slimy. Luckily it wasn't so slimy as to completely destroy friction, and I was able to chimney down without slipping.

"I did wonder, in passing, how I would get back up. But since I knew the top of that shaft would be watched by mantis people, I figured it was better to go all the way down and then find another way. So. Down it was. Down, down, down, down, *down* . . . until my ankles and hands were as sore as my back, and the slime had seeped through to my knees and shoulders and halfway up my sleeves.

"And then I slid a foot down, and the shaft abruptly vanished, leaving my foot kicking at thin air. It was a close thing, but I managed to keep from falling by bracing my back against one side and my remaining foot against the other. I folded myself in half and peered down around my legs, trying to get a glimpse of what lay below.

"This was almost impossible because it was dark as a cave down there—had been in the shaft as well—but there was the faintest of faint red glows outlining the end of the tunnel, now I concentrated to look. There was also a weak updraft that smelled, thankfully, not of biological decomposition, but of algae and, again, that tangy smell—which by now I thought was some kind of metal cleaner. Lacking my cane, I chose to sacrifice my wig and, plucking it from my head, let it fall. Sooner rather than later, there was a little, wet, *plop*.

"The updraft made it difficult to judge, but I guessed the drop was less than twenty feet. Short enough to jump, and even if the water was only a few feet deep I stood a good chance of making it without any broken bones, assuming I landed properly. So I maneuvered myself around as best I could, and then dropped, feet first, out of the shaft. I tried to keep my body as relaxed as possible, which wasn't very, I'm afraid.

"Fortunately the water was deep. I went in all at once and plunged down . . . *far* down . . . into cold depths that closed in around me and tried to hold me. So I wriggled out of my coat, kicked off my shoes, and swam back up to the surface.

"I came up spitting and gasping and absolutely determined to go back down again and fetch my cane. This took several tries, and by the time I finally succeeded I was cold and shivering and exhausted—and I had lost my coat and shoes. Luckily the water reflected some of the dim, red light, and by it I could just make out a huge mound of something rising up out of the water. So I made for that, paddling as best I could with one hand, and pretty soon I reached an uneasy mountain of . . . well, it was junk, really. I clambered up on top of it, nearly losing my limbs several times in the cracks between old pieces of molding, pipes, and metal struts.

"I climbed just far enough to get entirely out of the water, and then laid myself out across the pokey heap. I wasn't exactly in *despair*, you understand. Still not as bad as being strapped to a table without any legs. But it was *discouraging*, and I was tired. I lay there in the almost complete darkness and closed my eyes, feeling the cold from my wet clothes begin to seep into my bones . . . and *that's* when the music started. Oh, here we are!"

While she spoke Professor Odd had led them down a busy city street with towering buildings on either side, across a small plaza with a cinema on one side and a park on the other, and finally down a narrow street lined with trees. Here all the ground-floor properties were occupied by various kinds of restaurants; Chinese, Indian, Greek and Italian were all represented. There was also an Irish pub and a late-night café where crowds of people sat, typing away at laptops. A flickering sign above a recessed door that claimed it to be "Hel's Kitchen" made Alister feel vaguely uncomfortable. Just beyond it, however, was a brightly lit storefront with strings of yellow lights inside paper lanterns. The name was in the kind of pictograph writing Alister could never make sense of, but above it was a bright red dragon arched over the door, and it was to this sign that Professor Odd had led them.

The small Asian woman behind the little podium just inside the door looked tired, but her face brightened immediately at the sight of Professor Odd.

"Irashai! *Irashai* Oddo-san!" she cried out, bobbing up and down in excitement. *"Ninzuu ha nan nin desu ka?"*

Professor Odd smiled, held up four fingers, and replied, *"Yon-tsu,"* and then continued on in far more rough, but no less enthusiastic, Japanese.

The result was they were led at once to a quiet table in the back that was almost a booth, the walls around it were so high. The table was dark brown wood, polished to a mirror shine, and the placemats were made of woven bamboo. There was a narrow vase with a single sprig of cherry blossoms in the center, and on the wall above them hung a painting of a hoofed creature that seemed to be part snake and part billowing cloud. Alister had no sooner picked up the menu—which was mostly in Japanese but thankfully had lots of pictures—when there was a rumbling growl and the tramp of heavy feet and he looked up to find a large man with pale gray skin wearing a dirty apron standing next to their table. At least, Alister assumed it was male. It was hard to tell, since the person's head was that of an octopus, with eight curling tentacle-arms sprouting from where his mouth should have been (might still *have* been, under all those suckers) and a large, domed head—on top of which was perched a neat blue cap.

"*Tako-chan!*" Professor Odd shouted joyously, and Alister watched in bemusement as she managed to shake one of the person's mouth-arms with her own tentacle. There was another exchange in Japanese, and then the octopus-man lumbered away again.

"WHO WAS THAT?" Dave demanded.

"Tako-chan," said Professor Odd, as if this explained everything. "He's the owner. One of them, anyway. I just ordered. Don't worry, you'll *like* it." She sipped the water that had been set out for them, and sighed. "Now . . . where was I?"

"You said you heard music?" Elo reminded her.

"*Ooooh* yes of course!" said Professor Odd, her eyes misting over as she leaned back in her seat. "Yes, yes, that music was *very* interesting.

"It was so unexpected, for a start. I could tell it wasn't echoing down from the stage above—it sounded as though it was coming just from the other side of the mountain I lay on. It was . . . synthetic sounding, full of beeps and whistles and a pulsing buzz like the beat of a drum. It was . . . well, it was actually very nice, in its own way. So after listening for a while, curiosity got the better of me, and I dragged myself up and over to get a better look at where it was coming from.

"What I found on the other side was absolutely *marvelous* . . . At first I was a little confused, I'll grant you, since it looked for a moment like I'd stumbled back into the Oddity.

"There were *lights*, little ones, blinking everywhere. They formed the shape of a rough tunnel leading up out of the water—I could tell because the surface reflected the lights back up at the ceiling—at the end of which was a great big circular light, which flashed dimly every time there was a drumbeat. Er, buzz-beat.

"The walls and ceiling of the tunnel were covered in pipes, which must have been glass because they would also glow with respect to certain notes. Red and purple and blue and green—all represented different tones of beats and whistles. And something about the way this was so specific and consistent—green lit up *only* for a particular instrument, with different greens for different notes—that I got the impression the sounds were coming *from* the lights, not just flashing on cue.

"It was fascinating music, too, now I was listening properly. It should have been repetitive and mind-numbing, but there was variation under the repetition that seemed to be building toward something. My brain got interested following the narrative of the music, and at the same time the beat was so powerful and energizing it made me forget, for a little while, that I was cold and tired and wet.

"I half climbed, half slid down the back side of the mountain, and found myself knee-deep in water with a smooth, concrete floor beneath. Slowly I waded up the tunnel, my head tilted back to watch the light show produced by the music.

"It was amazing. Interspersed between the pipes were little bulbs—those were the blinking lights I'd seen first—with squares of light behind them that changed color with the chord progression.

"Then the music began to fade, and with it the lights, until I was left stranded in silent darkness, the water just over my ankles.

"'Hello?' I called experimentally.

"The response was a run of sharp notes down the wall next to me, which appeared as a single white light dropping between bulbs. It repeated, moving down the tunnel, until it stopped and the music began again—but different this time. And by its light I saw someone standing a little ways up the tunnel, looking down at me.

"I only glimpsed them for a moment, and then the music changed and they were lost to darkness, and when that area was lit again they were gone. I knew what I had seen, though: a medium-sized, thinnish person in black leather, with a very strange head. It was too small to be a human head—though they were otherwise human-shaped—and lumpy with little colored lights down either side of what would have been their jaw, if they'd had one.

"Then I caught movement out of the corner of my eye, and I thought they had reappeared—except this was a *different* person: shorter, with a tapered waist, and the lights on their head ran up in two lines from where their eyes should have been. I say *should* because, from what I caught of their face, they didn't *have* eyes where a human would. Instead there was a big lens in the middle, with two smaller ones on either side, and a bunch more in a line underneath these. They were supported by piece of metal like a rectangular chin, that had a depression front and center like a speaker. That was all I could make out before *that* person disappeared as well.

"'Who are you?' I called out into the music, but my voice got eaten up in the notes. I thought they wouldn't have heard, but then, to my surprise, the *music* started talking. You know how, with the right pitch and tone, a musical note can almost sound like a word? Well, this was that, only *more* so. It was difficult to understand, but the words were few and far apart, so I had time to puzzle them out.

"'*Weeeeeeeeeeee . . . are. The. Rooooooooooooooooo . . . bots.*'" Professor Odd sang the words in a hard, vibrating voice. "'*Weeeeeeeeeeee . . . runnnnnnnnnn . . . awaaaaaaaaaay . . .*'

"'Runaway robots?' I asked. 'That's fine with me, I ran away too. Er, what are you doing here?'

"'*Weeeeeeeeeeee . . . maaaaaaaake*—sorry, is that getting annoying? I'll talk normally then. Anyway, they said: 'We make *music*. We have no heart but a four-four beat. We are the robots who open up the extrascape.' Then the short one with the tapered waist reappeared at the end of the tunnel, silhouetted against the pulsing light there. I saw them bend down, rather stiffly, and pick up something off the ground. It was a helmet, I realized. Like a motorcycle helmet but with wires and cables hanging out the bottom instead of a chinstrap. The figure slipped it on over its head, fiddled with the wires, and then the helmet lit up with the same lights as were underneath it.

"'Two, zero, two,' said the music. 'Single B.'

Then the other figure—the one I'd seen first—stepped up next to them. They looked a lot taller, but I realized this was because they were wearing boots with heels almost as high as the ones Princess Die wore. They also picked up a helmet—this one had a big, bubble-like visor that reached back over the head, and had lights along the side to match the ones on the robot's jaw. When it was in place, the music said: 'Seven, one, three, D, H, C.'

"The chords grew louder, and in a crescendo the music said:

"'Together we are robots. Together we are *Extrascape.*'

"After that they stood there, looking at me blankly, and the music lulled. I realized they were waiting for me.

"I'm Professor Odd," I told them. "No numbers—not anymore. Just O, D, D. I'm afraid I'm a bit lost. Do you know if there's a way back up from here?'

"The music's lull faded into nothing, until the only light came from the robots' helmets—and the faint glow from the lamp behind them. It emitted a low hum, I realized, that never entirely went away.

"'Go back . . . *uuuuuuup?*' asked 202-B—the one with flat-soled boots and vertical lights. Their voice was quiet and granulated, and even though they were definitely *speaking*—not singing—every word they said *slid* into a note.

"'Yes, up,' I said. 'To the surface. The place with the arena. There's someone up there who's in trouble, and I need to rescue her.'

"'Up is not good,' said 713-DHC—the one in heels. Their voices were almost identical, but I thought 713 spoke in a minor key. 'Up means the monster.'

"'Monster?' I said. 'What monster? What's going *on* up there? Do you know?'

"The two robots looked at each other, the colored lights on their helmets flickering and blinking—*just* like the Oddity did when calculating a portal. Then they nodded in unison, a single bounce of their metal-and-glass heads, turned, and walked over to the big lamp.

"This lamp looked like a motorcar's headlight, only many, many times larger. I realized it was just like the giant search-light I'd stood on back up in the arena, only this one was old and battered. Of course it would be, considering we were in a garbage heap.

"713-DHC went around the back, and there was a scrape of metal, and a moment later an image of their face appeared in the middle of the light. It was a bit fuzzy, but I could see how there was now a single, powerful light shining in the center of their visor. This grew and grew, until the entire lamp was whited out, and then another image appeared, projected onto the plastic shell from the inside. I watched in fascination as a sort of video began to play. It showed an empty, deserted planet, with a black sky in which a huge gold-and-purple nebula rested. Stars, impossibly close, illuminated the gas and dust, and made the night on the desert planet almost as bright as day.

"'Long, long ago,' 202-B began, and a single chord hummed in the background of their voice. 'There was a lonely planet, with no star to guide it. It floated in space, looking for a star to call home. To this planet, there came the first peoples . . . '

"Now the barren desert was suddenly populated by lanky, humanoid-mantis shapes. They scurried across the desert, and slowly, like watching a time-lapse photo, a city rose from the plain of the desert, and the gold-and-purple nebula wheeled past overhead.

"'They built cities. They built towers,' 202-B went on. 'They made music, and the planet was not lonely.'

"'Where did the people *come* from, though?' I cut in. It was a little rude, but I was so curious I couldn't help it.

"'The people came through doors, doors in the sky,' said 202-B, perfectly patient and unflustered. 'They brought with them an advanced technology that allowed them to grow food from the sand and to alter the atmosphere so that it could support their life.

"'Their music floated out into space, and eventually many other species came to the planet in order to listen. Then came one who did not like the music . . .

"Now the projection showed a huge, crude ship: it was essentially a long tube with rounded ends, encrusted with little silver blobs, and eight stubby legs. One end of it had a huge, circular mouth, showing concentric rings of triangular teeth. It hovered over a city made of gleaming gold stone, and rained down fire. The city disappeared into dust, which in turn spread to envelop the whole screen, and the music in the background took on a mournful quality.

"'After that,' continued 202-B, 'the first people tried everything to make music the alien liked. Eventually, they discovered that certain voices from distant worlds would stop the alien in its tracks. But it would only listen for a single day—for the du-ration of one thousand songs—before it turned on the singer and devoured them.'

"The view in the lamp changed again. Now it showed a more primitive version of the arena, with a single figure dancing in the middle of it. As I watched, too stunned to say anything, the giant metal slug with the gaping mouth descended, tendrils extending from the opening, scooping up the little figure and carrying them away. The projection flickered through count-less versions of this scene, as around the stage a structure took form, growing in size and complexity, until I recognized the arena where I had seen Princess Die perform.

"'But that's *horrible!*' I cried. 'Oh, and I suppose they *lure* these artists with dreams of fame and fortune. That's why they built the arena with all the cheering holograms.' Then my brain caught up with what my mouth was saying, and I looked criti-cally at 202-B. 'Is that how *you* got tangled up in this? Why are you down here? How did you escape?'

"The image in the light flickered out, and 713 stood up and came around next to their partner. 'We did not escape,' they hummed.

"'We are the robots,' 202-B said. 'We do not care for fame and fortune. We are one with the music of the universe. Our music did not please the alien; we were rejected.'

"They didn't seem at all put out by this, and I couldn't say I blamed them.

"'Well,' I said, putting my hands on my hips. 'That's *something* to be going on, I suppose. How did you get hold of that nifty little video, may I ask?'

"'Many records are stored underground,' said 202-B. 'We are good listeners.'

"'I see,' I said, thinking very hard. 'Er . . . *Extrascape,* if you don't care for fame or fortune . . . how do you feel about *home?*'

"The two robots looked at me, their heads slightly tilted. They seemed puzzled.

"'Let me put it this way,' I tried again. 'If you can *help me* put a stop to this horrible, wasteful tradition, I can take you back *home.*' Oh, that looks *sugoi,* Tako-chan!"

Alister looked up with a jerk. He had been so absorbed by the Professor's tale that he'd missed the return of the octopus-man, who had arrived carrying a huge tray filled seaweed-wrapped bundles, dumplings, and little piles of pickled ginger and dollops of bright green horseradish paste—*wasabi,* he thought it was called.

There was a gurgling sound, and the blue dome of Dave's panvironment suit rolled back and Dave rose, like a little green sun, from the depths, his single orange-and-yellow eye gazing at the expanse of food in amazement.

Tako-chan set the tray carefully in the middle of the little table, took a step back, and bowed. Alister and Elo attempted to return the gesture, while Professor Odd somehow managed to bow using only her head and shoulders.

"Right," she said, once the octopus-man had left. Snapping up a pair of chopsticks she reached out and began selecting rolls and dumplings and putting them on the little plate in front of her. "There's *inari,* shrimp *nigiri,* eel, tuna and salmon *sashimi,* there's also three California-style *temaki,* one for each of us, and—I think you'll like *these* Dave—*salmon roe."* She pushed a little bowl of bright, orange-red balls toward Dave.

There was silence at the table for the next few minutes as Professor Odd devoured her serving of sushi. Alister ate slowly and experimentally. The *sashimi* was a little strange—just raw slices of fish—but the *inari* were nice, being rice wrapped in sweet tofu pouches, and the *temaki*—which was like a cone of rice wrapped in seaweed and stuffed with shrimp and avocado and dusted with sesame seeds—was surprisingly good.

The result was that Professor Odd finished long before any of them, and sat back with a sigh of satisfaction.

"That was good," she said. "Where was I? Oh, right, *Extrascape!* Well, since they were robots, and therefore reasonable, they readily agreed to help me. They had schematics for the whole complex, and we were able to take a disused maintenance elevator back to the surface. On the way, I learned a little more about them—the individual robots, I mean. It turned out they were originally part of a run of a thousand anthrobots (and numbered accordingly) meant for a variety of tasks. Each one had a characteristic, or set of characteristics, associated with them. 202-B, for example, was number 202 in the series, and B stood for either Bold or Brave or possibly both. Bold *and* Brave, I mean, not Both. Anyway, the letters behind 713 meant De-cisive, Honest, and Calm—though they had changed the D to mean *Disobedient* around the time they decided they preferred making music together to . . . whatever it was they'd been pro-grammed to do. Fascinating, really. They had such a mastery of sound, they could make music out of anything, not to mention play back all the songs they had performed out of their memory.

As we traveled up—and it took a while—I had time to think harder about what I'd learned. I began to realize that I couldn't simply whisk Princess Die away. I mean I *could* do that, yes, but it left the mantis people and that strange alien to keep on kidnapping and devouring people, which was no good. *Besides,* they were traversing universes to support this horrible prac-tice, which meant the atrocities were multiplied accordingly! I might save *this* version of Princess Die, but what if they went after her in a *different* universe? That's the problem when you start dealing with a multiplicity of worlds—you really have to be loyal to all versions of a person, even if some of those versions don't have the history you associate with the one you first met. And there were all the *other* musicians they'd kidnapped as well. That bothered me too, because they had been *robbing* universes of these people—and not only the people, but all the creative things they might have gone on to do! Artists are influential; their creations ripple out through the population, spreading in-spiration and gently shifting chances. Any one song may or may not drastically change the world, but cumulatively they are ex-traordinarily powerful.

"I had to put a stop to it before I tried to rescue Princess Die again. And to do that I needed to figure out what was *really* going on.

"'Look,' I told Extrascape when we were nearing the surface at last. 'Can you tap into the mainframe computer of this place? Like you did to get those histories? I need to look at more of their records.'

"'Certainly,' said 202-B, and put a hand on the nape of 713's neck. Their lights flickered in unison, and after a moment 713 said:

"'Now have complete access. Which records do you wish to see?'

"'Is there a list of all the singers they've kidnapped? All the ones that have been . . . sacrificed, that is? With what happened to them in the end, preferably.'

"'Searching,' said 713, and a little ring of lights appeared in the middle of their visor, blinking in and out so it looked like one light traveling in a circle. 'Records located. Displaying . . . '

"And they did. The circle of lights disappeared, replaced by a scrolling list of names. I recognized most of them from the file I had seen earlier, but now they were accompanied by a number, and a more detailed explanation.

"'L.B.H. Jones 1; songs: 982; status: consumed,' read the first entry. And so it went. I soon figured that the number after the name denoted which version of the person it was, the number after 'songs' was how many songs they performed, and the status was what happened to them. Almost all the song numbers were between nine hundred and one thousand, though a very few were significantly lower. Similarly, most of the entries were listed as *consumed,* though maybe a dozen were labeled *rejected.* I found Extrascape on the list: only one version, thirty songs, and *rejected.* They had by far the fewest songs, save one . . .

"Aside from Extrascape, there was only one other name with no multiples. It was M.E. Wren, and he was also the only one with just *one* song. Just one song. And he wasn't consumed *or* rejected . . . he was listed as *returned.*

"'This one,' I said, putting my finger on his name.

"'Marshal Evan Wren,' said 713. 'Human, male, home planet: Earth, 2005 A.D. Singer, songwriter, piano and geek rock.'

"'Yes, yes, I *have* heard of him—he's quite famous in some narratives. What *song* though? *What did he play?*'

"713 thought about this for a while, and finally came up with the song title: it was 'Queen of Rats.' Marshal Evan Wren sang 'Queen of Rats,' just once, and was *returned!*"

Professor Odd sat back in her seat and gazed at her audience significantly. When all she found were blank stares (and in Dave's case, some slurping sounds), she sighed heavily.

"You know 'Queen of Rats?' *They keep her bound in memories, trapped inside her own mind?*"

When Alister and Elo shook their heads, and Dave said, "I AM NOT FAMILIAR WITH THAT PIECE OF MUSIC," she rolled her head back to stare at the ceiling.

"It's a funny sort of song. Like a ballad," she explained. "Very, *very* long because of all the instrumental breaks. Its lyrics are half nonsense, half horror. Honestly I don't know what Wren was thinking of when he wrote it. Anyway, he wrote that song, and that was the song he performed in the arena, and afterward he was *returned home.* He was the *only singer* on the entire list marked as 'returned,' so naturally I got interested in the song. I'd only heard it once, though, years before, and I couldn't remember all the words.

"'Is there any way I could *see* that performance?' I asked Extrascape. 'They *must* keep records, right?'

"'Archives of the offerings are behind a lava flow,' 202-B told me. 'We cannot access without being attacked.'

"'But we remember,' 713 said. 'We remember everything.'

"And right there in the slowly rising elevator, 713 narrowed the beam of light coming out of their helmet, and projected an image on the far wall. Music emerged, too, out of the anthrobot's speakers, and though it was tinny and canned, I caught the words well enough.

"I watched Marshal Wren, standing behind an electronic keyboard, perform 'Queen of Rats' like his life depended on it. And it probably did, whether or not he realized. When the song finished at last, and the holographic crowds were still cheering distantly, a bright light shone down onto the stage, and Marshal Wren looked up, shading his eyes.

"713 must have looked up too, because the camera swung upward and *there* was the strange gun and the curling mist, and *above* that . . .

"Well, far above it all, against the bright nebula of the sky, was a creature like a huge, blocky, fat metal worm. It was covered all over with squares of metal, almost like something constructed from those interlocking plastic building bricks. From this angle I could see it had four sets of stubby feet, and instead of a face there was a circular mouth lined with teeth. This opened and closed like a diaphragm shutter, so the mouth almost looked like a giant eye at the same time.

"The huge alien bent down over the gun, and long, rope-like tendrils snaked out of its mouth-eye, twining around the contraption and rotating it so it was pointed directly at Marshal Wren. There was a noise that gave me an instant headache, a flash of light, and then Marshal Wren was gone, and the alien was drifting back up into the sky, while the stage below was suddenly swarmed with mantis people. The image blinked off, and I turned to find Extrascape looking at me curiously.

"'What is Odd planning?' asked 202-B.

"I couldn't help grinning back as I answered: 'I can *fix* this! I really can! That song is the key—oh, but I'll have to check on something first!' I was already thinking there must have been a huge misunderstanding at some point, and now I knew Marshal Wren and his silly little song were the key! I just needed to find which lock to fit it in, as it were. But I also needed to make sure that Marshal Wren actually did *go home*. So Extrascape and I had to creep through the basement of the arena, back to where I'd left the Oddity, so I could check. That was a bit tense, but they could disable surveillance cameras *literally* with a flick of their fingers, so we made it all right.

"Once we were back in the Oddity I had it do a search of all the present universes in which Marshal Wren was active. It found one that had a small blip in his history. Just the sort of blip caused by someone slipping in and out of the world. Someone not *me*, anyway. And sure enough, Marshal Wren was *still* there. Alive and well and very much still performing, too.

"I'd had to detach the Oddity from the universe with the arena to do this, so when we got back it had only been a matter of minutes, locally, even though the search had taken me hours. I'd also taken a bath and changed my clothes, and Extrascape had taught the Oddity how to play songs on her lights. She still does it, sometimes, you might have noticed. Anyway, I spent a lot of time thinking, and by the time we were ready to leave I felt I had a pretty good plan. It was a risky plan, but then any time you're dealing with a large number of militant people things are bound to get a little risky."

Professor Odd chuckled and shook her head. Then she glanced at her watch—which was the circular, flip-open kind, which she kept on a string in her pocket.

"Oh," she said. "We should probably start walking to the theater," and she waved down a passing waitress for the bill.

It turned out Tako-chan refused to accept money from them, so Professor Odd gave him a hug instead, and a light kiss on his broad forehead. Elo bowed. Dave waved. Alister said "Thank you," a bit awkwardly.

They went out the back of the restaurant and ambled down the alley toward the main street. Everyone, being rather full of fish, was moving slowly—except for Professor Odd, who skipped about as she continued to tell her story.

Part Two

"THE CONCERT—or rather, Princess Die's performance—was still going on when we got back, and the counter was reading 58/1,000. 202-B explained that they gave the performers breaks every twenty songs or so, and sure enough, after a couple more sets, some mantis people came and guided Princess Die off the stage.

"We were able to watch this happen—and read the number on the counter—because I'd been able to anchor the Oddity to a little aperture among the gun's struts and supports. It wasn't very big, and a little awkward because of the gravity difference, but it got us a great view. The only thing I couldn't see was what was going on directly above us, but judging by how many times the mantis people glanced nervously at the sky, I assumed the alien must be close.

"Once the stage was clear, I took a rope and tied it to one leg of the table and rappelled down to the net. I cut a hole in it using my sword-cane, and from there shimmied all the way down to the floor. Extrascape followed me, and by the time the mantis people returned we'd gotten ourselves sitting up on Princess Die's glittery piano; 202-B, 713-DHC, with me in the middle. I can't imagine what they thought, but Princess Die stared at us, wide-eyed, like she was really seeing things for the first time.

"Now, the first part of the plan was the riskiest, because we didn't have a good escape route, but I was fairly confident I could talk to the mantis people, since I'd managed to program the multiversal translator to work with audio. Also, Extrascape could speak the language perfectly, having had ages to listen to it.

"So when the first group of mantis people climbed up onto the stage I waved at them, and called 'Helloooooo' through my translator.

"That made them pause, so I hurried on before they could get any wrong ideas.

"'Please relax, I'm here to help. *Her,* mostly,' I said, pointing at Princess Die. 'But your lot as well. You see, I think you've gotten yourselves into a rather unfortunate situation. What with your *literal* alien overlord and all.' I pointed up, to illustrate.

"Oh yes, it *had been* the giant metal alien with the diaphragm-shutter mouth hovering over the stage that the mantis people had been glancing nervously at. It looked pretty much the same as it had on the video, only bigger and craggier. At the moment its mouth was mostly shut, just a small black circle in the center showed where it would open. But it was very tangibly *there,* looking down at the stage like some monstrous balloon animal. Every now and then little bolts of lightning would dance over its metallic skin.

"'Now look,' I went on. 'I know you think you've found a way to keep it from eating you or whatever, but I'm here to say you've *got* to stop kidnapping artists from other worlds. It's not healthy. Not for them, and not for the multiverse. So I propose you give me five minutes with Princess Die over there, and we'll see if we can't play this big guy a song that will send him away *forever.*'

"I thought I sounded pretty convincing, but I don't think the mantis people were listening very closely. What *actually* decided them was this huge, distant rumbling from above us, and the big alien's mouth began to open. Something flicked out of it, like a long narrow tongue, and almost as one the crowd of mantis people fled the stage, leaving Princess Die standing, bewildered, on her own.

"I was so worried about her—she looked ready to topple over—that I didn't see the long, gray, blade-like appendage that descended from the alien's mouth, slipping past the girders that supported the gun, until it cut through the net and crashed into the stage less than ten feet away. I hopped down off the piano and ran over to Princess Die, and before I did anything else I snapped the collar off her neck.

"She came more alive then, looked around and backed away from the debris thrown up by the alien's tongue, and then looked down at me and frowned.

"Then she said . . . well, she said some *very* rude words, but since she didn't seem angry at me I didn't mind.

"'Professor Odd, at your service,' I said, doffing my wig at her. (It was a replacement wig, orange I think.) That *really* made her look, but she came away with me willingly enough when I led her over to the piano.

"'This isn't Chicago,' she said, as if realizing it for the first time.

"'Nope,' I said, sitting her down at the bench. 'And those aren't people cheering, and this isn't a stage. Well, it sort of is, I guess. But not a stage as you would know it.'

"The tongue stabbed again, and I realized I'd have to hurry.

"I went on. 'It's a platform for people who can create a particular kind of energy. Music and words combine into something greater than the sum of their parts and pours out into the universe and—in this case—tames the big guy who's currently trying to impale us with his tongue.'

"Another stab. The only reason we hadn't been hit yet was thanks to the gun, which was blocking the alien's view of the stage.

"Princess Die looked around, then up at the huge alien. She blanched, but said, quite calmly, 'That sounds like a stage to me. So what do we do?'

"'Well, I'd like to run an experiment,' I explained. 'See, the people of this world have been using *music* to make the big metal guy in the sky not kill them. They think it's *appeasing* him or something. But *I* think something different is going on. *I* think the music has been doing something very, very different. So I'm going to try *asking him.*'

"'How?' she said. 'With your special speaking box?'

"'No,' I said, a little surprised at how well she was handling this. It was like nothing could fluster her. I think the stage could have caught fire, and she'd just calmly figure out a way to extinguish it. 'Well, *yes* I'm gonna speak with him. Her. It. Not sure what applies yet. But *first* I've got to get its attention.'

"I was interrupted at this point by another impact from the alien's blade-like tongue, and 202-B said: 'If we remain silent, we will be destroyed.'

"'*Yes*, right!' I said. 'I don't suppose you know the song 'Queen of Rats' by Marshal Wren?' I asked Princess Die.

"She frowned, and shook her head. I sighed. 'Oh well,' I said, 'I suppose I'd better sing it, then. You can play along, if you want, but Extrascape needs to do the music.'

"Princess Die peered at the two robots curiously, who were messing around in the back of the piano, making small zapping noises.

"There was a crash, and a piece of net fell down onto the stage, narrowly missing us.

"'Can I have your microphone?' I asked the Princess.

"Silently, Princess Die took off her headset and handed it to me, then reached behind her and unsnapped the little radio pack that was clipped to her belt.

"'Thanks,' I said, putting them both on. 'When you're ready, robots!'

"Now you have to imagine this scene. A huge stage, with a piano in the center of it, and on the piano are two skinny people in black leather wearing motorcycle helmets with lights on them and cables running down from their chins. One of them's wearing knee-high, stiletto-heeled boots, and the other's got a sort of metal corset thing around their waist. They're standing on the glittering piano, right? Okay, and next to them is a woman wearing a rhinestone bathing suit and platform shoes . . . and then there's *me*. I'm sort of . . . I don't actually remember. I think I was wearing my old green jacket, and of course the orange wig. But . . . I was me. And all around the edge of the stage the mantis people were crouching, and above us the net is being *shredded* by the alien's tongue. The hologram audience had flickered off, and so all the stands appeared empty. The light gun was still working, though, but the beams were random and undirected. And above all this, the giant metallic alien had rotated so it was almost vertical, with its mouth open all the way, and I looked up right at it as Extrascape began to play, and I can *see* its tongues—it had, like, five of them—poking out through the teeth, ready to strike. And *then* . . . you know what I did *then?*"

Professor Odd paused, and turned back to look at her audience expectantly. They were back on the broad thoroughfare now, and ahead, over the tops of some low buildings, Alister could see the curving roof of a huge covered stadium, lit from below by searchlights, and supporting colorful banners. On the street around them the traffic had thickened, and on the sidewalk they had been joined by a crowd of other people, most of whom were wearing elaborate costumes involving leather and glitter. It was an unusual combination.

"I can take a *guess,*" Elo said.

"YOU ATTEMPTED TO COMMUNICATE WITH THE ALIEN USING MUSICAL THEORY?" Dave hazarded. Professor Odd grinned and raised a finger.

"*Very* close! Actually, I think it was the words *in* the music that did it. 'Queen of Rats,' you see, goes like this . . . "

And, to Alister's surprise, she turned around and began to sing, right there in the open, as they walked through the city. She had a full, throaty voice. Not the most pleasant to listen to, but she more than made up for it with enthusiasm and, Alister was interested to note, almost perfect diction.

"*The Queen came down today,*" she sang, waving at their fellow pedestrians who were giving her curious looks. "*She rolled her sleeves, and I heard her saaaaaaay . . . All your passions and your fears, have brought nothing but my tears! Can you keep your motions wise? Or are you ruled by what's insiiiiiiiiiiide . . .* that's how it begins," she explained. "Which I think meant the alien. The alien was the Queen, who, for some reason, was annoyed by what the mantis people were doing. If I took the song to be *completely* accurate, then I think the Queen—er, the alien—was worried that the mantis people would get caught up in their passions and lose the ability to think logically and rationally. Now, you might think that's an awful lot to read into a song that was written by someone who didn't even *belong* to that world . . . but the moment I started singing, the alien stopped trying to tear apart the stage, and hovered above us, its tongues waving back and forth to the music. Encouraged, I kept going . . .

"*Then the rats they clustered 'round, they took up trumpets from the ground. In their hearts they played and played. They sang that they were not afraaaaaaid . . .* I think those lines mean the mantis people who ignored the aliens at first, and just kept right on doing their thing—whatever it was. So the song goes on: *But the Queen she took a broom, and swept them off to their doooooom!* That was when the alien wiped out most of the cities. *But rats are not so meek, they were back within a weeeeeek. They played at night under her bed, they put their music in her heeeeaaad . . .* that's when the mantis people started bringing in off-world musicians. *And the Queen she could not rise, but watched them dance before her eeeeeeyes!*

"This is where I started having to guess, but I took this verse to mean that the music confused the alien. Got in its head and messed it up, like the Queen in the song. Which was why the alien was stuck here. They literally *could not rise.* Anyway, next comes the bridge, which doesn't fit as well as the rest of the song, but I sang it anyway . . .

"*Oh, where have you gone? Was it something I did wrong? Where is my maddening Queen? What is it that she's seen?* Personally, I think it was things she *heard* that caused problems, but I'm getting to that. The song has a *really long* instrumental break after the bridge, and Extrascape launched into it with gusto. They'd paired themselves with the piano, which was in turn paired with the speakers, and they were playing things no human could play on that instrument. It got dissonant at times, enough to make Princess Die flinch, but when I checked, the alien's tongues were wagging almost happily, and I noticed two smaller apertures, like eyes, on either side of the huge mouth. These had been invisible till now, when they began to crack open. I fairly screamed the last verse, which was the really important bit, I thought."

"*They keep her bound in memories!*" Professor Odd fairly belted, causing the group of teenagers in fishnet stockings that were on the sidewalk ahead of them to jump and scatter. "*Trapped inside her own miiiiiind! Is it the rats she eats at night?*—that's the musicians the alien devours—*But she can't see her enemies, though they are not hard to find. They won her throne without a fiiiiiiiiiiiiiight . . .*"

Professor Odd's voice trailed off, coasting to a stop, to be absorbed by the clatter and boom of the city, and revealing the bemused muttering of the group of teenagers.

"The rats were the mantis people, of course," Professor Odd went on, unflustered. "They won the alien's throne—whatever that was—not by superior weapons, but by *driving it crazy* with the sound of music. Which isn't such a crazy notion in itself. Have you ever gotten a song stuck in your head that *wouldn't go away*? You know how *annoying* that gets? Well, imagine if that song is so fundamentally *different* from the type of music you find pleasant, it was like having a constant loop of bone-grating noise playing over and over inside your head.

"This was my theory: that the alien's preferred form of music was something so different from *ours* that what *we* found pleasant or exciting, *it found* like . . . well, like nails on a chalkboard. Which would be why the aliens attacked the mantis people in the first place. Sort of like humans who swat at flies because they find the buzzing sound annoying. Only in this case the flies came back and drove that human *mad* with the sound of their buzzing. So mad that human—er, I mean the alien—couldn't really *do* anything. Trapped inside their own mind, like the song said.

"Anyway, after I'd finished the song, and after Extrascape finished playing, I had to wait, looking up at the alien, until the little apertures opened completely and it stared down at us out of bright, glowy red eyes.

"'I'm pretty sure you can hear me,' I said, then. 'Now I've got your *attention*, listen up! I think its time you *went home* and left these people alone. Which you *can* do, if you could only *think* straight. Now, because our brains are so different, our music clearly isn't *your* music, so obviously we don't know any of your songs. But Extrascape here—' Extrascape waved '—are *very clever*. I'm sure if you, as it were, *hummed a few bars*, they could improvise something for you.'

"It was another long shot, but I guessed that hearing a bit of its own music would help clear the alien's mind. Sort of the way putting on a song you like can help your brain let go of unpleasant memories. And you know what? *I was right.*

"The alien sat there, dumbly, for a while, as all around us the mantis people went scurrying away. This was a clue, I now realize, though at the time I didn't figure out what it meant before the alien ... well. Heh. It did exactly what I suggested: it started humming.

"It was *awful*. Worse than nails on chalkboard. Worse than those high-pitched squirrel repulsers. Like a combination of the two but with this sort of *roaring* behind it that buzzed in your teeth and made your bones itch. I think some of it was below and some *above* my range of hearing, and I'm not sure whether that made it better or worse. It was so *painful* to listen to that I tried *not* to, so I couldn't really hear the tune—if there was even a recognizable tune.

"I pressed my hands firmly over my ears, and Princess Die did the same. We both ended up on our knees on the stage, cowering together. I thought, *if this is what our music was like to the alien, no wonder it went mad!*

"Then Extrascape joined in, and it became almost unbearable. I tried to make myself as small as possible, to let the sound wash over me, but it just burrowed into my head and rattled around in there, like a cannonball. I couldn't move. I couldn't *think*. And that was a small mercy, I suppose, because in retrospect the whole ordeal didn't last very long—though at the time it felt like it took *forever*.

"What I remember, though, is how the pain slowly lessened, and as bits of my mind came back online I crumpled to the floor and rolled over onto my back, next to Princess Die who was doing pretty much the same thing. Together we stared up at the great, blocky metal underbelly of the alien. Little lights flashed along its side as it wheeled around, and then, its whole body undulating, it rose up into the sky, higher and higher and higher, until it was just another speck of light amid the starry nebula, and then that speck was a twinkle, and then the twinkle went out.

"It took me a while to realize that the alien had taken the horrible music with it, and that what I was still hearing was the stuff bouncing around in my own head. In an effort to push the sound out, I shoved the headset mic aside and stuck a finger in my ear—to help me hit the right notes—and sang the bridge from 'Queen of Rats' one more time.

"'*Oh, where have you gone? Was it something I did wrong? Where is my maddening Queen? What is it that she's seen?*'

"As I sang the pain lessened, and I felt a surge of relief wash over me when Extrascape—perfectly unperturbed by the whole affair—obligingly picked up the tune. Once I'd stopped singing, however, they morphed it into something new. Something slowly building with excitement, joy, and *triumph*, I realized.

"'I'm no queen,' Princess Die mumbled next to me, under the music.

"'I didn't mean you, Princess,' I replied, a little groggily.

"She sat up, rubbing her temples, and looked around.

"'Wow,' she said, dully. 'This is pretty far out. I think I'm ready to go home now.'

"That got me to sit up all at once, which made me have to put my head between my knees for a moment while my blood pressure adjusted. 'Yes,' I said, once I didn't feel dizzy anymore. And then, when I realized what had just happened, I couldn't help letting out a little triumphant cry of my own. '*Yes!*' I said. 'We can *all* go home now!'"

Professor Odd spread her arms as they came around a corner, and there was the stadium, brightly lit and bedecked by colorful banners, the streets between them closed off with barricades and the entire place *swarming* with people. Merchants on street corners were selling t-shirts with Princess Die iconography on them, glowsticks, and little crowns with sequins. Above it all rose a huge billboard, with three faces on it. Two were motorcycle helmet–like masks, with colored lights on them. The one in the middle seemed human, but with cheekbones accentuated by prosthetic makeup, bright blue eye shadow, and long dark lashes. There was a splatter of rhinestones across the forehead, and the hair that had been sculpted into the shape of a crown above it was dyed a pale lavender. Across the bottom was written:

PRINCESS DIE: THE ROBOTS RETURN TOUR

Slowly their group slipped through the throng—Alister saw a number of people with horns, some of which looked quite real, wearing fluttery garments that glittered like morning dew—up the wide, concrete stairs, and through the vast glass doors. A wide, brown-skinned woman in a neat blue uniform took their tickets and gave them little wristbands with a bar code.

"I hope this will work for you," she said, handing one to Dave. "If not, go see the lady at information and she can make you a magnetic tag."

She didn't look twice at Elo.

"THIS WILL BE ACCEPTABLE," Dave said, curling the tip of his arm around it. "THANK YOU," he added, sounding touched.

Inside was even more crowded, and the costumes were even more magnificent. People dressed in skin-tight spandex next to people in extravagant ball gowns and people in sequined suits—with male and female representatives in each—milled around getting their pictures taken.

Professor Odd led them through the confusion with a purpose.

"It took a bit of doing to actually *get* everyone home, of course," she mentioned casually. "I was very cross with the mantis people, but when I saw how relieved they were that the alien was finally *gone*, I couldn't bring myself to berate them for how they'd handled the situation. Besides, that might have made them hostile again, and I wanted their help sending everyone home, since it would have taken *forever* using just the Oddity. But they were really quite a *reasonable* race, once they had the threat of sudden annihilation by giant alien removed, and they started up their own transuniversal machine without much fuss.

"I took Princess Die home myself. I could tell she was getting tired of the whole thing, and since Extrascape didn't seem too keen on staying either I loaded them all up into the Oddity—after I'd moved the portal to somewhere more easily accessible—and took everyone back to Princess Die's world. I'd thought after that I'd find a nice place for Extrascape to settle down, since they didn't want to go back to their native universe, but Princess Die had gotten very interested in them, and by the time I'd got the portal to her hotel room open, they had decided to give her world a try.

"'It'll be *amazing*,' she told them as they tumbled out into her suite. *'Real* robots—people won't believe it! I hope you don't mind being mistaken for guys in suits? I don't know if this world is ready for musical androids.'

"'Anthrobots,' 202-B corrected her.

"'Yeah, sure,' said Princess Die. 'Do anthrobots drink scotch? What about you . . . um . . . ?'

"'Professor Odd,' I reminded her. 'And no, I really shouldn't. Must get back and see all the other musicians are returned properly. I mean, they probably *will* be . . . but you can't be too careful.'

"She asked me if I would be going then. I said yes. She told me to come back and see her sometime. I got very flustered at that and hurried away without really saying anything. I *had* intended to go back, after I'd sorted the other musicians out . . . but . . . well . . . that took *longer* than I thought it would, and by then I really needed some sleep. And after that I decided I wanted a holiday, which was the first time I went to Geda, I think, and you know how *that* turned out. And after that there were the Rats of Alnitak, and then I got really interested in testing the event horizons of black holes and . . . well . . . one thing led to another and by the time I'd worked up the courage to go back, the Oddity's temporal lock had slipped and enough time had passed that I wasn't sure if Princess Die would even *remember* me . . .

"I did check in though, of course. Just to see how they were doing. Things got a bit rough for Princess Die—she spent six months in rehab, and everyone said her career was over. It was reported as a combination of anorexia and alcoholism, but I think it was post-traumatic stress from her ordeal. But she got through it, and went back on tour—*with* Extrascape as her opening act. Did very well from then on, and Extrascape eventually became quite famous in their own right. That's why I was so excited to catch *this* show. It's the first time they've performed together in five years. Oh, and Extrascape are out as *real* anthrobots now, so I'm excited to see what they do."

"You'll like it," said the usher who checked their ticket stubs and pointed the way down a hall to their seats. He was a young man with dark skin and black hair and an earnest look about him. He had clearly only caught the last few words of Professor Odd's monologue.

"It's their *first time* at a Princess show," Professor Odd told him, giddily.

"Ah," said the young man knowingly. "Well, you're in for a *treat*. You're down near the arena, by the way—they have a ramp to the left if you can't do stairs," he added, obviously for Dave's benefit.

"THANK YOU, I AM SURE I WILL MANAGE," Dave said as he rolled past. The young man didn't even blink.

"Hold on, hold on," said Alister, once they were a safe distance down the hall. It was much less crowded here—most people either being outside milling around, or already seated—but his voice echoed loudly. "You mean to say you just dropped Princess Die off and *never went back to explain things?* Just left her at home as if . . . as if the whole thing was a big, weird *dream?*"

"One that she came out of with a pair of musical robot friends?" Elo added.

Professor Odd wiggled her shoulders uncomfortably. "It just . . . didn't feel *right* . . . barging in, I mean. I mean, I don't *really* know her. I just like her music. A *lot.* But she doesn't know *me* at all. I'm just this weird person who helped her out once—and I can't imagine what she's made of it all. She was pretty out of her mind for most of it. She probably doesn't remember me. Not really. It would be *weird.*"

Alister gazed at Professor Odd an astonishment, while behind him Elo burst out:

"Weird? Since when have *you* been afraid of things being *weird?*"

"I felt *shy,* if you *must* know!" Professor Odd cried out, turning on them in a whirl of shiny orange coat. She took a deep breath, her chest swelling up like a pigeon's. "And I get very nervous meeting famous people. Famous people I admire, anyway." She turned on her heel and marched down the hall, turning off at the door labeled "Arena Level, A 030–060."

Checking his ticket stub, Alister saw it was indeed labeled "AL A 042" and he followed the Professor, but not before exchanging an eye-roll with Elo. Dave, impassive in his panvironment suit, trundled after them.

They encountered the promised stairs immediately, and Dave surged ahead of them by tipping sideways and rolling his barrel-shaped suit down them, using the gear around his midsection as a brace. He was waiting for them at the bottom, where there was another usher who, after a peek at their stubs, pointed to their right.

They came out around a buffer and there *was* the arena: the center of the stadium, one half built up into an elaborate stage like a spaceship, with the other half bare concrete packed with people. A living chain made of security guards ringed them in, and a small fence further separated the arena from the first row of seats. Once they reached AL A 039–042 and sat down, Alister found he was more or less at eye level with the lowest part of the stage. He was about as far away from it as one would be from the screen of a movie theater if they sat in the very back row, but after leaning around to gaze at the hundreds of rows of seats stretching up and behind them, he realized what good seats these really were. Only the people standing on the floor got closer to the stage, and Alister suspected they didn't have as good a view.

The stage itself was something to behold. There was a big semicircle that jutted out into the throng of people, and behind it was a bank of computer screens with little blinking lights and dials. The screens were playing computer-generated animations of nebulas, supernovas, and solar eclipses. Above this were two pods, large enough to hold a grown man, which were belching fog. They each had large letters stenciled across the lid, which spelled out CRYO. Between them was a chair—clearly meant to be the captain's chair—which stood empty. Beyond this the stage rose in a complicated framework of ramps and ladders and poles and catwalks, to where it was swallowed up by a rich, black velvet curtain.

"Here," said Professor Odd, pressing something small and soft into Alister's hand. He looked down to find a pair of yellow foam earplugs resting in his palm.

"Trust me, you'll need them," the Professor said with a grin, working a pair into her own ears.

"Gosh, *thanks,*" said Elo, putting on a pair of sound-dampening headphones.

"I AM GRATEFUL I HAVE MY OWN SYSTEM OF HEAR-ING," Dave announced, garnering a surprised look from their neighbors in seats 43 and 44. But the couple appeared more in-terested in taking pictures of the stage than the strange robot-like creature, and looked away again quickly.

After a while a voice boomed out of the high, vaulted ceiling, its words lost in its own echo and the roar of the crowd as everyone in the stadium—which had filled to capacity—began to scream. Everyone except Alister, Elo and Dave, who winced as Professor Odd jumped to her feet, sticking two fingers in her mouth and whistling loudly.

The voice spoke again, and now Alister saw how the lights on the stage were flickering wildly, sparks flying from a few places further up among the catwalks. Lithe figures in black leotards could be seen, jumping and climbing and running about up there, and the two cryo pods had been lit from within to reveal a dark, humanoid figure in each.

Listening carefully, Alister was able to discern words in the echoes this time around.

"Ladies and gentlemen and everyone between and beyond, robots, monsters and aliens . . . " the booming voice said. "Are you ready for *Extrascape?*"

Tremendous cheers, interspersed with beeps and whistles and some horrible screeching.

"Are you ready . . . for *Princess Die?*"

The noise, if possible, increased. Alister was glad of his earplugs.

"They have come a long way . . . " said the voice, over the cheering which refused to die down, " . . . from a galaxy beyond your imagination! Our Princess has returned from a journey of discovery, and she brings with her the envoys of a new age. An age of acceptance, an age of life! An age of revolution! Evolution! But most of all . . . an age"—something boomed, and a searchlight blazed upward, illuminating the rolling bank of stage fog—"of song! And! *Dance!*"

On the final word there was a huge clash of cymbals and a figure appeared, as if by magic, in the middle of the clear semicircle. For a moment they were enveloped in a pillar of golden light, and then the next their form solidified into a tall, slender woman wearing an elaborate platinum costume full of spikes and odd angles. She looked like she was wearing a giant crystal.

"*Ooohh-ooohh-oooooooh-ooh-oh, oh, oh, calling Professor Odd . . . *" sang the woman.

Alister nearly choked in surprise.

But he hadn't heard wrong. The woman repeated:

"Ooohh-ooohh-oooooooooh-ooh-oh, oh, oh, calling Professor Odd!"

Alister turned to stare at Professor Odd, his mouth agape.

"How *can* she not have remembered you?" he shouted over the din of music, cheering, and singing. "She put you in a bloody *song!*"

"It's just what she *thought* I was," Professor Odd said, a small, wistful smile spreading across her face. "What she remembered . . . "

From what Alister caught of the lyrics, he thought Princess Die must have remembered things remarkably well. There was a line about *"who has the answers I want to believe, who has a citrus wig of maple and bees . . . "* that seemed pretty accurate. Except for the bit about the maple and bees, which Alister put down to a case of mishearing.

Then Extrascape came out of their pods, and he forgot to listen to the lyrics for a couple minutes.

They did look remarkably like tall, thin people in leather suits with helmets on, but there was a jaggedness about their bodies, and a precision to their movements, that seemed just a little *off.* Their proportions were neither classically male, nor classically female, though 202-B appeared shorter and curvier, because of the corset it wore, and 713-DHC looked taller, because of the high heels. Their helmets were alight with colors and their hands glinted metallically. They marched down the steps to the lowest part of the stage, where a small panel had risen, and stood behind it. Almost at once the music redoubled, taking on subtle electronic undertones, and both the robots nodded their heads to the beat of the music. The crowd went wild.

When Alister could again hear what Princess Die was singing, he began to realize that the song wasn't *just* about Professor Odd (or, Professor Odd as Princess Die had perceived her). It also seemed to be about Princess Die's *feelings* about Professor Odd, if the lines *"When I'm lonely I just have to pretend that through the door is Professor Odd,"* and *"When I'm so low and everything seems wrong, I will try to find Professor Odd,"* meant anything. There was the continued refrain of *"Calling Professor Odd,"* interspersed with shouts of *"Want Professor Odd!"*

Then Extrascape began to chant, quickly, and without breaks to breathe, *"Onwards fusion-crazy, who's like a supernova—onwards fusion-crazy, who's like a supernova ..."* for at least a minute, while the music did funny things in the background, and Princess Die danced, until they closed with: *"Onwards crashing-crazy, crossed wires can't delete you, baby."*

"She's like a star, made up of all your dreams," Princess Die took over. *"She's like a star, she's burning through the screams ..."* and then went off into a language Alister didn't recognize. When the lyrics returned to English it was to repeat, *"She's burning through the screams, made up of all your dreams—my technicolor sta-a-ar, she's Professor Odd!"*

And then some words jumped out at him, from the midst of the music, the cheering, and the echoing refrain, *"Stuck on a stage, trapped in the thousand songs, I know I can call Professor Odd ..."*

Alister wanted to jump up and *shake* Professor Odd. It was *obvious* that Princess Die remembered, and from the sound of the song, she was probably *still missing* her. But he restrained himself until the music finished (*"Don't want drugs and fame, this fame's not a game. Won't worship your rod, want Professor Odd!"*), and he had a chance of actually being heard.

"How can you think she doesn't remember?" Alister screamed. "She's practically *pining* after you!"

"She's just trying to make sense of some very conflicting memories!" Professor Odd shouted back through the roar of the crowd.

On the stage, Princess Die had joined hands with Extrascape and was leading them forward to the edge, saying something along the lines of how *glad* she was to be back in San Jose with her very best robot friends—who were now able to be out of their helmets, as it were, about being *actual* robots.

"Professor," said Alister, trying to sound cross, even though inwardly he found the whole situation tragically hilarious. "If you don't go visit her *right* after the show is done, I shall be very, *very* disappointed! Forget being a fangirl for once—you *owe* it to her! *And* Extrascape!"

"I could talk to Extrascape," Professor Odd allowed, but she crumpled back into her seat and mumbled something else.

Alister pulled out his earplugs. *"What?"* he said.

"She's so *very* busy these days," Professor Odd repeated testily. "And I'm sure she'll be *exhausted* after the performance. I wouldn't want to bother her."

"I *really* don't think you'll be a bother—" Alister began, but one of the people in the row behind them had leaned down and was making annoyed *shushing* motions with their hands. Alister sat back reluctantly, but he caught sight of Elo waving at him from the far side of the Professor, and he left his earplugs out long enough to hear her say:

"Don't worry! If she won't do it, *I'll* open a portal into Die's dressing room *myself!*"

"You wouldn't—!" Professor Odd began, but at that moment the next song started up, and their conversation was cut off.

Alister passed the rest of the concert in a state of growing admiration. The trio performed song after song after song, some of which went on for a long time. Princess Die went through about five variations on her original costume, played a piano made of crystal, danced on the piano in five-inch heels, and at one point was lifted clean into the air by a set of ropes. Extrascape spent most of their time behind their little control panels, manipulating pieces of the set along with the music. The dancers in black crawled all over it, coming down to dance with Princess Die now and then. There were some slow songs, some fast songs, and some songs that went back and forth.

Princess Die's lyrics seemed to be rather complicated with a lot of hidden meanings. Alister wished he knew the secret to them. They seemed, to him, to be parts of a bigger narrative, and if he only knew the secret to the code they were written in he could understand that story. As it was he contented himself with enjoying the music, an interesting blend of orchestral rock and roll merged with Extrascape's electronic tunes.

There were a couple of breaks where Princess Die paused and talked to the audience, or talked to Extrascape. She went down to the edge of the stage to receive a gift from one of the people on the floor, and came back holding a rhinestone-studded vest with the words "woman of thunder" picked out on the back. She thanked the fan profusely, getting a little teary as she did so.

"Fans are so, *so* important," she said, putting the vest on. "You all probably know how I hit a low spot maybe a decade ago—right before I met Extrascape. I was a real mess, and it was a bad time. People said I was done. Washed out. A loser. But my fans always believed in me. It was my *fans* who got me through it, they really did. I wouldn't be here today without you, my fans."

Alister had to roll his eyes at Professor Odd, but he didn't think she noticed; she was watching the stage, enraptured.

The concert went on. Alister lost track of the songs—though he didn't think there were actually a thousand of them. Then it finished, but the people stayed and kept cheering. So Princess Die came back and did a solo piece, just her and the piano in the middle of an empty stage. After that there was still *more* cheering, so Extrascape came back and lit up the whole stage with their music. And then, when people still wouldn't go, they *both* came back and did a song together. This one was markedly different from all the other songs, and seemed a little off the cuff. Princess Die broke down laughing several times, and would pause to talk to the audience, telling them over and over how much she enjoyed playing for them. Extrascape did too, in their own way—though their words were woven in with the music, and Alister had trouble distinguishing them.

And then, at last, Extrascape and Princess Die left the stage, the house lights went up, and people began, reluctantly, to filter out.

"Right," said Alister, standing up and taking Professor Odd's elbow in a loose hold.

"Right," said Elo, doing the same on the other side.

"This is absolutely ridiculous," Professor Odd protested.

"I COULDN'T AGREE MORE," said Dave, as he followed the three of them out of the stadium.

Epilogue

Pᴿᴵᴺᶜᴱˢˢ Dᴵᴱ sᴛʀᴇᴛᴄʜᴇᴅ ᴏᴜᴛ as much as the tiny dressing room would allow. One would think that a venue as huge as the stadium in San Jose would also have a comfortable dressing room, but all the space had been spent on room for the stage and the audience, with almost nothing left for the artists and the crew.

This was all right for Extrascape, who just leaned themselves against the wall over their portable chargers and went into sleep mode, but Princess Die, despite her myriad stage personas of aliens, demons, gynoids, and metaphysical deities, was in reality only human—and not even a very young one anymore.

"I think I need a bath . . . of ice," she croaked, sipping at the tall glass of water that had replaced her traditional post-concert whisky since . . . well . . . since she'd met Extrascape.

Princess Die was a practical woman, and as such did not look too closely at the jumble of foggy memories she had of her "crash" as the press had called it. And she had crashed. Badly. Been right off the rails for a few months. Hadn't known what to think or what was real. There were memories of a strange, clicking language, and other, weirder things. She'd ended up putting them all into the song "Professor Odd" and then only thought about them when she performed it.

She was still thinking about it now, however, as she rolled the remaining water around in her glass, wishing it was something stronger.

"Who has the answers I want to believe?" she whispered.

There was a scratch on her door.

Princess Die leaned her head back and shut her eyes. She'd asked Carol, her tour manager, for ten minutes of absolute solitude, and she knew she still had six more to go.

"What is it?" she called, tiredly.

To her surprise it wasn't the main door that opened, but the little closet door next to it. A dark crack appeared, and from the other side were voices. Princess Die caught the words, " . . . *really a very bad idea* . . . " and " . . . *that never stopped you before!*" and then a furry, golden head pushed itself through the crack and looked around.

It looked like a dog. Or a wolf. Except it was too intelligent, and far too high off the ground. Princess Die had seen a lot of strange things since the convergence, but this was possibly the most surprising.

A humanoid wolf with gleaming, buttery-golden fur, wearing a purple jumpsuit, slid out of her closet and bowed apologetically.

"So sorry to bother you, princess," the dog said in perfect, slightly British-sounding English. "Only, it seemed like the best time. I'm sure you'll understand." Then she poked her head back through the door and called, "Better give her a push, Alister!"

"There's really no need for that," said a voice from within Princess Die's closet. It was the same as the first voice, and it sparked memories, distant as dreams.

A moment later the memories got a lot less distant when Professor Odd pushed her way out of the closet and past the golden wolf.

Princess Die knew it was Professor Odd at once, even though the woman was wearing a bright orange overcoat, and her wig was a swirl of orange and pink and blue. It was the same shaggy, flyaway cut that her previous one had been. The tentacle that she remembered, but hadn't had the courage to put in the song, was curled tightly under the woman's jaw, and her eyes were very large and dark. Like a cat's.

"So *sorry* about this," she was saying, pulling at the ends of her lime-green scarf. "I didn't want you bother you—know you must be tired. But they *insisted* I check in on you—and I wanted to say hello to Extrascape anyway . . . "

That was the voice. A little raspy, but so animated and *earnest*. Princess Die realized she was staring at her visitor with her mouth slightly open, utterly astonished.

Over by the wall, Extrascape whirred into life, the lights on their helmets running through the boot-up sequence.

There was a knock on the door. A real knock this time, on the real door, and a moment later Carol put his head in.

"Ten minutes, Die," he said. "I've got the very polite writer for *NewWire* dot com, also Johnny Bathory's manager called, asking if—" he cut off at the sight of Professor Odd and the wolf. "Oi!" he said, his normally bluff, pleasant face clouding over. "What are you—"

"*Not now*, Carol," Princess Die said, trying and failing to sound casual. But she didn't want to take her eyes off Professor Odd, lest the woman disappear on her again, and so her words came out rather sharp.

Carol, bless him, took the hint and backed out of the door, shutting it diffidently behind him.

*   *   *

The door shut with a clap, leaving Professor Odd to stare back at Princess Die almost defiantly. From his post on the stairs, blocking Professor Odd's retreat back into the Oddity, Alister saw a pair of long legs in fishnet tights swing off the little makeup table, and a moment later Princess Die advanced into view between Elo and the Professor.

Alister had to marvel at how, though the two women were of similar height and build, the closer you got to Professor Odd, the stranger she looked, but the closer you looked at Princess Die the more normal she seemed. She had a scattering of moles around her collarbone, and the backs of her thin hands were a little wrinkly. She was maybe in her mid-to-late-thirties, and that age showed rather more now that she had most of her makeup off.

Her face was also more expressive this way, and Alister saw her eyes widen, her mouth opened in a disbelieving *"oh."*

"You're real," she said in a small, hollow voice.

"Yep," said Professor Odd, wiggling her shoulders awkwardly.

Princess Die nodded to herself, and when Alister saw the small, triumphant grin spread across her face, he couldn't help feeling immensely pleased with himself.

"You saw the show?" Princess Die asked, almost hesitantly.

"Oh," said Professor Odd, clearly taken aback. "Oh *yes!* Yes it was *brilliant!*"

Elo coughed. "I'll just, er, I'll just *wait for you outside,* shall I?" she asked, then waved a paw at Princess Die's protesting expression. "You lot have *loads* to catch up on, I'm sure," she said, backing toward the door as she spoke. "Don't mind us. We'll wait. Have fun."

So saying she shut the Oddity's door with a quiet click.

In the tiny dressing room, Princess Die regarded Professor Odd curiously.

"I hope you don't mind if I ask the obvious, obnoxious question first," she said. "But . . . just who in the world *are* you?"

Professor Odd smiled, a little cryptically. "I'm just a *fan,* Princess Die. One of the many. Never underestimate the importance of a good fan base. But, to be honest, I think that lovely song you wrote does as good a job describing me as anything I could say."

"The Odd is back?" asked 713, their lights blinking fiercely.

"Odd is back," announced 202-B. They regarded Professor Odd critically. "You have lost your cane," they said.

"*Ah,*" said Professor Odd, turning around in the little room. For lack of a chair, she went and sat on a bundle of gymnastics mats that had been stuffed into a corner. "That's a rather long story . . . "

Alister and Elo and Dave sat up around the table for a few hours, but eventually they gave up waiting and went to bed. Alister was woken at some point, hours later, by the soft sound of singing coming from downstairs. Putting his head through his door, he looked down to find Professor Odd had returned, and that it was she who was singing. She'd lost her orange jacket, but had acquired a tuxedo-like coat with rhinestones on the tail, and her rainbow wig had been exchanged for a lavender one with long tresses pinned into a complicated hairdo like piles of whipped cream. Alister recognized it as one of Princess Die's signature wigs.

"How'd it go?" he called down.

Professor Odd looked up at him. She seemed a little wobbly. She grinned.

"It's *so* nice," she said. "It's so, *so* nice when artists really *appreciate* their fans." She climbed up the ladder and tottered over to her room, still singing softly . . .

"*When you're lonely you just have to pretend beyond that door is Professor Odd. You're not a looney, you can go tell your friends that you can call on Professor Odd . . . *"

Professor Odd will return in
"Davebot"

This story happened by accident, all because I sat next to an editor at an awards banquet back in 2012. She was working on an anthology featuring interpretations of the Green Man archetype in urban fantasy settings, and asked if I had anything for their consideration. I said no. Then on the way home this story popped into my head, and I wrote it down one afternoon when I was between projects. Amazingly enough, it was bought by that very editor and can be found in the Urban Green Man *anthology, from* EDGE Science Fiction and Fantasy. *It is technically a standalone, but because none of my stories are islands, it has a connection with the* Driving Arcana *story which immediately follows.*

ABANDON ALL ____

EVENING IN THE CITY. The cooling air is filled with the sound of traffic: the roar of cars; the grumble and screech of trucks. A train barrels through, adding to the din. The sky is half pale blue gray, half black clouds hanging ominously in the south. A soft wind ruffles the topmost leaves of a majestic oak tree, but there is no sound; the quiet rustling of the leaves is eaten up by the pervasive rumbling, honks and occasional squeaks of rush hour.

The sound washed over and around Marvin like a blanket. He had been born in the city, raised in the city, and to him the sound of car engines was as natural and reassuring as birdsong—when he noticed it at all. At the moment, he had other things to think about.

It was getting dark. That meant that the lights had come on along the pedestrian path that ran beside the canal, casting little circles of orange light that marched away into the distance. Marvin wished they hadn't: he liked dark places. In dark places he could hide. In dark places he was safe. He didn't understand why people were afraid of the dark. A place was a place whether it was light or dark, except that if it was dark and Marvin was in it, then people didn't see him and left him alone.

Marvin liked being alone. There was no one to hurt you if you were alone. His mother didn't like it. She said he had borderline social dysfunction disorder, or something like that, and encouraged him to make friends.

Marvin didn't like friends. His friends at school called him Starvin' Marvin, because he ate so much. The fact that he was also quite fat was hilarious to them, and they spent most of their time around him talking about how funny this was. Sometimes they pushed or poked him, just to make him squeal, and that was even funnier. They called him stupid and retarded, and talked about him like he wasn't there.

At that moment, Marvin was trying to avoid some of these friends. He had decided to take the detour home to avoid them, but was now realizing the error in his plan: the detour meant taking the pedestrian path over the freeway and along the canal and then through the abandoned cemetery. It was deserted at this time, which meant Marvin was alone. His friends were more likely to play with him if they found him alone.

Marvin hated playing with his friends. It was never any fun. One time they'd lifted him over the fence along the canal and he'd spent all afternoon trying to get out. His sneakers had been ruined, and he'd smelled of algae and bird poop when he got home. His mother hadn't been happy about that, though when he told her he'd been playing with his friends she cheered up. She always cheered up when he told her he had been playing with his friends, which was the only reason he kept doing it.

This evening, however, Marvin was tired and didn't want to play. So he walked quickly along the path, darting from shadow to shadow. He veered off across the cemetery, and here thankfully there were no lights.

There were also three teenagers lounging on broken headstones, drinking from bottles in paper bags. Marvin stopped dead in his tracks. These were some of his least favorite friends; they were the ones who had dumped him in the canal. Marvin thought about turning around and going home another way, but they had already seen him.

"Heeeey, look 'ere guys, it's Starvin' Marvin," said the tallest of the teenagers, a lanky boy with black hair and a thin beard.

"Hey Marvin, wanna drink?" said the shortest of the teenagers, a skinny boy with a buzz cut and a large zit on his nose.

"No, no thanks," said Marvin politely. He had tried one of their drinks before, and it had reminded him of the way his vomit had tasted when he'd had the flu last winter.

"Whatsa matter Marvin, you *scared* of a little beer?" said the middle teenager, a girl with her hair in pigtails and a book bag over her shoulder. She was the worst, because everybody liked her—including the teachers—and were forever telling Marvin she was a good influence on him and he should spend more time with her. This was because they never saw what she was like when she was alone with Marvin: she would stab him with her pencil and snap at him.

"Nah, nah," said the tallest teenager. "He's not *scared,* he's *hopeless.* That right, Marvin? You're *hopeless!*"

Marvin didn't think he was hopeless. He hoped, for example, that they would all step in dog doo on their way home. But he didn't say so.

The short boy chuckled. "Yeah, hopeless I'll say. Hey, hey Marvin—you know where you belong? In with *them.*" He pointed at one of the largest graves. Instead of a headstone it had a small house with a battered wooden door and words carved in blocks over the lintel. At one time ivy had grown over the front, and when it had been ripped away by some long-ago gardener, one of the blocks had been pulled free as well. Where once there had been a complete couplet, there now only read:

> *Abandon All ----*
> *Ye Who Enter Here.*

"That's s'posed to say '*Abandon all hope, ye who enter here,*'" the short boy chuckled. "That's from litra-cher, that is. Dante. Classic, man. Invented Italian. It means *welcome to hell.*"

Marvin peered at the little building. "I don't think so," he said carefully. "Hell is a big place. That is too small."

"What do *you* know about it, huh, *re-tard,*" said the girl. She pronounced the word 'retard' like it was two words: re tard.

"Hey, hey," said the tall boy. "Maybe Marvin should go in and see for himself, yeah? He'll learn a thing or two about *hell* in there!"

The other two thought this was a great idea, and before he could protest Marvin found himself stripped of his backpack and marched up to the door, which the short boy kicked open. They pushed him inside and hauled the door shut behind him, and when he turned around to try to open it again, he found it immovable. They probably had all their backs pressed up against it. In fact he could hear their muffled giggles close by on the other side.

Marvin turned around and sat down with his back to the door. He was getting hungry and wanted to go home, but though he explained this in a loud voice so his friends could hear, they only laughed harder. This made Marvin frustrated and a little angry.

But he was not afraid.

He sat in the dark, waiting for his eyes to adjust. At first he had thought the place was pitch black, but now he realized there must be a skylight up in the arched ceiling, for the longer he waited the more gray shapes swam into view.

He was in a little stone room with a large stone slab in the middle, on the far side of which was a dark doorway. Marvin considered it for some time, before deciding to make his way around the stone slab to peer cautiously through the door. Perhaps there was another way out?

He stepped through, into a pile of dead leaves, which gave way under his feet. He staggered, then tumbled down a steeply sloping passage, the leaves rustling and whispering all around him. He landed in another pile of leaves at the bottom and clawed his way to the surface, spitting twigs and bits of leaf out of his mouth.

He blinked. It was light down here. A dim, pale light, ghostly and white—not at all like the orange streetlights. Marvin was reminded of the time when he was ten and his mother had taken him to visit his grandparents in the country. He had gone outside one night to find the world bathed in pale white light, and the moon full and round and blindingly bright above him. This then . . . this was *moonlight.* Wonderingly, Marvin looked up.

High stone walls stretched up all around him, but there was no ceiling, and beyond that was an impossibly black night sky, pricked by impossibly bright stars. Sure enough, there was the moon, milky white with a faint aura around her. It was wrong, how bright the moon was, and Marvin got the uncomfortable feeling that if he were to climb the stone walls he would find himself in a completely different place than the abandoned cemetery.

Drifts of leaves, muted brown in the moonlight, half filled the room. It was absolutely silent, as if the whole world was holding its breath. And at the far end, resting on the leaves as though on a bed, was a human skeleton.

Marvin frowned. It was hard to tell in the moonlight, but he thought it was the wrong color: too dark, and some of the bones looked wobbly and wrong. Curious, he waded through the leaves toward it for a closer look.

It was a tall skeleton—much taller than he was—and the reason it looked so dark was because it was not made of bone, but of perfectly carved wood. Marvin could see the grains of it, like in his mother's best chairs, making patterns in the ribs and the skull.

There was something in the skull's mouth that glinted in the moonlight. Marvin reached forward with his hand . . .

No sooner had his fingers brushed the skeleton's wooden teeth than the whole thing shuddered and twitched. Marvin was so surprised that he fell backwards and could only stare in astonishment at what happened next.

A little green sprout, color vivid even in the moonlight, pushed its way out of the skull's mouth and twined around the side of its head, sprouting more leaves as it went. Another sprout appeared, twining up the other side. Their leaves grew shiny and wide, then opened revealing pale buds. These quivered a moment, then unfurled gracefully into white, star-shaped flowers.

At the same time more leaves were curling out from its eye sockets, pushing together in the center of its forehead. A sharp shoot sprang up between them, arching back from the brow like a crest.

Even as all this happened, the rest of its body was undergoing a similar transformation: leaves crowded out from its shoulders, covering its ribs and pelvis. Vines ran down its arms, joining the wooden bones together, and little green buds bloomed on its fingertips.

Then the skeleton—which was not really a skeleton anymore but a body made of leaves and vines and blossoms—sat up with a jerk (more leaves burst out across its shoulders), writhed to its feet (a curtain of leaves like ivy tumbled down its legs like the folds of a robe), arched its back, rolled its shoulders, and finally looked down at Marvin. Its eyes were two dark pools between the leaves of its forehead and its cheeks, with little points of light in them like distant stars. Its chin was bare and its mouth slightly open because of the shoots of leaves that poured out on either side.

Marvin was not sure what to do. Nothing he had ever read had told him what to do about wooden skeletons that sprouted leaves and came to life. So he did what he usually did when he met a new person: he stared, trying to figure out if they were threatening or not.

"Hello," said the leafy thing. Marvin didn't see its mouth move, and its voice had a swishy, rustling quality that made him think it was the *leaves* doing the talking, not the head.

Marvin decided the leafy thing was *not* threatening. It was too polite.

"Hello," he replied solemnly. "I'm Marvin."

"Hello Marvin," said the leafy thing with equal gravity. "Why are you here?"

Marvin sighed. He didn't like being asked questions. Answering them usually got him into trouble. But the leafy thing did not strike him as the same sort of person as his teachers or his friends. He felt like he could talk to it without worrying what it thought.

"My friends wanted to play, so they locked me in the hell house in the old cemetery," he said. A thought occurred to him. "Is this hell?"

The leafy thing rustled, but no words came out. Marvin thought it was laughing. Eventually it said: "No. I cannot be in Hell, and Hell cannot be with me. We are . . . incompatible." It pushed its finger buds together to demonstrate. The leaves of its face drooped then, as if it was sad. "You keep strange friends," it said. "When last I walked, friends took up arms against one's enemy, defended one's honor, brought one solace and comfort in times of trouble. They did not lock one in houses of the damned." The leaves of its forehead bunched together, crowding over its brow in a frown. "Do your friends do any of those other things?" it asked.

Marvin thought about it, and had to admit that they did not.

"Then," said the leafy thing, it's face firming up as it came to a decision. "They are not your friends."

The statement hit Marvin like a blow. *They were not his friends.* That made so much more *sense.* He felt a brief pang of sadness at the thought that this meant he didn't have any friends, but mostly he was so relieved not to have to call those horrible bullies—which was, he realized now, what they were— his friends, that he laughed out loud.

This puzzled the leafy thing, but it leaned back against the wall, folding its hands under the wide leaves hanging down from its chest, and waited patiently for Marvin to finish.

"I understand that now," Marvin said. "They only *said* they were friends, but they were not."

"They lied," said the leafy thing. Marvin found he liked how it stated things so neatly and clearly. It made it easy to talk to.

"I like you," he told the leafy thing. "What's your name?"

The leaves along the thing's shoulders rose and fell, like a sort of shrug. "I have been called by many names," it said. "I'm not sure which one you would know me by."

"Well," said Marvin, who had given a lot of thought to what he would have called himself if given the chance. "What do *you* like to be called?"

The thing ruffled its leaves, and its eyes glowed brighter.

"Green," it said decidedly. "I am . . . Green."

"Are you a boy or a girl?" asked Marvin.

"I am neither," said Green. "But you may refer to me as whichever you wish."

Marvin shook his head. "I won't call you either, then, if you're not. It's only fair."

Green was pleased at this. Marvin found, now he was grow- ing used to the face, that he could read its expressions better than normal human faces: something about the way its leaves perked or sagged confused him less than the way cheeks and eyebrows would bunch and squish.

"I think," said Green, "that we should go talk to your other friends."

"They're not my friends anymore," Marvin said, and felt warm and good just saying that. "They never were. I was confused."

"Still," said Green, offering Marvin one twiggy hand. "I believe we should explain how matters stand, don't you?"

Three teenagers sat in a cemetery drinking beer from bottles in paper bags. One of them, the tall one, said:

"He's been awfully quiet in there, think we should let him out?"

"He's jug . . . he's jug . . . " the shortest (and the drunkest) boy replied. "He's juz tryin' to scare uz. Yanno . . . make uz tink he'z inter . . . in trouble."

"He's prolly just waitin' for us to let him out. Thinks it's all a big game . . . re-tard." The middle one—the girl—giggled. So did the short one. The tallest—who was also the most sober— laughed nervously and glanced at the little crypt . . .

. . . and turned pale and let out a ragged gasping sound.

In the middle of the old wooden door had erupted a profusion of bright green leaves, and in the center of the leaves, stained a sickly green, was Marvin's pudgy face.

"Hello . . . children," said Marvin's face. But it was not Marvin's voice: it was too knowing, too old, too *wise*. It was the voice of something ancient beyond reckoning that knew each one of them personally. *Intimately.* It knew all their darkest little secrets, and it was not pleased.

The other two found themselves sobering up fast. All three of them stared at the green face in the door, speechless. The shortest one made a retching sound.

"I know what you've been doing," continued Marvin's face in the old, knowing voice. "I know what you've been dreaming. I know what you've been *fearing*." The old voice trailed off into laughter like wind in trees. When it spoke again it was definitely all Marvin now, and the face scrunched up in anger.

"You're *not* my friends anymore," he said. "You never *were!* And if you don't stop bothering me . . . I'll *get* you!"

As he spoke the last words the leaves writhed around his face, and it lunged forward out of the door, supported by tendrils of strong, black vines.

There was a crash and a tinkle as the tallest boy hurled one of the bottles against a tombstone, turned tail and fled. The other two followed suit, stumbling, blind with panic, until they found each other and hobbled off together at a stilted run.

Marvin stepped out of the door and craned his neck to watch them go. Behind him the vines and leaves retreated, weaving back together, and Green emerged, its disgorging mouth stretched into an unmistakable grin.

"That was good," Marvin said, when the sounds of the teenagers had dwindled to nothing.

Green didn't answer. When Marvin turned to look he found it staring back up at the lintel above the door, at the inscription missing a word.

"I see the problem," Green said, and bent over, sending shoots and tendrils out along the ground, searching. Eventually it found what it was looking for and stood up, a block of stone held in one hand. Carefully it reached up and fitted the block into the space of the missing word and stepped back.

"Oh," said Marvin, after reading what the inscription now said. "That's much better."

"I think so too," said Green.

Marvin was very late getting home. His mother was upset at first—she had been worried—but when she saw him all rosy cheeked and brimming with happiness she relented, and gave him a slice of pie with his dinner.

"I made a new friend tonight," Marvin said through his pie. "We played in that old cemetery."

"That's wonderful," said his mother. "Maybe tomorrow you can bring him around for dinner, I would love to meet him."

Marvin nodded vigorously, his mouth full of pie. It occurred to him, distantly, that there might be some complications involved with bringing Green home for dinner—he wasn't sure Green even ate human food—but that was a problem for another day. For now, he had a friend—a real, proper friend—and pie. He was happy. His mother was happy. Things would be all right.

In the cemetery, standing so still that any passerby would have mistaken it for a shrub, Green stood and listened to the sound of the traffic roaring in the distance. This world was drastically changed from the one it had known, but all the old principles were still in place. There was material to work with, and all things considered, Green was happy too.

Above and behind it, over the lintel of the door to the crypt, the repaired sign now read:

Abandon All Fear
Ye Who Enter Here.

The black clouds parted, and the moon shone down on the little cemetery. It was unusually bright that night.

You do not need to have read "Abandon All _____" to understand "The Earth It Weeps," nor do you have to read the nine Driving Arcana *stories which precede it—though I recommend it. But, as it is the first episode in the second* Wheel *of* Driving Arcana, *it is not a bad place to join the ride. It was written in the spring of 2015, and will be followed by* Driving Arcana *#11: "Out of Space" (coming in* Apsis Fiction: Aphelion 2017).*

The Earth it Weeps

Tulsa, OK
November

ON THE WHOLE, it had been a good summer. True, the move had been rough, but that was only to be expected. Marvin had been depressed for a month, and complained loudly about missing his friend. Whenever Sharon gently suggested he go make new friends Marvin would clamp down and go blank in a way that frightened her.

"I want Green back," was all he would say. "Green was my *friend.*"

This made Sharon unhappy. Because Green had been one of the reasons for their move in the first place. Well, *Lucas* had been the real reason, but if packing up and leaving town meant Sharon never had to see her ex-husband *or* deal with Marvin's creepy imaginary friend again, so much the better, she thought.

Marvin disagreed (though not about the Lucas part), and gloomed around their new house until school started, where by some miracle he met Rosie Thorn.

At first Sharon had worried that Rosie was another like Green—their names had a similar, plant-ish connotation—but she had turned out to be a perfectly real, flesh-and-blood girl, albeit a rather extraordinary one.

She was a perfect storm of mixed features: brown-skinned but light enough to show the permanent pink flush that adorned her cheeks, which was the reason for her name (her real name, Sharon didn't learn until much later, was Latasha). She had a mass of tightly curled black hair, trimmed to a small halo, and the most incongruously bright, brilliant green eyes. They practically jumped out of her face and stunned Sharon the first time she laid eyes on the girl, which was on the afternoon of Marvin's twelfth birthday.

Marvin had spent the morning sequestered in his room, playing the latest console game his grandmother had given him as a present. It was both a blessing and a curse, Sharon's mother being so finely attuned to what Marvin would find compelling and addictive. Sharon herself had been prepared to spend her Saturday like she always did: mired in housework and bills with the added stress of baking a birthday cake. Because what sort of mother was she if there was no cake?

As it happened she had been spared the trials of her new kitchen by the appearance, around three in the afternoon, of Rosie Thorn and her own mother, the former bearing a large parcel wrapped in gold paper, and the latter a cake box.

The surprising appearance of the girl was partially explained by her mother, who had the exact same eyes but was otherwise the opposite of her daughter in every way: Rosie was a soft, round girl with matching face, nose, and lips, while Audrey was narrow, sinewy and careworn. She had the sort of skin that went straight from white to red without any attempt at a tan, and blond hair whose artificialness was only belied by the woman's comparatively dark eyebrows.

She held the cake box out, almost apologetically.

"I'm sorry if we're interrupting your plans," she said. "But Rosie insisted—and she hasn't stopped talking about Marvin."

She was interrupted by a clatter from inside the house and Marvin bursting out into the yard to hug Rosie, sufficiently diffusing any lingering social awkwardness.

Rosie's present was a hammock, woven in rainbow colors. Sharon and Audrey had helped them find a place for it in the backyard, after which they had candles and cake and (for the adults) coffee. Fortified on sugar, Rosie and Marvin had rushed out to play in the yard. *Actually play,* like normal kids. Sharon had watched them from the porch, sipping coffee, and commiserating with Audrey about the trials of being a single mother. The subject of husbands was pointedly avoided, and by the end of the afternoon Sharon had been surprised to discover that she had made a new friend as well.

Things got easier after that. Marvin was happier. Her consulting business was not a complete train wreck. Sometimes Rosie came over after school, and sometimes Marvin went to her house. One memorable weekend they both stayed the night with Sharon's mother, and she and Audrey had gone hiking in the Ozarks.

It was, on the whole, a good summer.

And then September had happened. Not as badly or as dramatically as for Sharon's friends in St. Louis, who reported the events first with disbelief, then horror, and then dubious resignation.

Monsters and demons and a giant coming through the Gateway Arch. It was too much to believe. It was crazy. It was (literally) out of this world.

It was suspiciously reminiscent of the sort of thing Marvin would say about his friend, Green.

Green, from what he had told her, slept in a crypt, had no discernible gender, was sometimes a skeleton ("But not a fleshy one. Wooden. Like a chair.") and sometimes a tree. They ate sunlight and vomited flowers and could, when they wanted, make other plants get up and walk around.

Sharon had dismissed it as childhood fantasy, at first. Then, as her marriage and her ability to sleep had deteriorated, one night she'd found herself standing at the kitchen sink, staring out into their front yard, at a strange bush which should not have been there.

It had been difficult to tell in the dappled streetlight, but she thought the bush had looked back at her with eyes that twinkled. Like stars at the bottom of a deep, dark well. It had been smiling, blossoms and leaves pouring out of its mouth.

She had run back to bed like she was seven and had seen a scary shadow.

In the morning it had been gone.

Nothing like that had happened since they'd moved to Tulsa. Everything had been wonderfully, soothingly *ordinary*.

And then September happened.

Sharon had been woken by a sound in the middle of the night. It had sounded like Marvin, and because of that she got out of bed and padded over to his room. She'd barely pushed the door open when she heard another noise from outside, like someone breathing heavily.

It was something Marvin did when he was excited. The next moment Sharon had realized the reason she could hear it was because Marvin's window was open, and the moment after that she was running for the back door.

She'd seen them, clear as day. Marvin was swinging on the hammock, and standing behind him, pushing him back and forth, was a . . . a . . .

It was not exactly a skeleton. It was not exactly a bush. It was difficult to tell, with the backyard in the shadow of the house and the moon behind a thin cloud. Sharon was sure she saw *something* in the dark, but when she flicked on the porch light it was just Marvin.

Marvin on the hammock, looking happier than he had since their move.

In the end she'd scolded him for going outside in the middle of the night, put him to bed, and then sat up with all the lights on, trying to make sense of what she'd seen.

In the morning the news had been overflowing with the disaster in downtown St. Louis, and Sharon had had the sinking realization that she knew very well what this meant.

It meant that Marvin would start coming home late from school, covered in dirt with leaves in his hair. It meant that he would start telling stories about Green again. It meant he would sleep with his window open, and in the morning there would be a layer of flower petals on the floor. It meant that, when Sharon asked what he'd been doing and where he'd been, he would just say, "Playing with my friend," and *not* mean his good, kind, *normal* friend, Rosie.

And sure enough, that was what happened. Only this time Sharon *knew* she wasn't crazy. She knew to put locks on Marvin's window and to be there promptly to pick him up from school.

She spent more money than she should have hiring a landsca-
per to prune back all the trees around their house, so she had
clear lines of sight to the road in front and the fence in back.
She walked Marvin to Rosie's house after school, and insisted
Audrey walk him home if she couldn't do it herself.

But she still couldn't bring herself to tell anyone. What
would she tell them? I've seen a creepy plant person, in the
dark, playing with my child? He would come home with leaves
in his hair? He told funny stories about his imaginary friend?

Marvin's brain had always worked a little differently from
other people. "Special Needs" was what they called it, these days,
but Sharon didn't like that label. She didn't like the clinical di-
agnoses doctors gave Marvin either. Marvin was just . . . Marvin.
He wasn't stupid, but when people saw he was on the Asperger's
spectrum they tended to view everything he said through their
autism interpretive goggles. Anything at all outlandish that he
said would be dismissed out of hand. It was particularly aggravating because, in Sharon's own experience, the opposite was
true: Marvin was perfectly literal, he said what he meant, and
he didn't lie.

As for coming home disheveled, wasn't that a reflection of
her own failings as a parent? Couldn't she take care of her kid?

And the creepy plant person might have had some weight,
considering the pervasive phobia of child molesters, except that
Sharon had only ever *thought* she'd seen this person. At night. In
bad light. And it had disappeared as soon as she looked closely.

It was driving her crazy, being torn by what she knew she
was seeing and what she knew people would think of her, and
the tantalizing hope that, maybe, after the foofaraw in St. Louis,
people might actually *listen*.

Of course, one of the side-effects of the invasion of supernatural phenomena was that nutjobs were coming out of the
woodwork with their crazy stories, and now that they had an
actual thread of evidence to support their claims that ghosts
and demons and werewolves existed, they were *everywhere*. And
they seemed just as crazy and messed up as ever.

Sharon did *not* want to become like that. She was a *rational*
person, and she would deal with this like one.

Then Marvin went missing.

For fifteen minutes, he was missing. Somewhere between walking out of his last class and over to the parking lot where Sharon was waiting, he inexplicably vanished.

She had just enough time to panic, call the principal and get a search party going, when Rosie—who had, of course, joined in—discovered Marvin asleep under one of the trees which shaded the walk from the school to the gymnasium. He seemed confused upon waking, saying that he'd been playing in the park and asking where "they" had gone.

"Who's *they?*" Rosie asked.

"My friend," said Marvin. Sharon had practically picked him up and ran to her car before he could say anything else.

Then one of her clients—an older woman, staunchly Catholic, whom Sharon had always liked for her level-headedness—had casually dropped into the conversation that the reason she'd had to cancel her last appointment was because a demon had gotten into her plumbing and she'd had to hire an exorcist to get rid of it.

Sharon nearly spilled her coffee all over her computer.

"I *know,*" said Mrs. Doughty, seeing her reaction, but she was grinning conspiratorially. "Sounds practically *medieval,* doesn't it? But these are the days we live in, it seems. I talked to my priest, and *he* said they'd had a lot of incidents like mine, and they weren't really able to help. But he knew someone who was a specialist, and got us in touch and . . . *well.* I don't know what I was expecting, but it certainly wasn't—" the woman broke off, coloring a little. "He was *very* good. And professional. And got the demon out as clean as you please, and answered all my questions, and gave me tips so it wouldn't happen again. Not wackaboo at all. Cheaper than a plumber, too. Honestly I don't know how he makes his living—though I suppose with the re-cent spate of hauntings he must be very busy."

Sharon went still, mechanically drinking her coffee, while inside her mind spun in circles.

"I don't suppose you still have his number?" she asked after a minute.

Mrs. Doughty gave her a coy look. "Not troubled yourself, are you?" she asked.

Sharon felt her lips tighten. "It doesn't hurt to be prepared," she said.

Mrs. Doughty smiled, and slipped her a folded piece of notepaper without another word.

After her client had left, Sharon spent a long time staring at the number printed on the paper, wondering what to do. But though she entered it into her phone, she couldn't bring herself to call it.

Then she went to pick up Marvin from Rosie's house one day, and found the front door wide open.

It was a balmy autumn day and the Thorns had an indoor-outdoor cat, so this was not in itself an alarming sign. No, what sent Sharon's heart pounding was the scattering of red and orange leaves across the doormat, which formed a trail leading to the kitchen.

And there she had found them: Rosie and Marvin and Audrey too, sitting at the table which had put out shoots of branches heavy with nuts and ripe fruit. They were eating happily, and standing at the head of the table, flaming in colors of red and orange and yellow, was a person-shaped thing made out of bunches of leaves and twining vines. A bit of their skull—whorled and brown as polished mahogany—showed through around their chin, and a few vines trickled out of their open mouth.

They looked up at Sharon as she entered, their eyes like stars at the bottom of a deep well, and opened their mouth wider.

A faint rustling started around Sharon's feet as a soft wind whispered in through the open back door, shuffling the leaves which lay drifted on the floor. In the noise she thought she heard the sound of unearthly laughter.

She screamed. She wasn't sure what she said, only that she dove forward and grabbed Marvin by the scruff of his jacket.

Hands—human and branch-like—were grabbing at her. She was aware of Rosie crying, and of Audrey—*Audrey!*—pleading with her.

"Calm down," she heard. "This isn't what it looks like!"

She must have been enchanted, Sharon thought. Enchantments must be a thing now, like ghosts and demons and living tree skeletons.

She dragged Marvin out of the kitchen and somehow got them home. Marvin was crying. She was crying. She locked all the doors and spent some time hyperventilating on the living room couch.

Later, after Marvin had cried himself to sleep, after she had checked and re-checked, and none of the trees outside came to life and assaulted the house, she pulled up the contact on her phone that was just a number—no name—and hit "call."

Kansas City, MO

THE TRAILER DWARFED THE TRUCK. And considering the truck was a Ram 3200 with dual rear wheels, that was saying something.

Arcana gleamed in the afternoon sunlight, his deep red coat freshly washed and waxed, while the gooseneck camper crouched behind him, sleek and new and sparkling. With all its pocket sides expanded it looked like a small house that had been planted in the middle of the parking lot. In shining, chrome letters across the front was the word *Cougar.*

Standing beside it, sparkling with excitement rather than new paint, was its owner.

"*Well?*" said Jill Hamilton, smiling brightly. "What do you think?"

The two women who stood opposite her continued to stare, speechless, for some minutes. Then the tall, pale, bald one—the one dressed in black biking leathers with a broadsword strapped to her back—said in a faint voice:

"It's very . . . big."

"It has a *garage,*" said Jill, grinning hugely. "So we can haul Unicorn for you, if you get tired of riding."

The bald woman's partner, who was short only by comparison, folded her strong, brown arms over her chest. She wore jeans and cowboy boots and a cotton workshirt rolled up to the elbows. Her skin was the kind of of burnt umber that cooled to indigo in the shade. She reached up and scratched under her thick mane of frizzy black hair.

"At least he's keeping the animal theme we got going here," Selene Shields drawled. Her accent was hard to place: anyone

from the west or north would have called it "southern" but anyone actually from the south would probably have said "Texas." If
asked herself, the woman would just say "around."

"I *know,*" said Jill, swelling with pride. "Isn't it *awesome?*"

"But," said Clara Nordstern, screwing up her bright blue eyes
against the glare from the asphalt. "What is it *for?*"

Jill gave her a flabbergasted look.

"He's for *research,*" she said, somehow giving the impression
of rolling her eyes even though she kept them fixed on Clara's
face. "And, you know, *living* in? So we don't have to keep motel-
hopping. *Look,* I got him built custom: he's got extra lights and
ventilation in the garage so we can use it as an exam room if we
need to; a freeze locker, extra fridge, and I put in a mini chem lab.
With microscopes. And the bathroom doubles as a darkroom.
Oh, and there are bunks for you and Selene, if, like, you guys
ever need to sleep at the same time."

"How much did this *cost?*" Selene asked, sounding mildly
horrified.

"A lot," said Jill, airily. "But it's okay: he's pretty much covered by the grant I got from the Coalition of Concerned Scien-
tists. Apparently I'm not the only one with rational concerns
over how *little* we know about the supernatural." She grinned.
"Wanna see inside?"

With a sigh Selene gestured for the young woman to pro-
ceed, and Jill trotted around to the back and opened up the ramp,
her voice lingering even after she disappeared around the rear
corner of the trailer.

"This space can also double as a lab, if we get a large specimen like that worm. Also, storage for artifacts and samples . . . "
her voice faded to an incomprehensible mumble as she climbed
inside, Selene following with a bemused expression on her face.

Clara remained behind, regarding the trailer as though it
were a sign of the apocalypse. Which was unfair, she realized.
The world wasn't ending today any more than it already was.
Still, the trailer was a sign of Jill's increasing determination to
apply the scientific method to things which, in Clara's experience, took defying science as a personal challenge. She felt an
echo of the uncertainty she had first experienced when Jill set
off on her crusade, over a year ago.

But here they were, all three of them. Still alive and—in Jill's case—undaunted, despite slippery evidence and vampire attacks and demons and demigods and—in the case of the St. Louis disaster *real* gods. It was just another step on the road she'd been traveling for months already. But it was also a land-mark: Jill had always been serious about her quest, and now it seemed she might actually get somewhere.

The prospect was exciting and terrifying all at once. Because Clara knew better than anyone that there were things which were not only best left unknown but would become extremely prickly if you tried to get to know them.

She was roused from her bitter reverie by the harsh sound of an old-fashioned telephone, and it took her a moment to recognize it as Jill's cell phone. It sounded faintly muffled and came from the direction of Arcana's cab.

Clara sighed. Jill was one of those people who was an incredible multitasker, and so used her phone to the very limit of its smarts, but because she was so distracted most of the time she also had the bad habit of leaving it in random places.

Clara went over to Arcana and pulled open the front passenger door. Sure enough, lying there on the seat was Jill's sleek, black-and-steel tablet of a phone, its screen alight with the incoming call.

She had intended just to bring the phone to its proper owner, but when she saw the name of the caller she hesitated, a strange prickling going up her arms to settle at the base of her neck.

It was not quite fear. Clara was too familiar with that sensation to mistake it. But it was similar. Anticipatory and apprehensive at the same time.

"*Brrrinnnginging,*" said the phone, and Clara realized that if she was going to do anything she should do it soon.

Taking a gloved finger into her mouth she pulled the leather off her hand and swiped to answer.

For lack of anything better to say, she greeted the caller by name.

"Ariel Freeman," she said, her voice sounding stilted and blank, even to her.

"Whoa, okay, not Jill?" said the deep, warm, golden voice on the other end of the phone. But there was a ring of laughter behind the words, as though the speaker was smiling, as it went on. "Is that Claymore?" Then, more seriously, "Is everything all right?"

"Everything is fine," said Clara, robotically. "Jill left her phone in the truck, again. I am bringing you to her now."

"Nah, it's okay, actually. I got a case here: lady calls me, talking about some tree person who is trying to steal her son. Sounds serious. Thing is, I'm down in New Mexico at the moment with a really persistent haunting and I can't see myself getting out of here for at least another week. And this seemed like something more up your alley."

"My alley?" repeated Clara, surprised.

"I heard about the blood tree in Missouri," said Ariel, softly. "And St. Louis. Did your lot get out of that okay?"

"Yeah," said Clara. "We're okay. We're still in Missouri, actually. Kansas City."

"Well, ain't that perfect," said Ariel, the laugh returning to his voice. Clara wasn't sure why, but the sound made her feel warm inside in a way that was disturbingly pleasant. "This lady is in Tulsa. Name's Sharon Gilkey. I don't have her address, but I can give you her number. Also told her to call this one. Figured Jill would at least find it interesting."

Glancing toward the trailer, where Jill's voice could just be heard raised in excitement over the lab she had set up in the master bedroom, Clara couldn't help but agree.

"I'll tell her," she promised. "Do you have any idea what *it* is?"

Ariel sighed gustily. There was some blustering distortion on his end, as though from wind. Still, his words came across clearly when he said, "You know, to be honest it could be anything. Lady sounded pretty messed up when she called. But, from her description, I think it's some sort of green man."

"Green man," Clara echoed.

"Yeah, or a more general plant spirit," said Ariel. "Nature stuff's not my specialty, but I *would* take this one except . . ."

"Haunting. Yes, I understand," said Clara. She rolled her shoulders, feeling the weight of Bellatrix settling comfortably against her back. "We've been spinning our wheels for the last two months, I am sure Jill will want to investigate this. Even if she doesn't, I will look into it myself."

"Thanks," said Ariel, heartfelt. "But, be careful, m'okay?"

"The same to you," said Clara, stiffly.

There was proper laugh on the other end of the line at that. "If I was careful I wouldn't be in New Mexico right now," Ariel chuckled. Then, like before, his tone sobered quickly. "I'm just saying: things have changed since St. Louis, and not just with more *people* knowing about this stuff. There's more of *everything* out there, now. And what was always out there, it's stronger."

"I know," Clara said. She didn't say, *But I feel stronger, too. I don't know why, and it frightens me, but I know it's true.* "I'll call you when we're done; let you know how it went," she said instead.

This earned her another chuckle. "Thanks, Claymore. I'd appreciate that."

She should really correct him. Claymore was her name, but she was called Clara by choice. Only very few people called her by name anymore.

"Good luck in New Mexico," she said.

"Yeah, yeah, same to you. Bye."

"Good-bye," said Clara, but it was so faint she wasn't certain the man heard before the line went dead.

She stared at the phone for a long time. It had a passcode, but Jill had disclosed this to Clara in case of "extreme circumstances." After a minute Clara unglued her free hand and fumbled out the tiny notebook she kept in the inner pocket of her jacket. She grabbed a pen from Arcana's glove compartment and, unlocking the phone, went to Recent Calls and copied down Ariel's number in the book. Then she slept the phone and went around to the back of the trailer so she could put her head in the open rear door.

Jill and Selene were just visible through the inner door to the living area. Jill was sitting on the sofa with her feet up on the folding table while Selene paced up and down, looking in cupboards and examining the hidden nooks and crannies.

"This thing is a security nightmare," she was saying when Clara arrived. "I'm gonna have to make, like, a dozen ward pouches and put a heaven's array in each room. Clara," she said with relief as the woman stooped to enter the middle section of the camper. "Help a sister out here? How would you secure this place?"

"I would not attempt to sleep in it," Clara said, blandly.

"Well thanks for *that*," said Selene, rolling her eyes.

Wordlessly, Clara handed Jill's phone back to her.

"Oh, *thanks*," said Jill, leaping up to take it.

"Ariel Freeman called," Clara explained. "We have a case. It's in Tulsa."

"Oklahoma?" said Selene. "Great. Isn't this just a tour of all my least-favorite cities."

"Tulsa's quite progressive, these days," Jill pointed out.

"Uh-huh," said Selene, clearly unconvinced. "Maybe for *you* it is. But bible-belt nut-jobs aside, it's almost as bad as Cleveland."

"What's in Cleveland?" Jill asked.

"There are natural gates," Clara explained. "Built on a nexus of ley lines, they have a greater amount of supernatural energy, because it flows through between our world and the spirit one."

"Also, Tulsa's got some bad history, specially with my people, but also the natives. Although, this whole damn *country* has bad history with the natives. Kinda poisons the atmosphere, if yanno what I mean."

Jill frowned.

"No," she said. "I don't think so. But I want to learn." She stood up. "Right then. Tulsa. Clara, you want to load up Unicorn or—"

"I am riding," Clara stated, turned on her heel, and walked out of the trailer.

"Then I guess I'm driving," sighed Selene. "Unless you also want to learn how to haul a gooseneck?"

Jill sighed. "Something tells me I better."

Jill lasted longer than Selene expected: all the way to Carthage, at which point their run of clear highway driving was interrupted by the city, and Jill took the first exit advertising diesel and moved into the passenger seat while Selene was filling the tank.

For once Clara did not rush on ahead. She waited patiently astride Unicorn until Arcana had been refueled and lumbered onto the road again—this time under the more assured direction of Selene—and then followed in his wake.

"I think she's drafting us," said Selene, peering at the rearview mirrors. "D'ya think you could call her, ask her not to ride in my blind spot?"

Jill obligingly got out her phone, only to have it light up in her hands with an incoming call. It was an unfamiliar number, and Jill frowned as she answered and pressed the device to her ear.

"This is Jill Hamilton," she began, "may I ask who—"

She paused as a torrent of panicked words spilled into her ear.

"It's okay, I hear you," she said, at the first available opportunity. "No, I don't think you're crazy, Ms. . . . uh . . . sorry what was your name? Gilkey? Ms. Gilkey . . . Sharon? Okay, Sharon. Hi. We are actually already en route. We should be arriving in Tulsa in around . . ." she pulled the phone away from her ear to speak to Selene. "How long until Tulsa?" she asked.

Selene, driving one handed and pulling on a strand of hair with the other, shrugged. "Less than two hours," she said. "More, if we hit traffic. What part of Tulsa is she in?"

"We're just outside of Carthage," Jill said. "We can be at your location by this evening. If I could have an address?" She scrambled for a notepad while the information poured out of the phone. Jotting it down she passed it to Selene, who squinted at it, and then cursed.

"That's in Maple Ridge," she groaned. "Tell her we won't be there before eight."

"Right," said Jill. "Sharon? Are you there? Yes, it looks like we'll be there by eight."

"Ask her if she's in danger *right* now," Selene said.

"Are you in danger at this moment?" Jill repeated. She listened to the disjointed rambling, her face screwed up in concentration. After a while she covered the mic on her phone and whispered to Selene, "She says there's a bush person camped in her front yard, and her son keeps trying to go out and play with it."

"*Don't let him,*" Selene said immediately.

"I don't think she's going to," said Jill, wincing a little. "But, like, is there anything she can do before we get there?"

Selene frowned. "Could be anything, at this point. Hard to say. But tell her to put some iron down in all her doors and windows. *Real* iron, not that stainless steel crap. Lead works too, if she's got it. Oh, and if her house has a fireplace, tell her to light it. Or at least get some candles going."

Jill repeated these instructions to the woman on the other end of the phone, issued more assurances that they would be there within a few hours, and hung up.

"Definitely get Clara on the horn," said Selene. "Give her our destination, and put her on speaker: she knows more about this stuff than I do."

"This stuff?" said Jill, pulling up Clara's contact and hitting *Call.*

"Nature spirits," sighed Selene. "Whole 'nother bag of fish than monsters and zombies and crap like that. Closer to fairies and unicorns, but different."

"Like the god tree in River View?" Jill asked.

Selene shuddered, remembering the bloodthirsty, reality-warping tree. "Sort of," she said. "That was a kinda unique case. This? Could be a green man, like our boy Freeman says. Could be something more specific."

"What *is* a green man?" Jill asked, just as Clara answered.

"That depends on the culture and people," said Clara's voice, at the same time Selene said, "Depends on who you ask."

Jill prodded Arcana's controls until the bluetooth kicked in and Clara's voice could be heard out of the truck's speakers.

"Why do you ask?" was the first thing they heard.

"Freeman's referral gave us a call," Selene explained. "She's in Maple Ridge, 1123 Woodside Boulevard. If we get stuck in traffic on 44 I want you to go on ahead and scope the place. I think there's a wood sprite or something haunting them—not sure why."

"Names?" asked Clara.

"Sharon Gilkey," said Jill. "She has a son, at least. Don't know his name."

"Did she give a description?" Clara asked.

"She just said there was a bush person in their front yard," Jill explained.

"What kind of bush?" Clara asked.

"*I* don't know," snapped Jill. "She sounded pretty messed up. Said that it'd followed her from California and was trying to steal her kid. Or overrun the neighborhood. Said something about it possessing a friend of hers. But she was so upset, I don't know how much of it was accurate."

"For the time being, let's just assume it all is," said Selene.

"But it probably *isn't*," insisted Jill. "People who are upset don't make the best judgment calls."

Selene gave her a short, quizzical glance.

Like deciding to sell their house and run off to study the supernatural because their boyfriend got eaten by a chimera? the glance said. Jill ignored it.

"If it is a pursuing spirit, and it can possess people, this is serious," Clara pointed out. "We need to be prepared."

"Okay, okay," sighed Jill. "Yes, that's good. Just so long as we don't jump to any conclusions before we've had time to examine the evidence."

"*Yes, ma'am*," Selene said in a sing-song voice. "Clara, I meant to ask. What do you know about green men?"

"Do you mean plant spirits in general, or the actual Greenman?" Clara returned.

"There's a difference?" Jill asked.

From the speakers came a dusty sigh.

"The Greenman is an actual person," Selene explained in an undertone. "Kind of a god. One of the tricksters. Better to avoid him than fight him."

"He's real?" Jill asked.

"As real as Vjor," said Selene. "And a lot more present in this world. 'Specially with all the neo-pagans running around putting his face on bowls and doorknockers and stuff. They don't get half of it right most of the time, but it's enough to keep him nearby. I don't think anyone's actually *seen* in him modern times, but you get branches of him cropping up here and there. This could be one of them. We call 'em green men, though really it's green *people*. Plant-people, rose people, that sort of thing."

"Anthropomorphic personifications of plants," Clara informed them. "Some more human-looking than others, and their powers vary. Which is why I'm curious as to what sort of bush it is."

"Sorry," said Jill.

"I meant plant spirits, generally," Selene said. "Though it couldn't hurt to compare notes about *the* Greenman."

"All right," said Clara. "First, I do not believe there is *one* Greenman. I believe what we call the Greenman has been no less than seven different forest deities at any given time."

"Glad we got that sorted out," Selene said. "So what about spirits in general?"

"Dryads, as they are traditionally called, can be especially powerful and dangerous. However, they are not native to North America and so their powers are weaker here."

"But remember the gate," Selene said. "Lots of stuff that was confined geographically might have been spread around."

"Which is why I mentioned them," said Clara. "Dryads have transformative powers, and in large numbers can create pocket dimensions. They are easy to kill, however."

"Right," said Selene. "So what are our other possibilities? Do you think it could be a walker?"

"Walkers don't manifest spontaneously," Clara said, followed by Jill's demand of *What is a walker?*

"Walking tree," said Selene. "Rare enough, we can't really classify them beyond that."

"Like the Ents in *Lord of the Rings*?" asked Jill.

"Yeah . . . no," said Selene.

"They are more like the huorns," said Clara, seriously. "Which Tolkien lifted from the only surviving first-person account of a walker army."

"Ain't that that Welsh poem?" Selene said. "The *Cad Gothic-* something . . . "

"*Cad Goddeu,*" said Clara. "That was something else."

"What did you mean, they don't manifest spontaneously?" Jill asked.

"Walkers are normal trees given animalistic life and purpose," Clara explained. "That doesn't happen without serious supernatural intervention like a magician, witch, or forest deity."

"So if it is a walker, we'll have to hunt down whatever made it," Selene said.

"And then . . . what?" asked Jill.

There was an uncomfortable silence from the two hunters.

"If it's hurtin' people," Selene said heavily. "We really got no choice. Gotta rip it out."

"Dryads are a sign of a healthy forest," Clara admitted. "But they can prey upon humans: kidnappings and non-consensual transformations were not uncommon."

Jill frowned. This did not quite sit well with her, but then she remembered the panicked voice on the other end of the phone.

Her job was to *study* these things, so that they would be able to tell the difference between, say, a dryad and a walker or whatever, and know how it worked. First and foremost, however, there was a scared woman out there who, if Clara was to be believed (and Jill at least took what both her bodyguards believed very seriously) was in real danger, and Jill was not so single-minded as to ignore that.

They did hit traffic on 44, and Clara did go on ahead. Selene cursed her way to 412, whereupon they ran counter-commute, and things were easier until they had to skirt around downtown Tulsa in order to reach Maple Ridge. Here the traffic thickened again, and it was well past eight by the time she wearily steered Arcana down Woodside Boulevard, pulling up in front of a comfortably large house that was a good deal more exposed than its neighbors, thanks to all the trees near it having been brutally trimmed back.

Because of this it was easy to spot Unicorn resting in the driveway, and equally clear that there were no bushes—malevolent or otherwise—occupying the front lawn.

Pulling Arcana up in front of the house, almost to the next door's driveway so that the trailer didn't block anything, Selene set the parking brake with a sigh of relief, and pried herself out of the driver's seat.

Jill was already out of the truck and marching up to the front door, but Selene took the time to check and load Freddie, her trusty trench gun, and also saw that she had her iron knife in the holster at her hip and the little box of strike-anywhere matches in her shirt pocket. Going through her duffle of armaments and supplies to procure these items, she also discovered the little round talisman the witch had given her, back in St. Louis.

About the size of a half-dollar coin, it had a pin on the back, and the front was beaten silver, sculpted to look like the face of the moon. Half its face was stained dark, leaving a bright crescent on the other.

The thing felt cold and dead in her hand; not at all magical. Then again, you didn't take a gift from a witch lightly, let alone one as notorious as Faraday Isenfaust.

Selene pinned it above her shirt pocket, tapping it with one finger to be sure it would stay in place. Then she set Freddie against her back and crawled out of the cab—locking it behind her—before following Jill up the neatly tiled path to the front door.

Which door was in the action of being opened when she arrived, by none other than Clara, who greeted them with her sword drawn but held low.

"Any problems?" Selene asked as they stepped inside. Her first glance showed her a house which looked cluttered and messy in the way of a home whose family has been recently disrupted. Unopened mail lay piled on a nearby table, with coats and hats strewn haphazardly over pieces of furniture. Someone had made an attempt at clearing by shoving items under chairs and into corners, but they still made their presence known, intruding on the otherwise clean house like lurking monsters.

Clara's face twisted in frustration. "I think it *is* a walker, but a very strange one. Come in. Sharon, these are my colleagues, Jill Hamilton, Selene Shields."

Sharon Gilkey turned out to be an aggressively suburban-looking middle-aged woman with colored auburn hair and heavy foundation on her milky-white face. She looked, to Selene, like the kind of woman who wouldn't go out to the grocery store without putting on eyeliner, and the only reason she wasn't fully made up now was because of the disruption that was already evident in her house. She greeted them in a breathy, frightened voice, and barely managed to shake Jill's extended hand.

Selene though better of trying the same tack, and kept hers firmly in her pockets as she asked: "All right, Ms. Gilkey, what seems to be the problem?"

It took a little while for the whole story to come out. They had gathered in the living room after the travelers had relieved themselves and Selene had rechecked the wards Clara had set up, while Jill helped Sharon make coffee, before the woman managed to calm down enough to explain things clearly.

"It started in California, over a year ago," she began.

Just like we did, Selene couldn't help thinking.

"Marvin—that's my son—he came home one evening and he was just *filthy*—twigs and leaves in his hair and covered in dirt, and he said he'd made a friend. Marvin didn't—doesn't—make friends easily, so at first I thought, well, I thought, this is good. Right?"

"Sure," said Jill, nodding uncertainly.

"Of course!" said Sharon. "So I say, bring your friend home so I can meet them! But he doesn't, and he won't tell me their name—I mean, he did, but not their *real* name. Just the nickname he had for them. And he kept coming back late, and always with leaves and sticks in his hair, and always with the same excuse: 'I was playing with my *friend.*'" The woman grimaced.

"Finally I'd had enough, and I started picking him up from school. I told him if he wanted to see his friend they had to come visit us at *our* house. And that was when . . . " the woman paused, swallowing nervously. "You have to understand, I thought I was going crazy, at the time. My marriage was falling apart around me; I wasn't sleeping. So when I started seeing things, I just thought . . . I just thought . . . "

"What did you see?" Selene asked, trying not to let her impatience bleed into her voice.

Sharon Gilkey looked up at her, light hazel eyes a little too bright and intense. "I *thought* I saw this . . . sort of a bush? But tall, and kind of thin. Only . . . only it was in our yard, and I *knew* there was no bush there. I thought, maybe it's a big dog. But it was standing too still, and after a while . . . it looked *back.*"

Clara frowned, and Jill looked expectantly blank.

"How?" asked Selene.

"I thought," said Sharon. "I thought I saw its eyes."

"Can you describe them?" Clara asked.

Sharon pursed her lips, her brows knitting. "Sort of like . . . stars?" she said. "I was half out of my mind with anxiety at the time. But I thought they were stars, stars at the bottom of deep pits."

"Then what happened?" Selene asked.

"Well, I kind of lost it," said Sharon with a bitter laugh. "Left my husband, packed up and moved across the country to stay with my mom. Took Marvin with me. And . . . that seemed like the end of it. Things went back to normal. I started sleeping again. We moved in here this summer, and things *were* just fine, and then . . . " her shoulders slumped in defeat. "Then *September* happened."

Jill wiggled uncomfortably in her seat.

"Weird stuff started happening again?" Selene asked, sympathetically.

Sharon looked around nervously, as if she expected the monster to come bursting out of the walls. "Marvin started coming home with leaves in his hair again," she went on, her voice almost a whisper. "So I started walking him home from school, and dropping him off in the morning. But I saw *it* again. Like before, only I knew it was *real* this time. And then . . . " she breathed deeply for a few moments before going on. "Marvin *had* a real friend. This girl named Rosie. I let him stay at her house some afternoons, because her mom was home and could watch them. Yesterday, I went to pick him up and . . . and I found *it* in their kitchen! Just . . . like . . . sitting there at the table! With the two kids and Audrey, like it wasn't anything *wrong.* And there were leaves and a wind and I just . . . I just grabbed Marvin and ran. Got him home—he's still in his room—and I haven't been able to leave since."

"You haven't wanted to?" Selene asked, shrewdly. "Or you've *tried* to but you *can't?*"

She found herself met by Sharon's blank, frightened face.

"I don't *want* to," she whispered. *"It's* out there. I know it is. I hear its bones rattling, sometimes."

"Hold up," said Selene, as Clara blinked in surprise. "It has bones?"

"Wooden ones," said Sharon. "It looks sort of like a skeleton, only covered in leaves and flowers. There were vines and stuff coming out of its mouth. But I could see the skull shape, and its hands were like . . . you know, skeleton hands."

Jill looked between her two guards curiously, but Selene and Clara were equally at a loss.

"The name Marvin gave this creature," said Clara, softly. "What was it?"

"Oh, he just called the thing *Green*. And always *them* or *it*—I don't know if its male or female."

"Some things aren't," Clara said with a shrug. "Male or female," she added, seeing the woman's confused expression.

There was a faint pattering sound and Selene turned to find a small, pudgy form crouching in the hall. This resolved itself into a boy of eleven or twelve, his hair a neatly trimmed mop of brown, and the plain, pink face under it dusted with acne scars. When he met her gaze he froze, but when Selene said nothing he slowly crept backward out of sight, disappearing up the stairs.

"Marvin?" Sharon called, sharply. "Marvin, stop sneaking around. You're supposed to be in *bed.*"

There was a heavy thump, and a throaty voice on the verge of breaking called down, "Green is *not* bad! Green is my *friend!*"

"Marvin, it's dangerous and we don't know what it is," Sharon said, getting to her feet.

"My *friend!*" repeated the boy, and there was the sound of a door being slammed.

"Sounds like a green man of some kind," said Selene, once she and Clara escaped to the front porch to compare notes.

"The disgorging mouth suggests so," Clara agreed, with a short nod. "But it is not acting like one."

"Who's to say green men don't act like this?" Selene asked. "Befriending socially maladjusted children and frightening their overly protective parents?"

"Sharon Gilkey is not overly protective," Clara said mildly. "Merely frightened."

"That doesn't make this any easier," Selene pointed out. She rubbed her nose. "I am too tired to think about this right now. You wanna toss for first watch, or . . . ?"

"I will go first," said Clara, stoically.

"Thanks, sister," Selene said gratefully, and went to bed down in Arcana's back seat out of habit, before remembering that Jill had specifically mentioned that the sofa in the trailer could double as a bed.

It did, and proved so comfortable Selene slept hard and fast until one in the morning, when Clara came to change shifts.

Although the weather had been balmy, there was a cold sting in the air that night, and Selene brought her blanket with her when she set up on the front porch. Clara had been content to stand watch in the dark, but Selene switched on the porch light, and then went to sit just outside its puddle of yellow light. Drawing the blanket closely around her shoulders she laid Freddie on her lap, the barrel resting on the porch railing, and fought back against the tired ache that always settled behind her eyes when she had to take the midnight watch.

It didn't help that, as far as she could see or sense, there was nothing out there. As the world turned toward morning, occasionally a car would rumble past, but that was all. A gentle breeze blew through the neighborhood, rustling the remaining leaves and biting at Selene's ears. Eventually she took her hair out of its rough ponytail so that it fell in a thick blanket over her head and down her neck. Like that she was almost comfortable enough to fall asleep, and had to keep herself alert by mechanically examining each patch of dark yard and trees and street in turn. Even so she felt the tiredness creeping into the edges of her vision, like road fatigue. Her eyes ached, and if only she could close them for a moment . . .

There was a faint, but distinct, *pinnnnng* noise, like someone hitting fine china with a glass hammer. It rattled up her spine and jerked her out of her stupor, and she sat up straighter and looked around.

At first everything appeared as she last remembered it. And then, creeping out of the darkness so slowly she nearly mistook it for a shadow itself, was a bare, rootlike foot, its toes very long and burrowing into the grass of the lawn.

Training took over. Though her body protested and her hands shook, Selene was on her feet in an instant, her gun aimed at the creature she could just make out attached to the foot. Sparing a hand from her weapon she fumbled out the silver whistle she wore on a string around her neck. She slipped it into her mouth and blew a long, sharp note.

"Clara, someone's here!" she shouted, just to be sure, and wished Sharon Gilkey's yard had floodlights.

Likely in response to her call, the thing attached to the foot surged forward into the light, and only a lifetime of seeing disturbing, impossible things kept Selene at her post.

It did not look so much like a tree-person as a skeleton wearing clothes made of leaves. Selene could glimpse brown, whorled ribs peeking between the shiny, dark green ivy that covered its torso and fell in waves like the tails of a coat behind it. Bright, new green oak leaves decorated its shoulder, while its head was crowned with a halo of yellow and orange camphor. Its face was mostly covered with pale, green-yellow maple leaves, but she could see its bare jaw—complete with a set of little brown teeth—cracked open to allow the twining vines to curl out of it.

Its eyes were like bright green stars at the bottom of deep, dark wells. They sparkled as they alighted on Selene, and against every instinct she found herself wanting to lay down her weapon and step aside.

She felt split down the middle. One half of her—the half that was usually in charge—was screaming that this was a dangerously powerful wood spirit and it was walking right at her, while the other half was inexplicably convinced that it wouldn't hurt her. Which only made the first half more panicked, since she knew several creatures that relied on such mental tricks in order to catch their prey.

It was that panic which finally dragged her into action. It felt like she had to break physical restraints in order to move, but she aimed her weapon square at the thing's chest, and pulled the trigger.

Or tried to, anyway. With a sudden swell of horror she felt the gun come alive under her hands.

Literally. The wood of the stock was writhing, growing a tough bark and putting out delicate, green shoots. These had formed vines which twined around the barrel and the trigger, freezing it in place. Something soft brushed her chin, and she realized it was a young branch, grown up so big it was beginning to force her hands off the gun.

"Oh no you don't," she growled, ripping away at the soft new foliage.

She got a shot off this time, but it went wide and only tore at the creature's side. She could see it regrowing itself before the *bang* had time to fade away.

It was powering across the lawn now, a wind gathering around it which whipped the leaves on Selene's gun into her face. Cursing, she dropped the useless weapon and grabbed up her knife. She was feeling for her box of matches when the green person lunged forward, like a wave of foliage and twigs, its skeletal hands outstretched.

There were tiny, blush-pink blossoms on the ends of its fingers. Selene had time to notice them because the creature stopped, frozen mid-lunge, mere inches from her face.

It went so still it might almost have been a tree, except there were still the starlike eyes staring down at her.

Selene also froze. It was against her training, but something in her recoiled at the idea of striking such a vulnerable target.

The creature's mouth opened wider, and a torrent of vines came pouring out. They curled through the air between them, skittering over Selene's face and neck and shoulders—but never touching. A single tendril lifted the collar of her shirt, and she felt a *zap*—like an electric shock—jump from the moon talisman she had pinned there into the green thing.

It flinched away from her as if burned, the vines disappearing into its mouth and the leaves laying down flat against its wooden bones. Like that it looked more human than ever, until Selene noticed that its feet were still rooted in the earth. It was sending up smaller shoots all around it, their supple branches waving in the wind.

Then it reached out its hand—its real, skeleton one—and plucked the box of matches out of Selene's grasp as easily as she would have picked a flower.

There was a burst of growth around its face, and the leaves rustled, almost in mimicry of speech.

Except that it actually *was* speech. Selene was certain the creature spoke to her. Not only that, she was reasonably sure it asked her a question. And she could not for the life of her understand what it was or what her answer should be.

The next second the creature exploded into a confusion of leaves and twigs, the wind whipping it up and carrying it away—taking some clods of dirt out of the lawn as its feet detached—to reveal Clara, her sword raised and ready to strike.

Her face, always pale, showed paper-white in the porch light, and her mouth was a thin, narrow line. But her sword still rested in the ready position; she had not actually attacked.

"Check the back," Selene coughed. Her throat felt thick, and there was something tickling her nose, like pollen. Even so she shook her head at Clara's concerned look. "I'm fine—just *go.*"

Clara went, leaping into the darkness, her sword flashing once, then was gone.

Selene sank onto the porch steps and inspected what had previously been her shotgun. It was still largely gun, but the branches and twigs which sprouted from the stock were still there, supple and alive, and bled sap when she snapped them off.

She managed to clear the foliage from around the trigger, emptied the gun, and loaded a pair of blanks. Placing the barrel a few inches from a patch of undisturbed lawn, she fired twice, pleased at the shockwave of compressed air and smoke which resulted.

She put her regular rounds back in and was heading for the front door when it opened to reveal a bleary and panicked Sharon Gilkey—likely woken by her shots.

"It's all right ma'am," Selene assured her. "Pretty sure its gone—for now—just gotta check and make sure everyone's safe."

Yet even as she spoke she could feel the brush of leaves against her collar, and the lingering certainty of a question that she had left unanswered.

But there was still the security sweep to do, and only after it had been ascertained that everyone was present and accounted for—Jill and Sharon having set up in the living room and Marvin safe upstairs, refusing to come down—that Selene grabbed Clara and pulled her into the nearest bathroom.

"I think it got me," she said, turning on the vanity lights and inspecting herself in the little mirror.

"Where?" asked Clara, her gaze automatically darting to Selene's neck, abdomen, and legs.

"Not injured," Selene explained. "It barely touched me. And that talisman Faraday gave me just earned its keep."

Said talisman was unblemished, cold and ordinary on her shirt, if a little tarnished. That wasn't what caught her attention. She'd been having a prickling feeling in her nose ever since she'd come face to face with the creature, and now she could see why: a faint, yellow dusting of powder had blown out of one nostril, along with something tiny and yellowish-green. Like the smallest of small new leaves.

"Oh flaming *hells*," she said.

Clara reached around her and started running the water.

"Blow it out," she advised. "With any luck its still mostly in your sinuses."

"Yeah," said Selene, eying the growing pool of water distastefully.

"I'll get a bucket," said Clara.

Which was how Selene spent the next twenty minutes alternately trying to force her body to inhale water through her nose, and then violently sneezing it out again. The upshot was a lot of yellow pollen came out with it, and by the end it was entirely water.

Jill came in during the middle of it, exclaimed in dismay, and then collected some of the used rinse water.

"Do you think it's dangerous?" she asked.

"Don't know, don't care," said Selene. "Don't want it in me. Bad things happen when you carry around bits of monster in you."

In the end both she and Clara stayed up for the dawn watch, one at each of the house's two main doors, while Jill napped on the couch. Sharon came down around four-thirty and started making breakfast.

"I couldn't sleep," she admitted with a shaky laugh.

Selene couldn't blame her. She felt raw and wrecked inside, but blessedly clean. She kept taking long, slow breaths through her nose to make sure of the fact, for the certainty of the question still lingered in her mind, and it was beginning to alarm her.

Physical assaults were one thing. Selene had learned a long time ago how to anticipate, avoid, and if the first two failed, how to deal with the consequences of them. Something that got into your mind, however, and spread roots through your brain, was one of the few things she had nightmares about.

She remembered what Sharon had said about her friend Audrey and the girl Rosie, sitting around a table and treating the creature as if it were a family friend.

But whatever else Selene was experiencing, she felt no pressing need to go out and start hugging trees, so she did her best to push the question to the back of her head and concentrate on the things she *could* deal with.

"How did it get through your wards?" she asked Clara when they had been called into the kitchen to enjoy the fruits of Sharon's labors (which were a hearty mixture of hash browns with bacon and eggs over toasted frozen waffles, and some very strong coffee).

Clara shifted uncomfortably in her seat, which was a wooden chair made flimsy by her impressive bulk.

"It didn't," she admitted.

"Uh . . . " said Selene, and waved a hand at where she'd hung Freddie—still with a few leaves attached—on the wall. "I'm pretty sure it *got through.*"

"No, I mean . . . " Clara sighed windily. "As far as the wards are concerned, nothing got through. They weren't damaged or destroyed—and I tested them; they *worked.* They just . . . didn't affect whatever we saw last night."

"Yes, about that," said Jill, coming in and pouring herself a cup of coffee. "What *did* we see?"

"Pretty much what Sharon here described," Selene said, nodding at their host, who was putting another pair of waffles into the toaster. "Wooden skeleton with leaves all over. Eyes like stars."

Sharon Gilkey nearly dropped the frozen waffles on the floor.

"You really did see it!" she exclaimed.

"Uh, yeah," said Selene, giving the woman a sideways look. "It was kinda hard to miss."

Sharon gave a slightly hysterical laugh and left the waffles on the counter to come sit at the table and bury her head in her hands.

"It *is* real. It *is* real," she mumbled into the tablecloth.

"Entirely," said Clara, who was nearest. Awkwardly she raised a hand and patted the distraught women on the back. "You are not crazy, Sharon Gilkey. These things exist."

"Yes, but what thing *is* it?" said Jill, getting up and putting the waffles in the toaster herself. "Clara, you said it not only got through your wards, it didn't even *trip* them. That's gotta be diagnostic of *something.*"

"Unless," Selene suggested, hesitantly, "you did make a mistake."

"I did not," said Clara, unoffended, but iron-firm.

"Then, I don't know, can you think of *anything* that could do that? Is there anything your wards don't work against?"

Clara frowned, her pale eyebrows disappearing into the wrinkles across her brow.

"They will not rise for non-mage humans, animals, or other natural objects such as wind, rain, or leaves," she said, as if running down a mental checklist. "To be perfectly accurate, however, they are not *my* wards. They are part of the Greater Accord which was struck between Gilganar and Hecate, and function by invoking the Accord—which applies to all the entities named by Hecate, their derivatives, and all that came after."

"Sounds pretty thorough," said Selene, chewing a piece of waffle.

"It *is*," said Clara. "That is one reason why I use it."

"Do you think, maybe, some of these entities have developed a resistance to it?" Jill pondered. "You know, like an antibiotic-resistant strain of bacteria?"

Clara shook her head. "This doesn't work that way," she said. "It's more like . . . " she stopped, a stricken look crossing her face, then returning to settle behind her eyes. She looked across the kitchen at Selene's gun, her gaze sharpening on it, and her jaw clenching.

"Unless it was not named in the Accord," she said, her voice like a silvery rasp.

Selene stopped chewing to stare at Clara, her eyes like white dinner plates with black holes in them, they were so wide.

"Oh. Damn," she said.

The waffles popped up, making them all jump (though to different degrees).

"What does that mean?" Jill asked, taking the waffles out of the toaster and putting them on a new plate. She looked around curiously, trying to find their intended recipient.

"Those are for Marvin," Sharon said, pushing herself up from the table. She took the plate and began loading it with hash browns and eggs while Clara shook her head in answer to Jill's question.

Selene, however, dragged her attention off her colleague, and grimaced.

"It's always been assumed that the Greater Accord only applied to all supernatural entities which were . . . uh . . . *present* in this world at the time? Which was more than there are now, and since it also covers all the new things that have come up in the time since, that's pretty much everything. But it's *possible* there were things it missed. Things so old and ancient that even Hecate couldn't wrangle them into the bargain. Aether, Chaos, the Dark. The really old, primordial guys."

"That which came before gods, before the waking minds of men," Clara intoned.

"It doesn't really narrow things down, though," said Selene. "Seeing as we don't know what all existed back then. The oldest records of magic start with the emanations of Hecate, and no matter how many ancient manuscripts *claim* that was the beginning of all magic, practically speaking you gotta accept that there was supernatural crap going on long before her—just no humans around to organize our knowledge of it."

"It is what you might call the ultimate nature magic," said Clara. "The purest incarnation of the natural phenomenon, free from the interference of human interpretation."

"'Interpretation' meaning?" Jill prompted.

Clara pulled her shoulders down and then up again in one of her signature inverted shrugs.

"By interpreting the natural magic, we inevitably give it form. We anthropomorphize it, even when we don't intend to. Half of the magic happens inside our own minds and souls, so we can never observe natural magic in its unaltered state. Not while we're alive, anyway."

"To observe something is to affect it," said Jill nodding. "That makes sense."

"I'm glad it makes sense to *someone*," said Sharon, collecting utensils from the drawer and putting them on her son's plate. She poured a glass of orange juice and put the breakfast on a tray. "I'll be right back down," she said apologetically, and clattered out of the kitchen.

"So you think what we saw last night was one of these things?" Jill suggested. "But from what you and Sharon described, it sounded pretty anthropomorphic to me."

"Different emanations, different forms," said Clara. "If it is grown from stock exempt of the Accord, the Gilganian wards would not have risen to stop it."

"So what we know is that it's likely very, very old. Pre-humanity old," Jill said, pulling out her phone and starting a bullet list.

"Try pre-whatever the ice age was," said Selene. "Most people don't think Gilganar was human herself."

"Pre-Pleistocene?" said Jill, her eyes widening. "That's like, pre-*primates*." She paused to consider this. "But I suppose that's not inconceivable. Human beings have only been around for an infinitesimally small part of Earth's history, after all."

Selene rolled her eyes, but Jill was looking down at her phone and Clara ignored her.

"Something that old will likely not abide by the widely accepted rules," said the large woman, frowning thoughtfully. "There is no saying what it wants, or what it will do next."

She seemed about to go on, but the delicate moment of quiet was shattered by the sound of something crashing upstairs, and a moment later Sharon came down them, screaming. She was so upset it took a while for Selene to parse the panicked sounds into coherent words. When she did, she found they were:

"Gone! Gone! Marvin's *gone!* How did this happen? He was asleep when I checked in on him this morning—I *checked!* Where is he? *Where is he?*"

The poor woman broke down sobbing at the bottom of the stairs, while Clara practically leapt over her to go pounding up them to check for herself. Selene found herself stuck with a soggy and trembling Sharon Gilkey, trying to think of a way to calm her down.

So it was she heard the incoming call on the landline, and the message that followed.

It was another woman's voice, one she'd never heard before.

"Sharon?" it said. "It's Audrey. Look, I know you're mad at me and I don't blame you. You were *right* Sharon, and I'm sorry. But I think it's taken Rosie, Sharon. Unless she's with you. Tell me she's with you."

"Uh," said Jill. "Should I pick it up?"

"Yes, pick it up!" Selene shouted.

Beside her, Sharon had quieted suddenly. Wrapping her arms around her midsection she stared blankly at Selene out of red-rimmed eyes.

"It was after our kids," she whispered. "All this time, it wanted the kids."

"Hello?" said Jill's voice in the hall. "No, this isn't Sharon. My name is Jill Hamilton—I'm here about the plant monster. Yes, yes we've seen it. Rosie? Rosie is your daughter, I see. Rosie is . . ."

There was a shuffling on the stairs and Clara came down them. Her sword was sheathed but her shoulders were tense and she was walking in a fighting stance.

"No one upstairs," she stated.

"No, no she's not here," Jill said. "Neither is Marvin. Listen, may I come talk to you? In person? We're trying to figure out what's going on here and there's been some difficulty."

Sharon looked up. "I know where she lives," she whispered. "I'll take you."

Audrey lived in a slightly shabbier, slightly smaller house two blocks from the Gilkey's home. There were thick drifts of yellow and red leaves in the yard, and a huge rose bush half covering the front porch. On the steps, in the shadow of the rose, sat a small, thin woman with bleached hair, hugging her knees to her chest in a way Selene recognized as the "help-me-my-life-is-falling-apart" pose.

"I'll do a sweep," said Clara, and took off through the drifts of leaves to make a circuit of the house, while Selene started for the porch.

She paused when she realized they'd left Sharon on the sidewalk: the woman was staring at the porch and the rose bush as if it had come alive and spoken to her.

"Something wrong?" Selene asked, suddenly suspicious. She wasn't getting the uncomfortable tingle that usually alerted her to the presence of magic, but she was also keenly aware of the fact that her senses were not the best in the business.

"The . . . the rose," said Sharon, pointing with one trembling hand.

Selene looked at the rose bush, half expecting to see something terrible lurking in it.

But it was still an ordinary bush, as far as she could see. It had a few surprisingly bright red blossoms on it, and its leaves were very dark, glossy and green.

"What about the rose?" Selene asked, catching Jill's sleeve so the other woman wouldn't get any closer.

"Last time I was here," said Sharon, and made a motion with her hand, gesturing around her knees. "It was about this big."

Selene looked again at the overgrown bush, its thick arms tangling with the porch and its uppermost leaves brushing the roof's gutter.

"Mrs. Thorn?" Selene called. "Are you all right?"

The woman on the porch jerked her head up and stared at them. Her face was pinched with sadness and worry, but she did not have the mad panic in her eyes that had characterized Sharon Gilkey. Selene was also struck by the bright greenness of them. They were so bright they were almost yellow, and caught the light in a way that made them shimmer.

At the sight of Selene her face broke into a huge, relieved smile. She pushed herself up off the porch, brushing aside the overgrown rosebush, and came down across the stubbly lawn, one hand already outstretched.

"Yes," she said, still smiling at Selene like she was an old friend. "Yes, *I'm* all right. I'm so glad you could come—you must be Jill Hamilton."

"Uh," said Selene, uncertain what to do with the woman's proffered hand.

Beside her, Jill snorted with laughter.

"Actually, *I'm* Jill," she said, taking Audrey Thorn's hand. "This is my colleague, Selene Shields. We've got one more, Clara, who's securing your property."

Was it Selene's imagination, or did Audrey Thorn look momentarily disappointed? The expression was too fleeting for Selene to catch, but then the woman was laughing nervously, shaking Jill's hand and saying, "Wow, you're like . . . real professionals, aren't you?"

"Selene and Clara are the professionals," Jill said. "I'm a researcher, but we're all anxious to find your daughter. And Sharon's son. Can you tell us what happened?"

Audrey got a tight, unhappy look on her face at that, and glanced uncertainly at Sharon. Selene remembered the altercation that had occurred between the two women, but then Sharon pursed her lips and shrugged.

"I told them . . . my side," she said.

Audrey bit her lip and nodded. "Then I think you'd better come in and hear mine."

The inside of the Thorn house was even messier than the outside: drifts of leaves lay piled in the corner, and a wisteria vine had forced its way in through the kitchen window and trailed over the counter.

"It's blooming," said Jill, blankly, staring at the fragrant, purple flowers. "How is it blooming? It's *November.*"

"That's Green's doing," said Audrey with a tired sigh.

"Green?" said Selene, sharply.

"That's what Rosie called it," said Audrey, kicking leaves out of the way to pull out a chair. She sank into it with a sigh, gesturing for them to do the same.

Jill sat, as did Sharon, but Selene remained standing, staring at the glass-fronted cabinet against the far wall. It was the sort used to display fancy china, but in this case the shelves were occupied by little dioramas of gardens made of cut-and-glued paper. On top of it was a small shrine built around a faded snapshot of a man set in a frame of gilded ivy leaves. There was a jar of acorns with a black ribbon around the lid. On a silver chain was a pendant with the green man face—two eyes staring out of a face made of leaves. There were also several old, cloth-bound books, so worn their titles had been all but rubbed away, and a battered VHS of *My Neighbor Totoro*. A vase peeking out from behind the picture held a collection of dried flowers, including one made of black crepe paper.

The man himself was difficult to make out, since the picture was water damaged, and the subject backlit against an overexposed cloud of yellow. He was a young, black man. Selene could see that much. He had a scrubbly sort of beard and a smile that was visible in the bad lighting due only to the whiteness of his teeth. His eyes were screwed up in happy wrinkles of laughter, and he had let his hair grow out to the point where it hung down over his ears and brow like a sort of fuzzy, black plant.

" . . . Rosie's always had a special touch with these things," Audrey Thorn was saying, and Selene belatedly realized she'd missed a good chunk of conversation.

"She made friends with the crows last summer," the woman went on. "Started feeding them, talking to them. Then they started bringing her presents. A button, a coin, bits of ribbon. She's got quite a collection. Once it was a rare, old coin. And one time, when I'd lost my favorite earring in town, she went and told her crows about it and the next morning I found it on my windowsill."

"Wow," said Jill, frankly.

"My point is," said Audrey. "I'd gotten used to things being . . . a bit peculiar where Rosie was concerned. But it always seemed so harmless. They were *good*. Things—animals, nature—have always been kind to Rosie. Which made up for the way people would sometimes treat her."

"What do you mean?" Jill asked, and Selene turned around in time to see Audrey and Sharon exchange a significant glance.

"You haven't met her," said Audrey, pulling out her phone. "This should give you some idea." She held the little device up, and Jill peered at the screen, frowning. Selene wandered over and leaned in to get a closer look.

The image on the phone's background showed a little girl who was the perfect mix of Audrey Thorn and the man in the bad photo. Selene could tell, mostly because the girl had the exact same smile. And nose. And general coloration—though perhaps a couple shades lighter, with the addition of a few freckles. She also had the same bright, yellow-green eyes as her mother.

"When I took her to the Halloween festival I had two police officers—two *different* officers—come up and ask if she was bothering me," said Audrey, bitterly. "They didn't believe she was my daughter. *My* daughter. The one time I flew with her, I had this kind, concerned, *horrible* old lady tell me loudly how generous I was to adopt an African AIDS orphan. To her *face*." Audrey's own face had grown redder as she spoke. "The *worst* was when we first moved here. She was playing in our front yard and some dog walker started shouting at her to get off the lawn and go back Greenwood. I was so mad I threw a clod of turf at him. Rosie was scared and confused, which was how I ended up explaining the Tulsa Race Riots to a seven-year-old!"

Audrey stopped, her chest heaving, and looked up at Selene.

"You probably have some idea," she said.

"Probably," Selene agreed dryly. She didn't voice her opinion that everything Rosie had been through had probably been made more tolerable by having a white knight of a mother there to stand up for her, and instead jerked a thumb at the shrine on top of the cabinet. "So that guy there . . . "

"My husband, yes," said Audrey, a defiant tilt to her face. "LeShawn Thorn. Everybody called him Oakey, though, because he was a sort of tree doctor."

"Oakey and Rosie," said Selene. "Makes you the odd one out, don't it?"

"Not really," said Audrey. "His nickname for me was Audrey III." And like that her composure deserted her and she began to sob.

"Okay, okay," said Selene, patting the woman's arm. "I won't even ask why there's a shrine to him in your dining room. You want me to get you anything? Tea? Towel?"

"Paper towels in the kitchen, I'm fine," gulped Audrey. "I'm so sorry, everything—just—with Rosie and Green and all . . . I thought things were getting *better*."

"So did I," whispered Sharon.

"I guess . . . we do sort of have a whole plant theme going on with our family," Audrey was saying as Selene darted into the kitchen and found the paper towels. She also found Clara, hovering awkwardly in the back door.

"I found something," the large woman said.

"Urgent?"

From the other room: "Maybe that was why I was so accepting. And Green . . . never did anything scary or bad. Weird and amazing, yes, but not *bad*. Rosie liked him—it—I'm not sure. They could talk together, and sometimes I got the impression it was talking to me, but I could never really understand it. I just got the feeling of being asked a question, you know? But . . . but in a *kind* way. Green was kind. *Seemed* kind."

Selene was frozen with the roll of paper towels in her hand. Clara shook her head: no.

Selene jerked herself back into the dining room.

"What did it do with Rosie?" she asked sharply, setting the paper towels down in front of Audrey.

The woman took a towel and blew her nose gustily.

"Well, nothing, really. They'd go out and play together. And the crows seemed to like it—Green, I mean. So I thought, when Rosie wanted to sleep outside last night—and it was so warm—I thought . . . I thought it would be okay. So we made up a camp, for the two of us, and this morning she was gone."

Silently, Sharon reached across the table and took Audrey's hand.

"That was how we missed Marvin," she said.

Jill was frowning. "How do you know it was Green that took them?"

Sharon practically glared at her. "What else *could* it have been?"

"I had a dream," said Audrey, quietly.

"A dream?" said Jill, skeptically.

"What kind of dream?" demanded Clara, shouldering her way into the room.

Audrey looked up at her, blinking in surprise.

"This is Clara," Selene explained. "She's with us."

Audrey gazed uncertainly at Clara, who was looming over the table.

"There are dreams which come from inside us, from our minds and hearts. Then there are dreams which are given to us by other powers, when our minds reach out and touch the greater web of existence. Which kind was it?"

"I don't even—what?" said Audrey. "How can you tell?"

Clara did one of her inverted shrugs. "How much do you remember?"

"Just the general feelings," Audrey admitted. "There was wind, and leaves, and the sound of laughter. I felt light, like I was flying, but there was an anchor holding me down. And I was watching Rosie run away into a forest. I remember . . . it was okay, in my dream, because Oakey was in there, and would take care of her. But then everything got dark, and I heard this chanting—like a thousand tiny voices whispering at once. In my dream it was this—like a full-on poem, but by the time I woke up I could only remember the last line. It said: *The earth, it weeps. The earth, it weeps.*"

Selene felt something stiffen inside her, even as Jill looked up in astonishment.

"But isn't that—" she began, but Selene silenced her with a look.

"I woke up, and it was dawn, and Rosie was gone," Audrey finished. "And I knew, so was Oakey, and that she'd gone off with Green and there was no one to protect her. And I'd been wrong, all the time."

She looked miserably across at Sharon.

"I'm so sorry," she whispered. "It's just . . . after everything . . . I guess I'd hoped that, somehow, something good and magical was happening, like in a children's story. Where the monsters are friendly."

"Friendly monsters are usually the most dangerous," Clara remarked, but not judgmentally.

Jill took a deep breath. "All right then, where do we go from here?"

Selene looked across at Clara.

"I think it's time we ran a sweep," she said. "We can use Freddie as a point of reference—he's still got some of this Green magic in him—and I'd bet my bones that's where the kids are, too."

"Agreed," said Clara. "But first there's something you should see."

The Thorn's backyard was small, made even more crowded by the profusion of rose bushes planted along the fence. There were still the remains of Audrey and Rosie's camp: two inflatable foam mattresses laid out side by side, with tangled sleeping bags and damp pillows on top. In the center of the yard there was a bare patch of tilled soil, and in the center of this was a small, dark hole—as one might dig when preparing to transfer a plant from pot to earth. A set of bare, child-sized footprints crossed the open earth and disappeared into the rose bushes.

Selene knelt beside them and peered into the hole. At the bottom was a single, fat, shiny acorn.

"Huh," she said, and cautiously reached out a hand.

She felt the warning fizz on her talisman before her fingers touched it, and she withdrew her hand quickly.

"It's been here all right," she said.

"That's just Rosie's tree," said Audrey, broken and tired. "She plants an acorn every year, for her dad."

"What happened to him?" Clara asked, even as Selene followed the footprints to where they disappeared into the rose bushes.

"He left," said Audrey, tightly. "When Rosie was five. Went out to work one day and never came back."

"Did you file a missing person report?" asked Jill.

Audrey snorted. "Sure, much good it did. Everyone just assumed he'd run off. I don't . . . I didn't want to believe them. He loved Rosie more than anything, and he was so . . . *responsible.* He wouldn't have left even if he hated us both—and, we were never . . . we were *happy.*" She sighed. "But if he didn't run off it means something happened to him, and that's sort of worse. Because I'd much rather believe he was still alive somewhere, even if it meant I'd never forgive him."

"I understand," said Clara, simply, in tones that spoke very clearly that she *did,* and in ways Audrey Thorn could barely imagine.

"Oh, whoa," said Selene, pulling back a thorny branch and squinting down at the earth. Though it was dusted with fallen leaves it still held clear impressions, and so she could easily see how the footprints stopped abruptly under the branches.

Just . . . stopped. No backtracks, not even a cluster of prints from their maker standing in one place. There was left, right, left . . . and then nothing. As if Rosie Thorn had walked clean out of the world.

A shadow fell over her shoulder, and she looked up to find Clara had joined her. Wordlessly, Selene pointed at the tracks, and then backed out of the prickly bushes so the larger woman had room to move in.

She found herself standing next to Jill, who was looking at her shrewdly.

"What?" said Selene, though a part of her already knew.

"The earth it weeps," murmured Jill, unusually tactful. "That's from your verse."

"Yeah," said Selene. Her verse, from the Winchester Oracle, which had stuck in her mind even as the verses for Jill and Clara had clouded over as soon as she'd heard them. She wondered for a moment how Jill could remember, when she realized the woman probably had the whole thing written down. She sighed.

"And on the bough, before the storm, with a shattering, the earth it weeps," she said. "But I don't see how it has anything to do with this, or why *my* verse would wind up in Audrey's dream."

Jill bit her lip and frowned.

"Tell me about this sweep you and Clara are planning," she said, blessedly changing the subject.

"The whole idea is," Selene explained as Clara made little stone cairns at the north, south, east and west corners of Audrey Thorn's backyard, "is that every spirit or ghost or demon— basically, anything that don't rightly belong in this world— gives off a kind of *aura,* which you can sweep for if you know how to look. With demons, it's easy: just get yourself some mothwax and make a candle. For something like Green, something specific, you need an anchor. Something to tell the spell what to look for. Kinda like giving a dog the scent of a missing person. For that, we got Freddie." She hefted the unloaded gun, the single leaf which had unfurled over the course of the morning fluttering in the sunlight.

It was almost midday, and the November sky was a pale, washed-out blue. The leaves which remained on the neighbor's tree were bright red and falling fast, but in the Thorn yard the roses flourished and bloomed, basking in the weak sun.

"So . . . this is magic, then?" asked Audrey, sounding mostly curious.

"*Ehrm,*" said Selene, glancing over at Clara, who stood up.

"Sort of," said the tall woman, her shaved head gleaming from the thin sheen of sweat that lay upon it. "It is to magic as rhythm is to music. Something so old and rudimentary that no witch or magician would call it *magic*, but the two are not unrelated."

"It's a bit like what Clara did with her brother's sword, back in Chicago," Selene said to Jill. "Only, since I don't got any outstanding connections to Green we're gonna have to help it along a bit."

"What happened in Chicago?" Audrey asked.

"A demigod kidnapped Clara's brother and tried to get him to summon Loki," Jill explained, briskly.

Behind them, Sharon made a stifled choking noise.

Selene ignored her. Clara had dusted off her hands and was now assembling the pile of dry twigs she had collected and placed in Audrey's largest cast-iron skillet into a little pyramid shape. This done she took a small flask from her pocket and poured something that smelled like alcohol over the twigs, so it dripped down into the pan.

Replacing the flask she turned to the small cloth bag she had gotten out of her motorcycle's pannier, and from it took a hard, rectangular box of lacquered wood. She opened it to reveal a sharp triangle of waxy, grayish stone, a singed piece of metal, and a glass bottle half full of black powder.

"Uh . . . " said Jill. Clara sprinkled some black powder into the pan and removed the flint and steel. "I'm pretty sure I've got a safety light . . . "

"That will not serve our purpose," said Clara. "The fire is only a side effect of the flint reacting to the incantation."

"What incantation?" asked Jill.

"If you'll quiet down I think you'll hear it," said Selene, coming to stand over the pan and holding out her gun.

"Ready?" asked Clara.

"As ever," sighed Selene.

Clara knelt in the scratchy grass, and reaching under the pile of twigs she struck the flint sharply against the steel. At the same time, she spoke the incantation.

Selene wasn't sure what Jill and the other women heard. The language Clara used was not the one she was familiar with, and it had the unsettling effect of making the words bounce around in her head before evaporating, like something she'd heard in a dream. She knew from her own experience that they *meant* "rise and guide, see and steer," but they only worked if you spoke them in Sanskrit. Or, apparently, the language Clara used, because on the third spark from the flint a fire leapt up and consumed the twigs, devouring the alcohol and flashing warmly against Selene's hands.

There was an answering *twang* from her talisman, but she didn't need that to convince her that the spell had worked.

Freddie had come alive under her grip. Not so radically as the night before, but she could feel a faint vibration in his wooden stock, and he twitched in her hands like a dog eager to chase a bird.

"Whoa nelly," said Selene, bracing her feet. "We got a live one."

"Do not let go," Clara advised. "It will weaken the connection."

"No fear," said Selene, feeling the gun tugging her toward the rose bush which had apparently eaten Rosie Thorn.

"Can you get a sense of it in your mind?" Clara asked, hopefully.

Selene shook her head. "Freddie's got a sense though. Can you grab my ammo belt and kit? I think we're just gonna have to play follow-the-compass."

This was easier said than done. Freddie guided her with no account for fences or bushes or trees or houses, and in order to follow the path he picked out they were forced to go on a roundabout hike through Audrey Thorn's neighborhood.

Even more frustratingly, Freddie just seemed to want to lead them back to a point a little way past the rose bush in the Thorns' backyard. Secretly, Selene suspected there was something special about that bush, but since she couldn't imagine what that might be, she kept her mouth shut.

Then, on a circuit of the block that took them further from the bush than ever before, Freddie suddenly changed his tune, and Selene felt him jump under her hands as the pressure on him turned and pulled in a completely new direction.

"Okay," she said, stumbling off down the road. "I think we're going somewhere now."

She led, and the four other women followed: first Jill, then Sharon and Audrey, bewildered but determined, and finally Clara, who brought up the rear with her sword loose in its scabbard.

They meandered southwest, passing through more shady, residential neighborhoods, until they reached the Arkansas River, where there was some muddling around until Audrey pointed out the river trail that ran alongside it.

After that things went smoothly, as Freddie seemed to be leading them south along the river in more or less the same direction as the path.

"When did you first become aware of the Green's presence?" Clara asked, after they had been walking in silence for a few minutes, with no change in the direction indicated by Freddie.

"Late September, I think," said Audrey. "I remember it was right after that disaster in St. Louis. It was all over the internet, and I got stuck reading and lost track of Rosie, but when I went looking she was asleep under her favorite rose bush in the backyard. When I woke her up she was all full of stories about the magical green person who had come and played with her. I thought she was just describing a dream, but then the next day I actually saw it, standing out in front."

"What did you do?" asked Sharon.

"I went out to talk to it," said Audrey. "I know it sounds strange, but I didn't find it frightening or unbelievable— especially after what I'd heard from St. Louis. I introduced myself and explained I was Rosie's mother. I asked what it's name was . . . that was when I discovered I couldn't understand it. But Rosie came out, and *she* could understand it, and said it knew what I'd said. So I told it to take care of her and not to leave the backyard. And . . . that was it, really. They played in the backyard all day, and Green stayed while we ate dinner. It never seemed . . . I don't know . . . *evil*. Or bad, or dangerous. Maybe I was just going off how Rosie reacted—she's usually such a cautious girl, I couldn't imagine her befriending anything bad. Besides, the crows seemed to like it."

Sharon sighed heavily.

"But *you* had met Green before," Jill pointed out.

"Back in California, over a year ago," said Sharon.

"So its presence in this world predates the breach," Clara said, projecting so that Selene heard her clearly.

She needn't have bothered. Freddie was pulling her steadily down the path, and she could walk with one ear cocked so she could listen to the conversation behind her.

"Yeah," she said. "But it might have taken advantage of the upheaval to relocate itself. And it sounds like Rosie Thorn's not exactly a mundane kid."

"Excuse me?" said Audrey, sharply.

"I mean in the magical/not magical sense," Selene explained. "I'm a mundane, Jill's a mundane. Clara's . . . sort of mundane. I dunno. But the Isenfausts? They're *not* mundanes."

"Aren't they witches?" said Jill.

"Faraday is," said Selene. "But not being a mundane don't make you a witch. Tesla's a . . . a . . . what would you call Tesla?" she said, throwing the question back at Clara.

"A wondersmith," said Clara. "But I believe the term you are looking for is *lumenite*. Rosie sounds more like an accretor to me, however."

"A *what?*" said Audrey.

There was a windy sigh from the back of their group.

"An accretor is someone who has a . . . a natural attractive quality to the supernatural. *They* might not possess any remarkable abilities, but for some reason things that *do* will congregate around them. As opposed to a lumenite, who is anyone with a strong connection to the spirit world. It is generally accepted to be the opposite of a mundane—that is, one who doesn't have such a connection—and encompasses accretors, witches, magicians, and the thaumaturges: seers, mediums and prophets."

"That'd explain the crows," said Selene. "And Green turning up *there* right after the breach."

"By 'breach' you mean . . . that stuff that happened in St. Louis?" Sharon asked.

"Yep," said Selene, and would have been happy to leave it at that, but the woman was evidently curious.

"What *did* happen, actually?" she asked.

"An ancient god opened a portal through the Gateway Arch," Jill explained briskly. "As it was explained to me, this stirred up a lot of the supernatural entities already living in this dimension—there's more than one, apparently—and also let in a lot of new things from the dimension the god was in. That's why we've been seeing an increase in hauntings, possessions, and monster-sightings."

"Which god?" asked Audrey, with remarkable composure.

"Vjor," said Jill.

"I've never heard of him," said Sharon.

"Her, actually," Jill corrected her, gently.

"A *very* ancient god," said Clara.

"She's the original god of war, I guess," said Jill. "The only reason she's still around is because her name became our word *for* war. *Vee-yor,* war. You get it?"

"Wow," said Audrey. "Step aside, Athena."

"And she brought all this . . . *weird* stuff along with her?" asked Sharon.

"I don't think she meant to," Jill said, contritely, and didn't mention that the reason Vjor was there at all was partly because of her own actions.

"Yeah," said Selene. "But don't blame her. Sounds like this Green has been around for even longer, and if Rosie's an accretor, it probably didn't need any help finding her."

"Did her father have any of these similar . . . tendencies?" Clara asked, as tactfully as she could.

"Oakey?" said Audrey. "Not that I noticed. Not like Rosie, anyway. Except . . . and this isn't really so odd when you think about what some people are like . . . he did talk to trees a lot. As if they were people. He wasn't *crazy*," she assured them. "He didn't *actually think* they were people. But he'd talk to them a lot. And he did tell me that, if everything was quiet and peaceful, he could imagine that the trees were talking to each other. But it was all *imagination* and *make believe*—and he knew it."

They walked in silence for a while longer. The trail, wide and paved, curved along to match the bank of the river, taking them behind the backs of houses and under freeway overpasses.

Beneath one of these they passed the empty nest of a homeless person: a pile of sleeping bags on top of flattened cardboard boxes with a shopping cart nearby. Whoever had left it had stuffed the sleeping bag so it looked like someone was there to anyone who didn't look closely.

"You said he ran off," Clara remarked, once they were out from under the overpass.

"That's what everyone *else* said." Audrey sighed.

"And what do you think happened?"

The woman didn't answer at once.

"I don't know," she said eventually. "A part of me hopes he's still out there. But really, he just wasn't the sort of take off and leave his family—his *child*—no matter what anyone says. So I have to think . . . I think something happened to him."

No one said anything after that, though Selene found her mind involuntarily filled by all the *somethings*—none of them good—that could happen to a black man who was in the wrong place at the wrong time. She shook her head to clear it. They'd been walking for over two hours. Across the river she could see a collection of large buildings with signs for the Oklahoma Aquarium. Beside them a small strip mall with chain restaurants blocked their view of the city, while the river spread, gray and green and lazy, opposite.

The trail ended, but a narrow, two-lane road continued along the river, and they walked beside its shoulder as cars and trucks whizzed by.

"We should really walk on the left," Jill was saying. "Cars are more polite to pedestrians if you can make eye contact with the driver . . . "

Selene wasn't listening. For the first time since they'd got on the river trail, the tug on Freddie had changed direction.

Now it was pulling her insistently toward the river—specifically a thick copse of leafless oaks which grew between the river and the road.

"I think we're getting close," she said, and left the short-cropped verge and began forging her way through the tall, brown grass toward the trees. The other women fell in behind her, silent, though there was a metal *snick* as Clara drew her sword.

There was a narrow path, mostly overgrown and strewn with litter, which led into the heart of the trees, and for lack of anything better Selene took it. She found herself passing into a thick hedge of oaks, having to bend some branches back and duck under others. A few hollows with beaten drifts of light brown leaves showed signs of having been used as makeshift bedrooms in the past, though today the only remnants of human presence were an old, torn blanket and a lonely sock.

Selene climbed through the branches of a sprawling oak, and felt her hair catch on the mass of twigs. While she was untangling it she noticed that Freddie had gotten inexplicably heavier.

No, not heavier, she realized once she was on the far side of the tree. He was pulling her *down*. Down toward . . .

She almost didn't see the gully in time. It was choked with leaves and half hidden by old, dead branches. Just like the sort of primitive trap used to snag big animals. She reached out and grabbed a nearby tree, one foot swinging out over the hidden crevasse and sending an avalanche of acorns down into its depths. They clattered loudly, but when the sound had abated there was only the wind rustling the tops of the trees, and in the distance the rumble of a car.

"We are at a disadvantage here," Clara said. "We should not linger."

"Freddie says it's *down there*," Selene grunted, pointing.

There was a rustling and a crunching, and Clara appeared at her side, squinting down through the dead branches.

"I will be unable to cover you," she said.

"Then mind the civilians," said Selene, and slung Freddie over her back as she turned around and stomped a hole in the makeshift screen. Using the roots of the tree in front of her, she gently climbed down into the pit, cracking her way through more dead branches as she went. Still, she felt the weight of Freddie on her back, pulling her down, and knew she was headed in the right direction.

At least, she was reasonably certain until she came to the bottom of the gully—choked with moss and dead leaves and sticks—and the pressure from Freddie ceased.

She unslung the gun—not an easy task with roots and branches pressing in on all sides—and held it gently as she turned slowly around.

Nothing. Not even a twinge from her—

Even as the thought crossed her mind she felt a sensation explode out of the talisman pinned to her shirt. It hit her like a stroke of cold fire, causing her to buckle momentarily, shoving her face blindly into a mass of thorny twigs. She barely registered the pain over the energy that was flaring around the pendant. She took a step back . . .

. . . and she fell. *Tumbled* more like, as though a rabbit hole and opened up beneath her feet. She was upside-down—there was dirt in her face—instinctively she tried to roll, tried to round her shoulders and protect herself.

Then she slid to a stop in something soft and crackly, and came up spitting brilliant orange leaves.

Which was wrong, she knew. The oak trees' leaves had gone brown, and these were not oak leaves anyway. They were smooth and waxy, and smelled faintly of something fruity—maybe citrus?

She lay in the leaves for a while, mentally assessing the damage. Once the dizziness abated, however, she discovered with surprise that there was no damage. She had landed as softly as on a bed of feather pillows. Softer, actually, considering she was butt-down on an incline with her head above her feet and

Freddie in her lap. The only injury she'd sustained was a sharp bruise on her midsection, which she suspected had been self-inflicted.

Gingerly she sat up and looked around.

Weak, evening sunlight filtered down through a canopy of improbably green leaves, which stretched above her like the dome of a tent, their veins dark against the backlight of the sun. The ground she lay on was a tumble of soft, wet moss, partially covered with bright orange leaves. Craggy walls of weathered stone rose up to meet the canopy, and in their crevices grew a variety of ferns and creeping vines. There was a smell like orange blossoms, and motes of yellow pollen drifted through the thick air.

She was utterly alone, but the stone walls were riddled with narrow, dark holes, and from the recesses of one she thought she heard the sound of children laughing.

"Clara?' Selene called, turning herself around so she could look back up the way she'd come.

And froze.

There was no hole, no tunnel. No visible means by which she had arrived. There was only the rough stone wall, with countless tiny, curling ferns like green starfish on its face, and above that the leafy ceiling high above.

Selene checked her talisman. Nothing. Freddie was a dead weight—no life left in him. As far as their spell was concerned, she had found Green.

Except she couldn't for the life of her see where it might be. There was only rock and moss and ferns and piles and piles of leaves.

The *leaves.*

Selene fairly leapt to her feet, kicking around in the leaves looking for—she didn't know what. A wooden skull? A grasping hand? Something—anything!

All she found was more leaves, and at the bottom, smushed moss.

Taking in a deep breath she squared her shoulders and shouted, as loudly as she could, up at the ceiling. One meaningless word, just to see if she could elicit a response.

It felt like shouting into a pillow, the air was so thick and quiet. And again, nothing.

With a groan Selene pulled out her spare shot and loaded Freddie, saw that her iron knife was readily to hand, and set off to investigate the puzzling environment.

The thing that struck her hardest—aside from the lack of obvious exits—was the sheer *quietness* of the place. Not silence— there was the faint hum of insects and a trickle of water some- where in the caves beneath the rock—but it seemed as though the thick moss and ferns sucked up anything louder than a whis- per. Her footsteps were practically soundless as she approached the nearest tunnel opening, and even when she crossed onto bare rock it was with only the faintest tapping noise.

"Hello?" she called into the dark recess, and here the damp- ening blanket ended, for her voice echoed back at her, cold and chilly.

"*Hello*?" she called a little louder, into the tunnel next to it, the one she'd thought she'd heard laughter in.

No response, but again she thought she heard the faint sound of a child laughing. Not the spooky, falsely happy sound, but a delighted shriek followed by a bubbling giggle. There was also the mumble of another voice, too low for the words to be made out, but there seemed to be a conversation going on.

With one last look around the mysterious glade, Selene ducked into the tunnel and began feeling her way carefully along it.

She had thought she would need to get out her pocket flash- light, but just beyond the fall of light from the clearing she found the way lit by a tracery of glowing vines sunk into the rock. These opened teardrop-shaped flowers that shone from within with a lavender radiance. The path was dim, but they gave more than enough light to see by, and Selene was able to walk swiftly—if not exactly confidently—down the passage.

Sooner than she expected she saw daylight ahead of her, blocked by the twisting, thorny branches of some kind of bush. This turned out to be a rose bush when Selene got up close, and she blinked disbelievingly at the view beyond it.

She was looking into the Thorn's backyard. She could see the crater left by Rosie's plans to plant an oak tree, and beyond that the porch where she and Jill had stood earlier that day. On the ground beneath the branches, sure enough, were the mysterious vanishing footprints she and Clara had puzzled over. In fact, she could see both their own prints, so much larger and heavier, a little ways off.

She was just working up the fortitude to crawl through the thorny bush when she heard a voice behind her in the tunnel.

" . . . found another one!" she was pretty sure it said. It sounded closer, but still far away enough for half the words to be swallowed in echoes.

As far as Selene was any judge, she thought it sounded like Marvin.

She still found the prospect of escaping from the mysterious tunnel tempting enough to weather the bush, but then she heard the unmistakable sound of running feet, and with a muttered curse she turned back into the shadows.

She'd only gone a little way when she reached a fork in the tunnel she was absolutely sure had not been there before. On one side (the left) the glowing flowers were purple, while on the other they were warm and pink. And of course the sound of voices came down the new, unfamiliar, pink side.

Muttering curses which, were they to take, would have created even worse problems than those faced by Sharon Gilkey and Audrey Thorn, Selene stomped down the pink-lit tunnel, Freddie carefully pointed at the ground.

She kept hearing voices. Two distinct ones: a boy and a girl, each in that awkward stage of puberty where they hadn't fully settled into their full, adult form, and still retained the childlike ability to squeal at a painfully high pitch.

"Do we have enough?" said the girl.

"No, we need seven more," said the boy—definitely Marvin.

"I'll try the park again," said the girl, closer than ever.

Then Selene came around a bend and found herself facing the living, three-dimensional version of the girl she'd previously seen in the photograph.

Rosie Thorn was taller than she had expected—she must hit her growth spurt early. In the dim light of the flowers her eyes were too dark for their color to be apparent, but Selene recognized her face, and the bush of curls that framed it. Although, in person, Selene also noticed the thick scattering of freckles over her cheeks and the way the tips of her hair had been bleached to a rich, glimmering copper. Natural highlights, she realized.

"Hiya," she began. "Don't worry, I'm—"

The girl screamed, opening her mouth so wide it was like a dark red O, and then she was tearing off down the tunnel, away from Selene. Something clattered to the floor behind her, and Selene (after cursing herself inwardly) stooped down to examine it.

It was an acorn, shiny and fat, with its little nubby hat still on. Selene frowned and slipped it into her pocket.

"Wait," she called, tiredly, on the off chance the girl heard and would actually stop and give her a chance to explain herself.

Rosie Thorn was long gone, however, and all Selene found of her was, here and there, another dropped acorn.

There were no more forks in the tunnel, and Selene hoped she'd come across the kids before they had a chance to escape into the real world—for she was pretty certain everything from the time she'd fallen into the crevasse had been in a place that was, more or less, *separated*. What with the unnatural quiet and the green leaves and the distorted space—not to mention the glowing flowers.

When the tunnel ended, however, she found herself back where she'd begun: in the strange, leaf-covered well with mossy, rocky walls. She'd come out from another tunnel entrance, and though the light had almost gone from the canopy above, there was still enough for her to clearly see the two small figures who were crouching near the center.

One was Marvin, wearing a gray sweatshirt and torn jeans, his dark hair disheveled with twigs stuck in it. The other was Rosie Thorn, who was wearing cotton trousers so glaringly yellow Selene was shocked she hadn't noticed them before.

The two faced each other across a small depression in the moss, where they had piled a small mountain of acorns. Both had their fists clenched on their knees, and were staring at the collection with such intensity that neither of them noticed Selene's appearance.

For her part, Selene pressed herself back against the wall of rock, trying to regulate her breathing so she did not make any noise, and wondered if there was anything she could do that would not spook them.

Before anything occurred to her, however, Rosie said, "Come *onnnn!*" and Marvin said "It's coming!" and then the mountain of acorns erupted and, like a whale breaching the surface of the ocean, a brown skeleton thrust its head up through the tumbling acorns, vines twining and leaves unfurling and the mossy ground boiling as its shoulders and back emerged.

It put out one skeletal hand—bright green buds were showing at its fingertips—and pushed itself the rest of the way out of the ground. Dark leaves were tracing over its body, hiding the bones and falling in waves down its legs, almost in mimicry of a flowing robe.

It was completely covered in greenery now, with a single orange flower, tightly curled into a cone, crowning its head. The leafy skeleton knelt in the scattered pile of acorns and peered around at them with twinkling, starlike eyes.

"Did we get enough, Green?" Rosie Thorn was asking, while Marvin said, "Is she okay?"

Green didn't answer. It had spotted Selene and was staring at her, and under the weight of its gaze she felt the talisman begin to tingle.

Having learned from last time she holstered Freddie and put her hands up.

"I've just come for the kids," she said, trying to keep her voice steady. "Their moms are worried."

Still Green stared, and now Rosie and Marvin were staring too. Marvin moved himself so he was partially hidden by the Green's leafy dress, but Selene was aware of him staring at her sullenly from around a tangle of ivy. Rosie stood bravely facing her, her chin lifted in defiance.

None of them said anything, but Green straightened up so it could look down at Selene, and extended one hand—the bare, bony fingers protruding from a burst of curling, glossy leaves.

And then there was again the sensation of a question being asked, and though Selene screwed up her mind as best she could and tried to grab hold of it, she couldn't understand it. She shook her head.

"I'm sorry," she said. "I still can't hear you." She looked pleadingly at the children.

"Rosie, I'm sorry I scared you, earlier. I'm Selene Shields, I'm here to help."

"We don't need help," said Rosie. "*Green* is helping us."

"Helping you do what?" asked Selene.

"We're going to find my dad," said Rosie, clenching her fists as if daring Selene to stop her.

Selene felt her mouth come open. That couldn't be it. There had to be some angle, some other motivation. She looked at Green, whose eyes sparkled at her.

Now she was getting used to the creature's appearance, she realized it actually had a very expressive face. Only, just as with its words, she couldn't understand what those expressions meant. It was like looking at a person whose social conditioning had been tuned to a different wavelength. The leaves bunched and fluttered, giving her the impression of emotions, but nothing seemed to make sense.

The mouth, held open a crack by the vines that twined out of it from both corners, opened wider as a faint chattering escaped, like the whisper of wind in dry branches.

It was another question, Selene was certain of it from the way it tugged on her, begging an answer. But still she could not understand.

"I'm sorry," she repeated, and looked helplessly at Rosie. "Can *you* understand what it's saying? I can't."

But Rosie pursed her lips and said nothing.

The Green's shoulders slumped, the leaves drooping, and it withdrew the offered hand and extended the other one, pointing up at the darkening canopy.

"Green says you should go, then," said Marvin.

Selene shook her head.

"Not without you two," she said.

The leaves across Green's shoulders fluttered. Selene interpreted that as a shrug. It lowered its arm and tilted its head downward, working its rooty feet into the moss.

Selene felt the shuddering in the ground just in time to leap aside as a pillar of moss bulged up under where her feet had been.

It rose maybe two feet, and then stopped, only for another pillar to erupt directly beneath her, carrying her toward the canopy.

It was all she could do to keep her balance, dropping to one knee and raising a hand to break the impact against the leafy ceiling. She caught a glimpse of Green, staring up at her as she was carried away, and then she hit the canopy and her view was cut off as she was thrust into it.

Leaves everywhere, brushing her, whipping at her face. Selene closed her eyes and tucked her face into the crook of her elbow, trying to make herself as compact as possible.

Then the foliage around her turned dry and sharp, and she felt the sting of twigs scraping against her hand. The next moment she was fighting her way out through a tangle of dry brush, and there were hands on her—warm, living, leather-clad hands—and then she was being pulled bodily out of the crevasse and collapsing into Clara's arms.

"I have you," came the woman's steady voice in her ear, and only then did Selene dare lower her arm and look around.

Night had fallen while she'd been . . . wherever she had been. Jill had set up a makeshift camp in a clearer part of the wood, with an improvised floodlight tied to a nearby branch. Sharon and Audrey huddled beneath it, staring at Selene as though she had risen from her own grave.

"How much did I lose?" Selene gasped. She wasn't certain, but it was fully dark, and she could glimpse stars through the thinner branches of the trees.

"Two hours," said Clara.

"Well damn," said Selene, brushing dead leaves out of her hair, and staggering to her feet. "Thought it felt weird down there. I think I hit a pocket."

"A pocket?" asked Jill.

"What was in it?" asked Clara.

"What *happened?*" gasped Sharon.

"I found Green," said Selene. "And Marvin and Rosie—they're all right, as far as I can tell. But listen, Clara, I don't think Green kidnapped them. I think . . . "

She stopped. Though she was standing on hard, cold, *real* earth, she could feel a familiar trembling beneath her feet. And, faintly, from somewhere deep in the crevasse, there was a sound like hissing wind in bare branches.

"Flaming hells," she said, clutching at Clara's arm for balance. "I think it's *coming.*"

She felt Clara stiffen under her hand, then the large woman was pushing her aside, stepping between her and the crevasse.

Selene went, stumbling, and caught herself on a nearby branch. The trembling in the earth was strong enough now it was shaking the trees all around them, and causing the floodlight's beam to jiggle disconcertingly.

Something *was* coming up out of the crevasse: Selene could hear the snap of dead branches, and behind that, the windy rustle which she was beginning to associate with Green's voice.

And this time . . .

. . . this time there were words in it. Faint, but the same words repeated over and over again.

"I hear it," said Clara.

"Hear *what?*" demanded Jill, who was crouching with Sharon and Audrey well away from the crevasse.

"I cannot make out the words," Clara admitted, as if the other woman had not spoken.

"I can," said Selene, her mouth gone dry. "But only because I heard them before."

She was aware of Clara's pale face turning to stare at her through the gathering darkness, but Selene had eyes only for the center of the crevasse, which had opened to reveal a hungry, dark hole, and from within that hole a sweet wind was rushing, bringing with it a thin cloud of yellow motes.

"And on the bough, before the storm," Selene whispered, adding her voice to the cacophony already in her head.

And Green erupted out of the ground, sending waves of vines and blooming runners everywhere. Moss gushed out of the hole, pouring over the dead branches in a thick torrent of fuzzy greenness, and from its banks tiny white flowers blossomed. The air was suffused with the smell of new growth, sweet and wet and clear.

The vines ran along the ground, caressing the barren oak trees, and every tree they touched gave a shudder and put out new, green leaves.

The circle of living foliage radiated out from the hole, the wave of moss breaking on Clara's legs to flow around her, blanketing the ground. Jill gave a surprised shout, and something knocked into the tree that held the flashlight, sending it clattering to the ground.

In the ensuing darkness Selene blinked fiercely, willing her eyes to adjust. Already she could see a familiar purple light emanating from the depths of the hole, and soon the trailing, glowing vines were threading their way out over the moss. They illuminated the figure of Green, who was standing in a tumble of leaves with their feet sunk deep in the ground. They were stooped, pushing at the moss around their legs, and a moment later Rosie and Marvin scrambled out.

The children were red-faced and wide-eyed, but seemed happily excited. Then they saw their audience, and Rosie put a protective hand on Marvin's arm.

"*Marvin!*" shouted Sharon, and there was a cracking in the undergrowth as the woman pushed herself through the branches and vines, trying to get closer.

"Wait," said Selene, warningly, but Sharon was yelling over her.

"Marvin, what are you *doing?* Come back here, this minute!"

Marvin got a sullen look on his face, and shook his head obstinately.

"Rosie," said Audrey, who was sitting at Jill's feet. "Rosie, what's going on?"

"*Marvin,*" said Sharon, warningly.

"We're going to find dad," said Rosie, simply. Marvin nodded in agreement.

Audrey was shaking her head, however.

"No no, Rosie," she said, her voice more sad than frightened. "It doesn't work that way. Your dad's gone."

"Green says he's not," said Rosie. "And Green can do anything."

"Why is it doing this for you?" asked Clara, voicing what Selene thought was the first sensible question.

Rosie looked momentarily confused. She looked back up at Green, who seemed to have grown taller, though their shoulders were still hunched. There was a lot of new growth there: thick leaves forcing their way out like the collar of a cape.

The leaves of the creature's face shifted and its eyes twinkled. But it was Marvin who answered.

"Rosie was sad," he said, as if this explained everything.

"I—what?" said Audrey.

"Rosie was sad," he repeated.

Beside them, Sharon took a deep breath and looked up at the sky for a moment.

"Why was Rosie sad, Marvin?" she asked.

"She misses her dad," Marvin explained.

"But you can't do anything about that, Marvin," Sharon said, heavily.

"Green can," said Marvin. "I asked. It said yes."

"Green," said Clara, and this time she addressed the creature itself. "What are you doing?"

Green began to tremble, the leaves across its shoulders chattering from the motion. There was a bright tangle of glowing vines settling between its feet, and by their light Selene saw how it was not just the shadow of Green that seemed to reach up forever into the sky: Green *itself* was growing, rising slowly so that its head broke through the canopy of newly leafed trees, its body pushing them back as it grew, until it was as tall as a house at least. Its leafy skin was stretched thin, and Selene could clearly see the brown bones of its rib cage, and in place of a heart, a tangle of vines holding what looked like a clump of acorns.

Then with a fierce rushing sound the foliage which had been gathering around its shoulders spread out, sprouting long, thin, bladelike leaves.

Selene had often been struck as a child by the similarity between leaves and feathers, and sure enough, it turned out leaves could make *very* convincing wings. For that was unmistakably what was unfolding from Green's back: two giant wings made of long, strong leaves, slatted together in mimicry of primaries and secondaries and coverts. It beat them once, and sent a shower of motes down into the clearing.

Through the branches of the trees, Selene looked up into a face grown giant, the eyes brighter than any of the stars just coming out in the evening sky.

A hand reached down, and the two children used it as a step to climb up inside the creature's rib cage, where they arranged themselves comfortably: Marvin sat on one rib while he draped his arms over the one above. Rosie stood, gripping the next rib up, which passed around her waist, while she ducked her head out from under the one above so she could look down at them.

"Don't worry," she called down. "We'll be back before dawn."

"Green is *good*," Marvin insisted.

"Marvin," gasped Sharon, her face white from fury and terror. "Come down from there *this instant!* Or I'll—"

She broke off out of pure surprise as Audrey got to her feet and walked shakily across the springy new moss, to where the fall of leaves marked Green's legs.

"Audrey—no," said Clara, making a jerking motion as if to grab the woman.

Audrey looked at her—at both of them—and Selene saw her eyes were red and she didn't look afraid. Clara left her hand outstretched, but didn't stop the woman as she continued on, coming to stand at Green's feet.

"Mom?" said Rosie, uncertainly.

Audrey shrugged, then lifted her hands, almost pleadingly.

Moving slowly, and more gently than it had with the children, Green lowered its hand further, and allowed Audrey to stand on its fingers as it lifted her up, depositing her on its ribs along with the children.

"Audrey, what are you doing?" Jill shouted.

Audrey didn't answer. She crawled inside Green's rib cage and sat down next to Rosie.

Something prickled on Selene's mind. Something like a question.

She looked up to find Green gazing down at her curiously. Though its face was distant, Selene thought she could almost read its expression. She had the shape of the question in her mind, but *still* could not sense its meaning.

"Try again," she shouted up at it. "I almost had it that time."

Green extended its neck down, the leaves of its face fluttering.

It was monstrous and beautiful and dangerous and magical in all the ways Selene had learned to guard herself against. Because good things in this world don't come for free. Monsters were real, and magic brought curses and loss and death and grief.

And Green, who brought flowers and moss and played with children. Green, who breathed out fresh air like a spring morning after a rainstorm. Green, who made the talisman on Selene's shirt tingle—not in warning, she now realized, but in *recognition.*

Green, who reached out its hand, palm up, and in the rustling of its leaves asked,

Will you come?

"What did it say?" Clara demanded, but Selene heard her words only distantly.

She'd dropped Freddie somewhere in the moss. She didn't care. She stepped neatly around Clara to look up into the huge, crinkling face.

She'd been trained to dislike the shape of human skulls, but with Green, Selene had to admit there was a sort of beauty there. Like the rusting husk of a car with a tree growing through it.

"I'm not like them," Selene said, gesturing weakly at the three already seated in Green's chest cavity. "I'm not a lumenite, or even very friendly. I *hunt* things like you."

There was a bristling in Green's face, and it struck Selene that the thing looked *amused.*

There are no other things like me.

The words were easier to make out when she didn't expect to hear them with her ears. Rather, they turned up in the back of her head in the same sourceless voice that spoke when she thought to herself.

She shook her head. "Sorry," she said. "I don't think I'm compatible with your world."

But you are a part of it, said the Green. Its hand turned, and a finger the size of a soup spoon reached out and pressed, ever so gently, against the little round talisman.

Moonshield, it said, *will you come?*

Selene looked up. Marvin seemed to be getting impatient, but Rosie was gazing down at her curiously.

"It likes you," she said, sounding surprised.

Selene looked back up at Green.

Monsters exist, Selene reminded herself. Why not good monsters, too? Just this once.

Clara's protests were faint echoes in her ears as she took hold of the vines covering Green's hand and pushed herself up, swinging herself easily next to Audrey, who gave her a wet smile.

"Selene, what are you *doing?*" Jill screeched from the ground—which was suddenly a long way below her. Green had stood up.

"Ain't it obvious?" Selene called back down. "I'm going with them! Clara, find Freddie for me! I can't bring him this time."

Clara glared up at her, disapproval written all over her pale face. But she nodded once, firmly.

"Are you crazy?" Sharon screamed. "You can't just let them *go!* What is it—*give me my son back, you monster!*" She hurled herself through the moss and vines, as if she were going to pull Green to pieces.

Green, however, gave one beat of its gigantic wings, and with a great *whoosh* they were airborne, drifting away into the night sky like a seed on the wind. The shouts of the women on the ground were swallowed by the distance, and the world shrank until it appeared to Selene like a miniature model. It reminded her of flying in an airplane, when she could look down during their initial ascent and see the houses and highways below them so tiny, and the cars creeping along them at a snail's pace.

Here it was the same, except there was no thick, smudged window between her and the rushing night air, and instead of cramped plane seats she was clutching fiercely to the smooth bough of polished wood that passed for Green's fourth rib, her feet planted three more down. She felt the vines which curled around where Green's heart should have been tickling her back, and to her surprise she felt them push against her supportively when a sudden dip caused her to swing on her hold.

Next to her, Audrey had her own rib in a dead clutch, her face pressed against the wood and her shoulders tight. But below them, on the other side of Green's sternum, Marvin and Rosie were sitting in a tangle of vines and staring out at the night in amazement. Marvin had a bewildered grin on his face, and Rosie was laughing.

Up and up and they rose, Green circling to gain height over the sprawling city suburbs. The moon was high behind them, and much brighter than Selene thought it should have been. It bathed the twinkling lights of the city in a pale, unearthly light, and by squinting a little, Selene could see Green's shadow stretched over the ground: a huge, monstrous, humanoid shape with wide, spreading wings, their tips like ragged fingers grasping at the night.

When they had reached a height where the towers of downtown looked like termite mounds to their north, and the Arkansas River was a pale glimmer in a winding dark stripe cutting through the sea of city lights, Selene felt Green shift above them, and by looping an elbow around the rib at her chest and hooking the one below it with a leg, she was able to lean back and get a look at its face.

Green's eyes were blazing, casting the shadow of its skull onto the leaves of its head, and its mouth was opening wider, wider, wider. . . . Vines were spilling out of the corners, dark buds blossoming along their length, and Selene smelled the sweet scent of roses a moment before there was a huge, roaring gust.

It came from Green itself, she realized as the wind whipped by over her head. She heard it passing over the city and roaring in the branches of the trees. There was a faint clatter of garbage cans being knocked over, and a few car alarms went off—though the blaring honks were muffled by the distance.

Below her, Marvin giggled.

Green was hovering, its wings vibrating against the cool night air, and turning in a slow circle. The vines from its mouth had extended and were drifting through the air like curious snakes, probing and testing. They had come around and were facing the dark swatch of a county park to the west of the city, when Green sucked in the vines and dove toward the earth.

Selene felt the wind in her hair, saw the world rushing up toward her, and was strangely unafraid. Marvin and Rosie were shrieking in joy, Audrey was crying a litany of "Oh god, oh god, oh *god!*" but inside Selene's mind everything was cool and calm as a pool in winter. She heard the whistle of wind in leaves, and imagined huge wings folded in a falcon's dive as they plummeted toward the ground. Closer, closer. . . . She could make out the individual houses with their cars in the driveway—there was a dog in one yard, barking its head off.

Wooden bones creaked, and with a thrilling swoop they pulled even with the ground and then began a gentle rise over the rooftops, drifting just clear of the power lines. Green's trailing feet brushed the tops of the trees, and its wings stretched from rooftop to rooftop across the quiet streets.

"It's like the dream I told you about!" Rosie shrieked to Marvin. "Just like it!"

It was nothing like any dream Selene could remember, but it certainly felt like one.

She could see the few people who were out clutching their hats as the wind Green brought hit them, yet though many looked skyward, none seemed to see them. None, at least, save for the small boy carrying the trash out of the kitchen. He dropped the bag and stared at them, eyes wide in astonishment.

The animals also knew something was there, though Selene couldn't imagine what the neighborhood dogs thought they saw. Maybe a wooden skeleton the size of a small airplane with a wingspan to match, covered in leaves and vines and carrying people in its rib cage.

They were moving swiftly over the houses now, listing westward, away from the bright lights of downtown. They passed over a long stretch of two-lane highway leading out of the city, and finally veered off over a dark expanse of trees to the south. Green circled again, tightening and descending with each orbit, until all Selene could see were the prickly tops of trees choking a remote gully.

Huge arms descended on either side, and Green landed on its hands and knees, pulling its wings in and pressing its torso down so that it was only a drop of two or three feet to the ground.

Rosie and Marvin swung themselves down with shouts of "We're here! It's here!" and Selene followed suit, then turned back to help Audrey. The woman's hand was cold and shaking, but there was light in her eyes as she joined Selene on the ground.

"Well," she said. "That was *something.*"

There was a groaning sound above them, and then a lightening as Green began to shrink, pouring itself down to the ground beside them, until it stood up again, more or less the height of a regular human. Now it carried the bundle of acorns in its hands, and its wings were gone.

Marvin was still shouting "We're here! We're here!" and Rosie ran up to Green expectantly.

"He's close, isn't he?" she asked, and the leafy creature nodded.

"Who's close, Rosie?" her mother asked.

"*Dad,*" said Rosie, as if this should have been obvious.

Selene looked around the shrubby little ravine. It ought to have been too dark to see anything, but the moon was still shining unnaturally bright, and by its light she thought she could make out a break in the undergrowth, where perhaps there had once been an old vehicle track. Other than that, the place looked like it had been undisturbed by humans for years.

She felt her heart sink as she realized what sort of state Oakey Thorn was likely to be in, if he was truly nearby. Judging by the stricken expression on Audrey's face, she suspected the woman had come to the same conclusion.

"Rosie," she said, tentatively. "Your father's not . . . we don't know for certain if he's still alive."

"Green says nothing truly dies," Rosie announced, with the certainty only an adolescent could muster. "It's only broken down into component parts and reforms into new things."

Selene opened her mouth to point out that once it was a new thing the old thing didn't exist anymore and if that wasn't a kind of death she didn't know what was, but decided against it.

Green had paced over, leaving a trail of vigorously growing plants in its wake, to stand next to a particularly thick pile of dead brush, so old and decayed that it was almost dirt. A young oak tree was doing its best to put down roots there, but had only reached a height of about three feet.

Green put out a hand, and the tree took life and slid away off the pile, leaving it relatively clear. There was a shivering in the creature's limbs, like the rattling of wind in the trees, though in the gully the air was perfectly still—almost stagnant. There was a hissing noise and Selene saw that the vines trailing from

Green's mouth were growing even longer, trailing down its front and testing the air like curious snakes. It shivered, causing its leaves to rustle, and in the rustling Selene thought she heard its voice. It began to sway, leaning forward and back, and with every forward lean it dropped an acorn into the pile of brush. And with every dropped seed, the rustling intensified until Selene could make out the words.

And once again, she found she knew them.

"What's it saying?" Audrey asked, clutching her arm and leaning close. But already Rosie and Marvin had begun to chant, pumping their fists as they watched the heap of decaying brush.

"With—a—chattering!" cried Rosie.

"*Shattering*, Rosie," Marvin corrected her.

"Oh, right," said Rosie. "With—a—shattering!"

"With a shattering!" said Marvin.

The words were throbbing inside Selene's head. She turned to Audrey.

"With a shattering, the Earth it weeps," she said, just as Green dropped the last acorn into the pile.

There *was* a shattering then: the shattering of dried, dead wood as it broke apart and was swept aside in tiny splinters, stinging Selene's arms when she raised them to shield her face. When the small storm abated it was to reveal a bare patch of earth, stripped clean of brush and foliage, with dark pools of liquid oozing from its surface.

Anyone else might have thought it was tar or molasses, but Selene had seen enough to recognize it as old blood, even before the sharp, coppery smell hit them.

"*Yee-urggh!*" said Rosie, covering her face.

"Ya might want to stand back," Selene told Audrey. "This could get ugly."

Green glanced at her then, its eyes twinkling merrily, and Selene thought it looked amused. Then it turned and walked forward into the growing pool of blood. It bent, and reaching out a hand, grabbed at something that was hidden in the muck.

It came up holding another skeleton hand—only this one gleamed pale in the moonlight, though it was still stained dark with blood.

"Oh *no . . .*" said Audrey, but Selene had no attention to spare for the woman.

The hand had been followed by an arm, and the arm by a shoulder, and then with a grinding wrench the skull came free, lolling off the neck at an odd angle. After that the torso, which still had the tattered remains of a shirt partially covering it.

Behind her, Audrey had started to cry.

"No, no, *no, no, no,*" she sobbed.

The children, however, watched the grim scene with serenity. Marvin even looked the tiniest bit bored, while Rosie was leaning forward, fascinated.

For her part, Selene forced herself to watch, even though a part of her—the part that remembered all too well what they found under the blood tree outside River View—was beginning to feel queasy.

Now the body—for it was a body; there was enough flesh left below the chest for the smell to become immediately noticeable—was clear to the hips, and its other arm flailed free to clutch at Green as it continued to struggle out of the wet, bloody earth. Even so the body hung heavily off Green, who continued to tug at it until only its feet were buried. Then, cradling the pale skeleton with its ruddy, tattered clothing and scant fleshy remains, the creature lowered its leafy face and breathed out a stream of yellow dust.

It washed over the bloody skeleton in waves, sticking to the bones and quickly germinating into tiny mushrooms and fungi. A thick fuzz of pale green moss stole over the bones, covering them in a soft, springy coat. The body clutched at Green with both hands—the only parts of it where the bones still showed— and gave a convulsive shudder.

A moment later green buds burst from all over its mossy skin, growing quickly into vines and trailing branches. Large, glossy leaves spread over it, and the next thing Selene knew there were two strange, plantlike humanoids standing in the clearing, their hands joined and their heads bowed together.

For the breath of a moment the little gully was soaked in silent moonlight, the only sound being a faint rustle of a gentle wind in the leaves of the two green men standing in the center of it.

Then, with a creaking of wood and vines, the humanoid that had previously been the body of Oakey Thorn straightened up and looked at them curiously. His eyes were darker, the light in them a reflection of Green's, and they shuttered briefly as he blinked.

Yet though his face was covered in leaves, and there was a crown of lichen covering his head, enough of the shape and humor remained, that even though Selene had only ever seen that face in a badly lit photograph, she found it immediately recognizable.

Rosie and Audrey had even less trouble. The woman dropped to her knees with a faint cry, while her daughter gave a delighted shriek and ran at the green man, whose face broke into a white-toothed grin as he bent creakingly and stretched out his hands, catching up the girl and lifting her into the air. Peals of laughter rang through the night, accompanied by a deep, hearty laugh that sank into Selene's bones and warmed them. Nothing bad could come from a creature that laughed like that, not if the world had any rhyme or reason to it.

Still Audrey did not move, but sat with her knees sunk in the twigs and brambles, until the newly risen green man settled Rosie on a broad shoulder and turned to look at her. His smile faltered, and he extended a hand almost apologetically.

"That's not possible," whispered Audrey.

"Anything is possible," said Marvin, "when you're with Green." He walked boldly up to Oakey Thorn and shook the outstretched hand. "I am Marvin," he said. "I'm Rosie's friend."

Oakey Thorn—and the name had never been more fitting, Selene thought distantly—inclined his shaggy head and shook Marvin's hand gravely. Then it looked up and stared at Selene, curiously.

"Hi," said Selene, weakly. "I'm . . . uh . . . I'm just along to make sure no one gets hurt."

Oakey Thorn seemed to find this amusing. He laughed, his open mouth revealing white teeth and a glossy, green tongue. Unlike Green itself, no vines or shoots fell out. It made his face altogether more human looking.

"Oh my god," whispered Audrey, bringing her hands up to clutch at her face. "It *is* you . . . "

The green man nodded. Dragging his feet through the earth, he came to stand before the kneeling woman and reached down, helping her to her feet.

On his shoulder, Rosie kicked her feet and looked expectantly at Green.

"Now what?" she asked.

Green looked back at them, its starry eyes shimmering in their dark hollows, and once again Selene saw it begin to grow, rising above them into the night.

Now we go home, it said, in a voice like chattering leaves and sighing wind.

Selene and Marvin rode back on Green's shoulders, each one with an arm twined into the vines covering its neck. By looking back as far as possible Selene could see Oakey Thorn, who was walking at their side, his daughter on his shoulder and his wife clutched to his chest. Tall as skyscrapers they both were, and their huge, lunging strides ate up the miles of road leading toward Maple Ridge. Downtown Tulsa was a tight knot of bright lights on their left, while cars whizzed by far below. Judging by the lack of crashing and swerving, Selene guessed they were once more protected by the strange sheen of half-invisibility that Green carried with it.

Only half invisible, she decided, after an owl swooped down, circled a huge head curiously, before flapping off again. Every time they passed a house with a dog she heard frantic barking, and once she spotted a mad streak across a lawn as a cat took fright and sped away.

They forded the river with much splashing, but the water only came up to the giants' knees, and soon they were across and stepping carefully between the tightly packed houses.

Though Selene recognized the neighborhood, she was so far disoriented that it came as a surprise when she felt Green begin to shrink under her hand, and then they were tumbling into the Thorn's backyard, Rosie and Audrey joining them as Oakey Thorn withdrew back to his original height.

He'd continued to flesh out, in a leafy way, over the course of their walk. Now Selene could see bark-like skin showing through the gaps in his leaves, and there was definitely more of the shape of the man in his shoulders and torso. Yet his hands remained skeletal, and his feet were still buried in the ground. When Rosie tugged at his arm, trying to coax him in the back door, he shook his head.

Things do die, Selene thought, sadly. *And even if they stay with us, somehow, it's never the same.*

Audrey seemed to understand. She was holding onto Oakey's other arm as if she were afraid he would vanish.

There was a faint, haunting whistle, and Selene turned to find Green was standing, its back very straight, and its mouth open to let out the long, pure note.

The sound lit a shiver of nerves that ran down Selene's spine and settled in her feet, making her soles itch. Then Marvin stood up next to Green and began to sing along.

It should have sounded terrible: the unearthly voice and the husky, adolescent one, singing a strange harmony together. Yet the combination proved surprisingly intriguing, with elements of the Green's fantastic, terrifying magic, and Marvin's solid, everyday humanity.

The two of them began to rock back and forth, their voices going stronger, and everything after that took on the nature of a dream. Selene could only watch, her body feeling fuzzy and far away, as Oaky Thorn came to stand in the little crater Rosie had dug to plant her acorn. He worked his feet into the earth with a satisfied sigh, and stretched his arms up, up, reaching into the sky.

Rosie and Audrey joined hands, and after a confused moment Selene joined them. Together they began to dance a slow step around the green man, and all the while the voices sang, and he reached higher and higher into the sky.

His arms branched, his head was swallowed by his shoulders; his legs fused together and new green leaves exploded from the crown of his head.

He became a tree. More than that, he became a great oak with a gnarled trunk and thick, beautiful branches that reached up and out, overshadowing the little house in a protective embrace. He might have reached up to the stars themselves, which looked closer in the strange moonlight, or he might have crouched low over the rooftops. His branches swayed and rustled in the wind, and still Marvin and the Green sang on, long after Audrey and Rosie and Selene had ceased to dance, dropping to lie, exhausted, among the tree's roots.

They should have grown cold in the night air, the sweat drying on their skin as a cool breeze rippled through the backyard, but to Selene if felt as though warmth radiated out from the roots of the tree, and far from being hard and uncomfortable they caressed her back and shoulders like loving hands. The stars were caught in the branches of Oakey Thorn, sparkling like tiny jewels in a dark crown. She had never seen anything so beautiful.

Despite everything that had happened, despite her experience and training and everything she knew, Selene felt a wave of peaceful contentment wash over her, and in the ensuing lull found herself drifting inexorably toward sleep.

There was a stirring in her gut; the last, feeble efforts of the old habit that prevented her from relaxing unless there was someone on guard. Rolling her head to one side, she saw that Marvin and the Green were still standing. They stood with their backs to the tree, the boy with his hand tangled in the creature's flowing skirt of leaves.

Green would keep watch, Selene knew. They were on Green's ground, and nothing would dare encroach upon it.

Nothing would be allowed to.

Sometimes the monsters are good.

She only knew she slept because a time later she woke to find Green crouched over her. The moon had set and in the relative darkness its eyes glowed like greenish embers.

"Something wrong?" Selene mumbled, unsticking her mouth from sleep paralysis with some difficulty.

In the dark it was utterly impossible to read Green's expression, but there was a shifting of the leaves around its face that suggested something. A frown? A raised eyebrow? A hint of a smile?

It is going to be a hard winter, the Green said, its voice like the rustle of leaves and the clack of bare branches. *But do not doubt, the glory of spring will come again.*

A tendril reached out, sliding over the ground, and tapped its end against the little talisman still pinned to Selene's shirt. Again she felt the fizz of magic passing between them, not a warning, but a greeting. One piece of old magic recognizing another, and calling out to it.

Keep reflecting, said Green, its voice so soft Selene thought she might have imagined it. The words echoed in her head, mixing with the memory of its song, and she let herself be lost in it; in the wind and the whisper of leaves and the great, strong branches, studded with stars.

Selene woke to a bone-chilling cold and a hard piece of wet root digging into her side. Someone had put a blanket over her, and she could feel the bite of the brisk morning air around its edges. It did nothing, however, for the damp that was seeping up from the ground she lay on, and she groaned as she pushed herself into a sitting position.

The sun was in the act of climbing over the eastern rooftops. Already the uppermost branches of Oakey Thorn were tinged with gold, yet still incongruously green in the sea of reds and yellows of the surrounding trees.

Selene gave a shiver, her waking mind taking stock of the events from the previous night and demanding answers.

Audrey and Rosie lay a few feet away, curled into each other and half covered by a battered sleeping bag. The tree that had been Oakey Thorn was as solid as ever—and just as solidly a *tree.* Not a man.

There was no sign of either Marvin or the Green.

There was a shout from the front yard, and a moment later the back gate burst open and Clara came hurtling through it. She carried Freddie slung over her back and her sword was out, but she stopped dead and lowered it when she caught sight of Selene—and the tree. Her icy blue eyes widened, and she rocked a little as Jill, not so quick to react, bumped into her from behind.

"What's going on?" Sharon's voice carried over their shoulders. "Are they there? What's *happened?*"

"We're here," said Selene, wearily. She felt cold and achey and a little empty inside. As if she had been filled with wonder and delight, but all that had bled away with the rising of the sun. The world was going back to normal—the new, dangerous normal where monsters were everywhere and ready to eat you. And yet . . . *and yet*.

There was still a giant oak tree where before no tree had been.

"I'm not sure what happened," she admitted, as Rosie and Audrey stirred.

"Where did he go?" Audrey asked, blinking around at them.

"Where did who go?" Clara asked.

"Oakey," she said. "He was here. He carried me home on his shoulders."

Selene looked at the woman. She looked meaningfully at the tree. She looked back to find Rosie staring up into his branches with a growing look of delight on her face.

"He's *here*," she shrieked, jumping to her feet. "He's *here!* He came *home*, Mom! And he's not going to leave!" She ran forward and embraced the huge, rough trunk, pressing her cheek into it and closing her eyes. Then she stepped back and, throwing her arms up, began a slower version of the dance they had performed the night before.

"Dad's back!" she announced, proudly. "Dad's *back!*" She did a cartwheel.

"That's a *tree*," said Jill. She looked uncertainly at Selene. "That *is* a tree, isn't it?"

Selene shrugged.

Clara sheathed her sword and came over to stand under his branches. They did not seem impossibly high anymore; just the height of a normally large, well-grown oak tree. With respectful caution, Clara pulled off one of her gloves and laid her bare hand against the dark bark, her brow pinched into a frown. When she stepped away she looked wonderingly at Selene.

"What sorcery is this?" she asked.

"'S not sorcery," Selene sighed, climbing stiffly to her feet. "It's Green's magic. That *was* Oakey Thorn. Might still be, in a way. Even Green can't bring the dead back to life, but I suppose it can give the dead new life. As to *why* it did it . . . I got nothing."

"I did *tell* you," said a husky voice from the back porch, and they all turned to find Marvin standing in the doorway. He looked tired and pale, but he'd brushed his hair. He was also wearing one of Audrey's aprons. "Green is *good*."

"Marvin!" cried Sharon, apparently torn between relief and anger. "Can *you* explain this?"

Marvin shrugged, implacably.   "I made eggs," he said. "There's toast, also."

Selene discovered she was ravenous, as were Audrey and Rosie. Marvin confessed to having eaten the first panful of scrambled eggs, and sat smugly on a stool in the corner while the rest of them ate and compared notes.

"We tried to follow," Clara explained, carefully arranging a layer of egg over her dry toast. "But as soon as you cleared the treetops you disappeared. I tried recasting the sweep, but I couldn't feel anything from Freddie."

"Then we tried to go back to Audrey's house," Jill said. "But we couldn't."

Selene stopped chewing long enough to give her a surprised look.

"There was a spatial distortion," Clara explained. "Every time we approached, the road would turn or we'd come to the cross street beyond without ever passing this house. It was what convinced me you were here the whole time."

"Yeah," said Jill. "It was really wonky. Kind of like the wood around that blood tree, only there was space *missing* instead of space added."

"I stood watch as close as I could," Clara said. "Just before dawn I felt something give, and suddenly I could see the house again. And the tree. That was when we arrived and found you."

Selene scratched behind one ear and nodded.

"That makes sense," she said. "It felt sorta like we went . . . well, we went into a halfway place, if you know what I mean? We were still in this world, but Green had its own little bubble of reality that traveled around with it. We went walking through the suburbs, and the only things that noticed were animals . . . and this one kid."

"You can only see Green if it wants you to," Rosie piped up. "That goes for everyone, even me and Marvin."

Clara nodded in acceptance. Then she looked across at Selene, her eyes very cold and blue in the slanting morning light.

"How did the tree happen?"

With a sigh, Selene explained about their walk out to the gully, the raising of the body, the transformation it underwent, and finally how it came back to the house and turned into a tree. She didn't mention Green's last words to her. That felt private, somehow. Not that she couldn't talk about it—just that it would have been rude to share.

Clara let out a low whistle when she'd finished.

"Wow," said Sharon, glancing out the window at the tree with new respect.

"But how did Oakey Thorn wind up in that gully in the first place? And how do you know it was him?"

"I recognized him," said Audrey, quietly.

The gathering around the table went silent for a moment. Then Selene pursed her lips and said:

"As to how he got there . . . maybe the wrong kind of assholes found him. Got carried away. Maybe a cop thought he'd stolen a car and chased him; thought it was easier to dump the body than do the paperwork." She shrugged. "Pick the one that makes you the least miserable. Only thing I can tell you: I don't think he did anything wrong, and I don't think it would help to know the truth." She squinted out the window, where the rising sun had lit the new green leaves of the giant oak a bright, yellow-green. "He came home," she said. "That's more than you can say for a lot of folks who disappeared."

Jill chewed thoughtfully on her breakfast, and didn't ask any more questions.

"So," said Sharon in a small voice. "Is there anything to be done? About Green, I mean. Or do we just have to live with it?"

Clara looked up, ready to respond, but it was Marvin who answered.

"Green's gone," the boy said, quiet and subdued.

Rosie put her knife and fork down with a clatter. "What do you mean its *gone?*" she cried.

Marvin shrugged.

"Said it had other things to do. It told me there was going to be a bad winter, but it would come back at the end of it."

"Oh," said Rosie, beginning to eat again. "Well, as long as it comes back, I suppose that's all right." She smiled over at her mom. "In the meantime, Dad will take care of us."

Audrey reached across the table and took her daughter's hand. There were tears in her eyes, but she was smiling.

Sharon sighed. "And it was such a nice summer."

"If anything bothers us, I'll talk to them," Marvin said.

His mother gave him a blank look. He stared back, a little defiantly.

"Just because someone can't talk the way you do doesn't mean they're not talking," he said.

Sharon looked helplessly at Jill, who shrugged.

"Count yourself lucky," said Selene. "You came out of an interaction with the oldest god I've ever met, and you're not only in possession of your family, your soul, and your livelihood— you've actually benefited from it. That doesn't happen very . . . " she paused. "That's never happened before."

"Maybe this supernatural leak won't be so bad," said Jill, with painfully naïve optimism. Selene found Clara's gaze across the table, and the larger woman shrugged (down, then up) impassively.

Selene was inclined to laugh, bitterly, but then she looked down and saw the talisman pinned to her shirt.

Just this once, she decided, she would live in hope.

After breakfast there wasn't much to do but help Audrey tidy up, though Jill insisted on taking samples from the Oakey Thorn tree. These turned out to be bark scrapings, since Rosie would not allow her to cut any of the branches. Selene privately agreed, though she wondered what the family would do when the tree grew large enough to interfere with the power lines.

They walked back to Sharon's house alone—the woman and her son having elected to stay and help clean the leaves out of the Thorn residence. Selene felt stiff and tired, but no more so than could have been expected from a night spent dancing and sleeping on the roots of a tree. And there was still the lingering peace and serenity she'd felt, looking up at the stars through the branches. It would fade with the coming days and the new challenges and dangers that inevitably awaited, but for now she clung to it, wanting it to last as long as it could.

"So, what *was* the Green?" Jill asked as they walked. "Was it a . . . I mean, was it *the* Greenman?"

Clara looked thoughtful, but Selene shook her head.

"Naw," she said. "I think it was older than that. It felt like . . . I dunno . . . maybe the thing that the Greenman came from? Like, the oldest possible incarnation of plant magic."

"A primordial deity," said Clara. "Like Chaos, like the Dark. The name fits: Green. It was the Green."

"Plants have been around an awful long time," Jill allowed. "Much longer than animals. Why appear human?"

"Probably the form that it felt we'd relate to the best," said Selene. "Could probably make itself look like anything, if it wanted."

"Did you understand what Marvin said, about it being a hard winter?"

Selene shivered.

"Likely, it means the next entity we meet will not be so . . . benevolent," said Clara, and Selene reluctantly agreed.

They turned down Woodside Boulevard and there was Arcana, squatting in front of the huge trailer, just as they had left him. Selene suddenly felt the call of the sofa bed, and her pace quickened.

"Forget what I said earlier," she told Jill as the woman unlocked the trailer and opened the door. "This thing is gonna be a lifesaver, I can tell."

Clara remained outside while her two companions disappeared into the trailer. She wandered off down the street and took out her phone.

It took her almost five minutes of going over in her head what she wanted to say before she worked up the nerve to make the call.

Ambient car noise greeted her after the third ring.

"Freeman, how can I help you?" came a voice, almost drowned out by the sound of the wind and engine.

"Ariel?" said Clara. "It's me. It's Claymore."

"Well, hello there stranger," said the warm, golden voice. There was a humming and the sound of wind abruptly vanished, as though a window had been shut. "So, what's up?"

"The green man you told us about," Clara said.

"Yes," said Freeman. "How did that go?"

Clara told him.

"Wow," said Freeman, when she had finished. "Wish I'd come. Sounds nice. Better than what I got."

Clara considered the ramifications of what she was about to say, then asked:

"Are you all right?"

Ariel Freeman chuckled. "Yeah," he laughed. "Yeah, I'm all right. Just . . . it's been messy, you know? Demon here, demon there. Ghouls too. And . . . I don't think I'm losing my touch, but that just means they're getting stronger." He sighed.

"If you ever need help . . . " Clara began, and found she couldn't finish.

"I'll call you?" said Freeman. "That's sweet of you to offer. Really."

"You should," said Clara. She took a breath. "You have my number, now."

"I do?" said Freeman. "Holy crap, I *do*. Awesome." It was hard to tell over the car noises, but he sounded pleased. "Right. For sure, I'll call you. If anything comes up."

Clara wasn't sure what to do with that.

"Be safe, Ariel Freeman," she said.

A distant laugh. "And the same to you, Claymore."

The phone went silent in her hand, and Clara slipped it into her pocket without looking. Wearily she turned and began walking back toward Arcana, and the black bike parked on the curb beside it.

It seemed to Sharon that the three women in the big red truck took the last of the warmth with them when they left. There followed a cold snap that had her digging out all the warm clothes she'd only worn once a year back in California. Only this snap dragged on and on, and she had to have someone come over and fix the furnace.

Marvin was better, though. Rosie came over every day, and Audrey had them for dinner on Thursdays. There was no sign of Green, though the strange oak tree remained. Sharon still wasn't sure about that, but when the first big storm ripped through, Audrey's house was the only one in the neighborhood that didn't get a branch dropped on it.

Bother what the creepy leaf person had said, Sharon decided. She'd had a good summer, and come through autumn all right. She'd invite Audrey and Rosie and her mother over for Thanksgiving, and they would have Christmas and New Year's and, no matter how cold it got, they'd have a good winter, too.

A fierce wind rattled the panes of the kitchen window. It warned of more storms and worse things beside, but Sharon ignored it. She put on a scarf and got a pot of water boiling. Rosie and Marvin would be home from school soon, and they always liked it when she had hot chocolate waiting for them.

In the backyard of Audrey Thorn's house, the great tree that had once been Oakey Thorn shifted its branches in the sharp wind. It was not an ill wind, but a dangerous one, and the tree stooped protectively over the house.

Under its branches the air was calm, and one brave blossom still clung to the rosebush that sat beside it, gleaming red against the spiny, dark green leaves.

*

Cold winds blow beyond my window
They sing of hope and mystery
But I know that they're only siren voices
They want a repeat of my history
(History)

Still the voices whisper to me in the night
Paint pretty illusions on my wall
And in this darkness I begin to hope I'm wrong
Hope that I might somehow get it all, oh-ah!

I have dreamed of summer nights
I have dreamed of an autumn's call
Was it worth the dream of a flight
To wake and find myself in fall?
O-oh no

So I stand between two worlds joined hand in hand
With all their contradictions plain to see
Though I never thought the dark could be so kind to me
Now it seems I might have to believe
O-oh,

no

I have dreamed of winter snows
I have dreamed of an awesome spring
Even as the darkness grows
I can hear the wind and the wind sings
O-oh, ah!

Sings of a place where I belong
Sings of a tree rising high and tall
(Rising high and tall)
If I could believe this song
I would never fear to take the fall
(Never fear the fall!)
O-oh yeah

Take the
take the fall
Never
fear the fall
Take the
take the fall
Never
fear the fall
Take the
take the fall!

—The Fall/*Technorhyme*

The Arcana crew will return in
"Out of Space"

When I first conceived of The Adventures of Bouragner Felpz *I wrote down two volumes' worth of short story titles, which were to cover (with only two exceptions) the shared adventures of Bouragner Felpz and Corianne Birch. These have since appeared in* The Adventures of Bouragner Felpz, Volume I, *and the last seven issues of* Apsis Fiction. *This story, however, is a little different. It is a novella, the first of three which will become the third volume of* Felpz *adventures, and comes chronologically in the latter half of Volume II. It was written over the summer of 2014, and will be followed by the second novella:* The Hand of Rishké, *coming in* Apsis Fiction: Aphelion 2017.

The Wolves of Riddlemoor

Foreword

THE FOLLOWING STORY takes place largely in the summer of 2326, between the events of "The Goblin's Fiddle" and "The Silver Chimera," though it has nothing to do with either of them. I did make a passing reference to it at the beginning of "The Hidden Road" as part of my introduction to Tida Hammin. So for my loyal readers, know that this narrative begins before those events, when I was still living in Redling with Bouragner Felpz, but does not close until some years after I moved away to Stanton Leaning. It offers a fuller explanation of how Tida and I met, and also references events from all the preceding stories—though you need not have read them in order to enjoy this one.

Corianne Birch
Stanton Leaning
Spring, 2338

Chapter 1:
An Unexpected Visitor

"HAVE YOU CONSIDERED, Corianne, how all living things are, essentially, *invaders*?" Bouragner Felpz asked me one morning as he lingered over breakfast, and I, ensconced in my corner by the window, attempted to write.

"Hmm?" I replied, not paying him much attention. My friend was apt to begin conversations as though they had been going on for some minutes already in his head—which I fancied was often the case—and I had learned in my long years of cohabitation with him that the best course of action was one of good-natured indulgence. "No," I said. "I don't believe so."

There was a clattering as he pushed the sausages about on his plate, but no following sounds to indicate that they were fulfilling their ultimate purpose. Instead my friend continued:

"It has always been my belief that humans did not spring, fully formed, into being on every continent and island that they currently inhabit. No no, we are all *too alike* for such a sudden and universal emergence. So you can imagine how pleased I am that the academic world is finally giving credence to the excellent theory, first proposed by the Azoan scholar Gai, that humans evolved from a small population in central Saffara and thence spread, over the course of several thousand years, to form our current diaspora. And so it follows, since humans are not so unique among the animal kingdom as we like to imagine ourselves, that the same can likely be said of many other animals. Our cousins the elves, giants, and roags, most notably."

"I beg your pardon," I said, for I had, against my better judgment, begun to listen, and now I wondered if I had perhaps missed something in the beginning. "Rogue whats?"

"Not rogue," said Felpz. "*Roag*, which is the proper way to address members of the species that have been, somewhat condescendingly, referred to by humans as *dwarfs*. Which is a highly offensive term among their people, I'll have you know."

I turned to look at my friend, and found him sprawled half out of his chair, his lavender dressing gown flung open to reveal the plum-colored waistcoat and matching, pinstriped trousers he'd elected to wear that day. He was smiling at me, a little ruefully.

"I learned this recently," he added. "To my sorrow. But that has little bearing upon the point I am trying to make: that *all* creatures are, simply by living, *invading* a space. Even the first primordial algae were invaders upon the pristine slate of this lifeless planet, and the invasion of *land*"—he huffed a laugh—"what a great conquest that was. My point is, everything is an invader, at some period in time. To consider yourself a native is just to say the invading happened before you came along; but you are still a product of that invasion. Likewise even if you were not born to a place, if you live there long enough, and unobtrusively enough, your invasion may be interpreted to be anything but what it actually is. Which I conclude by drawing your attention to the interloper who is currently invading the northwest corner of our sitting room."

That got me to look around in a hurry, but in the corner referred to, I saw only the usual jumble of books and oddments and baubles stacked haphazardly on a couple of armchairs. A pair of Felpz's slippers—embroidered with purple pansies—rested on the seat of one of these chairs, while the other held a broomstick, two volumes from the *Encyclopedia Magica,* and a curious wine bottle that appeared to be filled with black smoke. I frowned at it, wondering if the bottle contained—as I had suspected when I first saw it—some sort of spirit or genie. But Felpz had brought that bottle home himself, ordered me not to touch it, and then left it on the chair, apparently forgotten. If anything it was a hostage, not an invader.

"I'm afraid I fail to see the implied invader," I admitted. "Though I will give you your point, even if it appears irrelevant."

"But, my dear, it is completely relevant," cried Felpz, leaping up and maneuvering through the clutter to stand beside the chair with the broomstick and bottle. "Look a little closer, will you? See how he has hidden it in plain sight?"

I looked again, and then I saw it, peeking out from behind the broomstick: another stick, this one knobby and thick and polished, carved with dark runes and wound about with a leather thong that must have served as a loop to be hung from, and also to hold the collection of talismans that were attached to the staff.

For staff it was, and if anything was more obviously a wizard's staff I could not think what it would be. Even to my magically inept eyes the thing fairly glowed with an aura of mystery and wonder.

"My goodness, Felpz," I said, rising from my seat. "Wherever did that come from?"

"From Delpheon, judging by the wood," said Felpz, leaning over the staff but having a care not to touch it. "Originally, at least. I see there is mud on it that smells of something rather more local—one of the moors, I think. There is a name here, inscribed with Delpheonian letters: *Gandlyn Wale*. Which means nothing to my mind. But his staff implies that he should: for this is the staff of an *enhauron*."

"Bless you," I said automatically, then realized that he had not ended his sentence with a sneeze, as I had thought, but with an actual word.

"Forgive me," I said, ducking my head when he turned to give me a hurt look. "What is an . . . an *en-how* . . . er?"

"*En-how-rron*," said Felpz rolling the R with slow precision. "It is another invader from Delpheon; a word with no exact Kyrish translation, to be precise. In plain words: they are quite the most remarkable form of magical being." He turned back to study the staff. "And I mean that literally: you will find *enhauron* in all species of sentient animals, for they are not a human construct, like a wizard or a sorcerer. Also, unlike all other kinds of magic user—which are really just names for an occupation, like violinist, equestrian, or doctor—an *enhauron* is an *enhauron* whether they want to be one or not. They are the purest embodiment of magic that a living organism can be—which makes them extraordinarily powerful, if a bit limited in their scope of skills."

"How fascinating," I said. "And you mean to say one was *here*, and left that staff? Whatever could they have wanted?"

"That I do not know and cannot guess," Felpz said. He shrugged to himself. "Well, no point in delaying, I suppose. Let us ask *Enhaur* Gandlyn Wale what has driven him to seek me out!"

With these words Felpz reached forward and took up the staff, lifting it carefully by its midsection before grasping the knob at the top and rapping the end on the carpet.

He had not finished this motion when the air in front of him shimmered and a man appeared there, one hand outstretched so it rested below Felpz's own on the staff.

He was in all regards one of the most extraordinary characters I had ever seen—and this in a long life full of extraordinary characters. Not since Lilith Maugs's dramatic appearance had I been so fascinated by one of our visitors.

In height he was nearly as tall as Felpz, and just as lean. He was also surprisingly young—closer to twenty than thirty, I thought—with light auburn hair swept back from his high brow and tied at his nape by a piece of green ribbon.

That was another thing that made me stare: though his clothes were conservative enough in their form, in color he was as striking as Felpz—save that where my friend wore all shades of purple, this man wore shades of green: a deep, forest-colored suit could not conceal the bright green cravat nor the emerald waistcoat. His shirt—from what I could see of it at the collar and the cuffs—was pale moss. All this should have clashed horribly, yet somehow the nature of the greens blended together, putting me in mind of a spring wood, when all the trees are leafing out in their myriad viridian hues.

The man turned sharply around, taking in his surroundings, and I caught a glimpse of a narrow, pointed face with soaring eyebrows, a sharp nose, and bright, pale green eyes. They seemed to me to not belong in a human face—even one so finely crafted as this man's—but instead might have been more at home in that of a dragon—or even a demon. The sight gave me a momentary shiver.

"Dear me," said Felpz, politely removing his hand from the staff. "Forgive me, but you are far younger than I imagined."

The man cleared his throat and cast his eyes briefly downwards. "Yes, well," he said in a pleasant, rumbling voice like thick velvet. "We must all be born sometime."

Felpz smiled at this, and retreated to the breakfast table in a flurry of lavender dressing gown, where he began setting out a fresh cup and saucer. "Quite right," said he. "Well then, *Enhaur Wale*, may I offer you some refreshments? And then you can tell me why you were compelled to leave your staff in my sitting room."

"I require nothing in the way of refreshments," our visitor said, a little stiffly. "And I apologize for the intrusion, but I had to be certain to see you. It is . . . well, it's an embarrassment, seeking help like this, but as you have already noticed, I am somewhat lacking in experience, and I would very much appreciate your advice."

Felpz paused in the middle of pouring the tea, then shrugged and finished anyway. He motioned Wale to sit, and handed him the cup and saucer when he had done so.

"It would be an honor to assist you," he said, resting himself on the arm of a nearby chair. "If Corianne doesn't mind the interruption to her morning, you may begin immediately. Or we may move our consultation into my study . . . "

"Oh, no, please don't," I spoke up at once. For though I was loathe to have my work upset, I had come to recognize the beginnings of stories, and I was so fascinated by the peculiar young man that I was determined to document this one. "Please, carry on," I urged them, and discreetly got out a fresh notebook.

Felpz turned and looked expectantly at the man, who had laid his staff across his knees and was holding his tea awkwardly. "At your ready, *Enhaur* Wale." said Felpz graciously.

The man sipped cautiously at his tea, then balanced it on the arm of his chair. Folding his delicate, long-fingered hands together he cleared his throat again, and fixed Felpz with a piercing, pale green gaze.

"I suppose I had better give you some background. To that end, I must ask that you refer to me as Wizard Gandlyn—it is the title by which I will most readily be recognized, and the fact of the matter is, aside from you and your companion here, no one outside of Delpheon knows I am an *enhauron*."

Felpz raised his eyebrows at this, and our visitor continued.

"It is only a matter of convenience," he admitted. "I wish to avoid the difficulty of explaining to people what an *enhauron* is. Since I am in my peregrine at the moment, and having gained employment as the parish wizard of Riddlemoor, it seemed easier to allow the residents to assume that was all I was. I have studied the laws of wizardry extensively as part of my peregrine, but also in order to fulfill my duties," he said earnestly, and I saw Felpz nod in approval.

"How very responsible of you," he said, with real admiration in his voice.

"These duties have, until recently, been little more than a cursory performance of the traditional tasks of a parish wizard: participation in council planning, consulting with farmers and herders upon the state of the ambient magic, and appearing at all the appropriate social functions." Here Wizard Gandlyn smiled in a faintly pained way, as though this last item caused him the most grief. "For the most part, the responsibility of tending to the local magics and related creatures has fallen upon my neighbor, Morgrainne Deerling of Deerling Hall. She came from a long line of magicians who have kept a field of care in that area for the better part of the last thousand years, and it was impressed upon me at the outset that, apart from my civic duties as parish wizard, my greatest responsibility was not to get in the way of the Deerling magician's work. This, it turned out, was made easy by the fact that Magician Deerling was of an accommodating nature, and was patient with me in the first months—when in my zeal to perform my duties I might have overstepped my bounds. Morgrainne was understanding, and for the past year we have cleanly divided our territories, so that Morgrainne took care of the wild magics and any large distur-bances that occurred, while I looked after the more mundane concerns of the local villages, and never did our two fields min-gle. In this way we avoided any unpleasantness, and though I thought of her as a worthy colleague, it appears she thought even more highly of me. For you see, Magician Deerling died suddenly, last month . . . "

"Oh dear," said Felpz, as Wizard Gandlyn fell silent, looking hard at the floor. "Do not tell me she has left you her field of care?"

"No, nothing of the sort," said Gandlyn, sighing a little. "It turns out she has a distant cousin who has been roped into that job, a girl by the name of Clarkia Aldeer. I have gotten the next worst thing: I am to mentor this new mage and see her settled into her position at Deerling Hall."

"Oh," said Felpz, with gentle sympathy. "That is not so ter-rible. A field of care is not so different from a parish of humans, and provided the girl has a grasp of practical magic, you need only hold the head of the horse, as it were, while she gets on and finds the reins."

"If it were only that," said Wizard Gandlyn, running a hand over his brow, "I should not be here asking for your help. No, I have come because the matter is entirely more sinister than that. I mentioned that Morgrainne Deerling died suddenly—

well, I do mean *suddenly*. So suddenly, I feel there must have been a foul component in her demise, but since the police feel no need to investigate and I am hardly qualified to do so on my own, there is little to be done. Only that I worry for this girl— young woman, really, I hear she is almost eighteen—who might be stepping, not only into a great responsibility, but also into very real danger."

Felpz's eyes, which had sharpened as Wizard Gandlyn spoke, now narrowed as he gave the other man a grave stare. Taking a deep breath, he moved himself from the arm of the chair to the seat of it and, leaning forward to rest his elbows on his knees, spoke earnestly to our visitor.

"Tell me," he said, his voice low and quiet as a cat's purr. "In all exactitude."

Wizard Gandlyn returned the look with one of equal intensity, and pursed his lips. "That will require a long and sprawling explanation," he said.

"Then by all means, begin," said Felpz, leaning back as he folded his hands behind his head and shut his eyes. "We have time, let us not waste it."

The wizard seemed taken aback by Felpz's actions, but he drew himself up and gamely began.

"It is not my place to lecture you, a native of this country, in the history of Riddlemoor. But I must rehash a little of it, just so that what follows will make sense. As you may know, the Deerlings are one of the oldest families in those parts. According to their records—which go back a good deal further than those kept at the county seat—they were descended from a joining between an Aldonican magician and one of the deer people who used to live on the moor, before the moor was even a moor, when it was a part of the great northern forest that was so shamefully decimated near the beginning of your recorded history. A fanciful notion to some, but the family took it seriously—as do I. My own heritage is not entirely human, and so I do not take claims of such interbreeding lightly. It is a documented fact that such mixes usually produce powerful magic users, and the Deerling family have all been talented mages. So powerful is their hereditary magic that their members are required to keep that name above all others. Even in the case of cadet branches, like the

Aldeers, who moved away from the moor and have grown further distant, they have only condescended to *combine* the name with that of their spouse. This made it easy to fill the seat of power at Deerling Hall, until a strange and brutal catastrophe befell them—it would be some thirty years ago now—which left them with only this one elderly matron, Morgrainne, to look after the place."

"This catastrophe," said Felpz, frowning. "Can you be more specific as to its nature? For as it happens I was not present in this world at that time."

I could have told Felpz of the bizarre fate which had befallen the Deerling clan—as I recalled reading articles about it at the time—but since Wizard Gandlyn seemed readily able, I let him continue.

"It was not a pleasant business," said the wizard in a flat tone. "It struck like a plague, but a very specific one: it affected only those who were in the direct employ of the Deerling estate, and the family members themselves, of course. It is such an unusual thing there is really no way to describe it except to say, bluntly, that they all turned into trees."

Felpz blinked at this. "I am sorry?" he said.

Wizard Gandlyn nodded. "Trees. From what I hear it was not a peaceful matter, either. The transmutation would come about slowly: first as a general stiffening of the limbs and a roughness of the skin, progressing to difficulty in bending over and a fondness for sunlight. Eventually the victim's feet would begin putting out roots whenever they stood on soil, burrowing into the earth, while crowns of leaves would sprout from their heads. They lost a gardener this way, I believe; the man turned into a tree one afternoon, and no amount of magic could turn him back. And considering they had at their disposal four of the most powerful magicians in the country, that is saying something.

"After that they took to keeping sufferers inside, as that seemed to delay the process, but what happened then was worse: the victims would become stiffer and stiffer, bark slowly creeping over their skin and their blood turning to sap, while they lost their ability to eat, and slowly withered. One, at least, died this way, and after that, many chose to become trees as quickly as possible once they were afflicted.

"The first Deerling to show symptoms was Malarch, Morgrainne's daughter, who had been deeply involved in trying to restore the sufferers. Malarch's young son soon followed, as did the leader of the family, Professor Raven Deerling—Morgrainne's father. The only ones who remained, at this point, were Morgrainne and her brother—who were both showing the beginning stages of the disease—and their elderly mother, Lada, who was not a Deerling by birth but only took the name when she married their father.

"With her daughter and grandson growing more wooden every day, Morgrainne and her brother sought feverishly for a cure. It is unknown what they eventually found, save that it led the two of them to wander out onto the moor one night, where they then went missing for three days. Numerous search parties were launched, but they were all in vain.

"Until, one night, a late shepherd taking his flock home across the moor stumbled upon a strange procession: crossing his path as though they aimed for the very heart of the moor were all the people who had been turned into trees. Malarch and her son were among them as well, with branches sprouting from their shoulders and leaves for hair. They were all bleached white, and moved stiffly, dragging their feet and leaving a burrow of torn earth in their wake.

"Taking fright the shepherd ran home, but the next morning they were able to follow the track of tilled earth—which had begun to sprout with saplings overnight—to a dell near the center of the moor, where they found a young, thin forest, dominated by a spreading oak. At the base of this tree was Morgrainne, asleep with her arms wrapped around its trunk. She had but hazy memories of the preceding days, but it was understood that the oak was all that remained of her brother, Sorden, and that the forest was comprised of the people the shepherd had seen the night before.

"Morgrainne was returned to her home and to her distraught mother, and was soon discovered to be very sick—but from an entirely mundane ailment. Nevertheless she was weak for several months, and had trouble with her memory for almost a year following. It came as a surprise to everyone when, two years after the event, she took the seat of power in Deerling Hall, after her father, and proceeded to manage the field of care just as he had before her. She hired new staff, and seemed to forget about the entire incident. She spoke as if her whole family—save her mother—had died of some strange illness. Her mother, by now very old and weak herself, was the only one brave enough to talk to her about it, and when she died a few years later, the events quickly passed into the realm of local myth and gossip; but only the sort whispered behind closed doors and never to Magician Deerling's face. In fact, I was only made aware of the catastrophe's existence after Morgrainne had died, since one of her neighbors—a Mrs Tida Hammin—seemed to think it important that I know. I had to spend some time corroborating Mrs Hammin's story, but once I had, I found that Morgrainne's own death took on a much more sinister tone.

"Now that is all out of the way," Gandlyn said with a small cough. "I may go on and speak of the event itself. It is only recently that I have been able to put together a coherent narrative, since at first no one wished to talk about it. Since it came out I was to be the one to shepherd Morgrainne's successor, however, I was able to use that as a lever to pry the facts out of her servants and staff—not to mention her doctor.

"She died . . . well, this is almost as bad as the case of people turning into trees. The truth is no one is quite certain *how* she died, only that her lifeless body was found, early one morning, by the groundskeeper on his first rounds. She was lying in the middle of a bridle path that runs along the edge of the house's gardens, separating them from the moor itself. This in itself was odd, for though she was known to walk it during daytime, she never went at night. Though she was a hale and hardy old woman, with an unparalleled love of nature, Morgrainne had a singular dislike of the moor at night, and seldom went outside during it. There was some practicality to this, as there have been signs of wolves upon the moor in recent months, and the shepherds are taking extra care with their flocks."

Felpz, surprisingly enough, perked up at this, his attention narrowing like a searchlight upon the wizard.

"Wolves?" he said. "There have been no wild wolves in Kyreland for almost two thousand years. How have these come to Riddlemoor now?"

Gandlyn shrugged. He seemed a little annoyed at being interrupted.

"Of this I do not know," he said. "The moor was very much Morgrainne's territory, and I found it best not to think of it too much, since I had no right to meddle in its affairs. They might be escaped dogs, for all I know, or a particularly brave family of werewolves. The fact was, it made Morgrainne wary of going out at night, and so it was strange that she should have been found where she was.

"Stranger still, there were marks and abrasions upon her face, as though she had fallen on it, though she was found on her back, looking up at the sky. The rest is difficult to describe, but I had the man who found her—his name is Hortall—draw me a diagram, and I have it here."

Reaching into a pocket of his coat Wizard Gandlyn withdrew a folded piece of brownish paper and handed it to Felpz. My friend hardly glanced at its contents before passing it to me.

It showed in rough outlines the shape of a large house with expansive gardens, and there was a path running between the boundary hedge and a low stone fence (labeled on the map as being no more than three feet tall). A thick X marked the location of the body, while around it were dotted little marks, which at first I thought were a mistake, before I realized they looked a bit like paw prints.

"What are these?" I asked, holding the paper up and pointing.

Wizard Gandlyn fixed me with his pale green stare, and it was only my vast experience of being stared at by frightening, magical things that allowed me to hide the strange thrill that shot through me.

"Those were footprints," the wizard told me. "Noticed by Hortall, but gone by the time help arrived. They were, as he described to me, those of a giant dog—or wolf. They were scattered all around Morgrainne's body, and upon closer inspection he found they led down the path towards a gate—you will find it marked—that leads onto the moor, whence they vanished."

"But the body—it was not harmed?" Felpz asked, taking the drawing back and peering at it with new interest.

"Aside from the superficial damage from her presumed fall," said Gandlyn stiffly, and I was reminded that this woman had been almost a friend to him. "There was no sign of violence. No sign at all, in fact, of what could have caused her death. It was thought at first that she had had a heart attack, but when I consulted her doctor he admitted there were no conclusive signs of that either. I attempted to involve the local police, with the hope that one of their necromancers might be able to ask Morgrainne herself what had happened—I certainly had some questions of my own for her, as you might imagine—but they were singularly uninterested. An old woman who had a history of illness had been found dead; they felt it was a waste of time." The wizard's lip curled contemptuously, revealing a glimpse of straight, if yellowish, teeth. "I did, however, manage to convince her doctor to perform an autopsy—after I had confirmed Tida Hammin's incredible story—and in doing so he discovered two extraordinary things: firstly, and impossible to miss, her blood had turned to sap, just as the victims' of the plague thirty years ago had. Secondly, and what was probably the cause of her demise: her heart was missing."

Felpz, who had been resting his head on one hand, jerked upright.

"Missing?" he said.

"Positively vanished," said Gandlyn, a light of cold triumph in his eyes. "Dr Narriott could not credit it. He said all the veins and arteries simply led to a messy tangle where her heart should have been."

Felpz rubbed his chin. "Was there anything out of the ordinary about the veins—aside from the sap they carried?"

"Not that Dr Narriott could find," the wizard replied. "You must understand I was not allowed to examine the body myself—I only discussed it with the doctor afterwards."

Bouragner Felpz frowned, but gestured for Gandlyn to continue.

"In light of what I now know of her family's history, not to mention her grotesque end," he went on, "can you understand why I am concerned for the well-being of her successor?" This last was spoken with an undertone of defiance, but Felpz seemed not to notice. He had spread the little diagram upon his knee and was examining it closely.

"Yes, yes," he said airily. "I can easily understand. Can you tell me which direction she was facing when they found her?"

Gandlyn seemed put off balance by this change of subject, but he righted himself quickly and answered Felpz's question:

"That is somewhat difficult to divine," he admitted. "Being that it appears the body moved after she fell—perhaps by her own death throes. But Hortall thought she was facing south— that is, *away* from the gate. He postulates that she saw something on the moor that frightened her, and she ran from it."

"Hmm," said Felpz. "And this postmortem repositioning did not strike the police as something worth investigating?"

Wizard Gandlyn leaned his head back and regarded our ceiling as if the sight of it gave him strength. "They were pleased to think that Hortall had arranged her so, and simply forgotten to say—even though, when I asked, the man denied having touched her more than was absolutely necessary to tell that she was dead."

"How disappointing," said Felpz, sympathetically. "But let me not add to your troubles, Wizard Gandlyn. I think you are right to be concerned for this young magician—Aldeer, you say her name was?"

"Clarkia Aldeer," Gandlyn said, lowering his gaze again. "A distant cousin of the Deerlings, but she was the one named in Morgrainne's will. Born in Azo, I hear, though her parents moved to Beranica when she was young."

"North or South?" Felpz asked.

"South," said Gandlyn. "She is arriving by boat—that was one of the reasons for the delay; not only did it take ages to contact her, but with the Ardaman monsoon season starting early she had to take the long way around. Her ship landed in Grey-wall this morning, however, and she is taking a riverboat up to Redling tomorrow afternoon—hence why I am here."

Felpz turned and stared out the window—where we were suffering through one of our muggy, hot summer days—and was silent for some moments. Although I could tell his mind was working at a fantastic pace, physically he became so still that he nearly disappeared into the furniture, becoming closer to an inanimate object than a human being.

To his credit Gandlyn seemed to appreciate my friend's eccentricity, and far from becoming impatient, he appeared to relax for the first time that morning; leaning back in his chair he crossed his legs, and finally deigned to drink his tea, though it must have been stone cold by that time.

At last Felpz gave a small shudder and drew his attention in from where it had wandered on unseen paths, back into that little room, and trained it once again upon our visitor.

"It seems to me your first course of action is an obvious one," he said, shrugging slightly. "I would recommend you discharge your duty to this young woman: go retrieve her from the docks, and present to her all the information you have just divulged to me. If Morgrainne Deerling thought her a suitable successor, she must be at least mature enough to handle the perils and oddities attendant upon being a master of a field of care. I, in the meanwhile, will make my own independent investigations, and we may meet again tomorrow night, and once I have had a chance to lay eyes on Miss Aldeer, I shall be better able to recommend what precautions should be taken. As it stands, the whole matter is too vague, too nebulous, for me to give you any specific advice—except to say that it sounds as though many of these problems stem from a lack of communication on all parts, and we should not allow that to continue."

"I agree," said Gandlyn, gratefully setting his tea aside and rising to his feet. "Wholeheartedly," he added, turning his staff over in his hands so that the end rested on the floor. "Then I shall see you tomorrow night."

"Would seven suit your purposes?" Felpz asked.

"I am sure that can be accommodated," Wizard Gandlyn said in his stiff way. "Until then, farewell, magician."

"*Enhauron,*" Felpz returned, touching his brow.

Gandlyn Wale nodded curtly, rapped his staff on the floor, and both he and it disappeared with a faint inrushing of air.

Felpz immediately sprang up and threw himself upon the spot where our visitor had last stood. He crawled over it, picking over the chair and inspecting the abandoned tea cup.

"Curious," he said, lifting the dish to his nose and taking a careful sniff.

"Felpz?" I asked, somewhat befuddled by his actions. Though I thought the character of Gandlyn Wale was indeed a curious one, it was not nearly so interesting to me as the story he had told.

"That man is a deep one, Corianne, have no doubt," Felpz said, rising and returning the cup and saucer to the table. "I find it interesting that he hides his status as an *enhauron*—usually they are well respected, even in this country. And did you notice his color?"

"All the green?" I said, grasping at Felpz's train of thought. "Yes, I thought it was quite remarkable."

"More remarkable that he did not make any allusions to it," Felpz said. "Though perhaps that is understandable—I have held the color purple for so long that I forget it is often the first thing people see about me—but his color felt fresh; recently acquired, that is to say."

I frowned to myself, realizing that my friend spoke of his peculiar relationship with the color purple. His title of the *Purple Magician* was not idly taken; he held true power through that color, and it saturated all the magic he did. This affinity came, I had learned, from an ancient caste of spirits known as color demons—whose powers had, over the course of history, percolated through the ranks of magic users. I was still not entirely certain how Felpz had acquired his color—it had been hinted that a duel with a fairy was somehow involved—but I was not surprised to learn that there existed magic users who represented the rest of the rainbow.

"Do you mean to say he is the . . . would it be *green wizard?* as you are the *purple magician?*" I asked.

Bouragner Felpz sniffed. "Green wizard has its own specific connotations," he admitted. "Pertaining mostly to plant and nature magic—of which Gandlyn Wale appears singularly uninterested. But there is no doubt he has the color green. It is a small omission—perhaps he simply trusted me to make my own observations and to take from them what I would—but it is a surprising one for someone who seemed so invested in my complete understanding of events."

"I do not see why you harp on it so," I said a little testily. "What does it matter that he does not wish to divulge every last detail about himself?"

Felpz shrugged expansively.

"His story is, in many regards, incredible—and based primarily on second-hand sources. Though I would like to think the best of everybody, especially my fellow thaumaturges, the fact remains that being a powerful magic user does not preclude you from being a pernicious villain—quite the opposite, in fact."

"My dear Felpz," I said, laughing a little at the absurdity of it. "You do not mean to say you suspect him of being the perpetrator of this unpleasantness? Why, he must not even have been *born* when that tragedy befell the Deerlings."

"Apparent age can be deceptive," Felpz said, wagging a finger at me. "As you should well know. But I may be rowing up the wrong tributary, as well. The facts as he presents them are troubling, but not unbelievable. No, they speak to me, in whispers, of something I ought to recognize. Trees and wolves, Corianne, *trees and wolves,* and the ancient, unwritten history of Riddlemoor. Were I half as clever as you make me out to be in your stories, I should be able to solve this entire mystery from those three tenets alone. Alas, I am not omnipotent, and I must prostrate my mind before a greater power if I hope to sort this mess out."

"Greater power?" I wondered aloud. "What arcane being do you intend to call upon this time?"

"Why, no being at all," said Felpz, shrugging out of his dressing gown and throwing it over the back of a chair before disappearing into his bedroom. He emerged moments later, dressed magnificently in a deep purple frock coat and holding a matching top hat, which he set firmly upon his handsome head before making for the door. "I am going to the *library,* of course," he said with a wink. "Please don't expect me back before tomorrow evening. That should be enough time for you to get a satisfactory amount of writing done, is it not? Good, then I will leave the matter of dinner in your capable hands. Good-day, Corianne."

So saying he left our little apartment, and I heard him clattering down the stairs and out the door. Shaking my head I poured myself another cup of tea and attempted to wrench my mind away from the story I had just heard. But the idea of the bleak moor with the sound of wolves upon its downs and the once-humans trudging across the earth, their roots leaving a tilled course in their wake, lingered in my mind. I regret to say I made little use of the peace and quiet bestowed on me by Felpz's absence.

Chapter 2:
The Beranican Heiress

THE NEXT MORNING brought a heavy, warm summer rain followed by such oppressive humidity that it quite negated the pleasing, clean-washed feeling that usually followed such storms. Thinking of Clarkia Aldeer, newly arrived in this country and about to be thrown into a sinister predicament, I couldn't help but feel sorry for the poor woman. Surely our country could have provided her with a better welcome than this? But that is Kyrish weather for you.

Bouragner Felpz followed shortly after the rain had ceased; as dour and dripping as the weather, he tripped up the stairs and flung himself across the sofa, where he began to steam faintly.

"I take it the library was less than helpful?" I asked sympathetically, trying to hide my own disappointment—secretly I had been hoping that he would have been able to solve the problem before Clarkia Aldeer ever set foot in our apartment, but now I realized the likelihood of this was sharply diminished.

"The library was exemplary," Felpz moaned from under the crook of his arm—which had been thrown dramatically across his face. "It was singularly obliging. The trouble was it simply did not have the information I was seeking."

The arm raised, and he gazed back at me out of tired, anguished eyes. His hair had streaks of grey in it this morning, and his face looked even more crinkled than usual. "I recall things about that area," he sighed, "from my own, early memory. The Riddle Moor was even a part of my old kingdom. Do you know why it is called that? Because the moors there have a magic about them: space within their borders is apt to slide and twist and stretch. It is a sort of magic not uncommon among woods, but highly unusual in open country. To cross the Riddle

Moor, it was said, was like solving a puzzle or a riddle. I recall further things too; echoes of stories, ancient even in my youth, of when the moor was covered in trees, a corner of the Great Forest that covered Cairdra and much of Kyreland. That forest was decimated by the arrival of humans and now exists only in stranded clumps, scattered throughout the land. I thought—I hoped—that the library would have records with which I could corroborate my memories, but I find nothing of use; all that remain are legends, and those only deal with the moor after the trees had gone."

"What legends were these?" I prompted, hoping that perhaps there was some kernel of knowledge hidden within that my friend had missed.

"Oh, they were mostly to do with the moor and people getting lost in it. How one might come to a pleasant dell or vale, but never be able to find it again. How paths could not be made to run straight, and fences were forever being bent out of shape. There were also a few concerning the proverbial Deerling ancestors: the deer people who had remained after their wood had gone, and later interbred with the local human population. There were also accounts of wild moor people who lived in stone houses under the earth, like barrows. The stories made them out to sound like savages, but I think they were probably hoblins."

"Hoblins?" I asked. "Do you not mean *goblins?*"

"Not at all," said Felpz, his feet twitching in annoyance. "*Hoblins* are another matter entirely—though they are related to goblins—they fall in well with elves and creatures of dream, but tend to avoid humans. You don't find them in this realm hardly at all anymore, and I doubt whether any remain, even in the heart of Riddlemoor."

"Did you discover anything that would explain the return of the wolves?" I asked.

"No . . . " groaned Felpz. "For all I can tell, the wolves disappeared from that area along with the forest. That must have been the connection to trees and wolves I was sensing earlier, but I have no idea as to why they would be back now. And I have *too many* ideas when it comes to the strange enchantment that befell the Deerlings. I do not wish to bore you with them. Have you ordered dinner yet? If not, I shall, and then I will rack my poor excuse for a brain so that I might have something more constructive to tell the Beranican heiress when she arrives."

Felpz did as he said, and although dinner arrived promptly, our expected guests did not. It was nearing suppertime, and the food was hot only because Felpz did not allow it to cool, when at last there was a ring of the bell, and I heard our housekeeper answering the door. This was followed shortly by the second appearance in as many days of the Wizard Gandlyn, and the first time I ever set eyes on Clarkia Aldeer.

The first thing I can say is that she was no girl at all, and if she was only eighteen then she was the most worldly looking person of that age I had ever seen. She had a face as brown as a nut and wriggly black hair, while her eyes were a golden hazel. She was a slim, wiry person, though this was partially masked by the baggy trousers and loose coat she wore. Her cheeks were flushed and red, and she fairly sprang into the room, as though she were expecting to meet an adversary in it.

What she thought of Felpz, lounging behind the table in all his luxuriant glory, or for that matter, of *me*—I had put on one of my better dresses for the occasion—I could not tell. Her face shuttered at the sight of us, her nose twitching a little, and she looked around the room with an air of detached curiosity. But always her body was vibrating faintly, as though some hidden energy was coursing through it.

"Miss Aldeer," said Gandlyn Wale in his formal, stiff manner. "This is the magician Bouragner Felpz, and his companion, Corianne Birch. Magician, allow me to introduce Miss Clarkia Aldeer, the new keeper of Deerling Hall."

"It is my pleasure," said Felpz, rising gracefully and giving a low bow, while I merely nodded. Miss Aldeer struck me as the sort of person who found such formalities boring at best, and insulting at worst. The look she gave Felpz was certainly not an impressed one, but she swallowed whatever reservations she held and made a little bow in return. I remembered then how Gandlyn had mentioned she was a native of the matriarchal nation of Azo, and though I had no idea what sort of society she had left behind in South Beranica, from what I had heard that was still very much a wild and savage place, and her clothes and manner bore this out. If anyone could face what was waiting at Riddlemoor, it might be this young woman.

All this I sorted out afterwards, but such was the forcefulness of her personality that I find all my impressions of Clarkia Aldeer's character stemmed from what I perceived in those first few moments—and I was not far wrong.

"Mr Felpz," she said, her thick, angular accent very prominent. "I don't know if you Kyrish mages have a thin skin or if things really are as bad as Mr Wale describes, but I can say this: I like to handle my own affairs. I've found my way through some pretty rough places back home, and if I can't manage one patch of wet, rainy fields then I'm not much of a wizard. And I do mean *wizard*, if you please. I've never been to any fancy school for magic or anything else, and I ain't got no paper says I can put *magician* in front of my name."

She broke off there, for Felpz had begun to laugh.

"My dear," said he; "Please do not let your lack of *accreditation* stop you; I received no formal schooling either, and yet I am very much a magician. But choose whatever title suits you best, and don't feel the need to justify it to anyone. You have a right to tell others what sort of mage you are; they hold no such power over you. As to whatever assistance I can lend; I promise to do so purely as per your request. If you go to Riddlemoor and find it well within your means then you may think no more of me. If, however, as I strongly suspect, you feel the need for some advice or guidance, I will be ever at your service. Which I would recommend: magic changes with distance, and mages not born of Kyreland sometimes have difficulty adapting to it . . . " here his eyes flickered almost imperceptibly to Wizard Gandlyn, but fixed back on Clarkia Aldeer so fast I could not be certain. "In any case," he went on, "as you are here, if there is any matter—however small—you would like my input on, please do not hesitate to ask." He gestured to one of the open chairs.

Clarkia Aldeer tilted her head and gave my friend a considering look, but she came around and sat down (Wizard Gandlyn doing the same) and crossed her legs casually.

"There is something," she admitted. "It is the reason we were late, actually, and I have not shown Mr Wale yet—I was hoping I could figure it out before we came to visit you. He told me all about what happened to Morgrainne yesterday," she added, reaching inside her coat and pulling a small cloth bundle out of an interior pocket. "I have no idea if this could be related, but this morning, well, I found *that* on the breakfast tray the hotel left for me."

She had set the bundle down on the table as she spoke, and teased at a corner of the cloth until it came away, revealing a small, grey, stone fruit.

If Wizard Gandlyn and Bouragner Felpz had been cats, I imagine their hackles would have come up, and one or both would have started hissing. As it was they straightened in their chairs, and the wizard's neck seemed to elongate as he craned his head to stare.

Felpz descended upon the table, coming to kneel before it so he could peer closely at the little object without touching it. He inhaled deeply, through his nose, and turned his head this way and that.

"There's the echoes of a spell on it," Clarkia Aldeer said, as if stating the obvious. "Who put it there, I can't tell. But it's strong stuff. I couldn't turn it back."

"And you are naturally good at things of that kind?" Felpz asked, interrupting his examination of the fruit to glance up at Aldeer.

The young woman shrugged. "What one wizard has done I can usually undo," she said. "It's pretty easy. Usually."

Felpz gave her a respectful look, and then turned back to the stone fruit. "May I?" he asked, reaching out a hand.

"Be my guest," said Aldeer.

Gently, using only the tips of his fingers, Felpz picked the fruit up and looked it over, bringing it to his nose, his mouth, and one ear. He frowned, then offered it to Gandlyn.

The wizard bent forward and took the fruit, then gave it his own minute examination. I noticed that, contrary to Felpz, Wizard Gandlyn merely held the stone in the palm of his hand and glared at it, as though demanding it give up its secrets.

"It is indeed an enchanted fruit," he declared. "It is not a natural stone."

"Let Corianne see it," Felpz said, getting to his feet again.

The stone was duly passed to me, and I put on my reading glasses to give it a better look. It was smooth and dark and speckled with white, and formed the shape of a small peach or apricot. It was not a perfect specimen; there was a dimple on one side as though the fruit had been bruised when it was still plant flesh, and a rough place where something had pecked at it early in the fruit's life and the skin healed over. Now, of course, all was hard stone, and it sat cold and heavy in my hand.

"How very peculiar," I said, passing it back. "And rather upsetting, I imagine."

Clarkia Aldeer shrugged. "What was more upsetting—to the staff, anyway—were the huge, muddy paw prints that got left in the hall."

Felpz, who had gone to stand looking out the window, whirled around so fast his coattails flared out.

"Paw prints?" he said.

"You did not mention those earlier," Wizard Gandlyn said, grimly.

"Yes, well," said Aldeer with a roll of her eyes. "They faded away on their own, before the hotel staff even had a chance to clean them. But I got a good whiff of magic off them, and I was trying to follow their scent through this very loud and confusing city of yours. That's why I was so late meeting you."

"Did you find anything?" Felpz asked at once.

"Not as such," said Aldeer. "I found a lot of dogs, of course, but none of them were the kind to leave fading footprints. I was able to follow the trail out of the hotel and down the street to a park, but I lost it there. I went all over the park but found nothing, so I tried a more general search. That turned up a few spots—down by the docks and by another hotel—but they felt faded and dry; a day old, at least."

"This magic that you smelled," Felpz said. "Can you describe it?"

Clarkia Aldeer screwed her face up and inhaled deeply. "Earthy," she said. "Foreign, like everything here is—you're quite right about magic changing with distance—and maybe I couldn't find any more traces because *everything* feels weird to me. But it was definitely *not* an ordinary dog. It was really big, for starters, and felt more . . . I don't know . . . *wild*."

"A wolf," said Gandlyn, bleakly. "What you are describing is a wolf."

Aldeer frowned at him, making the center of her face wrinkle and her little red mouth pucker up like a prune. "Unless the wolves here are even weirder than the rest of the magic," she said. "They'd never come into this city."

"Wolves are generally not here," Felpz explained. "Kyreland hasn't seen wild wolves in over two thousand years."

Aldeer stared at him. Then she shook her head and laughed. "I might have to hire you," she said. "Just to explain local history to me. I tried to read up on the voyage but . . . well, it didn't go as planned. But if you have any ideas about where this stone fruit came from or those paw prints I'd love to hear it."

Felpz's expression darkened, and he looked down at the floor for a moment before answering.

"It strikes me as being ominously similar to the circum-stances of Morgrainne Deerling's death," he said, casting a glance at the wizard. "There were paw prints nearby then as well. Prints that faded with time."

Wizard Gandlyn pursed his lips. "I have already explained that to Miss Aldeer," he said.

"Yeah, but if there's someone—or some *thing*—out there that wants to do me harm, it's a funny way of going about it, don't you think?" Clarkia Aldeer said, showing a surprising rationality about the whole matter. "If you can get close enough to turn a part of my breakfast to stone, then getting at me should hardly be more difficult."

This gave Felpz pause, and he smiled at the young woman in surprise. "I think you underestimate your natural defenses," he said mildly. "But you are right: this does not strike me as an overt threat. A warning, perhaps? Or even . . . a simple message."

"A *message*?" echoed Aldeer. "About *what*?"

"That I do not know . . . yet," Felpz said, reaching over and plucking the stone from the woman's lap. "May I keep this? For the next few days at least; there are one or two avenues of in-vestigation I would like to explore, and having this ready might help speed things along."

"That suits me fine," said Aldeer with a shrug. "I had planned to spend a few more days in Redling, anyway; if I'm going to be the 'lady' of anywhere I'm going to need a new wardrobe, and I'm told there's more likely to be tailors who'll suit my needs here than in Greenwitch. Now I can draw on the allowance Morgrainne left me, I thought I'd see to it I arrived at this place properly dressed at least."

"A fine idea," said Felpz, pocketing the stone. "Corianne knows a good seamstress, if you do not yet have one in mind; and I know for a fact she has no qualms about unusual requests."

Wizard Gandlyn cleared his throat. "It does make things a little more complicated," he pointed out. "I had intended to accompany Miss Aldeer back to Deerling Hall, but if she intends to stay here beyond tomorrow I cannot do so: I have duties at Riddlemoor that will not stand to be neglected any longer, and I must return to tend to them."

He stopped, and looked earnestly at Felpz, a question hovering in the air, unspoken. I thought it to be along the lines of *"Would you escort her?"* but Felpz took it entirely differently.

"Then do so, my good wizard," he said. "You can see she has a clean nest to land in. Meanwhile, if Miss Aldeer feels at all adrift in this city, I cannot recommend a better guide than Corianne; she has lived here all her life."

Once more I felt the wizard's intense, pale green gaze upon me, and tried to put on my best, world-weary expression. He seemed about to object, but Clarkia Aldeer took it out of his hands by saying:

"To be honest I wouldn't mind a guiding hand, at least for the first day or so," she said. "If Corianne doesn't mind."

I did mind actually, rather a lot, but since I could tell Felpz was planning something, and that I was a crucial part of this plan, I only smiled and nodded and said it would be my pleasure. I made arrangements to meet Aldeer at her hotel for breakfast the next morning, before taking her to Mrs Grissom (the tailor Felpz had mentioned). Gandlyn sat and watched us stonily as we did so, then, when we were at last ready to begin upon our dinner-gone-supper, he excused himself and left in a whirl of green coattails.

"I hope they're not all as prickly as him out there," Clarkia Aldeer said as she piled her plate with food.

"I doubt it," said Felpz, his eyes lingering on the door where Gandlyn had last been seen. "Our wizard friend is of a peculiar make; I would not take anything he does at face value."

He paused then, and I wondered if he would voice his suspicions to Clarkia Aldeer, but he said nothing more. Instead he went on to talk of amusing, mundane things; unrelated to the grim events that surrounded her arrival in Kyreland. This seemed just the thing to lift the woman's spirits, and after the meal, she bade us a cordial good-bye before marching boldly out into the night.

Felpz seemed relaxed enough, but I noticed how he stood at the window, gazing off into the city, well after our visitor's footsteps had died away. I guessed he must have been following her progress back to her lodging using his own magical powers, for after about twenty minutes he relaxed and came away from the window.

"She's a strong one, and not too dull," he said as he passed me on his way to bed. "One might hope that she will cut through the fog that surrounds her on her own, but that is a lot to ask of any mage—especially one so young. Have an eye out for her, would you Corianne? It would mean the world to my peace of mind."

"I most certainly shall," I assured my friend, unable to sound bitter. "Though what I could do that she cannot must be very small."

"Perhaps so," said Felpz with a shrug. "But your powers, where they do exist, are no less important. Have a care, I beg; she may have need of you before long."

With this he disappeared into his rooms, leaving me to stay up half the night trying to cram an extra day's worth of writing in—but mostly pondering the strange mystery that had only deepened with the events of the day.

It was a Thursday, according to my journal, that I met Clarkia Aldeer for breakfast, as promised. There were no more of the mysterious stone fruits, and we passed the meal in idle chatter. Aldeer—or *Clarkia* as she insisted I call her—was overflowing with stories of both Azo and South Beranica, and though ostensibly it was I who was supposed to be telling her about Kyreland, I feel that she told me more of her homeland that I managed to tell her of mine.

Afterwards we walked down to Mrs Grissom's, and after seeing the two women introduced and well on their way to plotting Clarkia's new wardrobe, I popped over to say hello to my old friend Milky, who kept the carpenter's shop next door. We spent the remainder of the morning puzzling over the case together while Milky varnished tables.

"Thanks kindly for the warning Miss Cor," he said to me with a lopsided smile.

"Warning?" I returned in surprise.

"Way Felpz is carrying on, he'll be dragging both of us into this before it's over, you mark my words. I probably have another week—which I'll be putting to good use you can be sure—but it looks like he's got you fairly slammed."

I took this to mean I was already embroiled in Felpz's plans, with which I could not argue. As if to hammer this point home, Clarkia came wandering in at that moment, having left Mrs Grissom with enough work to last her several weeks.

"Though she can have one suit ready by tomorrow morning," she told me with satisfaction. "That one I'll wait for, but the others we agreed will be shipped when they are ready. It means I will only have to spend one more night in this city, which is a relief to me. Is it always so loud?"

Milky chuckled, and I assured her it would no doubt be quieter in the country. Finding it was nearing lunchtime, and that we were all happy with each other's company, we took our midday meal together at Valaire's. Milky spent the time animatedly recounting anecdotes of Felpz's previous cases, which I think Clarkia found reassuring.

The only disturbing event of the day occurred as I walked Clarkia back to her hotel. I'd elected to take her by way of Reidway Park, thinking that she might find the trees and hedges—though carefully cultivated as opposed to the wilderness of Beranica—a refreshing change from the oppressive machinery of Redling. It was here, pausing in a patch of shade to gaze out through the trees, that Clarkia suddenly froze and gripped my sleeve sharply.

I could not speak before her other arm rose, pointing urgently back the way we had come. And there in the shadows of the bridge we had just passed under, I thought I saw, for a moment, a huge, canine shape, its ears outlined in dark triangles against the bright patch of sun beyond the tunnel. Then a wind swept through the upper branches of the trees, causing a raven that had been perched above to fly off, cawing throatily as it went.

Somewhere in the disturbance the form disappeared, fading into the shadow or into the stones.

Clarkia gave a shout and took off after it. She sounded more angry than frightened, but I found myself temporarily frozen stiff in shock. Then I realized I was standing, paralyzed, watching the woman Felpz had set me to look after go racing headlong into the shadow of the tunnel, and I forced myself to follow her.

It was all for naught, however, as I came upon Clarkia standing under the bridge, walking back and forth and sniffing, as if she were a dog herself trying to find a scent.

"Did you see it, Corianne?" she asked me, not stopping her pacing. "That wasn't no vision; I felt it too."

"Indeed so," I said, looking around curiously. There was no sign that any animal had been there; not even any paw prints—and the earth was suitably soft and damp in the tunnel, perfect for preserving marks.

"I tell you this is *not* menchable at *all,*" Clarkia said, her Beranican accent becoming even more pronounced. "If something takes issue with my presence, let it come out and *say so.* Less of this lurking and hiding; it gives me an itch." She shivered her shoulders expressively, and was in a stormy mood the rest of the way back to the hotel.

I left her there and made my way swiftly home, eager to report to Felpz, only to find him absent. He remained so until late that night, and I caught him only because I waited up long past my usual bedtime. When he did come, it was with a heavy step, a defeated slouch to his shoulders and a sour twist to his mouth. His investigations had not gone well at all, but he would only give me the vaguest hints as to their nature. Still, he contrived to bemoan his failings to me for almost an hour before I was able to make a report of my own day—leaving out my candid conversation with Milky.

He frowned at my description of the vision, and smiled ruefully upon hearing Clarkia's reaction.

"Yes, I do believe I understand *exactly* how she feels," he said, stretching out on the sofa with his hands behind his head. Letting out a long sigh, he propped his feet on the armrest and unceremoniously kicked off his shoes. "The worst of it is, I do not think I will be able to accompany her to Riddlemoor tomorrow—and I do not feel comfortable sending her there alone. In Redling I have enough influence to keep her reasonably safe, but that ends at the edge of the city."

He let this statement hang in the air, gathering weight, until I lost my patience and blurted out what I knew he meant to ask:

"Felpz, do I take this to mean I must expand my role as guardian spirit to include a trip to Riddlemoor?" I spoke partially in jest, but Felpz gave me such a look of supreme relief that I knew I had hit my mark.

"Oh, *dear* Corianne," he said, smiling benevolently at me. "That would be *more* than ideal."

So it was that I found myself waiting at Redling City Central beside a hastily packed travel case the next morning, along with Clarkia Aldeer and her veritable mountain of luggage.

"Gandlyn suggested I send much of it ahead of me," she said, a little bitterly. "But as I told him: this here is my life, bundled up and shipped from Mackanaw with me, and I'll be damned if I let it out of my sight."

And as we waited for the train that would take us out of the cramped city and into my country's wild north, I considered Clarkia Aldeer's slim frame and steely determination, set against a turbulent and uncertain future, and thought I understood very well her desire to keep what solid reminders of her old life she still possessed close at her side. Though she was now dressed smartly in the suit Mrs Grissom had rushed through for her—a heavily altered man's waistcoat and trousers with a light navy blazer—she had topped this with a battered, wide-brimmed hat of the sort used to keep sun off one's face and shoulders, and was still wearing her cracked leather boots. Thus she appeared refined and Kyrish about her body, but on either end were clear indicators of her free, forthright life in a hot, far-away country. Watching her direct the loading of her luggage once the train arrived, and then following her swaggering step up into our compartment, I couldn't help but think that she was bringing with her a kind of fierce, southern wildness of her own—and one that would be a match for anything my country threw at her.

Saying a silent prayer that I would be at least able to keep pace with this woman, I settled myself into the train and prepared for our long journey to the high, grey-green expanse of Riddlemoor.

For those of my readers who have never been, allow me to pull back a little ways in order to better describe the stage upon which the following narrative will be played out.

If one travels north from our country's capital, taking care not to cross the River Kyre, one will eventually run into its main tributary, the Gyrehass, which flows down out of western Cairdra and through the moorlands until it joins the Kyre at Stillgate. Between these two points it flows through the town and outlying villages of Greenwitch, to the south of which extend the warm, rolling hills of the midlands, now thoroughly cultivated—while to the north stretches the Riddlemoor; a vast expanse of wild moorland, filled with bleak hills and shallow valleys, studded with peaks of frowning rock and harboring treacherous mires and marshland in its northernmost reaches. The great forest of Kyreland that once covered its hills—as it did much of the country—might have been all but eradicated, but the moor still retained its wild, untamable heart. It has served as a muse of poets, writers, artists and composers in its long history, Tenor Claybridge having famously kept a summer house on the moor that only he could reach.

There were no villages on the moor—they hugged the Gyre-hass like the lifeline that it was—but there were a number of households along its southern edge, some of which were quite far advanced into the hills. Chief among these was Deerling Hall, which was not only the largest house, but also the most remote. After the train ride to Greenwitch—which was as far as that mode of transport could take us—it was an additional hour of swiftly trotting coach before we set eyes on our destination.

It took us far longer than the travel time, of course, because we had to contend with Clarkia's baggage. The carriage that had come down from the Hall was not nearly big enough to carry all she brought, and since the young woman adamantly refused to let it out of her sight we were obliged to wait while a cart was hired, and all of Clarkia's trunks and boxes and crates loaded into it. Thereupon she caused further stir by insisting on driving the thing herself.

"If I cannot ride, then at least let me hold the reins," she told the poor lad who had come with the cart. But she let him ride in the back, amongst the boxes, so that he could drive the cart home again the next day.

I rode in the cart as well, squeezed in next to her on the little bench. The driver of the carriage, who was none other than the groundskeeper, Hortall, threw up his hands in despair and had to settle for leading us out of the town.

This did not take long, and once we were clear of the little cluster of houses, our way became strikingly obvious: few roads reached up into the moor, and at every intersection were wooden signs, carved in the shape of arrows, upon which were written the names of the destinations to which they pointed. The words DEERLING HALL were always prominent, and we merely had to follow the arrows out across the rolling moor.

This was not so desolate at first. Grazing pasture was grazing pasture, after all, and we passed numerous herds of fluffy white sheep, bound by ancient stone walls that crisscrossed the moor like raised ley lines. These slowly were replaced by wild, long-horned cows, and eventually the fences gave way and the hills grew a little steeper.

These were very green from grass and moss, and though their skin was punctured at odd intervals by crags of dark grey stone, there was not a single tree in sight. Low shrubs and bushes were the tallest things that grew on the moor, and these were constantly bending and whipping as waves of wind came pounding over the hills. Once, such a gust struck our caravan of two, making the loose ropes and straps securing the luggage flap about fiercely, snapping like angry turtles. It lifted the hat clean off Clarkia's head, releasing a whirl of the dark, curling hair that had been trapped under it.

Clarkia hissed in annoyance, reined the horses to a stop, and stood up upon the footboard to shout words into the wind that boomed and echoed, disappearing into the distant grey sky.

I saw Hortall stop his horse and stare back at us, surprised, but the wind abated immediately, and a moment later, almost guiltily, her hat came drifting down out of the sky to land on her knee.

"Thank you," she said primly, sparing a hand from the reins and jamming the old hat back on her head.

"At least the elementals here are the same as the lot back home," she told me under her breath once we were moving again.

I nodded and bit my tongue, not wanting to say that I had felt nothing abnormal about the wind. I had such a limited grasp of magic, even after all the time spent living with Felpz, and it pained me to admit it.

We passed the remainder of the journey in relative peace—the gusts of wind seemed to follow us across the moor, but they never again struck us directly—and I was able to wrap myself firmly in my shawl such that the evening air could not chill me.

We were lucky it was summer, for it was past eight o'clock by the time we crested a gentle rise and saw, across a wide, flat plain, a dark, spiky house with sprawling grounds. The only trees for miles were clustered at its sides, like frightened chicks around their mother hen. The sun, putting in a brief appearance between the clouds and the horizon as it set, sent a shaft of golden light across the moor, gilding the domes of the hills and setting fire to the uppermost peaks of the house's steeply slanting roofs.

Hortall had to stop the carriage and point out the view to Clarkia.

"There lies Deerling Hall," he said to her, smiling encouragingly. "Your domain, and the home of your ancestors."

He made it sound very grand and majestic, and I could not help but appreciate the sight: Deerling Hall looked like a black ship upon a swelling green sea, bravely setting forth across the misty moor. In that light, touched by the dying sun, I think I could have been proud to call it my home.

Clarkia Aldeer, however, reacted conservatively. She made agreeable noises in response to Hortall's introduction, but once he was a safe distance in front she turned to me and whispered: "Some of my ancestors, anyway," and I was reminded yet again that she was as much, if not more, a product of a wild, foreign country than she was of this desolate place. I could only nod sympathetically as we slowly approached the house. It grew larger and larger the nearer we got, until finally its great gate loomed above us, blocking out the sight of the all-surrounding moor.

A young woman who bore a striking resemblance to Hortall opened this gate for us, and then jogged behind until we reached the front doors of the Hall itself. These were very tall and decorated with iron filigree in the form of antlers, and were cast in shadow by the bulk of the house. Here we were met by an older couple and a younger man, who stood outside the doors in a neat line, the young man coming forward to hold Clarkia's horses while she climbed down from the cart, and the lad who had waited so patiently came around to take the reins.

"Well come to Deerling Hall, Magician Aldeer," said the female half of the mature couple. She had striking, jet-black hair with electric jolts of white in it, piled formidably upon her head, but this was the most intimidating thing about her. In build she was rather short and wide, and she wore an old-fashioned black dress with a lot of black lace and a matching black apron. She had gleaming little blue eyes and peered out at the world from a circular face covered in wrinkles. She had a sonorous, commanding tone, even though she stepped forward and curtsied respectfully to her new mistress.

"I am Mrs Wreath, your housekeeper—if you did not recall from the dispatch," she said, a little curtly.

To my relief, Clarkia seemed to like this woman's direct way of speaking. She walked right up and shook her hand—much to the older woman's surprise.

"Glad to meet ya," said Clarkia Aldeer. "I do remember your name, but I'm afraid I can't put the others I've learned to the faces here, except for Hortall back there," she jerked a thumb at the man who was climbing down from the carriage.

"That is . . . understandable," said Mrs Wreath, grappling for control of her features. She seemed not to know what to do with the handshake, and looked relieved when Clarkia released her. "May I introduce your cook, Mr del Garren," she said, gesturing at her male counterpart. This man had white, tightly curling hair and a beard to match, and he was even wider than Mrs Wreath. His skin was dark and ruddy—almost as dark as Clarkia's—and his eyes were surprisingly bright and green.

"Call me Hewlith, please," he said, with a pronounced Cairdrian accent. "I'm afraid my cuisine will be very different from what you're used to, but I'm hoping we might learn from each other, eh?"

If Clarkia had liked Mrs Wreath, she fairly loved Hewlith del Garren—who even I had to admit looked like a singularly lovable person—and leaned forward eagerly to ask him what exactly his cuisine *was,* but Mrs Wreath swept on.

"The young man helping to unload your cart is our new footman, Mr Roke, and here is young Jaria, our gardener."

Jaria came trotting up just then and I was struck once more by her resemblance to Hortall. They were both pale skinned and dark haired with large, brown eyes, and though Jaria's face was dusted with freckles and Hortall's was smooth; though he was old and craggy and she was fresh and supple, they shared so many small mannerisms in the way they moved and spoke it was impossible not to assume they were related. My suspicions were confirmed a moment later when Jaria, dropping a significantly more sloppy curtsy than the one performed by Mrs Wreath, said: "Jaria Hortall, at your service. I'll just help Father put the carriage away and then I'll get on with the unloading."

When the young woman—she must have been within a few months of Clarkia's age—paused after this, uncertain, Clarkia shook herself and nodded. "Sounds good," she said, at which Jaria Hortall ran off after the carriage, which was being led around to the back of the house.

"Great gods, what have I stepped in?" I heard Clarkia murmur to herself. "Well, Mrs Wreath, have you got any more cast members to introduce to me? Or can I and my friend come inside and have some dinner—which I don't care what it is, Hewlith, as long as it's hot."

Mrs Wreath had not, and so we followed them up the steps and into the Hall, which was as impressive inside as it was out, but I was too tired by this point to take much notice of it. It was odd, how one could be so tired after a day spent essentially sitting down, but that is travel for you.

We took dinner in a small room off the kitchen ("This isn't regular at all," Mrs Wreath said. "*Servants* used to eat here, when the house was better staffed, but I thought the dining hall might be a bit much for you, after your journey.") where I ate the bowl of hot, hearty soup that Hewlith put down in front of me, and tried to keep my eyes open long enough to see Clarkia safely to her room.

"I am sorry that we've had to dust off one of the guest rooms so quickly," Mrs Wreath told me as she led me to my quarters. "But we didn't know you were coming until you got down off that cart. I sent Roke on ahead to turn down the bed in this one—oh *good* he has. Well, there you are, Mrs Birch. And how long, may I ask, will you be staying?"

I looked at the woman hard, my fatigued mind not wanting to think so far into the future.

"For as long as it takes, Mrs Wreath," I told her, trying to put a little of Felpz's commanding tone into my voice.

It must have worked, for the housekeeper left me alone after that, and I was able to stagger over to the large, soft—if rather musty—bed, and collapsed down onto it with relief.

Whatever sinister fate lay over Riddlemoor, or whatever plots might be brewing in Deerling Hall, I knew I could not face them in my current condition, and so I surrendered myself promptly to sleep, and to whatever the following morning would bring.

Chapter 3:
Deerling Hall and Its Neighbors

FOR THE NEXT PIECE of my narrative I had to ask Felpz to send me the reports I wrote for him during my first weeks at Deerling Hall, so that I might have references beyond that of my own memory. Upon examination, however, I find that they provide so clear and complete a picture that I intend to save myself the trouble of writing everything down all over again by simply reproducing them here. I have edited them, since in my hurry some sentences were muddled, and I have attempted to remove repetitive passages, but otherwise they are unchanged.

Deerling Hall, July 22, '26
Dear Felpz,

I got the note you sent via raven requesting thorough reports from Riddlemoor, and I have to say I was intending to write to you anyway, but since you specifically asked that these reports be *thorough* you'll have to forgive the lateness of this letter, since it has taken me three days to find the time to write everything down.

First let me assure you that there seems to be no immediate danger, and we have not had any cause for alarm; no mysterious wolves or paw prints, and everyone hale as could be. Deerling Hall is an imposing house, even without all the mourning dresses and black drapes, but the people in it are a colorful bunch, which even the pall of Magician Deerling's death cannot mute.

In addition to Erren Hortall, of whom you have already heard, there is his daughter Jaria, who is ostensibly the gardener but also serves as an assistant stable hand or wherever else she is needed. Inside, the house is run by a surprisingly blunt housekeeper called Mrs Wreath. I have even more respect for her since I have learned her given name is Beneficent. She could, I am sure, manage a household many times this size, for the only other servants are our Cairdrian cook, Hewlith del Garren, and the footman, Roke. I have yet to learn his first name—for all I know Roke *is* his first name. He seems an earnest young man, eager to please, and I fear a little too impressed with his new mistress. He is at that awkward stage of being all long limbs and knobby elbows, and hair that no amount of grease can tame. Clarkia, thankfully, is made of steel where I was soft clay at her age, and seems completely impervious to romantic attraction. Instead she has set herself with commendable vigor to learning the ways of this place—though it appears she does this precisely in order to defy them.

I realize I am a poor judge of magic, but I will try to relay what I have seen of hers as accurately as possible. She seems to use words of power more often than you—or perhaps they are just words and she finds that speaking aids whatever other magic she is doing. Whatever the reason, it makes it easy to notice when she is performing magic, and I think the staff finds this a relief—since she does it all the time.

Magician Deerling made do without a maid, and Clarkia is just the same. Who needs a maid, or even a housekeeper, when one can summon hot water and command one's bed to make itself? Clarkia uses her magic for all this and more, and many times has my morning rest been ruptured by her vigorous shouting when the magic does not do as she wishes. This was quite frequent on the first day, when she was still adjusting to Riddlemoor's magic; she explained it to me like the difference between swimming in a river and swimming in an ocean, which I confess I can only imagine, but lately she has become more fluid and proficient.

However, since she seemed content to stay at Deerling Hall for the first few days, it gave me the opportunity to do some exploring of my own. I wished to familiarize myself with this landscape as well, knowing you would doubtless ask questions if I did not.

To begin with I should describe Deerling Hall itself. As I said before it is a large, imposing place. Easily big enough for a multigenerational family with a full staff (which it used to house), it is a square, blockish building, with two wings protruding from either side. Despite its height there are only two floors—not counting the attic and the cellars—and this allows the ceilings to be very high. Every room feels a bit like a cathedral, airy and dark. The motif of antlers—befitting the Deerling heritage—is everywhere, sometimes in the pattern of the wallpaper, sometimes in picture frames, and others worked into the architecture and furnishings. I've received no less that seven new bruises from inadvertently running into pronged chairs, tables, door frames and bannisters.

The gardens are as austere as their surroundings, containing a stand of cypress trees that act as a wind buffer for the cold northern breezes that blow in every afternoon, and several acres of lawn cloven by neat hedges. This is ringed by a bridle path, and that bounded by a low stone wall which separates the grounds from the wild moor. Clarkia and I walked it on the morning after our arrival, as Clarkia felt it was her duty to see where her predecessor had met her end.

I confess I found nothing out of the ordinary; the scene having long since been cleared away, but Clarkia spent a long time walking the length of the path on either side of the moor gate, her nose raised to the sky, like a dog casting for an elusive scent.

The place is not all grim coordination, however. The stables—overseen by the elder Hortall—are comfortable, and house no less than three very fine horses. It turns out Magician Deerling was a keen rider and kept, in addition to the sturdy cob who pulled the carriage, a graceful red hunting mare and a modest but reliable-looking bay gelding.

"Jaria has been exercising them," Hortall explained when he showed us the stables. "Bangle is a good worker, and he'll pull the carriage if need be. I recommend keeping him, but Mrs Hammin has expressed an interest in Scarlatta if you feel she is superfluous."

"*Superfluous?*" gasped Clarkia, who had been gazing at the red mare with more open emotion than I had seen her yet display. "She is the most beautiful thing I have seen since leaving Mackanaw! No, no, I should not think of selling her. Unless we do not get on, which I hope we will."

I worried then that I would forever be chasing Clarkia across Riddlemoor by horseback, but here she showed unusual prudence, being satisfied to exercise Scarlatta on the grounds the first few times they stepped out together. This was just as well, since it appears Scarlatta has as much character as Clarkia, and the two did not mesh well at first, the former leaving the latter in one of the hedges during their first gallop.

"She *is* particular about her leg cues," Clarkia said, plucking leaves and twigs off her person as Jaria, who'd intercepted the runaway horse, came leading her back. "I shall bear that in mind in future!"

While Clarkia worked out a compromise with the horse, I went on and explored the gardens which were attached to the stables. These contained, aside from a glorious vegetable patch, a modest orchard of apple, peach, pear, and apricot trees—all of which were in their full summer splendor. In the center of this little oasis of trees was a gazebo, which has become my place of refuge when the echoing heights of the house become too much. I am sitting in it now, as a matter of fact, and from my seat I can see the turrets and spiked walls of Deerling Hall rising above the green crowns of the fruit trees, and beyond that the black silhouettes of the cypresses. The sky is a gentle blue, but there are clouds building in the north and Jaria thinks it will rain tonight.

Yesterday Clarkia announced that she and Scarlatta had come to an accord, and that she was now ready to ride out and explore the moor. I quailed inside, knowing that I would have to accompany her and not looking forward to spending the day in a saddle. Jaria came to my rescue, however, when she offered to take Snowflake—that is their cob—with the dog cart so that I might ride in more comfort and she could serve as a guide. Clarkia found this suggestion agreeable, and by ten we were outside under a cloud-veiled sun, setting out from Deerling Hall into the wide-open moor.

Jaria guided us on a perfunctory circuit of all the main neighbors—though we did not visit every single house due to time constraints. She was happy enough to talk of them however, I think finding it easier to speak candidly to me than to her mistress. She is a sharp, clever girl, and I do not think she will be a gardener all her life. She has a great gift of perception and a clarity to her opinions that speaks of long thought—and though she was frank with me about the nature of the moor's inhabitants, she was always fair in her assessment and did not gossip.

From Deerling Hall we rode west—which was the only way the road led—and took the first branch north on a long loop that included two of the Hall's closest neighbors: Mothwitch Farm and Raven's Landing. The former was a sprawling estate kept by a family named Connally, and there we were greeted quite warmly. It seems Deerling Hall is a patron of that farm, and in order to secure the new mistress's continued clientele the dog cart was summarily loaded with cheeses and nuts. Darby Connally, the farm's patriarch, came out and offered to give Clarkia a grand tour. Clarkia excused us on the grounds that we had a lot of land to cover if we were to make it all the way to Greenwitch and back, and citing our close proximity promised to come visit again.

"They are a good family, the Connallys," Jaria told me as we left the farm behind. "The old man, Darby, has been a friend of the Deerlings since before the plague. I was a little worried, since they weren't best pleased to hear a foreign magician was being brought in to take Morgrainne's place, but he seems to have gotten over that."

"Morgrainne was well loved then, I take it?" I asked.

"Oh yes, mother, she was like the root of all the moor families. Any troubles or problems with the moor, people would go to her and she'd get them sorted out quick as anything. Why, there was one time she made the moor paths run straight for an entire week, all because little Ani Connally lost their new mare, and they needed the moor to hold still until she could find her way home again."

This caused me to ask after the exact nature of the moor, and Jaria's response lasted us all the way to Raven's Landing.

It turns out the spatial changes are not random or whimsical, but operate on something of a pattern. Not so mechanical that it can be predicted with absolute certainty, but rather the way a river will have recognizable pools and currents: some places are easier to reach than others, some are nearly impossible to visit, while others still are easy enough to get to but only if you visit them in the correct order.

"Take Lathecliff," she said, pointing to a spiky promontory of stone out on the moor. "You'd think it'd be easiest to make right for it, no? But going to Lathecliff from here is nearly impossible. You'd get so turned around you'll end up farther away from it than where you started. But if you take the hill trail from behind Raven's Landing—I'll point it out when we get there—that leads you further west, well, that might *seem* like it's taking you away from Lathecliff, but once you get to the summit of Iron Hill you can make a swing to the east and you'll be at Lathecliff in no time. And from Lathecliff, even though it's so far northeast of us, is the fastest way to Wizard's House—even though *that's* just outside Greenwitch."

"Fascinating," said I. "Does this follow in reverse? Is it easier to get from Lathecliff to Iron Hill, I mean?"

Jaria screwed up her face in a frown. "Sometimes, but not always. Don't think of it as spatial folding, if you know what that is. It's not so much two places coming to meet each other on either side of a wrinkle in space, but more like . . . aye, it's more like space gets uphills and downhills. That's the best way to describe it. It's downhill from Iron Hill to Lathecliff, and from Lathecliff to Wizard's House, but it's *uphill* from Wizard's House to Lathecliff.

"Of course it gets a bit confusing there, because Lathecliff and Iron Hill are both downhill of *each other,* and they're both uphill of Deerling Hall, which in turn is *downhill* from Wizard's House."

Perhaps to you this makes perfect sense, but I soon felt my brain becoming overloaded trying to visualize all these invisible and contradicting uphills and downhills in the nature of space itself. Jaria was sympathetic, and explained that many of the residents of the moor developed a sensitivity to these changes, and could usually get about fairly well. The sheep were always getting lost, however. Their solution was to mix goats in with the sheep; for the goats could navigate the moor better than anyone.

"Most houses around here keep goats, or they borrow one from Mothwitch. Deerling Hall is one of the few that doesn't, on account of the fact we always had Morgrainne to sort the moor out for us."

"She could flatten out the uphills and downhills?" I asked.

"Aye, and do more besides, but then only in emergencies. Ah, here's Raven's Landing—mistress, have a care, Dr Verdemeister does not like unexpected visitors." This last was to Clarkia, who had ridden on ahead and was now pausing at the start of a drive that led to a tall, tower-like house built on top of a low, stony hill.

Dr Radja Verdemeister, I learned, was the sole inhabitant of Raven's Landing, and a reclusive Elgan native. It was generally assumed that she made a special study of birds. She lived in a house well known to attract ravens, and on one of the few occasions that she deigned to entertain visitors, a large book detailing the lives of polar terns had been seen on her coffee table.

"Honestly I couldn't say for certain what she does. Malta Connally makes deliveries there once a week but never sees her. We hear her though; she goes out owl-calling at night on the moor. So if you hear a strange hooting at night, be not alarmed. She frightened the hair off Mrs Mills-Hardy one evening, but she is harmless enough."

As we had made no prior arrangements, we left the bleak outpost that was Raven's Landing without calling upon the house, and made our way down, past the trailhead for Iron Hill, and thence back to join the main road, where it began sloping gently down into the vale of the Gyrehass—now just visible as a vibrant band of yellow-green and deep blue cutting across the lonely grey moor.

At one bend in the road Jaria reined Snowflake in and called Clarkia back. "This is a good path to know about," she said, and pointed to a little green road that broke off from the main drive and cut through a hedge onto the moor.

"I know it looks like a shady moor path if there ever was one, but that'll take you straight to Merrybriar House, reliable as rain."

"Merrybriar? Who lives there?" Clarkia asked.

Jaria explained that it was an older couple—a pair of retired solicitors—Mr Joryford Hardy-Mills and Mrs Element Mills-Hardy. "We better not miss paying them a visit," Jaria explained. "They're the exact opposite of Dr Verdemeister; if you pass by without visiting they will know of it, and then you will never hear the end of it the next time your paths cross. Which they will make sure happens sooner rather than later."

"Then let's not give them cause for grief," said Clarkia gamely, and pointed Scarlatta down the little green road.

You will be proud of me, Felpz. At least, I hope you will. I thought all on my own to ask Jaria if there were any hidden roads on Riddlemoor. She did not seem to know what I was talking about, however—though that may have been because I described them so poorly. It has been many years since last I thought of them, you understand.

Merrybriar House was as lively and welcoming as Raven's Landing had been cold and aloof. A low house built under the lee of a steep green hill, it was covered in honeysuckle and morning glories, guarded by magnolia trees and formidable rose bushes. As we approached, a friendly yellow dog loped out to greet us, and by the way Scarlatta reacted (reaching down to breathe into its trusting face) I gathered that Morgrainne must have been a frequent visitor.

The dog was followed shortly by a wide-set man at least a decade older than myself. Nevertheless he came walking briskly down the hill behind the house, a telescope under one arm.

"Saw you coming a mile off," he said in brusque but pleasant tones. "Signaled to Mrs Element that you were on your way. Should have the luncheon ready by now."

I will not bore you with the details of that luncheon, but rather give you my impression of the Mills-Hardy household—since that at least may be useful to you.

They are both extremely inquisitive, energetic people, and quite eager to pour Clarkia into the mold left empty by her predecessor. There was much presumptuous talk of " . . . when you get the north road reopened" and " . . . finish seeding the southern hills" and " . . . don't let that Delpheonian discourage you from lifting the fog when it comes on too thick, the clear spell has done wonders for stargazing."

All these, I assumed, were various projects that Morgrainne had discussed with the Mills-Hardys, and which Clarkia—judging by her politely vague answers—had no prior knowledge of.

Recognizing her plight for what it was, I begged that I was a stranger to these parts, and asked for more information about our surroundings. Information that both halves of the couple were more than happy to provide.

I learned from them that Hortall had originally been in their employment, having moved to Riddlemoor with them. Merrybriar had made a loan of him and his young daughter to Deerling Hall when they became aware of Morgrainne's difficulty in keeping steady servants, and the elder Hortall had liked it so much he had decided to stay.

"Not that we begrudge you in the *least*," Mrs Mills-Hardy assured Clarkia, who'd looked a little worried at hearing this. "We're quite happy with Pennbrook, and we were only glad to be able to help."

They were also eager to share more details about Dr Verdemeister than Jaria (who was taking her lunch with the aforementioned Pennbrook in the stable yard). From them we learned the woman was in her sixth decade, had been educated extensively abroad, and came to Riddlemoor precisely to study the unique magic of the native ravens. Indeed, Mr Hardy-Mills had once glimpsed her through his telescope (the top of the hill over Merrybriar having a good view of Raven's Landing), leaping from the highest tower only to disappear into an explosion of feathers and go flapping off into the sky in the form of a great, black bird.

"I hear her house is full of birds," Mrs Mills-Hardy told us, delightedly. "That she's let the upper rooms fall into ruin, with the windows always open, so they can fly in and out as they please."

Mr Hardy-Mills then asked where next we were bound, and when it came out we intended to go all the way to Greenwitch before coming back via Wizard's House, he recommended we pay a visit to Dr Narriott—the county physician.

"Always good for the magicians and the physicians to get acquainted," he said. "Narriott's a fine fellow, and a good man to have on your side. Oh, but they'll be passing Hovergate, won't they? Best ride past as if you have urgent business in town. That's Tida Hammin's domain, and if she catches you you won't escape until she's fed you four courses and pried all your secrets out of you."

Mrs Mills-Hardy nodded and made a *tsking* noise. Then she asked Clarkia what things were like in Beranica, and if they all spoke that way down there.

In all we spent a good three hours in the company of the Mills-Hardys, and only managed to escape because Jaria appeared and deferentially pointed out that if we were to make it back to Deerling Hall by dinnertime we would have to leave soon. Even so, the couple followed us outside, and would not stop talking to Clarkia until we were all mounted, and Clarkia interrupted them in order to say good-bye.

"Thought I should get you out of there," Jaria said as soon as we were out of earshot. "What with Hovergate next, and we can't afford to avoid Tida Hammin either."

"Mr Hardy-Mills suggested we put off visiting Hovergate until some other trip," I remarked, seeing Clarkia's expression.

"What, and give Mrs Hammin the snip?" said Jaria. "Well, I suppose you might, but it'll be more trouble than it's worth, in the end. Hovergate and Merrybriar had a bit of a rivalry going, with regards to who could ingratiate themselves with Deerling Hall the most. You'd best give Hammin a fair crack at you—she's not a bad egg besides."

Clarkia groaned. "I'll take this as part of my new burden," she said, and spurred Scarlatta down the drive.

Hovergate House lies on the outskirts of Greenwitch—barely on the moor at all. It was once a very grand estate run by Lord Hovergate. That family went bankrupt at the beginning of this century, however, and the lands passed into the care of the last Lord Hovergate's steward—a man named Argentius Bullrose—who later married the same Tida Hammin who now lived alone at Hovergate—having been widowed some five years ago. Upon her husband's death she made the rational decision to parcel the estate and rent it off to her former employees, cutting back until she had only the house and its immediate grounds, where she seemed perfectly happy to spend her days, living off the income from her lands and deriving entertainment, it seemed, by getting into the business of everyone in close proximity.

I have to say, Felpz, that I found her a most trying person. While she was polite enough in showing Clarkia around the grounds and presenting a friendly interest in her experiences at Riddlemoor so far, she contrived to attach herself to me as we walked up to the house, and began putting me all manner of questions. Which would not have been so bad, except the woman was as keen as a shrew and perceptive to boot. She connected me at once with you, and asked right out when you would be arriving at Riddlemoor to solve the problem of Morgrainne's death.

I tried to give vague answers, since I did not want to lie, but I didn't wish sensitive information in the hands of this notoriously talkative woman. I asked her in return why she thought Morgrainne's death was problematic, which she brushed aside with a very impertinent question regarding your success rate when it came to cases like these. You'll be happy to know I did not give her the satisfaction of an answer to that one.

A short description: Tida Hammin is roughly my age, a little taller and wider, and her hair is improbably yellow—I believe she colors it artificially. She wears fine, fashionable clothes, but doesn't seem to be an overly vain person otherwise. She certainly doesn't hesitate to take part in the more messy aspects of running her estate: many of the gardens she tends herself, which she had been at when we rode up. All these admirable traits make it even more aggravating that she has such an abrasive character, and I was wholeheartedly relieved when we escaped from Hovergate.

It was getting on in the afternoon, so we made a brief stop in Greenwitch, calling on Dr Narriott. I found him to be a lean, grey-haired, respectable man. He was pleased to meet Clarkia, and generously offered her any information she desired with regard to Morgrainne Deerling. This Clarkia accepted gladly, and we left the doctor's practice with a thick envelope full of papers.

We took an alternate route back to Deerling Hall, one that followed the Gyrehass downstream a ways before striking out across the moor. It was a pleasant ride in the late afternoon, and very nearly warm. The thickly forested banks of the river made an agreeable change from the barren moor, and I felt their loss keenly once we were again headed towards home.

This road was less used than the other, and mostly covered in grass.

"It's the wizard's road," Jaria explained. "And he mostly gets about on foot."

"By wizard do you mean that Gandlyn fellow?" Clarkia, who was riding beside us, asked.

"Aye, him and all the wizards who came before," said Jaria, nodding.

Clarkia's mouth clamped shut at this, and she got a sour expression on her face that I remembered from Redling. I puzzled over this all the way to Wizard's House, for it did not seem to me that Clarkia so much disliked Gandlyn, but that she took special care to *not* show concern for him. I find this worrisome, considering her age and the doubts you have expressed to me about the man.

Whatever ominous current might have been lurking beneath the surface, it was rendered moot by the fact that Gandlyn was out when we arrived at his house. This was a sprawling, tumbledown affair, though there were signs that someone had been about fixing the place up. There was a new, bright wooden fence separating the front garden from the road, and a trellis with young vines climbing up it beside the front door. A giant oak tree spread its branches over the whole place, the lone tree we had encountered since leaving the river.

Jaria halted the cart by the sign declaring the place "Wizard's House" and hitched Snowflake to one of the metal rings attached to it.

"You'd best leave Scarlatta here," she advised Clarkia. "He may be out, but the eagle sometimes hangs around."

"An eagle?" said Clarkia, not bothering to hide her interest in this. "I didn't know you had eagles here!"

"Strictly speaking, we don't," said Jaria, with a wry grin. "And Kierel's not the sort of eagle you'd be familiar with. She came with the wizard when he shipped down from Delpheon, but there's no knowing where *he* found her. She's a *snow eagle*," she added, giving me a meaningful look.

I'm sure you now know exactly what we were going to find, but I regret to say I did not recognize the term. My mind went straight to *snowy owls* and I imagined that Gandlyn must keep an exotic raptor as a familiar or even a pet.

And I suppose exotic raptor is not so bad a description of a snow eagle, but it did not prepare me for the creature that reared up above the house as we approached and stared down at us out of keen yellow eyes.

I do not know how much variation there is in the appearance of snow eagles, but Kierel is twice the size of Scarlatta, and a perfect, pristine white—save for her head and breast, which have a faint black mottling. I have no way of guessing her age, but she looked very strong and healthy from what I could see.

It is a good thing I have had practice with dragons and griffins, because otherwise I am sure I would have run away shamelessly. Kierel looks big enough to be a griffin, even if her tail is short and feathery rather than long and feline. Her talons are sharp and black, and left gouges in the thatched roof of the house. Gouges that I soon spotted all over the structure: clearly she used the roof as an improvised nest.

She made a rattling sound in her throat as we approached. It did not seem threatening, but coming from such a huge bird it was very hard to interpret otherwise.

Jaria, however, was unfazed—bless her.

"Hallo Kierel," she said, walking up to the eaves of the house and making a short bow. "Is the wizard home? I've brought Magician Aldeer from the Hall to pay a visit."

Kierel answered with another rattling caw, and Jaria turned to Clarkia. "She says . . . " the woman began, but Clarkia cut her off with a wave of her hand.

"I got that part," she said. She was looking a little stunned. "Out on his rounds, is he? Well, can she tell him we came by while he was gone? Tell him Clarkia says hi, that sort of thing."

Kierel made a hissing noise, and turned her head to one side so as to give Clarkia an intense, one-eyed stare.

"If it's not too much trouble, please," Clarkia added hastily.

Kierel ruffled her feathers and then turned her back on us in order to preen.

"That's as much of an answer as we'll ever get," Jaria said with a shrug. "But I'm glad you understand her—I can only pick up her general intent. But Wizard Gandlyn promises she understands us—just doesn't always listen."

"That's . . . reasonable," said Clarkia in a small voice, and she rode behind us very quietly all the way back to the Hall.

So much then for the inhabitants and neighbors of Deerling Hall. I have elected not to provide details on the residents of Greenwitch itself other than Dr Narriott, as I fear that would bloat this report beyond tolerability. Today has been relatively quiet, though Clarkia and I spent some time after breakfast going over Dr Narriott's report. I found nothing in it that Gandlyn did not already tell us, but I have asked Roke to make a copy, which I will send along to you as soon as he has it finished.

I hope you are doing well, and that whatever lines of investigation you are pursuing have been fruitful. Rest assured I will write again soon.

With kindest regards,

Corianne

Chapter 4:
A Troubling Encounter

Continued letters from Corianne Birch to Bouragner Felpz, July 2326

Deerling Hall, July 24, '26
Dear Felpz,

I know you have made it clear that your work prevents you from taking a direct hand in the matters here at Riddlemoor, but I would greatly appreciate your input on something that occurred yesterday. I would normally discuss it with Clarkia or Gandlyn, but as they are intimately involved I do not think bringing my knowledge of it to their attention would help anything.

First let me say that things had been quite peaceful since my last report, with Clarkia settling in nicely and even receiving guests with good grace. The evening after I wrote last saw both the Merrybriar couple and Dr Narriott coming to dinner, and the day after (yesterday), Tida Hammin invited herself over for tea.

My opinion of this woman has not improved—quite the opposite, in fact. I have tried not to blame her for what transpired, as I do not believe it was her intention to cause trouble. Still, without her the whole mess might have been avoided.

It began innocuously enough. Around nine this morning, just as we were finishing breakfast, there was a piercing, rattling call from the front door, and Roke ran in bearing a tattered envelope in one hand. Apparently, Kierel had landed like a small, feathery avalanche in the front courtyard, and thrust her huge, deadly beak at him until he saw the letter clasped within and took it from her. She was waiting, he said, as though expecting a reply.

Despite the letter's dramatic delivery, it turned out to be a simple message declaring Gandlyn's intent to visit Deerling Hall that afternoon, to make up for missing us when we called upon him. Clarkia frowned at the letter, as if it gave her personal offense, but scribbled out a positive reply on a corner of the paper, tore it off, put it back in the tattered envelope, and went outside to give it to Kierel herself—much to Roke's relief.

Perhaps you, with your greater experience of human nature, have already guessed what was building between Clarkia and Gandlyn, but though I did steel myself to be particularly alert, knowing that you had reservations about him, the coming storm still took me by surprise.

How it happened was this: Just as Hewlith was preparing afternoon tea, who should come trundling through the gate but Tida Hammin, driving a dog cart behind a giant bay gelding. She greeted Jaria, who was in the front courtyard when she arrived, and threw her the reins before pulling down a huge hamper from the cart and letting herself into the hall. This I learned later; the first I heard of her visit was when she called, *"Cooey!"* at the top of her lungs.

I was sitting in the front drawing room at the time, filtering through more of Dr Narriott's incredibly dry autopsy report, and went with all innocence into the hall to greet whoever had slipped past Jaria, Roke, and Mrs Wreath.

"Ah, Corianne!" said the woman, beaming at me. *"So* good to see you again! You are still here? That is wonderful; Giancarla and I baked far too many pasties this morning, and I find myself in need of mouths to feed them to. Say you will help—my household is unable to keep up with our combined cooking!"

Unable to defend myself against this attack of generosity, I could only invite Hammin to join us for tea, and sent Mrs Wreath, when she appeared, down to the kitchen to tell Hewlith not to bother himself; for Hammin had at least been honest about the sheer amount of food she had brought: enough, I should think, to feed a small army—and all of it crisp and fresh. When Clarkia eventually put her head into the parlor it was to find Hammin and I in the process of covering the little table with plates stacked high with meat pies, fruit pasties, buns, rolls, and biscuits.

"Gods deliver me," she said, her eyes widening. "What have I done to deserve this?"

"I *am* sorry for the intrusion," Tida Hammin said, leaving a tray precariously balanced on the edge of the table (I had to dart forward to save it sliding off onto the carpet) and rushing over to take both of Clarkia's hands, which she shook between her own. "As I told Corianne, I come to you in distress. Giancarla and I . . . " and she launched into a repeat of the excuse she had given me.

I laid out the remainder of the food, trying to control the sour feeling that was crawling up my throat. It was clear to me that Hammin had come just to get a good look at the new magician's household—no doubt so she could report back to the rest of Greenwitch.

Clarkia must have come to the same realization, for though she was perfectly polite—in her own blunt way—she let very little of her recent activities slip out.

It was a difficult act to maintain, since Hammin kept coming at us from odd angles, trying to induce us into saying more than we wished. She did this by heaping our plates high with pasties and rolls, pouring us tea, and talking almost nonstop about what Greenwitch was saying about Clarkia. It was all so wildly inaccurate that I felt my chest swell in irritation, and when Hammin stopped for a moment, I very nearly blurted out a refutation to these falsehoods—which was, I realized just in time, exactly what Hammin wanted.

She changed tactics after that. Turning her attentions to Clarkia, she kept asking presumptuous questions along the lines of, "I suppose you'll want to get rid of those dour cypresses now, won't you? Morgrainne wouldn't hear of it, but I never thought they belonged here." And, "Have the wolves been bothering you? They were keeping the Mills-Hardys up all last night." And, "I have an extra goat, if you wish to explore the moor. I know Morgrainne didn't need one, but with all respect, she was a native of the moor . . . "

Clarkia only smiled tightly and nodded, and never said much more than "Ah," and "I see," and "How interesting," but her demeanor grew steadily colder and harder the longer Hammin kept at it.

It was almost a relief when Roke put his head in and announced that Wizard Gandlyn had arrived, and Clarkia fairly shot out of her seat to greet him. This left me to bear the full force of Hammin's curiosity, and I weathered it with the fortitude born of knowing that reinforcements would soon arrive.

Five minutes passed, however, and neither Clarkia nor Gandlyn appeared. Ten minutes, and Hammin began to wonder aloud what had become of them. She seemed satisfied to continue pestering me with questions, however, (Was I getting any writing done at Deerling Hall? Had the moor inspired me? Did you have any insight that I could share with her?) until almost half an hour had passed, and I felt it within my rights to get up and inquire after our missing companions.

You can well imagine my dismay when I was told by a nervous Roke that the two had barely exchanged greetings before they left the hall and began walking towards Iron Hill.

This confused me mightily, until I remembered Jaria's explanation of the peculiarities of the moor: it was "uphill" from the Hall to Wizard's House, so they must be taking the route via Iron Hill to Lathecliff, and thence to Gandlyn's home.

What with everything you told me, and that I had heard about the moor, not to mention the strange fate of the Deerlings, I was gripped by a horror at the thought of Clarkia alone on the moor. And while I might have been comforted to know she had another wizard with her, the fact that it was *Gandlyn* disturbed me.

It was an agonizing decision, but since I knew I could not abandon Hammin—much as I disliked her company—I sent Jaria after them, on the pretext of making Gandlyn a present of some of Hammin's baking. I then returned to entertaining the unwanted guest, and spent the remainder of the afternoon in an increasing state of anxiety.

Hammin was finally induced to leave when dinnertime approached and there was still no sign of either Jaria or Clarkia, and I was wondering whether I could eat anything at all when there were voices in the courtyard, and I ran outside to find the two young women had returned—and both looked utterly unhappy.

Jaria was white-lipped and stared at the ground, her shoulders slumped, while Clarkia tried to mask her displeasure with a veil of anger. Neither of them said more than a word to me, and Jaria took the first opportunity to disappear into her gardens. Clarkia was stony and silent throughout dinner, eating mechanically and sometimes pausing to stare off through the long narrow windows, to where the moor was going through its brief, golden phase before being swallowed by the gloom of night.

"I don't think I like the magic here, Corianne," she said eventually, and that was all she said until after we had finished the meal and retired to the library for tea. Then she threw herself into an armchair and, crossing her face with an arm, said in a low groan:

"Thanks for sending Jaria after me. It was lucky you did, all things considered."

"I am glad she was of help," I said, timidly—since I was uncertain how far my actions had been responsible for the woman's ill mood.

"Oh, I wasn't so happy when she first turned up," Clarkia admitted. "I cursed you—harmlessly, don't worry—at length. But in the end it was a good thing. That . . . that blasted moor. And Wale is the most irritating man I've ever had to deal with. He is so *polite* about everything, you can never tell if what you've said has offended him, but his face is so wretched: it always looks like he's plotting some horrible revenge or something."

"He does have an . . . excessively serious nature," I said. "Did he say something in particular?"

Clarkia shut like a trap at that question, and stared hard up at the ceiling for some moments before replying:

"No. No, it was more his overall behavior." She let out a grumbling sigh—a surprisingly deep noise for one of such a slight frame—and reluctantly uncovered her face. "But he is not important," she said, as if trying to convince herself. "The fact is, Corianne, I saw another one of those wolves . . . "

I shall paraphrase now, since the story she related came out in bits and pieces over the next two hours. What happened was, Jaria interrupted Clarkia and Gandlyn's conversation (though what this conversation was I do not know), and when Clarkia turned back to look at her she had seen the silhouette of a wolf standing against the pale sky.

How can a silhouette be seen in broad daylight? I hear you wonder. Yes, so do I, but those were the words Clarkia used. She cried out then, and pointed, and both Gandlyn and Jaria saw it too.

As quickly as this happened, the wolf vanished from sight. Clarkia took off for where she had seen it, leaving Gandlyn and Jaria on the road.

When she reached the top of the hill where it had appeared, she found paw prints—ringed with freshly grown sprouts—that led down the other side. Following them, she found they disappeared at the bottom of a dell, but upon casting her gaze skywards she saw the wolf again, this time farther off. She described it as being tawny in color, like an amber shadow, but she was unable to see more detail than that.

More chasing led her to another clump of paw prints, but these were already fading—the sprouts having matured at an amazing rate, filling in the depressions left by the creature's feet, and those depressions vanishing even as Clarkia watched.

From there no other wolves could be seen, though Clarkia thought she saw, from the top of that hill, a clump of bright green trees nestled in a nearby vale. She was about to make for them—thinking they must belong to a house or farmstead—when she heard Jaria calling for her.

There followed a most trying time where the two women completely failed at finding one another. Clarkia described it as the moor moving pieces of itself around, like dinner plates on a table, so that even at times when she could *see* Jaria on a nearby hill, something always happened to force them farther apart again.

Understandably frustrated, Clarkia set about trying to keep the pieces of the moor still until Jaria could find her, but this was impossible. "Like trying to keep a waterfall together," were her words.

It was Gandlyn who eventually came to their aid. He flew down on Kierel and plucked Clarkia off the side of the hill, before putting her down next to Jaria.

Clarkia, it seems, was so embarrassed about this that she sent Gandlyn away, saying that she could find her own way home. She proceeded to wander the moor almost at random—"Raven's Landing, Merrybriar, even Hovergate, Corianne! I saw them all—from a distance. And other, stranger places besides. Do you know there is a collection of jagged stone pinnacles somewhere in the far north reaches? Like the weathered spikes of a dragon's spine"—until at last she gave up and let Jaria lead them home.

But they had gotten so lost that even Jaria had trouble finding Deerling Hall amidst the shifting moor. It was only when Clarkia, growing close to despair, admitted that the moor had gotten the better of her, that they crested a hill and found themselves looking down on the hall.

"You know, Corianne, I think it *let* us out, once it made me admit to my arrogance," she finished ruefully. "But I know better now, and tomorrow I am going back out there. I will find that wolf—and when I do I'll make it explain everything."

I naturally asked to come along, and Clarkia agreed—providing I rode a horse of my own, so we could go off the road. I saw no other alternative, so I accepted the proposal.

I have now been up past reasonable time writing this to you. Tomorrow we go out onto the moor, and I do not know what we will find. Assuming we are returned to civilization at the end of our journey, I will send you a full report.

In the meantime, I worry about Clarkia, and whatever it was Gandlyn said or did that has upset her so. I feel if I only knew then it might help confirm or dispel the misgivings you had regarding the man. Your insight would be greatly valued.

Wish me luck for tomorrow friend, and write back soon—these terse notes delivered by raven do little to boost my confidence in this role you have cast me in—until then I will remain faithfully yours,

Corianne

Raven's Landing, July 25, '26
Dear Felpz,

One good thing, at least, has come of this day: I have solved the mystery of Gandlyn Wale and Clarkia Aldeer and what went

on between them. That is all. Everything else has flown so far
out of my grasp that I can only beg you to come out to Riddlemoor as soon as you can. I am writing this—as you will have
seen—from Raven's Landing, in the hope that one of Dr Verdemeister's birds will reach you more swiftly than the post. Because I believe the sooner you learn of what has happened, the
sooner you will be moved to join me here.

Clarkia and I rode out first thing this morning, after a light
breakfast. We packed supplies for a day on the moor, as well as
extra blankets and coats—for though the morning was sunny,
fog lying low in the north suggested a chill afternoon. Clarkia
rode Scarlatta, of course, while I was bundled up onto the gelding, Bangle. Jaria accompanied us on Snowflake. It being years
since I last sat astride a horse, the beginning of our journey was
marked by me relearning how to balance. Luckily, Bangle is as
steady and patient as horses come, and put up with my flailing
and grabbing of his mane with admirable fortitude. Even when
Clarkia insisted we trot, in order to cover more ground, I was
able to stay on thanks to his even gait.

Because I was mostly concerned with my mount, I didn't
pay much attention to the direction we went at first. Clarkia led
the way, taking the first footpath onto the moor that we came
to. Jaria protested, but Clarkia declared that it was time she and
the moor got acquainted with each other, and rode boldly out
among the hills.

The moor remained relatively tranquil at first. As I became
more comfortable in the saddle I found I could look around. I
saw Deerling Hall holding steady behind and below us, its sharp,
black shape a striking blot on the pale green moor. Before us
the land stretched out in lumpy, grey-green hills, dotted with
outcroppings of grey stone. We had some rain the night before,
and everything was fresh and wet, sparkling in the morning sun.

The path led us up the side of a wide hill, and at the top
Clarkia stopped and stood up in her stirrups, leaning forward
and scenting the air—almost like a hound. Then she dis-
mounted, tossed the reins onto the ground (Scarlatta promptly
started grazing), and scooped up some of the soft, wet soil between her fingers. She held this for a while, eyes tightly shut,
and then put it back, patting it down so there was little sign that

the earth had ever been disturbed. Flipping the reins back over her horse's neck she fairly levitated into the saddle.

"Now I have directions," she announced happily, and led us off the path and down the back side of the hill.

I caught Jaria giving me a curious look, and I could only shrug in response. My guess is that she was communicating with some elemental spirit, but you will be a better judge of that than I.

Down the hill we went, into a wide vale with a marsh at the bottom. Here Jaria protested again, warning of places like these: the water sat under the earth, and it was impossible to tell whether firm ground or an endless, sucking cavern lay beneath. I was inclined to agree with her—it reminded me of the sinking land we encountered down in Hexindale all those years ago— but Clarkia rode fearlessly across it—though she did stop from time to time, reaching down to brush the tips of the tall grasses that grew thick and yellow-green from the mucky ground.

"Just follow my trail," she told us confidently.

This was fairly easy, as Bangle seemed to think of Scarlatta as his leading mare, and was happiest when walking with his nose almost touching her tail. Snowflake took issue with the mud and danced around a little. Jaria had some sharp words with her, and the two eventually followed.

Nevertheless it was a relief to climb up out of the bog and onto the harder, stonier side of the hill beyond. Clarkia let Scarlatta gallop up this, and Bangle—seeing his friend leaving— followed suit. Luckily I had ahold of his mane already, and so was able to cling to his back until we reached the top. There Clarkia had stopped to scent the air again, and so Bangle stopped as well.

I was out of breath, a little shaky, and bits of my anatomy were beginning to ache. Clarkia, on the other hand, looked more vibrantly alive than I had yet seen her. Cheeks flushed a deep magenta, her mouth was pulled into a triumphant grin when I at last managed to regain control of my steed.

"I have him, Corianne," she told me. "The trail is faint, but I *have* him!"

"Have who?" I asked.

"The wolf, Corianne, the *wolf*," she replied. "I got a good whiff of him yesterday, and I am sure this is the same one."

"I must take your word for it," I admitted as Jaria rode up on the lumbering Snowflake.

"Then stay with me," Clarkia said, no doubt to the bewilderment of our companion, and took off along the ridge of the hill.

Though I was mostly concentrated on riding at this point, I did manage to have a look around, and it was with quiet resignation that I realized I could no longer see Deerling Hall, or the road, or any sign of civilization. Whether or not Riddlemoor was living up to its name, it seemed that we had been swallowed by the rolling hills.

Clarkia did not seem to mind, however; she rode with confidence down the spine of the hill, through a shallow valley— mercifully dry—and then up a steep tor with a rocky crag at the top. Here she stopped again, and this time I could see why:

Growing around the base of the rock were little circles of tightly packed pink, yellow, and white flowers, their leaves bright golden green and curling vigorously into the air.

"These!" Clarkia exclaimed, leaping down once more. "These are the flowers I saw in his paw prints! He leaves them, like tracks, after his tracks vanish."

She went down on her knees and inspected the flowers, but I noticed how she never touched them.

"Have an eye out for these," she said, mounting again. "I do not think he leaves them idly."

We continued our rambling on the moor, and though we never encountered anything excessively strange, neither did I see a single familiar sight. Clarkia found several more patches of flowers, but no tangible evidence of any wolves.

We took our lunch in the lee of a half-fallen spire, which provided some shelter from the wind that insisted on following us over the moor, and in the afternoon, at Jaria's behest, we began making our way home.

At least, that was the intent. For as soon as we had a definite destination in mind the moor became a constantly shifting landscape. Hills took ages to climb, and descending the other side we found ourselves back where we had started. Clarkia took this in good spirits at first, speaking to the moor in reasonable tones, but slowly she became visibly frustrated.

I turned to Jaria, in the hopes that she might be able to puzzle out a way home, only to find her looking so desperately unhappy I realized she must be as lost as we were.

Then, in accordance with the capricious nature of the moor, we came around a hill and discovered not only a path, but a familiar figure walking on it.

"Father!" Jaria called, and waved desperately.

Hortall—for it was he—looked up and saw us. He gave a little start of surprise, and stopped.

"Milady?" he said, lifting the brim of his wide hat as Clarkia trotted down to meet him. "How is it you are here?"

"Blame this blasted moor," said Clarkia, laughing in relief. "I thought I had it sussed, but it must have sussed me. Where are we, can you tell?"

"Why, milady, you are beyond Lathecliff, very near the far reaches." His face—wide and brown and wrinkled—twitched, and he gazed piercingly over our shoulders.

Turning, I saw that Jaria remained someways up the hillside; she had reined her horse in and was staring off at the horizon beyond us, her whole body a tense arch.

Following her gaze, I saw movement on the hill opposite, and a moment later this solidified into a low, canine form, moving swiftly towards us.

"Away, milady!" cried Hortall, moving to put himself between Clarkia and the charging wolf. Clarkia was having none of it, however, and jumped off Scarlatta—who promptly bolted—and shouldered her way past Hortall.

"Hold you!" she shouted at the wolf, which was less than a hundred feet away. It was of a tawny, honey color, with a white belly and face, and left a curling trail of bright yellow-green leaves in its wake.

It was by all accounts a beautiful creature, its legs long and graceful, its coat gleaming in the sun, while its eyes blazed with a bright green light.

Everything moved too fast for me to act. I'm afraid I was no help at all, Felpz; I can only tell you what I saw, in snatches as I held Bangle in a tight circle to prevent him running off to join Scarlatta.

The wolf ran straight at Clarkia, who squared her feet as if to do battle with it, but at the last moment it took a great leap, soaring clean over her head, and landed with an explosion of grass and petals on the ground beside Hortall. In the next moment it was upon him, its forelegs at his shoulders and its head at his throat.

Jaria screamed—as did I—and Clarkia shouted angrily.

Then, as quickly as the wolf had struck, it was leaping away with a yelp—for Hortall had drawn a small knife from his belt and slashed at it. It retreated up the hill, away from us and from Jaria, and crouched there, growling, while all around it little pink and yellow flowers thrust up through the earth and unfurled their petals.

"What the *hell* did you mean by that?" Clarkia screamed at the wolf, even as she went to Hortall and stood protectively over him.

I felt Bangle shudder under me, and trusting his sense for danger above my own, I looked keenly around our environment. That was how I saw, before anyone else, two more amber wolves appear on the hillside behind Hortall's attacker. Their ears were pinned back, and even from a distance I could hear their growls.

We remained in this strange standoff for what felt like a minute, when the tension was broken by the rattling, croaking call of a raven. I was aware of it as a flash of black on the pale sky, rising up from the hill behind us. Risking a glance, I turned back to see its wings stretched wide as it coasted down towards the ground—to where another wolf had risen into view, standing at the peak of the hill where a jumble of rocks created a natural pedestal.

Unlike the others, this wolf was dark, its shaggy head a black silhouette against the light blue sky. It also appeared larger, and stood calm, regal, surveying us as though we were actors in a play. The raven came to light on its withers, and then the wolf raised its head and let out a long, mournful howl.

I tell you, Felpz, the sound sent shivers down my spine in a way that no animal's cry ever has. It was as though it bored into my head and rattled down through my body.

So transfixed were we by this sight, not a single one of us noticed what became of the tawny wolves—I only know that when I turned around to look for them they had vanished, leaving only a scattering of pink and yellow flowers.

The dark wolf on the crag stared at us for a minute, before disappearing behind the hill with a flick of its tail—carrying the raven away with it.

Clarkia barely had time to cry out, when we were abruptly cast in shadow and from out of the sky came a call—sharper and longer than that of a raven—and the next moment Kierel alighted in a flurry of white wings where the wolf had stood a moment before. A figure in a neat green coat slid off her back, and Gandlyn came striding down the hill.

"What has happened?" he asked, in his abrupt way.

For answer, Hortall groaned, clapping a hand to his neck, where he had begun to bleed profusely.

"What do you *think*?" Clarkia snapped, going suddenly bitter. "I got it *wrong*, just like you said I would! Go ahead and gloat now—see if I care!"

Gandlyn, to his credit, only gave her a hurt, puzzled look, and went over to kneel beside Hortall.

It was horrible, Felpz. The wolf had bitten him quite badly, and it was only thanks to Clarkia's practical knowledge of frontier medicine that he did not bleed to death there on the moor. Gandlyn did what he could, and Jaria rode down and helped them lift her father onto Snowflake, though she was crying and shaking. I stood by and held the horses, feeling useless, and worried for Scarlatta—who had disappeared entirely.

"Not that way," Gandlyn said sharply when we went to take the path on which we had found Hortall. "Raven's Landing is closer."

I had only a moment of misgiving before Clarkia took the matter out of my hands by agreeing. Gandlyn sent Kierel on ahead, and he and Clarkia walked together in front, leading the way between the hills, while Jaria led Snowflake and the injured man, and I, in order to keep an eye on everyone, brought up the rear.

Like this I could not help overhearing the conversation shared between Clarkia and Gandlyn, and though under ordinary circumstances I would have made a greater effort to not eavesdrop, considering your reservations about the man I felt it was my duty to monitor their conversation.

"I suppose you think me a fool," Clarkia was saying bitterly.

Gandlyn make a noncommittal noise, halfway between a grunt and a sigh.

"If you think that was meant to *impress* me—" she continued, before Gandlyn cut her off.

"Good *grief,* Clarkia, I would not know where to *start* trying to impress you. I seem only able to do *wrong* in your book."

"Whatever have I done—wait, don't tell me," Clarkia sighed. "It is not just the magic that is different here. All the social niceties are turned on their heads as well—and I was never much good at them, even back in Beranica."

"You are not alone to blame," Gandlyn said, his voice milder than I had ever heard it. "I'm afraid no one has ever dared even *try* to court me before, and I took it badly."

"You are well within your rights to reject me," Clarkia said bitterly. "No one would blame you, least of all me."

"That would, I think, be somewhat dishonest," Gandlyn admitted softly.

"Really?" said Clarkia, head bobbing up to look at her companion. In this way she spotted me out of the corner of her eye, which I took as my cue to fall further back and let them continue their conversation in more privacy.

Which is how I came to fill in the gaps in my knowledge of their relationship. I confess I was thrown off-balance by the confirmation that Clarkia, far from disliking Gandlyn, felt very much the opposite, but upon consideration I see how she was using her icy demeanor as a cloak. I do not know if this is peculiar to her character, or if it is simply the way people behave in Beranica, but I can't help feeling a little sorry for Gandlyn.

Yet I think you may set whatever reservations you have about his character aside, for he led us safely and swiftly to Raven's Landing. There we found Scarlatta dancing outside its gate, her reins held by a tall, austere woman with messy black hair and thick spectacles.

Dr Verdemeister is a strange woman, but not as unlikable as her house and reputation make her out to be. She brought us inside without question and turned over her ground-floor study to us while Gandlyn flew off on Kierel to fetch Dr Narriott.

Hortall was by this time very pale and drifting in and out of consciousness. Clarkia had stopped the bleeding by magic, but beyond that she was unable to help him. It was a tense hour we spent in that room waiting for the arrival of the doctor, during which Dr Verdemeister fed us sausage sandwiches and cups of strong, dark coffee. Clarkia and I ate gratefully, but Jaria was understandably without appetite. She spent the whole time sitting at her father's side, holding his hand and trying to keep him engaged in conversation, and would not be removed even when a ruffled Dr Narriott appeared and turned everyone else out.

The four of us—Gandlyn included—retreated to Dr Verdemeister's library then, which is where I am writing this letter. It is a big, comfortable room that stretches up for the height of many floors, with ladders leading up and down at intervals, though many of the shelves have been converted into nests for Dr Verdemeister's birds. When I look up I can see smooth, feathered heads with gleaming black eyes gazing down at me. One has to be careful of their droppings, but thankfully the place is well ventilated and so the smell is not too bad.

While we waited for Dr Narriott to finish with his patient, Dr Verdemeister finally asked for an explanation, which I gave her readily enough—leaving out the conversation I overheard between Gandlyn and Clarkia.

At my description of the wolves, Dr Verdemeister trained her gaze on me with supreme intensity. Her spectacles, which are very thick with dark rims, served to magnify the power of her eyes, which are surprisingly bright grey with flecks of blue.

"Auch," she said, nodding. "So you have seen the *woodwolves*. Strange that they should attack Erren Hortall—they are normally such shy creatures."

"What did you call them?" Clarkia said, sitting up straight in her seat—a borrowed tuffet from another room, as the library only had a pair of chairs.

"Woodwolves," said Dr Verdemeister. "Wolves of the old Riddlewood. You did not know of them? Fah, well, I suppose it isn't surprising. No one believed me when I said *I* had seen them; everyone I spoke to is convinced wolves are extinct in

Kyreland. But these wolves are not, though they are very rare. I see them more often now that Magician Deerling has gone. I think we are experiencing another *Zaubergezeitenändern.*"

"Another what?" asked Clarkia.

Dr Verdemeister blinked at her. "*Zaubergezeitenändern,*" she said. "You do not have a word for it in Kyrish. It is when there are two or more magical forces, and one is superior, and there is a *shift.* One force recedes and another comes rushing in to take its place, like the tides. *Zaubergezeitenändern.*" She shrugged.

"You'll have to explain that a little more in-depth," said Clarkia. "How does this apply to the moor? I thought the moor had its own magic."

"The Riddlemoor has its own magic, yes," said the doctor, nodding her shaggy head. "But it is like a canvas. A blank field. Other magics run across it. Two biggest magics, as far as I can tell, are the woodwolves and the Deerlings. Deerlings, they come from the elk, from the deer that used to live in the forest. Woodwolves are same. Now, this was so long ago there is very little evidence left, but I think it likely that the woodwolves hunted the Deerlings. For a long time it was woodwolf magic that ruled. Then the forest gets chopped down, the Deerlings move out of the wood and live with humans. Their magic grows stronger, and they drive the woodwolves out of Kyreland."

"And now the woodwolves return . . ." Gandlyn said, heavily. "And it appears they have not forgotten their old enemy."

"Not enemy, not necessarily," said Dr Verdemeister, shaking her head. "Just two opposing forces." She brought her knobby, veined hands together. "When they balance each other out, there is no harm. No violence. It is only when they struggle"— she pushed her hands against each other, causing the tendons in her wrists to stand out—"and contest each other"—she rammed her hands together—"then there is trouble. There is pain. There is conflict." She nodded at the door which led to her study, where Dr Narriott and the Hortalls were.

Clarkia was silent at this, tugging on a loose lock of hair and chewing on the end of it.

"Doctor," said Gandlyn. "I regret that I have not held conference with you sooner."

Dr Verdemeister made a sound like *"Pschaw,"* and waved a hand at him. "I am no magician. I just observe. And listen. Anyone can do that."

Her eyes lingered on me then, as if recognizing me in some way, but only for a moment. Then there was a knock at the door and Jaria put her head in. Her face was pale and tearstained, but she seemed to have her emotions well in hand.

"Dr Narriott has finished," she announced. "He wishes to speak with you." She nodded to Clarkia. "But I am to say that father cannot be moved tonight. Perhaps tomorrow, if he is stronger then."

It was at that point that I began crafting this letter. I have been writing steadily for the better part of four hours now, and it appears we are all imposing on Dr Verdemeister for the night—all save Gandlyn and Kierel, who departed to take Dr Narriott home again.

All I have to add now is that the threat of the wolves is very real: Hortall is expected to make a full recovery, but he won't be able to speak for some time. I am worried about Clarkia, for she does not seem at all discouraged from continuing her exploration of the moor. But I am, Felpz. I am afraid. I am afraid for her, and for the safety of everyone living on the moor. For if Dr Verdemeister is correct in her observations, and the Deerlings have been the ones ruling the magic of the moor for the better part of recorded history, what upheaval is coming, should the tides of magic turn?

I will seal this now, in the hopes that it will reach you before the morning. Please respond as quickly as you can,

Corianne

Deerling Hall, July 26, '26
Dear Felpz,

I know you received my last letter, for Dr Verdemeister assures me the raven that took it delivered it directly into your hands. I can only assume something of even greater import has taken your attention, but I want you to know that the whole moor has erupted at the news of Hortall's misfortune. The Connallys are organizing a wolf hunt, of all things, to track down and kill the beasts responsible. Since Gandlyn has refused to have any part in it, they are petitioning Clarkia to lead them—and she, poor girl, cannot refuse when it was her own servant who was attacked. (Hortall is still recovering, by the way, and growing stronger by the hour.) If she goes, I am going with her—though I can barely walk after all the riding I did yesterday.

I hope this finds you well, and that whatever business has you tied down in Redling will be concluded soon, so that you may join me here; you are sorely missed.

Sincerely,

Corianne

P.S. There was another sighting of the wolves—the first time by anyone other than ourselves or Dr Verdemeister. Tida Hammin said she saw a large black wolf trotting along the road from Greenwitch last night. It has only served to fan the flames of the locals, who are showing a disturbing enthusiasm at the prospect of a hunt.

Chapter 5:
The Wolf Hunt

Continued letters from Corianne Birch to Bouragner Felpz, July 23–26

Deerling Hall, July 29, '26
Dear Felpz,

Your last letter was so vague I cannot tell what you do or do not want me to tell you, so I've decided to put everything down here. It may take a while, for as you will see, the events of the wolf hunt took a turn that no one could have anticipated. Only now, a full day after the events, am I able to put them to paper.

We rallied at Mothwitch Farm early in the morning, and I was surprised at the number of people that turned out. In addition to the older Connallys, there was also a large delegation from Merrybriar, though Mrs Mills-Hardy announced she was staying behind with Hawthorn Belledge—Darby Connally's wife. Dr Narriott was there as well, on a stunning white gelding, no less, along with a pair of fierce young women from Greenwitch who represented the southern chapter of the Aldonican Hunting Club. They had brought with them a small pack of

lean, long-limbed dogs with keen, narrow faces and shaggy, silver coats.

"Hyberian wolfhounds," Tida Hammin told me with barely
concealed excitement. "We were lucky to have them. This isn't
a fox hunt, after all."

Yes, Tida Hammin was there too. It surprised me less than
you might think, for the hunt had become the talk of the moor,
and I doubted Hammin would miss it. What did surprise me
was that she came on a smart, dapple-grey draft mare, which she
rode with evident expertise—though the horse was so wide it almost looked as though Hammin were sitting astride a table. She
was accompanied by her own groundskeeper, a long-suffering
man with a dark face and grey hair, and he carried with him two
imposing rifles.

This was typical of the attendees, who had all brought
firearms of some sort. It served to drive home the message that,
for all the good-natured excitement that saturated the atmosphere, we were ultimately on a mission of death.

Clarkia watched the hunters assemble with a sour expression. We had spoken little since our return to Deerling Hall, but
I knew in her heart she was against the hunt, and also doubtful
about her ability to lead them across the moor.

"Jaria would have been a better choice," she had confided to
me over dinner the previous night.

Jaria, however, was bound to her father's side, anxiously
tending his every need. I could not blame her, even though the
senior Hortall was showing every sign of making a full recovery.

So it was Clarkia, sitting straight and tall astride Scarlatta,
who waited by the gate onto the moor for the rest of the hunters
to assemble.

There were fourteen of us in total: myself and Clarkia, Darby
Connally and his eldest daughter, Ani, Tida Hammin and her
groundskeeper, Dr Narriott and the two Aldonican hunters, Mr
Hardy-Mills and *his* groundskeeper, as well as his gamekeeper,
valet, and stable hand.

We rode out onto the moor a little after eight, with the sun
still low in the east but muted by the fog that had not yet lifted.
Clarkia, I could tell, was reluctant to actively look for the wolves,
and at first only led us past Raven's Landing, up Iron Hill, before

striking out for Lathecliff. We passed several clusters of pink and white and yellow flowers, but as Clarkia did not remark upon them, neither did I.

Although Clarkia could choose not to hunt the wolves, the dogs had gotten no such message, and when Lathecliff was looming high before us, one of them began to bay, and his mistress signaled that a wolf had been scented.

We changed direction after that, striking out to the west and riding deeper into the moor. Clarkia and I fell behind—I out of necessity as I did not trust myself to gallop, and Clarkia out of reluctance. Still, our horses being horses it was impossible to let the herd get out of our sight, and I kept Bangle at a brisk trot so he would not panic and try to gallop.

Then one of the hounds howled, a blood-curdling sound that echoed around the moor and made my hair stand on end. There was shouting from the front of the group, and I saw the dogs take off in a streak of silver, followed closely by the Aldonicans and Dr Narriott.

There was nothing for it but to gallop then, and I was only saved by the fact that Bangle, in addition to having the steadiest gait four legs can give, was also perfectly happy to follow wherever Scarlatta went, so I had no need to steer and only clung to his neck as we pounded away over the hills.

I lost track of where we went. The moor became a blur of grass and stones and cloudy sky, but I think we headed mostly northwest. I wasn't able to get a good look, however, until we—and thus Scarlatta and Bangle—came to a halt at the base of a steep tor with a rocky outcropping at its peak.

"Surely, I know this," I gasped, breathless, to Clarkia. "Were we not on the other side when we had our encounter?"

Clarkia gave me a hard look, nodded curtly, and pressed a finger to her lips.

"I saw him!" cried Hammin's groundskeeper from the thick of the group. "Saw his tail disappearing into those rocks!"

"Circle around then!" commanded Dr Narriott. "Cut off his path of escape before we send in the dogs!"

This was done, the dozen other riders spread out around the hill. Like that the wolf could not escape without passing in range of at least three rifles.

"If he comes *our* way," Clarkia hissed at me, a warning in her words.

"No fear," said I. "I've nothing to shoot with even if I did share their sentiment."

Which I did not, I realized. For although I recognized the wolf as a natural threat—and possibly an enemy of Clarkia—I also understood the importance of the animal, and knew that killing it would not help you lift the veil of mystery that hung over Riddlemoor.

It never came to that, however.

When the hounds were released they charged at the rocks, but before they ever reached them the wolf stepped out, like a lord emerging from his castle, and glared down at them.

Never have I seen such noble animals turned humble so quickly. The dogs fairly fell over backwards and crawled away from the wolf—which was the same dark wolf we had seen that fateful day.

It was not black, but a very dark, rich brown, with a warm tinge about its paws. It stood out sharply on the pale grass, and I saw how, though it stood and watched us alertly, its hackles were not raised. Even so, it gave out such a strong feeling of menace and power that we were all rendered immobile for a moment.

Dr Narriott was the first to regain his senses. Bringing his rifle to bear he sighted past the hounds and took aim at the wolf.

Clarkia cried out in protest. The gun fired.

The bang was eaten up by the shrieking of birds—*ravens*, I realized—that burst forth from the muzzle of the gun in place of a bullet. They flapped around Dr Narriott's head, their wings cutting at the air, before they flew off, dissolving into black smoke.

While the hunters sat in stunned silence, the dark wolf lifted its head and howled. It was not like the howl of the dogs, eerie and primal, but low and mournful—almost musical. It stirred in me a sudden desire for the chase, to catch that beautiful animal and discover its secrets.

It must have had the same effect on the others, for when the wolf turned and ran down the hill, slipping between Darby and Ani Connally (whose guns fired doves and sparrowhawks when they went off), all the hunters turned and followed. I was so caught up that I might have been swept along with them, had Clarkia not come forward and grabbed Bangle's bridle, at the same time pulling Scarlatta's head around to her shoulder to prevent her bolting.

"Stay," she commanded me. "That is not the wolf *I* am seeking." And she held us there until the other horses had disappeared over the next hill, the sound of their hoofbeats and the baying of the hounds eaten up by the fog.

"Were the birds your doing?" I asked, once our mounts had quieted enough that Clarkia could let go of my reins.

"I wish," she replied. "No, as far as I can tell it was the wolf who did that. Which puzzles me; he seems unlike the others we have encountered."

"You mean the brown ones?" I asked, seeking reassurance.

Clarkia nodded. "The ones who leave the flowers. The dark wolf leaves none. I believe he is from a different pack, you might say. Now, if we can get around this hill perhaps we can finish what we started two days ago."

So saying she led us up and over the hill, skirting around the rocks, and then down into the valley—which was indeed the same place where Hortall had been attacked. The ground was slightly disturbed, and there was a sprinkling of telltale flowers dotting the slope of the far hill.

Clarkia followed them, and I, seeing little choice, followed her. In this way we crested yet another hill and found ourselves looking down on a wide valley filled with odd stone pillars.

It was an eerie sight, Felpz. The vale was wide and green, with thick drifts of the flowers growing in its middle, where a hidden watercourse must have run. The pillars varied from five to twenty feet in height, and similarly in girth. Some were cracked, and lumps half covered with grass and flowers showed where fallen stones now lay. What gave me a chill, however, was when I realized the pillars were not obelisks or any naturally occurring formation: they were petrified *trees*. Oaks and beeches turned to dark grey stone, traced with pale green lines from the creeping vines that sprang from the flowery earth.

"Is this not the place you found earlier?" I asked Clarkia, who had ridden down amongst the stone forest, coming close to what had been a slender birch and leaning over to sniff it.

"No," she replied, her voice distant and distracted. "No, this is very different."

I followed at a respectful distance, unwilling to ride in among the strange trees—though because Bangle wished to remain as close to Scarlatta as possible this was a constant struggle.

"I sense . . . two magics here," Clarkia said eventually, coming to join me on the edge of the wood. "There are the flowers, which are the calling cards of the wolves that attacked Hortall, but these trees . . . they are under a very different enchantment."

"Can you tell whose it is?" I asked.

Clarkia shook her head. "I will tell you what it reminds me of, though," she said, her face grim. "It reminds me of the echo I felt about that stone fruit that appeared so mysteriously back in Redling."

This sent a shiver down my spine, and I found myself looking around nervously.

I was not wrong to do so. There on the hill above us, gazing down out of the cloudy sky, was a wolf the color of honey with a white mane and chest. Around its feet, green buds were unfurling into pink and yellow flowers—some even running up its legs to tangle in its fur.

I gasped and pointed.

"Ah," said Clarkia, who did not seem to recognize the danger we were in. "*There* is my wolf." She stood up in her stirrups and called out to the animal. "Hello! Come down and talk, won't you? I've been told by some that you are by rights my enemy, but I don't know why this should be. I'd rather not fight, if it's all the same to you."

The wolf stared down at us, its lupine face unreadable at such a distance, but I did notice how its ears were raised and alert, and that its hackles were down. But while it showed no outward sign of aggression, neither did it acquiesce to Clarkia's request. Instead, after observing us for a few moments, it turned and trotted off along the hill, towards the low end of the valley. It left a little trail of flowers in its wake, though these quickly withered and disappeared back into the turf.

"Stay even with him," Clarkia said to me, and steered Scarlatta down the valley, so that she kept pace a little ways behind the wolf.

In this way we were led past the wood of stone trees and out into a wide, circular vale ringed with stone-topped hills. A cloud of birds rose from the nearest one at our approach, cawing and scraping at the sky with their wings. They reminded me of the birds that had erupted from the guns, and I wondered at the nature of the dark wolf—for its magic certainly took a different form than that of the tawny one.

Speaking of said wolf, I thought for a moment that it had abandoned us, but then I saw movement upon a nearby hill, and realized that it had somehow camouflaged itself among the grass and heather there. It was moving swiftly now, streaking off down the hill to the bottom of the vale—which was more akin to a caldera, really—where it was joined by two more wolves, both honey-backed with creamy manes and white bellies. Together they ran, and we followed at a trot—the landscape being open enough we had no fear of losing them now.

Coming further into the caldera, I saw that its center was filled with something dark that glimmered slightly in the uncertain sun. At first I assumed it was a lake of some sort, but as we drew nearer, and I heard the gentle rustling of leaves, I realized that the dark thing I saw was the many crowns of trees, forming a deep green canopy. They grew together thickly at the bottom of the caldera, rising out of a veritable sea of white and yellow and pink flowers. Crashing in among these, our horses left black tracks through their midst, throwing up their sweet scent into our nostrils and disturbing the bees which had been busy down among them. These rose in protest, and Clarkia at once brought Scarlatta down to a walk.

We had no need to rush anyway, for I could see the wolves waiting for us at the edge of the wood, clustered around the base of a spreading oak. There were easily a dozen of them now, and they watched us with an alert single-mindedness that made me feel uneasy.

I must have transmitted my trepidation to Bangle, for he balked fifty yards from the wood and refused to go any further. Scarlatta made it within thirty yards, but then she too stopped dead, and not even Clarkia could get her to move. Eventually she turned around and rode back to me.

"Corianne," she said, "you have followed me faithfully, and showed only support. I can't thank you enough, but I've got to ask for a favor now. Dismount, and hold Scarlatta while I go talk to them."

I agreed to this after a moment of inner turmoil, and though I was kicking myself the whole time as I watched Clarkia approach the wolves, wading through the sea of flowers, it turned out to be the right decision.

The wolves did not attack. They did not growl or even flatten their ears. They watched her expectantly, perhaps a little warily, but made no move until Clarkia stood barely a yard away, where she stopped and put her hands on her hips. Then the wolf who stood nearest the center stepped forward, ducking its head submissively, and let something dark and heavy fall from its mouth. I heard whatever it was land with a dull *thud,* and then the wolf was backing away once more, disappearing between the flanks of its packmates, and then the whole crowd was retreating into the wood.

"Won't you speak to me?" I heard Clarkia cry, moving as if to pursue them, but she stopped herself before she got to the trees, and looked down in consternation. She bent, and fishing among the thick flowers, came up holding something the size of an apple. She gazed at it, transfixed, and then up at the trees rising before her. She took a step back, and then another, and another, until, walking backwards, she nearly ran into Scarlatta's nose.

"Whatever is it?" I asked her, pushing the horses away. "Another stone fruit?"

"No fruit," said Clarkia, her voice a little hazy, and suddenly I noticed how pale she had gone, with a red blush standing out sharply on her drawn cheeks.

Without taking her eyes off the trees, she raised her hand limply, and offered its contents to me. I bundled the reins into one hand and plucked the strange object from her palm, noticing at once how heavy it was.

It was indeed another stone, but as Clarkia said, it was no fruit. It was the size of my fist, lumpish, with the veins and arteries still preserved where they ran along its outside. For it was perfectly shaped in the form of a human heart, and I nearly dropped it in shock when I recognized what it was.

"What on earth does this mean?" I exclaimed.

"I don't know," said Clarkia. "But I just realized where we are, Corianne. I should have known the moment I saw those trees, but I had to get practically under them before I smelled the magic. That's how complete the transformation was."

I looked up at the grove again, Clarkia's words stirring memories such that, when next she spoke, it only confirmed my suspicions.

"That is Deerling Grove," she whispered. "Those trees— some of them, at any rate—are what became of Morgrainne's family."

I looked again and felt a horrible chill spread through my limbs. Though the trees appeared normal enough, the thought that they had once been human was disturbing in the extreme. It brought back memories of an adventure from my childhood, the case of the Helk girl who had been turned into a tree. I wondered if those trees still contained human spines at their cores, as Helk's tree had.

Our morbid consideration of the scene was interrupted by a shout from the ridge of the caldera, and looking up I saw the horizon darkening with the shapes of riders, who poured over the edge and came galloping down to us.

It was the hunt, I saw soon enough. Dr Narriott and the Aldonicans riding close behind the wolfhounds, with the Connallys on their heels. There was no sign of the dark wolf, however, and while I looked around for it, Clarkia snatched the stone heart from my hand and thrust it into her pocket. She also took Scarlatta off my hands, for which I was grateful—the arrival of the other horses having excited the mare.

"What is the meaning of this?" Dr Narriott said as he rode up, reining his horse in hard.

"We made our own chase," Clarkia replied simply. "I take it your hunt was not successful?"

"Oh, he led us on a merry dance," said Darby Connally, red in the face and breathing hard. "If I didn't know better, I'd say he was toying with us. That's no ordinary wolf, in any case.

Powerful magic. A werewolf, I'd wager." He left off, looking expectantly at Clarkia.

The woman only turned her back so she could mount, and once settled again in the saddle, she shrugged. "I am not concerned with the dark wolf—it was not the one who attacked Hortall."

"But if a werewolf is running wild on the moor, it is your duty to . . . " the farmer trailed off under Clarkia's icy glare.

"To what, Mr Connally? Round him up like an animal? Do you fear for your animals, for your lives, because of this one person who has done you no harm?"

"I don't know what the werewolves are like where you come from," said Darby Connally, a little affronted. "But around here, any that take pleasure in using their abilities to harass the populace are not to be tolerated. As a magic being it falls on the magician in charge of—"

"Yes, yes, I see," said Clarkia, waving a hand to cut him off. "Very well, I will take care of your werewolf problem—though I don't see what it is. In the meantime, you'll be happy to know I've found out where the wolves that attacked Hortall live."

"Did you now?" said Dr Narriott, full of sharp interest.

Clarkia nodded. "They come from that wood, doctor, but I don't recommend you take your hunt into the trees. I don't need a local guide to tell me that's Deerling Grove there, and I for one have no desire to step under their branches."

Dr Narriott looked up at the trees in alarm, as if seeing them for the first time. The rest of the hunt, which had gathered around us, all turned to look.

"That can't be possible!" I heard Tida Hammin exclaim. "There was never more than a dozen trees—one for each of the Deerlings and their servants."

"Well, there are more now," said Clarkia with a shrug. "Maybe they are not all transformed humans—unless there has been a succession of missing persons of which I was not aware."

Silence greeted this, and the hunt regarded the wood with new respect. I took the opportunity to struggle back up onto Bangle, and sat there while the riders from Mothwitch and Merrybriar rode cautiously around the wood—led by Dr Narriott and the Aldonicans.

Nothing came of their exploration, however, and no more wolves were seen. Though it was barely midday, the fatigue of the chase had caught up with us all, and the pall cast by those gloomy trees was enough to take the fire out of even Darby Connally's belly. The hunt ended ignobly by turning for home, Clarkia managing to lead us back to the main road with minimal trouble. This pleased her, but she was the only one in remotely good spirits when we returned to the solid yard of Mothwitch, and thence dispersed to make our separate ways home.

I was fairly bursting with curiosity by this time, yearning to discuss the stone heart with Clarkia, but we were corralled by Tida Hammin, who contrived to ride with us right to the gates of Deerling Hall, pestering us with questions the whole way.

Clarkia, to her credit, answered with good nature and told a fairly honest account of our adventure—minus the gift of a stone heart, which I thought was prudent. Hammin did think it odd that the wolves simply disappeared into the wood without doing anything, and wondered about this aloud and at length, with a hopeful inflection at the ends of her sentences, as if encouraging Clarkia to fill in with her own speculation. This Clarkia steadfastly refused to do, and though I feared Hammin would pursue us all the way to our dinner table, she was put off by the presence of Kierel at the gates of Deerling Hall, and bade us a mercifully brief good-bye before riding off into the afternoon.

All Clarkia's good cheer vanished at the sight of the giant eagle, however, to be replaced by a jittery, nervous energy. She lingered outside the hall until Roke had taken charge of both horses, and stayed close by my side as we entered.

We found Gandlyn in the library, where he practically threw aside the book he had been reading to pass the time, leapt to his feet, and then stood there, awkwardly, uncertain what to do next.

"You heard of our adventures?" Clarkia said, throwing herself into a chair and putting her feet up on the nearest table. I winced at seeing her muddy boots so close to fine old books, and carefully pushed them out of harm's way before taking a seat myself.

"Dr Verdemeister sent a raven to say you had found Deerling Grove," Gandlyn said, his voice hard as a bed of granite. "I did not know ... I could not imagine ... " he trailed off, like a man in a wood who has lost the path. He looked around himself, then back up at Clarkia, and with more feeling than I had yet seen him express, said: "What did you *find?*"

Clarkia rolled her head over the back of the chair to give me a look. I confess I was stumped for a moment, but then I made the decision to trust Gandlyn—I hope it was the right one—and I nodded encouragingly at her.

Clarkia then related to Gandlyn everything that had transpired that day, right down to her discovery of the stone heart. The wizard listened gravely to the whole story, never interrupting, with his fingers knitted together and his brow a mess of concerned wrinkles.

I tell you, Felpz, though they both have a strange way of showing it, I think there is a strong mutual attraction between these two. Make of that what you will.

"This . . . stone heart," Gandlyn said, once Clarkia had finished. "May I see it?"

Clarkia hesitated, but only for a moment, before passing the object in question over.

Gandlyn received it with his characteristic gravity, and spent some time inspecting it; holding it up to the light, turning it round in his hands, and tracing the veins with his fingertips.

"This is a human's heart," he said, dully.

"Can you be sure?" asked Clarkia. "I thought the size was about right, but I've never seen a human heart before."

"I have," Gandlyn said blankly. "This is the heart of a mature woman, who had at some point in the past suffered a considerable amount of stress."

"You sound very sure of yourself," I remarked.

"I have studied human anatomy to some extent," came the curt reply as the wizard returned the stone heart to Clarkia's waiting hands. "I find that practical knowledge enhances thaumatic acumen."

I let this be, since Clarkia seemed eager, now she had a confidante with magical knowledge, to pour out her theories regarding the heart.

"I make it out to be the same enchantment as what affected that fruit I found in Redling," she said, taking her foot off the table and leaning forward. "What puzzles me is it doesn't feel like the magic of the wolves—even though they are the ones who seem to be behind these . . . gifts."

"I confess," said Gandlyn heavily, putting his head in his hands, "that I have never set eyes on these wolves, and so I have no basis with which to corroborate your comparison. I can say with some certainty that it is the same magic affecting this heart as that fruit, though this feels stronger, in a way. As if the fruit were but practice, and this was the end goal."

"Are we not overlooking a rather important point?" I put in, unable to be left out. When I had the two mages' attention, I went on: "If this was once a real heart, as the fruit in Redling had been a real fruit, then there must be a dead body to go with it. One cannot live with a stone heart, let alone a stone heart that is *missing*."

They looked at me blankly, and I could have shaken them.

"Gandlyn, did you not say that Morgrainne Deerling's body was *missing* its heart?" I said. "And this, you say, is an old woman's heart, and I think it safe to say poor Morgrainne did suffer a great deal of stress during her long life."

They stared at me, Felpz, as if I had gone mad. Then they stared at each other, and then down at the stone heart, still resting in Clarkia's hand.

"Oh *gods!*" the woman cried, letting it drop and roll across the floor as she recoiled. Gandlyn let out a stream of Delpheonian that sounded like a curse, then put the back of his hand against his mouth.

I pushed myself out of my chair and went over to pick it up, placing it heavily on the table between us. "Morgrainne's family was turned to wood," I said, looking to Gandlyn for confirmation. When the man nodded, I continued. "This is not. You both agree the magic affecting it is different from the wolves—who seem to be aligned with Deerling Grove, at least. Therefore, I put it to you that there is *another* source of wizardry upon this moor, distinct from the wood or the wolves or anyone in this room."

"Oh," said Clarkia, suddenly seeing the picture. "The dark wolf."

"The dark wolf?" Gandlyn said.

"The wolf we saw when Hortall was attacked, the one with the raven," Clarkia explained. "We saw him again today; he led the hunt on a diversion and disappeared without a sign. And he turned all their gunshots into birds."

"Do you think he is a rival?" I asked. "Perhaps the wood wolves are trying to warn you of him."

"It seems like," said Clarkia, twining a strand of hair absently through her fingers and chewing on the end. "And I promised Connally I'd take care of him for them. Blast."

Gandlyn gave an odd sort of shiver. "If he is a mage capable of besting Morgrainne Deerling," he began, and then stopped. Clarkia was looking at him with a hard, pointed expression, one that clearly made Gandlyn reconsider his next words. "I can only offer whatever assistance you may require," he finished, settling back into his chair as if awaiting judgement.

Clarkia found this agreeable, however, and the two spent the remainder of the evening discussing stratagems for finding and capturing the dark wolf. Gandlyn, I noticed, was quite deferential to Clarkia, only disagreeing when the latter put forward a truly reckless idea.

I left them to it so I could go eat supper, resigning myself to another day spent chasing Clarkia across the moor—now in pursuit of a dangerous mage. How I wished you were present, Felpz, how I wished.

What came to pass, however, was not what I had planned. It turned out two days of hard riding was more than my body could handle, and I woke the next morning with my muscles all aflame and my joints stiff as rusted steel. I had a headache and could barely rise from my bed.

"Never mind," said Clarkia, when she came to visit me. "Mrs Wreath will look after you. And don't worry about me. Gandlyn and I are going on foot, and will remain together at all times."

This only served to increase my worries—though not for the reasons you might expect. But I consoled myself with the knowledge that Clarkia clearly knew herself, and in any case Gandlyn had shown himself to be a reliable ally thus far.

So I have spent this day recuperating, and trying not to tear my hair out with worry. Writing this letter has taken most of the day, and now I hear voices in the courtyard. Gods willing the couple has returned safely; I will tell you shortly.

Yes, they are back, with nothing to show for a day spent searching the moor. I will leave this report here, then, and close with yet another request for you to come to Riddlemoor. I have done my best, but even you must admit I would be no match for a malevolent magician.

Sincerely yours,

Corianne

Chapter 6:
What I Found On the Moor

NOW I MUST LEAVE BEHIND the crutch of my old letters and move on to events which were not recorded as such at the time. However, as they are fairly burned into my memory, it has not been difficult to put them to paper after the fact.

First I feel I should add, since he is only mentioned in passing in the previous chapter, that Hortall recovered swiftly under the care of his daughter, and by the second day after the hunt was up and about again, pottering around the gardens and fretting over the orchard. His wound was still wrapped in bandages, and he carried his arm in a sling, but he was otherwise as fit as a fiddle. I came upon him in the orchard the day after Clarkia and Gandlyn's fruitless search, and he detained me for the better part of two hours, asking about the hunt and what we had found. I found him a pleasant man, if a rather hard one—the springy sinew of his daughter having manifested in him as something like horn or carved bone. Smooth and pleasing to the touch, but firm and ungiving if pressed. His salt-and-pepper hair was cut in a neat fringe all around his head, and he kept his beard impeccably trimmed. Hard little eyes like black stones peered out at me from a face as brown and considerably more weathered than Clarkia's, and he was so persistent in his questions that I would have become annoyed—except that I felt he was entitled to his curiosity.

He was disappointed to learn that no wolves had been shot, and though he said nothing against Clarkia, I could tell he was not pleased by her conduct. Which was only understandable, I

supposed. I assured him Clarkia had only the moor's best interests at heart, to which he grudgingly agreed.

But then he said something that gave me pause.

"Good old Lady Morgrainne had only the moor's best interests at heart," he told me, his voice grumbling like a barrel full of
gravel. "An' look what happened to her. It don't do to treat with
those wolves. It don't *do*. They're the enemy of all Deerlings—
even those what don't keep the old name. But our Clarkia's still
a *deer*, and that makes her prey."

Questions blossomed in my head like fireworks at this. *Was
Morgrainne in contact with the wolves? Did Hortall believe the stories
that implied that the Deerlings came from actual deer? Did he know who
the wolves were?* Unfortunately at this point we were interrupted
by Roke, who came around the corner and quite impertinently
told me he had a message from Tida Hammin.

"Whatever does she want with me?" I asked, annoyed.

"Strictly speaking, she doesn't want you," he said frankly, but
with an apologetic nod. "It's Clarkia she wants, but as the mistress has gone out I thought you ought to take it—being that
she mentions she'd like to see you as well."

"See *me*," I began, and then registered the earlier part of the
man's sentence. "Clarkia's gone out *again*?" I asked in alarm.

Behind me, Hortall made ominously disapproving noises.

"Yes, ma'am," said Roke, momentarily humbled by my out-
burst. "Just after you went outside, actually. Said not to tell
you," he added, going a little red.

I rolled my eyes. Clearly the young woman was beyond my
control, and I resigned myself to handling what affairs were
within my grasp.

"Let me see the note," I said, extending my hand to Roke.

"No note," replied the man, standing up a little straighter.
"Just a message. Mrs Hammin says she'd be pleased for Miss
Clarkia to join her picnic on Iron Hill, and if Mrs Birch would
come along then all the better."

I hesitated. But, I reasoned I was getting nothing done here,
and if I visited with Tida Hammin, there was a chance I might
learn things from her rather than the other way around. So I
nodded.

"I'll saddle Bangle for you then, shall I?" Roke asked.

I shuddered at the thought of more riding, and waved him away. "No, no I shall walk," I told him. I paid my leave to Hortall, and went inside to fetch an extra shawl and an umbrella—for the clouds were low and ominously potent.

The road was wet but not mucky when I set out on that fateful day, the grass of the moor wet and silvered from earlier rain. The wind, though damp, was not chill, and I soon warmed from the walking. It felt good to move my legs after so much time in the saddle, and soon my joints were feeling better. So it was that, despite the gloomy weather and my lingering worry over Clarkia, I was actually in a pleasant mood by the time I reached Iron Hill.

Which mood turned sour all over again when I arrived at the top of the long climb, where I could look down over Raven's Landing, and found it deserted. No sign of a single person, let alone a picnic. For a moment I was hurt and confused. I wondered if Tida Hammin had by some means divined my dislike of her, and had called me out here as a prank.

Then there was movement behind one of the granite outcroppings that dotted the summit, and a flap of blue cloth was the only warning I had before the woman herself stepped into view and hailed me.

She appeared somehow smaller and more unhappy than I remembered her. Gone was the expansive goodwill and inquiring gaze. Now her mouth was drawn tight, and her eyes were cast aside, avoiding mine.

"Mrs Hammin," I said, keeping my tone carefully neutral—for I guessed now she had an ulterior motive for calling me out here. What that could be filled my bones with nervous excitement, but I calmed myself with the knowledge that, should her motives be malevolent, at least Clarkia was safe away—and besides, if she did mean the woman harm, why include me in the invitation?

Then she began to speak, and all my misgivings evaporated— to be replaced by a very different breed of excitement.

"Mrs Birch," said Hammin, her voice as tight and nervous as her face. "You must forgive the misleading nature of my message—I thought a picnic might fool the servants into thinking this was another one of my innocent gossip-gathering missions—and I had to be careful not to raise suspicion."

"I'm sorry?" I said, a little unbalanced by her words. "I confess this is not what I expected, but you have cast me out to sea with your talk of suspicious servants. What on earth do you wish to speak of, that our meeting might raise suspicions?"

"Is Miss Aldeer with you?" Hammin asked, peering around me.

"Alas," I said with a shrug, "she took to the moor while my back was turned. So it is only I."

Tida Hammin rolled her lower lip into her mouth and bit down on it. She glanced about to either side, toying with the long hems of her sleeves and rocking back and forth on her feet. Then she gave her shoulders a little shake, and seemed to come to a decision.

"You'll have to do, then," she said. "You have the ear of that Magician Felpz, anyway, so I think you're a better one to speak to about this."

"About *what?*" I asked. It was an effort not to add "—*you maddening woman.*"

"About the murder of Magician Deerling," said Tida Hammin, blinking her eyes very wide. "Yes, the *murder* of Morgrainne Deerling. And the return of the woodwolves."

We gazed at each other, each in a different kind of shock; Hammin seemed amazed that she had said those words aloud, while I was simply amazed, period.

"Follow me," the woman said, beckoning. "We should not remain still while speaking of this."

Together we walked down the far side of Iron Hill, in the direction of Lathecliff, but at the bottom Hammin struck off across the heather, following a path that was little more than an animal track. I was growing annoyed by this point, but my curiosity compelled me to follow close behind, and soon I was rewarded when Hammin began to speak once more.

"I feel I owe you an apology, Mrs Birch," she said, with surprising contriteness, once we were well away from Iron Hill. "I have made rather a pest of myself ever since you arrived. Some of it was general inquisitiveness, but I was further motivated by my own suspicions. I may be a gossip by nature, but I do try to control the impulse. Lately, however, the things I have been hearing have driven me to pry even more than usual."

"What such things could these be?" I asked, with what I thought was commendable patience.

"It started with a rumor I got from Kinner—my gardener—who heard from Dr Narriott's assistant that Morgrainne Deerling's heart was not missing, as Gandlyn was told, but that it had been *turned to stone.*"

I stopped in my tracks at this, staring at Tida Hammin's back—which had also halted, and now slowly turned as the woman looked around at me. Her face was white and her voice deathly serious as she went on.

"I had no proof at the time, but I set myself to finding out everything I could about the Deerlings, in an effort to untangle the mystery of Morgrainne's death. For it was all too similar to the strange affliction that had caused the demise of the rest of her family."

With an effort I managed to swallow my heart—which had jumped to my throat at Tida Hammin's revelation—and managed to choke out the words: "But her family was turned to wood—into trees . . . "

Tida Hammin nodded curtly, as if she had already considered this. "I did not say it was identical; only that it was *similar.* In any case, it raised my suspicions, and caused me to research, and in doing so I discovered many things about Morgrainne that seem to have been forgotten.

"Did you know she not only accepted the presence of the wolves on the moor, but was actively trying to forge an alliance with them? I got that out of Hewlith after four hours in the kitchen with him. He let it drop quite by accident, and I felt bad for having teased it out of him, but you must admit it casts a whole new light upon the situation."

It did indeed, I realized upon reflection. Considering what Dr Verdemeister had told me of the Deerling's history, and the mutual animosity between them and the wolves. That, and the fact that the wolves appeared to be aligned with the forces that had turned Morgrainne's family into trees.

I pointed this out to Tida Hammin, who nodded understandingly.

"Exactly," she said, with a sharp gleam in her eye. It made her look altogether more interesting and formidable than the bumbling, superficial gossip I had taken her to be at first, and belatedly I began to realize what a huge misjudgment I had made. "I was equally disbelieving at first, but it only stoked my determination to get to the bottom of it. I am ashamed to say I contrived to get a peek at her personal journals, on the pretense of visiting Mrs Wreath. Oh, do not tell her I did so—for I don't believe she noticed at the time and I am deathly afraid of what she would do if she knew. We don't call her Mrs Wrath at Hovergate for nothing."

"Of course," I said, still dazed by this cascade of information.

"Thank you," Tida Hammin went on, marching briskly over the moor. "I cannot recall her words exactly—I was reading very fast, you understand—but the gist seemed to be that she thought the wolves were important to the health of the moor's magic. There was no mention at all of her family—it was as though she had forgotten them."

"That tallies with what I heard as well," I managed to say. "Gandlyn told us she seemed to forget what had become of her family after they turned into trees."

"Yes, that was the impression everyone got," Tida Hammin sighed. "But I thought . . . well, I thought she *must* remember, deep inside, and that surely she was bent on finding a cure for them. But unless that was covered in a different part of her journal—which is possible, I grant you—it seems the public's impression, for once, was correct."

"But you said she was murdered," I prompted, my voice quiet and hollow. I kept thinking of the stone heart, and the stone fruit before that, that the wolves had presented Clarkia. If it was Morgrainne's heart—I shuddered to think—then where had they gotten it? And where had they gotten the stone fruit, for that matter?

"*Yes,*" said Tida Hammin, pausing so I could come up next to her. "And the reason I called you out here so urgently is . . . I think I know who killed her."

All around us the moor was very quiet. Even the wind had slacked off, and the air hung, heavy and expectant, between us. I was suddenly conscious of how very isolated we were, and how little I knew of Tida Hammin, and what other unexplored depths that bluff countenance concealed.

But she continued to look concerned, and now she was twisting her hands together so roughly I worried she would do her fingers an injury.

"I only received this information this morning," she said. "Otherwise you can be sure I would have spoken to you earlier. But did you know that on the night of the twenty-seventh Dr Narriott's office was broken into? Well, it was—and he did not alert the authorities, nor did he tell anyone—save his valet, who had to come and help clean up the mess. But the valet mentioned it in passing to the butcher's delivery boy, who is a particular friend of my cook's own daughter, and she told her mother, who in turn let it drop in conversation with Kinner, who, knowing my interest in the matter, told me."

I blinked. "I fail to see how this has any relation to . . . " I began, but she cut me off.

"The twenty-seventh was the night before the hunt," she explained, a little breathlessly. "Where Dr Narriott was *so* exercised in finding and killing those wolves. Now, I *know* the wolves gave Miss Aldeer *something,* but I don't know what. But I *do* know that it was Dr Narriott who performed the autopsy on Morgrainne, and it is his word alone that her heart was missing. And Kinner told me that Beldin told him that her daughter—anyway, that he had heard that Dr Narriott woudn't tell his valet what had been stolen, but only looked in one place—his safe box, which had been pried open—and seemed most distressed at what he found there. Or *didn't* find, more likely. And I thought . . . well, you can probably guess what I thought."

"That Dr Narriott killed Morgrainne Deerling by turning her heart to stone, took it out of her during the autopsy so his crime would not be discovered, and kept it hidden in his office," I recited, numbly.

"*Yes,*" said Tida Hammin, with such intensity that her voice came out in a breathy hiss. "My *guess* is that it was the heart that was stolen. And what I wanted to ask you and Clarkia, straight out, is if *that* was what the wolves gave her during the hunt."

We had continued to walk, and now were come to a gentle dell between two green hills. A soft breeze blew down between them, lifting a little of the heavy potency of the air, but it did nothing to soothe my nerves. Now I was conflicted all over again, torn between taking Tida Hammin into my confidence and thereby possibly gaining an ally, or continuing to be loyal to Clarkia and keeping what cards I had flat against my chest.

The choice was taken out of my hands, however, when I looked up to see a flash of black wings cutting through the sky, and a raven dove down out of the clouds. It slipped between us, coasted up to the top of the nearest hill, and came to rest on the shoulders of the huge, shaggy dark wolf that had just appeared over the crest.

My heart, so carefully tamped down, leapt into my throat again. A wild fluttering, like a trapped bird, took its place, and only distantly did I feel Tida Hammin clutch my arm.

The wolf did not move, only looked down at us with a curious tilt to its head. The raven began to preen. Though they made an ominous pair, I could not help but feel that they were no threat to us. I remembered how it had been the tawny wolves who had attacked Hortall—not the shaggy dark one. Indeed, it had gone out of its way to lead the hunt astray without harming any of its members. In light of this revelation regarding Dr Narriot I considered it unlikely that the dark wolf was the third party whose magic had turned the fruit and heart to stone. Certainly it was not behaving as one who wished Clarkia harm. So it followed it likely meant us no harm either. And it struck me what a fortunate meeting this was, since it gave me the chance to do what Clarkia had been trying to do for days: speak to the dark wolf.

So I took a step off the path, toward the hill, and made a sort of curtsy. Tida Hammin, who had let go of me, remained on the path, and made a small sound of protest.

"I do not believe he is our enemy," I said, hoping against hope that this was true. Then I raised my voice and addressed the wolf himself.

"I know that you are a very magical creature," I began. "As such, I expect you understand what I am saying perfectly. Well, I am Corianne Birch, a friend of Clarkia Aldeer, and if she were here she would have a lot of questions for you. As she is not, I can only ask, if you are able, please tell me who you are and what you are doing here. If you are a foe, what do you have against Clarkia? And if you are a friend, why do you hide yourself out here?"

The wolf did not answer, but stood for a moment longer before disappearing behind the hill.

It was monumentally frustrating, and in my annoyance I strode further off the path and was halfway up the hill in pursuit before I realized what I was doing.

I heard Tida Hammin shout a warning after me, but I did not heed it. I could only think of the coy wolf and his raven attendant, and how disappointed Clarkia would be if I told her I had seen him only to lose him again.

When I reached the top of the hill, for a moment I despaired. The moor stretched out around me in a vast, grey-green sea, and there was no sign of the wolf.

There was, however, a little ways off, a familiar outcropping of jagged black rocks at the top of a steep tor. This I recognized as the selfsame hill where the hunt had encountered the dark wolf—as well as the place from which the wolf emerged when Hortall was being attacked.

It mattered not that each time I had seen that hill it had been in a different place upon the moor. I knew it for what it was immediately, and set off towards it, determined to reach my destination no matter what tricks the Riddlemoor played.

But it seemed for once the moor was pleased to let me go where I wanted, and I reached the hill sooner than I expected. Circling its base, I discovered that, apart from the hill itself and the rocks crowning it, nothing was the same as the last time I had been there. Gone was the dell on the far side with the trail, and the terrain surrounding it was harder and more rock-strewn than the soft turf which the hunt had ridden over.

I climbed the hill slowly, in zigzags, and kept an eye out for ravens. None came, however, and when I reached the top there was still no sign of the wolf.

It was the first time I had been in among the rocks, and upon closer examination I found that these were no natural jumble, but a carefully constructed cairn with a hollow interior. Peering inside, I saw that the earth within was well trampled, with a bed of dried leaves in one corner. There was also a little cooking pot, a lamp stand, and a small leather satchel. Everything was arranged with such precision that it was difficult to imagine a wild animal living within, and I found Clarkia's theory that the dark wolf was in fact a werewolf-magician more and more likely.

I considered prying into the contents of the satchel, but reasoned that if we were to make an ally of the wolf that would not be the best course of action. So I removed myself and went to sit on a handy rock just outside the cairn's entrance.

From there I was pleasantly surprised to find I could see a great deal of the moor laid out below me, from the ridges of Lathecliff to the swell of Iron Hill, down to the spires of Raven's Landing, and even a dark smudge that must have been Deerling Hall. Far away to the south crept a tendril of bright green and blue with a patch of reddish brown where Greenwitch lay. Though I could not see the path on which I had left Tida Hammin, I could make out the main road where it turned towards Hovergate, and was pleased to see how close it looked. Indeed, almost everything I could see appeared closer than it should have been, and I wondered about this place, and how often the wolf must have sat here and kept watch over the moor.

No sooner had I thought this than I saw the wolf approaching from below. I did not see where he came from, only that suddenly he was there, standing in plain sight below me. He was so carefully obvious I could only guess he wished to be seen, and I was more than happy to watch him as he slowly made his way up the hill.

You might think me foolish, or brave to the point of stupidity, to let such a powerful animal approach me. You might imagine that I grew more and more nervous with each step the wolf took towards me. You might imagine how my pulse quickened, how my palms sweated, and how my breath came faster and faster.

All this is perfectly reasonable to expect, of course, but in actual fact I felt nothing of the kind. Instead, as the wolf approached, I felt first a sense of extreme excitement, then of relief, and finally, one of pure, fond annoyance.

For as the animal drew closer I saw for the first time his color—which had so far been masked by him appearing against the pale sky—was not, as had been claimed by others, *black,* but neither was it the dark brown that I had seen earlier. It was too warm for brown, and shimmered in the cloudy light with a faint iridescence. And when the light caught it just so, the color of the fibers was not brown or even red, but a bright, rich *purple.* And when the wolf drew closer still, I looked into its piercing, light brown eyes, and found I knew them.

I stood up from my seat, put my hands on my hips, and advanced down the hill towards the wolf.

"My friend," I said as I went. "I do not know whether to shake or embrace you, but I *am* glad you are here, though you might have *told* me what you were about instead of having me write all those letters!"

The wolf twitched an ear and put his head to one side. He looked more apologetic than I had ever seen my friend, and I relished the sight, even though I continued to glare at him.

Then the animal gave a sort of shrug and stood up. As he did so his body hastily rearranged itself, first to accommodate standing on two legs, and then growing clothes instead of fur—which retreated from the hands and face—until it was my friend Bouragner Felpz who stood there, in the blackest purple coat I had ever seen, smoothing down his dark brown hair, which had retained a little of the wolf's shaggy mane.

"Oh Corianne," he said, his voice rather rough, but with all the familiar tones. "And here I had hoped to surprise you. All in good spirits, of course. But you must admit it was an admirable disguise?"

"Completely inscrutable," I assured him, my relief and joy at seeing my friend finally overpowering any fragments of bitter frustration. "I'd never have guessed if I hadn't seen your color—you cannot keep the purple off you, it seems, even when you are a wolf."

Felpz looked so chagrined at this that I almost felt sorry for him, but he shrugged a moment later and grinned at me.

"It would not have lasted much longer," he said ruefully. "Now that Clarkia is so persistently searching for me, I have been working as hard to avoid her as I have been to untangle her case."

"Why is it so important that she not know you are here?" I asked.

Felpz's face darkened a little. "It is not so much that I wish *her* not to know, but that I wish certain persons to believe I am elsewhere, when I am really here. Certain persons who, should *Clarkia* know, would certainly find it out from her."

Immediately my mind went to Tida Hammin, whom I had left so recklessly upon the path, and I shivered to think of all I had told her.

"Oh Felpz," I said. "If you mean that Hammin woman, then I am afraid . . . "

"What, Hammin?" said Felpz, blinking in surprise. "No, no, she is as trustworthy as a rock and contains as much malice as a glass of fresh milk. No, *Hammin* is not the one to worry about, nor is Gandlyn, I am happy to say—you were quite right about him."

"Then Dr Narriott—" I began, but Felpz raised a hand to quiet me. This turned into a sweeping gesture, and a moment later a large black raven descended from the sky to alight on his outstretched wrist.

"Yes," said Felpz to the bird, and I regretfully fell silent as the two conversed. It was a curious thing, for I could only hear Felpz's side of the conversation, which went thus:

"I am able to go on by myself from there—yes, *thank you,* you have been most helpful. Give my regards to the good doctor, and tell her I may yet have need of that tower room she so generously offered. Yes, speed well."

So saying he flung the raven up into the sky, where it flapped off into the misty grey clouds.

"Only one person knew of my presence here," he told me guiltily as we began to descend the tor together. "I had to confide in Dr Verdemeister in order to receive the supplies I needed to conduct my investigation. She makes a singularly good intelligence agent, Corianne, and I hope the two of you have a chance to become better acquainted. But now I think I've done all I can as a wolf, and it is time I made my presence known. An event is coming that, unless handled with the utmost delicacy, could spell disaster for not only our client, but the entire moor."

"I don't suppose you'd be inclined to explain that in greater detail?" I asked dryly.

"In good time," said Felpz, shooting me an apologetic smile. "Now, however, I think we should go collect Mrs Hammin—for there are things I wish to discuss with her. And I will need you back at Deerling Hall well before Clarkia returns—never mind the walk, I will take you there myself."

"Why is it so important that I be present there?" I asked, hurrying to keep up as Felpz extended his stride over the coarse heather.

"Because I believe the greatest danger to her lies, not on the moor, but within her own hall," Felpz said gravely. "From the first, it always has. Even Morgrainne did not see it."

"What on earth do you mean, Felpz?" I asked, beginning to grow impatient. "If you know who the villain is, then tell me!"

"Because I do not yet *know* who they are," Felpz hissed. "I have my suspicions, of course, and they have been wrong before. But I can tell you you have nothing to fear from the cook, Hewlith—in fact go to him first for aid if I or Gandlyn be not available—ah, here is Mrs Hammin."

What Tida Hammin thought when she saw us come walking down the hill, practically arm in arm, I cannot imagine. But I saw her eyes widen and her lower jaw drop, and she barely managed to compose herself before we came within speaking distance.

"My dear . . . Mrs Birch," she began, stumbling over her words. "I did not think you would return so . . . my goodness. Is this your magician, then? Is this Felpz?"

"I am, madam," said Felpz, touching his forelock in place of his missing hat. "Though you can take my presence as a piece of fresh information best left to cure a while, if you please. I find myself in need of information, and past experience tells me you are the one to ask."

To her credit, Tida Hammin took my friend's sudden appearance in stride, and schooled her face into a concerned and interested expression.

"Whatever I know is at your disposal, I am sure," she said, bobbing a short curtsy. "But may I ask where it is you came from? Last I saw, Corianne was chasing a *wolf*."

"Just so," said Felpz, smiling broadly at her, and let that matter rest there. Taking her gently by the arm he began leading us down the path towards Hovergate, talking as he went.

"I wish to speak to you about the doings of one Dr Narriott," he said. "Has he had any unusual visitors of late? For, as you seem to suspect, it *was* a stone heart which Clarkia found on the hunt—one which I have not, alas, had a chance to examine—and I believe it came from his office."

Tida Hammin was taken aback by this, but she recovered herself quickly. "Mr Felpz," she said. "I don't know why you should think I would know such things."

"Really, Mrs Hammin, you do not give yourself enough credit," said Felpz in good humor. "I happen to know that you keep a close eye on all your neighbors—not just the ones on the moor. For as you seemed bent on observing all around you, I put myself to observing *you*. And I know how often that modest little telescope you keep in your study is turned towards Greenwitch, and how industriously you write in that little notebook of yours. So tell me, who has Dr Narriott been seeing, up to and after his unfortunate break-in?"

Tida Hammin puffed up a little at this, partly out of indignation at Felpz's frank tone, but also with pride.

"I cannot give you such detailed information off the top of my head," she told him. "I will have to consult my notes. Which, if you will accompany me to Hovergate, I shall have no reservations about handing over to you."

"Then onwards to Hovergate," said Felpz, reaching for my hand. "Take hold, Corianne, we are losing time dawdling here, and time may be of the essence."

Still in a daze of surprise and confusion, I took my friend's hand, and at once felt the moor begin to slide past us. It was a disconcerting feeling, as I was already put off balance by Felpz's appearance and his ominous words concerning the staff of Deerling Hall, and his traveling magic only served to compound my feeling of things flying out of my control.

But I could only walk on to Hovergate, towards what I hoped were answers and enlightenment.

Chapter 7:
Tida Hammin Shows What She Can Do

MRS HAMMIN—OR TIDA, as I have come to call her—was a whirlwind of productivity when properly motivated; she bustled us into Hovergate, past a surprised footman, and into her private study. This was a room I had not yet seen, and it struck me as singularly homely and functional; no superfluous decorations or fancy artifacts, packed with bookcases and housing a large writing desk at one end, as well as a generous bay window with a little telescope set up in front of it.

"You'll be happy to know it can't see Deerling Hall from here," Tida assured me when she caught me looking.

"I almost wish that it did," mused Felpz, coming to stand beside the telescope in its stand. "It might have helped our case immensely. But in the meantime; you mentioned notes concerning Dr Narriott?"

Tida nodded, went to a shelf that was stuffed full of papers and journals, and pulled out two little books under the N heading.

"Most of the first and half of the second," she said, handing them over to Felpz. "But if you're looking for evidence of how he killed Morgrainne Deerling, I'm afraid you won't find it in there."

"I do not think it was Dr Narriott who killed Magician Deerling," Felpz muttered as he began to page through the books. "Though he most certainly had a hand in it. He would have had contact with someone at the Hall, however . . . "

"Why are you so certain it *was* someone at Deerling Hall?" I asked, putting my hands on my hips.

Felpz raised his eyes and gazed off over our heads for a moment.

"The stone fruit," he said at length. "The one that was left for Clarkia in Redling by the woodwolves. The magic affecting it is the same as that which afflicts the once-human members of Deerling Grove."

This came as a shock to me. "Deerling Grove?" I repeated. "But those people were turned to *trees,* not stone."

"Yes, our villain changed their method in the intervening years," said Felpz, going back to the book. "It remains that their magic is practically identical; I have spent enough time amid the grove, comparing it to the stone fruit, to be sure. It only remains for me to verify that the heart and the fruit are under the same spell, but if Clarkia is certain then that is only a formality."

"You mentioned the woodwolves," Tida said cautiously, apparently realizing how dangerous it was to distract Felpz when he was about other business. "Do you mean the tawny beasts like the one that attacked Hortall?"

Felpz snapped the book shut and looked up sharply, but he did not seem aggrieved. Rather, he stared at Tida very hard, as if the key to the puzzle was hidden in her face.

"Yes," he said after a moment. "The woodwolves. I know they left the stone fruit for Clarkia because they told me so. They told me much, in their way, once I proved I was no threat to them. They are possibly the main reason—aside from the natural deterrence of Corianne's presence—why Clarkia has not yet come to harm. They are singularly invested in keeping her safe, which is odd." He bent back down over the book.

"Why is that?" I asked, impertinent in my curiosity.

"Because the Deerlings were the enemy of the Wood," said Felpz quietly, his eyes skimming over the pages. "The great Riddlewood that once covered this moor. As I told you, it was destroyed with the coming of humans, chopped down for fire and timber and the building of ships. It was out of this holocaust that the Deerling family rose to power. *Trees and wolves*, did I not tell you so at the beginning? It all comes back to the trees and their wolves. The wolves *are* the forest, you see. Or at least the physical manifestation of the magic guarding it. Why do you think they are called *woodwolves*?"

"I am sorry," I said. "You mean to say that a magical wood has guardian spirits in the form of *wolves*? It does not seem to fit."

"It makes more sense when you consider the circle of life," Felpz said, still with his nose in his book. "A tree cannot run, cannot move. It is literally rooted to the spot. Deer and other herbivores feed off trees and plants. Is it not so surprising, then, that when the wood creates magical guardians, they would take the form of an animal that, in turn, hunts and kills the *deer*? Remember that plants do not feed only off of sunlight, but off the earth and the decayed carcasses of animals. What better ally to a tree then, than a wolf?"

"And *that* is why the Deerlings ought to be the enemy of the woodwolves!" Tida said, the pride in her deduction lighting her face aglow. "Not because wolves hunt deer, but because the deer ate the wood!"

"Yes," said Felpz, distractedly putting aside the one notebook and opening the other. "Which is why I am still puzzled at the woodwolves dedication to Clarkia Aldeer. It suggests that they have some need of her—that, or Morgrainne Deerling's attempts at forging an alliance with them were more successful than anyone thought."

"But if you say Dr Narriott was not the one who killed Morgrainne, then who *did*?" Tida said, exasperated.

"Someone as clever and subtle as they are powerful," said Felpz, but slowly, as if his mind were elsewhere. He closed the notebook and put it aside. "I believe it is time I went to Deerling Hall," he said at length. "Yes, and then I will bother Gandlyn to raise poor Morgrainne's body—I really must be sure it is *her* heart before we continue—and Clarkia will want the confirmation as well."

"Did my notes not help at all then?" Tida asked diffidently.

"Oh no, they were *extremely* helpful," said Felpz with a glimmer in his eye. "It was of great interest to me that Jaria Hortall was the one to deliver Morgrainne's body to his practice. Is that not out of the ordinary?"

Tida shrugged. "It is less remarkable here than in Redling, I suppose," she said. "Why?"

"Nothing," said Felpz. "A piece to a puzzle that is still full of holes, that is all. Well, Corianne and I shall leave you here then, and make our own way home. I daresay Clarkia will be returning to the Hall soon, and I dislike the thought of her in it alone."

My friend was silent on our return journey. As if in response to his mood the weather turned heavy and dark, and as we came into view of Deerling Hall it finally made good on its promise and let loose a torrent of rain. Yet not a drop of it touched either Felpz or I, but slid off an invisible bubble that appeared above our heads, and we arrived at the front gate perfectly dry.

Our approach had not gone unnoticed, and the entire staff poured out into the front courtyard just as they had when Clarkia arrived. Only now they stared more openly, and with surprise and excitement rather than respect.

Felpz regarded them with hardly concealed amusement, his gaze drifting over Hewlith del Garren, Mrs Wreath and Roke, but lingering on Jaria until the young woman began to color, at which point they passed on to her father, who met his gaze with fortitude.

"How very . . . *kind* of you to greet me," said Felpz after a time, causing the younger members of the staff to shuffle their feet uneasily.

"Excuse me for speaking out of line," said Hewlith, perfectly unapologetic. "But to be honest we have been expecting you to put in an appearance ever since Mrs Birch arrived. And, well, it was of particular interest to us that it was really you."

I saw Felpz's eyes crinkle in amusement at this.

"Not that I wish to disappoint," he said, stepping past the line of servants. "But I am only dropping in for the evening. Please, as you were," and he strode into the Hall, leaving me to hurry in after.

"Interesting," he murmured to me once we were ensconced in the library. "You did not mention that the staff of Deerling Hall were all talented magic users."

"I did not know that," I admitted, shamefully.

"Well some of them do conceal it," Felpz said with a shrug. "Hortall, for one, is much more than he appears—as is his daughter."

We were speaking in whispers, wary of being overheard, so we were made immediately aware when Clarkia returned, sweeping into the hall like a whirlwind and fairly bursting the doors of the library off their hinges as she came storming in.

"It was *you!*" she cried, pointing an accusing finger at Felpz. She was flushed red all over her brown face, and her curly dark hair was wound in tight, dripping ringlets. A small pool of water was slowly forming around her feet.

"*You* were the black wolf!" she repeated, spitting water.

Felpz leaned back in the chair he had been sitting in, folding his hands over his stomach and smiling beatifically up at Clarkia.

"How long have you known?" he asked.

"Since I came back here and felt traces of your magic all over my front courtyard," said Clarkia. "As a wolf or man you leave a distinct scent, and I finally recognized it. Oh, Gandlyn will be beside himself—you had him *completely* fooled."

Felpz smiled briefly, but then his expression clouded over again.

"Is Gandlyn *here?*" he asked.

"No, but he may be summoned easily enough," Clarkia declared. "Shall I?"

"Please do," said Felpz. "The more allies we have the better. Especially considering what must be done tonight."

"Tonight?" said Clarkia, shedding a fresh shower of water as she jerked in surprise. "Where are we going?"

"Nowhere," said Felpz, placidly. "Only out beyond your orchard. I intend to exhume Morgrainne's body, so that we may put this mystery to rest for good."

Clarkia stared at him, flabbergasted, for almost a minute. She had begun to steam faintly, her clothes drying as we spoke, and the puddle around her feet shrinking. Outside I heard the patter of rain against the stone walls of the house, and knew the summer storm that had been building all day was truly upon us.

"You'd better explain," she said. "You must have information I don't."

Felpz did explain, briefly and precisely, what he had already told Tida Hammin and myself. When he finished, Clarkia's expression was pinched and unhappy, but she promptly got out the stone heart—which she had been keeping on her person for safety—and Felpz produced the stone fruit—and the two magicians bent themselves over the library table where the objects had been laid, deep in conference, until Gandlyn arrived.

It must have been some sort of magic signal that alerted him, for I know Clarkia did not order anyone to take him a message, but there he appeared, his green suit damp and his auburn hair dark from the rain.

"Gandlyn," said Felpz briskly. "Come here and see what you make of this."

Not questioning Felpz's presence, Gandlyn came over and regarded the stone objects. His fine, sharp nose wrinkled, and he straightened up almost immediately.

"They are undoubtably from the same magic," he said grimly. "Can there be any doubt that this is Morgrainne's heart?"

"What doubt there is I hope to have dispelled before the morning," said Felpz. "I know it is a course of action that may be distasteful to you, but I think it is time we had a look at Morgrainne's body ourselves, and see if there is yet something she can tell us."

Clarkia pursed her lips at this, but not in a way that implied she disagreed. She was nodding even as she said: "There is a little cemetery specifically for Deerlings, just beyond the orchards. Morgrainne is buried there, along with her ancestors."

"Yes," said Felpz with a grim smile. "I know."

Clarkia gritted her teeth and nodded. "No point putting it off then," she said and made for the door.

What came next was unpleasant in all ways imaginable. The morbid nature of our mission aside, the rain had not let up one iota, and despite Felpz's best efforts to keep the water off of our backs he could not prevent it soaking the tools, the ground, or the cloth we spread out to receive the coffin. Mercifully all three mages showed no compunction about using their powers to speed the digging process, nor were they hesitant to levitate the coffin out of the grave. But we were all wet, tired, and hungry by the time we got it out, and then Felpz declared we would not take the body indoors, but examine it there and then.

"I would not wish to disturb your staff unnecessarily," he told Clarkia, but I knew the real reason was that he did not wish any of the staff to know what we were about.

The family graveyard was a quiet and somber place even on the best of days. Lying beyond the orchard, it was bordered on one side by lines of apricot trees, and on the other by a low stone wall, which was all that separated it from the great green moor. I had avoided the place as long as I had been at the hall, and now—in the dark and the wet—I wished even more fervently to be elsewhere.

Felpz made a light—a cool, bluish one that cast us all in deathly white—while Clarkia pried the lid off the coffin and Gandlyn redirected the rainfall.

Taking my eyes off what lay within, I couldn't help but notice how, while Felpz had created an invisible barrier that the rain splashed off, Gandlyn caused it to part smoothly and fall on either side of us. Two magicians, I pondered, with two ways of achieving the same end. I wondered if Clarkia would employ yet a third method for keeping us dry, but was distracted from my musings when Felpz leaned over and began unwrapping the shroud that covered the body within the coffin.

Do my readers really want to know what the body of Morgrainne Deerling looked like, six weeks dead and in the ghoulish pale light of Felpz's magic? I think not. Some writers may delight in describing such things in all their gruesome glory, but this one does not. Readers who enjoy the morbidity of a good corpse will have to content themselves with knowing that it was whitish grey with blotches of black liquid where the remaining blood had pooled, and the eyes were mercifully closed.

Morgrainne Deerling had been buried in a fine black dress, and this Felpz peeled off her shoulders with extreme care, leaving as much of it in place as possible. But there in the center of her chest, clear for all of us to see, were three long, black stitches. These he plucked out with equal care, and reached to begin peeling back the flaps of scored skin.

It was at this point that I became very interested in the behavior of the rain, and so I cannot tell you exactly what he found. But I can recount the words which were exchanged between the three mages.

"Dr Narriott reported that her heart was *missing,* and that all the veins and arteries had grown together!" Clarkia said, sounding more annoyed than anything. "Looks more like someone *ripped* the thing out of her."

"Then that settles it," said Gandlyn.

"Not quite," said Felpz.

"Oh *gods* what are you *doing?*" Clarkia groaned, and I looked down just in time to see Felpz reach into the corpse's chest cavity.

Almost as soon as Clarkia spoke, however, Felpz removed his hand and brought his fingers up, closer to the light, where he rubbed them together. A fine greyish powder fell from between them.

"Stone dust," he said. "I do not think we need check and see if the stone heart fits. Clearly that is the real reason she is dead."

"I do not see how you cannot be certain that Dr Narriott is the villain here," said Gandlyn, folding his arms and looking away. I was reminded, then, that he alone of our number had actually known Morgrainne Deerling in life, and felt a stab of pity for the young man.

"Oh, I am fairly certain he is *a* villain," said Felpz placidly. "But not the only one present in this narrative. But first, let us put Morgrainne back to rest—I am sure she will forgive us if we keep her heart a little longer, as it will prove invaluable in catching her killer."

This was done, and though I could only stand by uselessly and watch the three mages work, it was with relief that I saw the body made decent again, the coffin closed, and the whole thing lowered into the ground once more. Felpz carefully worked over the grave, bringing the dirt back in and regrowing the light layer of grass that had sprung up across it. In this way we left Morgrainne's gravesite identical to how we found it, and removed ourselves from the graveyard in a somber line.

We did not go back to the house, but stopped in the gazebo where Felpz changed his light from cold and blue to bright and warm, and had Clarkia produce the little stone fruit and stone heart, which he held under the glow for us to see.

They rested, one in each of his palms, dark grey and speckled white, the one a perfect match of the other.

"This spell," Felpz said, weighing the objects against one another, "is like nothing I have seen before. It takes the premise of transfiguration almost to its extreme conclusion. It is as though these objects *never were* a beating heart or a ripe fruit, but were grown this way—as stone. It strikes me as the kind of magic one does not idly do. Whoever did this must have taken years to develop the skills, and in those years, they would have needed to *practice.*" He held up the stone fruit, and I could see clearly now that it was an apricot—a large one, similar to the variety grown by Jaria in the orchard in which we now stood. I felt my heart sink.

"One fruit or even one hundred would not have been enough," said Felpz quietly. "And what do you do with stone objects which, by their very nature, you *cannot* turn back?"

Clarkia frowned and worried at her lower lip. Gandlyn said: "I can think of several options, but which one the magician took I cannot say."

"If the others are nearby then we might not need to waste time hunting all over this wretched garden," Clarkia pointed out. "Give me the stones, both of them, and I will see if I can't sniff them out."

The objects were passed to her in due course, and she held them both—one in each hand—for a full minute, her eyes narrowed to slits and her nostrils flared. The two men stood respectfully back, Gandlyn with his hands clasped contritely and Felpz with his arms folded.

Then, just when I was beginning to fidget, Clarkia gave a jerky little nod, as if she had surprised even herself, and said: "This way, I think ... "

We followed her back out into the rain and the wet night, and by the light of Felpz's persistent yellow orb, she guided us through the orchard until we reached a small gardener's shed that stood not far from the house. Here was where Jaria kept her tools, I knew, and her father's also. I had seen them both go in and out of it, and I felt my nerves sing with anticipation as Clarkia opened the door.

She had to do so by magic, for it had been locked. A distant frown crossed her face, and then with an angry jerk of her chin the door flew open, revealing a dark, dirty interior hung with shovels and spades and rakes. Pots were stacked in one corner, and crates used to harvest fruit when the season was ripe, filled half the little room.

Clarkia stepped boldly inside (Felpz's light followed her), and looked around keenly. Then she made a dart for a couple of crates that were covered by a moldy canvas, and tore it away.

Something dark and heavy and hard tumbled from the folds of the cloth and clattered on the floor. By the yellow light within I first saw the neat stacks of stone fruit in their trays, and later, once Clarkia moved aside, the dozen more that had spilled onto the earthy floor. They were dark in the yellow light, and some were more misshapen than others, but they were all recognizably the same as the two specimens that Clarkia held.

"Good *gods,*" said the woman, her Beranican twang coming out heavily in her surprise.

"Now *that* is final," I heard Felpz say as Clarkia looked up to stare at us in surprise and horror.

Gandlyn sucked in a sharp breath, and then whispered, "The Hortalls," and took off in a mad dash for the house.

"Hold on!" Clarkia shouted after him, pushing her way out of the little shed. "You're not confronting them without me!"

"I would advise against—" Felpz began, and then stopped, for Clarkia had shouldered her way past him and was now on Gandlyn's heels. He sighed, smoothed down his coat and hair, and then offered his arm to me. "Come, Corianne, I believe we can let the younger folk lead the way in this case," he said, as we began to walk, sedately, back to the hall.

The reason for Felpz's relaxed attitude became clear when we arrived to find the house in an uproar and the Hortalls nowhere to be found. In the time it had taken us to walk back, Clarkia had raised the entire staff—some of whom had already gone to bed—and now a small army was pounding up and down stairs, looking in bedrooms, and in some cases quite literally overturning furniture in search of Hortall and his daughter.

Felpz stood in the midst of this chaos like a calm, dark purple pillar, while around him orders and questions were shouted in such close proximity that they rendered each other unintelligible. Every now and then he would take out his pocket watch and check the hands, then put it back and continue waiting, patiently.

Thus it was to us that the wet, tired, and confused stableboy who wandered into the hall around one in the morning came rather than to Clarkia or Mrs Wreath, and Felpz took the damp letter he carried while I fetched him a blanket and snuck into the kitchen to brew some hot tea.

When at last it became clear that the Hortalls were long gone—along with Bangle and Snowflake—and the panic had died down a little, both Clarkia and Gandlyn came and found us in the hall, where we stood over the recuperating messenger.

"Hello, what's this about?" the young woman asked, coming up and putting her hands on her hips.

Felpz, who had been shamelessly reading the letter the boy had brought, carefully refolded it and handed it over to Clarkia.

"I am remiss," said he. "I could have saved us all a great deal of trouble—including our present difficulty—if I had simply left things to Tida Hammin."

Frowning, Clarkia inspected the letter, then read it aloud.

"To Corianne, Clarkia, or Magician Felpz, be warned: I am certain your villain is Erren Hortall, and he has every reason to do Clarkia an injury—and by extent, any who come to her defense. Advise you apprehend him with the greatest of care. See me for further details if necessary. I will await a reply. *T. H.*"

Clarkia looked up at us, her eyes wide, as Gandlyn took the letter from her lax hand and read it for himself.

"*Hammin?*" he said, the confusion evident in his tone.

"A valuable ally," Felpz said with a small smile. "She also had suspicions regarding Morgrainne's death, and conducted her own private investigation. One which, I have to say, has proved to be even more effective than my own—though perhaps more trying on her neighbors."

"She says she will wait for a reply," Clarkia said, peering over Gandlyn's elbow. "I don't think I could sleep a wink tonight. Don't suppose she's up for a visit?"

"I think Tida Hammin would be more than happy to speak to you in person," said Felpz.

"Don't you think it dangerous?" I asked. "To travel across the moor, with the Hortalls at large?"

"I believe we have less to fear from the Hortalls tonight than at any other time," my friend replied. "For tonight they are on the run. Tonight their thoughts are of flight and for their own safety. No, tonight of all times is the night we must move. I suppose the police should also be notified . . . " he said, a trifle regretfully.

"I have already alerted Sergeant Lecreux of the Greenwitch constabulary," Gandlyn said. "She is their chief of magical affairs," he explained at Felpz's sharp look. "I made her aware of my misgivings at the first, and warned her something like this might happen."

"Well, let us hope she has a level head and a competent arm," said Felpz with a shrug. "Now, I suggest you all collect what articles you might want in the coming twenty-four hours, and then we should be able to reach Hovergate before the sun rises."

Indeed the sun had not risen by the time we trudged through the entrance to Hovergate, but there was a lightening to the sky upon the eastern horizon, though with the heavy clouds the rest of the sky was as dark as ever.

Tida was awake and met us with commendable cheer and energy—though her unkempt hair and wrinkled clothes suggested she had had as unsettled a night as we. As such I felt entirely unrepentant appearing as I did, with my skirts all wet and muddy and my own shameful hair stuffed under a bonnet, and in company of the equally dirty Clarkia and Gandlyn. Felpz, of course, had contrived to look as trim and clean as if he had just stepped out of his dressing room, though there were lines under his eyes and a heaviness about the set of his head that spoke of our night's escapade.

"Come in, come *in*," Tida insisted, ushering us into her warm and well-lit parlor. "I hope you'll forgive me, but I sent my staff to bed. No use them losing sleep over this as well. Come in, Wizard Gandlyn, this will be of interest to you also."

Tida's parlor, it appeared, had been turned into an extension of her study, with the addition of a half-eaten cake and a huge pot of tea. Crumbles and scribbles of notes cluttered the table, and cups and saucers were balanced on stacks of books.

"I have not been idle in your absence," Tida said, unnecessarily. "I had hoped my note would reach you in time, but as you have all come I can only assume that Hortall has taken flight? Well, he *would*."

"His daughter is with him too," Gandlyn said, grimly.

Tida frowned at that. "Jaria," she said, placing the woman at once. "Yes, that is to be expected. Unfortunate, though; I had hoped maybe she was not embroiled in her father's schemes. But what schemes they are, it only makes sense that he had an accomplice."

"You said in your note that he had every reason to harm me," Clarkia said, her forehead a mass of wrinkles. She looked so wild and fierce, in her disheveled state, that I thought Hortall must be either very brave, or not a little stupid, to mean her harm.

Tida nodded emphatically. "Magician Felpz thought it was someone at Deerling Hall who was responsible, and so I spent the remainder of yesterday going over the history of every member of your staff in an attempt to narrow it down. Did you know that Hewlith del Garren was involved in the Mairrith Student's Revolution as a young man? Fascinating—I should like to ask him about it—but that is not pertinent to these events. What *is* is what I discovered about Erren Hortall."

She paused in order to pull a long sheet of paper from the clutter. It looked to be a scroll, to which had been affixed various newspaper clippings, notes, and transcripts from books. Each entry was marked with a date and a place on a thick black line that ran the length of the paper. At the top of this was printed: HORTALL'S HISTORY AS NEAR AS I CAN MAKE IT in careful block capitals.

"It was no easy task," said Tida, the pride evident in her voice. "But once I found the right thread, well, look what was attached! The trick was figuring out where Hortall had come from, before he *was* Erren Hortall. Yes, that was an assumed name—which I had known ever since he came to Merrybriar—but I had not bothered to look further back. He was born Erren Derrel Ellan, to Ranish immigrants, not far from Greenwitch. Ellan being such a very Ranish name, I figured he changed it so as to make himself more employable to Kyrish masters. Now, however, I see he had a much more sinister motive.

"You see, Ellan is the Ranish word for *elk,* and the family of Ellan traces *their* lineage back to a *Kyrish* magician who married a Ranish witch and was cast out of his family for doing so. Further research shows that this event matched the disgraceful departure of one Roddard *Deerling* about three generations ago—of whom all that is said is that he made an unfavorable marriage and was thence disowned. Well, remember in those times the Rani had no nation of their own, and were relegated to traveling caravans, passing from country to country. It was commonly assumed he married a girl from one of these nomadic carts, but what became of him afterwards was a mystery—until I traced the Ellan name back to the unnamed Kyrish magician—whom I am *convinced* was the same Roddard Deerling. The Deerlings being so loathe to let go of their name, it's only fitting that he chose his adopted family's word for a kind of deer as his new one."

Tida said all this with a fire in her eyes, and I had to admit she had a right to her pride. Her rather outrageous claims were backed by carefully collected notes and references, which had all been pasted onto the timeline.

"So . . . Hortall is a distant Deerling," said Clarkia heavily.

"Only as distant as you, by my calculation," said Tida, raising a warning finger. "And *that* is where I believe this trouble started. For the Ellans were poor, and when the then Erren Ellan discovered he was descended from such a wealthy and powerful family, is it no wonder he would aspire to come into his inheritance?"

"Then why did he not simply knock on the front door and introduce himself?" Clarkia asked.

Felpz sighed heavily. "You must remember, his claim to Deerling blood had been disowned. Legally, he had no right to inherit—in fact, the name *Ellan* would have been more of a hindrance than a help."

"So he changed his name," said Tida. "And positioned himself as close to the seat of Deerling power as possible. Where, I can only assume, he has been crafting his scheme ever since that mysterious plague rendered the family line so weak. Imagine his frustration, then, when *you* showed up—a cousin as distant as himself, and pulled from the very ends of the earth—to take what he believed was rightfully his."

Clarkia, who had gone pale as she listened, pursed her lips. "But how *was* he to inherit, if that was his ultimate goal? Setting himself up as my groundskeeper doesn't sound like the best way to go about that."

"I can think of several avenues which he could have pursued from that position," Felpz said. "He might not have cared so much for the title, but for the power, and would have been happy to remain a humble servant so long as he held great influence over the sitting magician. Or he might have intended to supplant the Deerlings with his own lineage once he had successfully weeded them out. It interests me that you make no mention of Jaria's mother, Mrs Hammin. For she comes after the harrowing of the Deerlings, and so Hortall must have married at some point."

"Oh," said Tida, and looked a little chagrined. "That takes no digging, Mr Felpz. It's common knowledge among us moor people, but not widely talked about. There was some argument over whether they were actually married, you see; she was a brewer's daughter from Greenwitch, and barely sixteen when she ran off with Hortall. They were together for all of a year, during which time she got with child, and tragically died giving birth to Jaria. It was . . . well it was a very sad matter all around."

Felpz's face twisted into something unpleasant. "How convenient for Hortall," he muttered.

"Oh, Hortall was devastated, you can be sure," said Tida, but then reconsidered her words. "At least, he appeared so."

"Yes, I expect he did," said Felpz grimly, looking across at Clarkia. "This Jaria," he said. "I have not had to pleasure to meet her in person. What was your impression?"

Clarkia, still looking a little dazed, shrugged. "She's competent enough. Reliable, trusty as a rock, I thought. Then again, I would have said the same of Hortall if you'd have asked me last week."

Felpz turned down the corners of his mouth. "One can hope, I suppose, that Hortall kept her in the dark regarding his plots, but I wouldn't count on it—and if we meet them together, be prepared to face her as an enemy."

"You mean to confront Hortall," Gandlyn said. It was more a statement than a question.

"Not before I sleep on the matter," said Felpz, brightening. "And I am still waiting on one last ally. I also wish to interview Dr Narriott, before I pursue his master. But first, sleep, I think. If you don't mind, Mrs Hammin, I saw a soft-looking sofa on the way in here, and by your leave I will avail myself of it for the next two hours. I suggest the rest of you make similar arrangements."

I don't believe any of us got much sleep that morning, although Tida graciously offered up her own bedroom to Clarkia.

Gandlyn disappeared on Kierel at first light—I don't believe he slept at all—while Tida and I made use of her guest room.

By this point my sentiments for her had taken a one hundred and eighty degree turn, and I was now feeling downright ashamed of what I had written in my letters to Felpz. Seeking to alleviate at least some of the heavy weight that was pressing on me, I explained as much to her, and sincerely apologized if I had ever been gruff or rude.

"Oh," said Tida, from where she lay on the little cot borrowed from her housekeeper's room (she had insisted I take the bed). "I am quite sure I deserved it. I was being patently obnoxious— even if I had ample cause. I fear I become perfectly shameless when driven in such a way, and all I can do now is apologize for giving *you* such grief. Rest assured, if you ever need something sleuthed out and don't wish to make a harpy of yourself, please call on me; I will be delighted to do it for you."

I had to laugh at this. "Please," I said. "If you would do me the honor of claiming me as a friend that should be more than enough."

"That sounds like a marvelous idea," said Tida. "I think I shall. And now, as your friend, I shall give you some friendly advice: rest your eyes, and see if you can't manage a little sleep. It is what I intend to do."

I did as I was told, and though my body was still alive with nerves, and the creeping morning light was doing nothing to lift the ominous shadow that hung over my friends, I did feel somehow relieved, and against all expectations I fell into a deep and all-consuming slumber.

Chapter 8: *The Guardians of Riddlewood*

I WAS WOKEN BY A LOUD RAPPING at the door. Sitting up, a wave of confusion washed over me upon finding I was not in my own bed, nor in my borrowed one at Deerling Hall. Then I spotted the bundle of rugs and wisps of yellow hair that marked Tida Hammin's nest, and the events of the previous day and night came rushing back. I groped for my watch upon the bedside table and had to blink at it for several seconds before the hands came into focus.

It was nine o' clock on the thirty-first of July, and by my estimate I had been asleep for only two hours. A fine duration for a nap, but hardly enough to replace a lost night of sleep.

"What is it?" I asked, my voice thick, for the rapping had continued.

"Dr Narriott," came Felpz's voice through the door. "Now is our chance to interrogate him."

At the sound of the physician's name Tida Hammin fairly levitated out of bed and began pulling on her dress and shoes even before she had got her eyes properly opened.

"We will be down immediately," she said, sounding far more awake than she looked. "Do not leave without us, I beg!"

There was an amused silence from the other side of the door. "And Corianne?"

"Yes, Felpz, I am *coming*," I said, fumbling for my own clothes.

It was with a bitterness in my mouth and my heart, as well as aches in my joints and my head, that I followed Tida down to a rushed breakfast.

All of which dissipated when I saw the comfortably rumpled, weathered figure of Milky standing in the hall, holding his cap respectfully to his chest, and speaking in a low voice with Felpz. He looked up as soon as he heard our steps on the stairs, and gave me his brightest grin—all straight, white teeth, contrasted sharply by the ugly scars on his cheeks that gave even his friendliest smile a sinister twist.

"Told you we'd both get caught up in this, 'fore it were over," he said.

"My dear Milky," I said, coming down the stairs as fast as my aching head would allow. "How good it is to see you here! Has Felpz told you all?"

"All he's willing to say," said Milky, giving Felpz a cheeky look. "Sounds like a perfect ball gown you've got going here. Can see why you'd want all the help you could get."

"I thought it prudent to acquire further assistance," Felpz said. "Helpful as Mrs Hammin and Dr Verdemeister have been," he said, nodding to Tida. "Allow me to introduce Edhard Thorn, the best carpenter in Redling, if you ever have need of one, and a particular friend of mine."

Milky bowed and made his pleasantries with Tida, who first looked at him a little sharply, but then decided she liked what she saw. In the meantime Felpz took my elbow and led me through to the dining room, where Clarkia and Gandlyn had been engaged in an intimate conversation at the far end of the table—their half-eaten breakfast plates abandoned near the center.

"Fortify yourself," Felpz said, handing me an empty one and pointing me towards the sideboard. "Dr Narriott is currently in the custody of Sergeant Lecreux, who holds enough regard for Gandlyn to allow him to question her prisoner, but I understand they have a special investigator coming with the eleven o'clock train, so we must hurry."

Taking my friend's point, I poured myself coffee and took two bread rolls—one for myself, one for Tida—and went to find the woman and tell her of the situation.

We all took different routes to Greenwitch, there being no mode of transport suitable for our number. Clarkia rode with Gandlyn on Kierel, while Milky and I walked with the magical augmentation of Felpz. Tida took her own cart, saying she would hear what Dr Narriott had to say from us, and that she had her own business to attend to. This was well enough, for when we arrived at the police station in Greenwitch the sergeant on duty looked a little put out at our number.

"I can let the magicians in to see him," he said, sourly. "On account as Lecreux said you'd be along. But the other two must wait outside."

"No, Corianne must come," said Clarkia firmly, much to my surprise. "Your insights have always been so helpful," she explained to me while the sergeant grumbled loudly.

He did allow me into the tiny interview chamber, and I saw now why he had been so reluctant to let us all in. The room was meant to hold only two—the interviewer and the detainee—and with the four of us on the other side of the table there was a certain amount of squeezing to be done in order to get the door shut.

Dr Narriott looked much changed from the tidy, mature man I remembered from the wolf hunt. His hair was unkempt. There were dark circles beneath his eyes, and his clothes had obviously been slept in. He gazed at us blankly, his eyes traveling from Felpz, to Gandlyn, to Clarkia, to me. Then he shut his eyes and put his head in his hands.

"Whatever possessed me to meddle in the affairs of magicians," he murmured. "Damn and blast it to hell."

Felpz rolled his eyes.

"There shall be no blasting of any sort here today, I assure you," he said dryly. "What I wish for is information; if you are forthcoming I see no need to make this any more unpleasant than it already is."

Slowly Dr Narriott raised his head and stared at us.

"I cannot claim innocence by ignorance," he said. He sounded like a man whose spirit had been broken—or at least seriously wounded. "I knew what Hortall was planning. Knew it all along. But I never killed anyone, and I never wanted anyone to *be* killed."

Felpz raised an eyebrow and looked over at Gandlyn, who gave him a stony stare in reply.

"And yet," Felpz said. "A woman is dead. And you did nothing to prevent it—and you were involved in concealing the truth about her fate. Why?"

Felpz had a terrible way of asking questions that demanded answers. I felt the tug of the power behind his *"Why?"* even though it was not directed at me. To Dr Narriott it must have pulled like the tides, for his words came tumbling out of him after that.

"Hortall explained—he made it sound so reasonable, too—that it was all to do with the magic. The magic of the moor . . . it's *important* somehow. Important to the country. Morgrainne Deerling wasn't taking care of it properly. We look like a nice little town, don't we? Well, it is mostly a façade. Everything is slowly drying up—people moving away and fewer coming in. Hortall said that's to do with the magic going sour from lack of care. Said he needed help taking care of the moor. He is really a Deerling himself, did you know?"

"An offshoot," said Gandlyn, coldly.

"As distant as myself," Clarkia remarked.

"He is the most powerful mage I have ever known," said Dr Narriott, his bloodshot eyes gone wide. "The way he explained it, everything we did, we did for the betterment of the moor. Because *he* was the true heir to Deerling Hall. So I helped him as best I could: I gave him reports on Morgrainne Deerling, I told him of her worries, her cares, such as those she shared with me. Lady forgive me, I broke my vow of patient confidentiality . . . but when he came to me asking that I violate her body's dignity, even in death, I told him I would not. I did not *want* to, you understand. But he made it clear to me that, if it was discovered Morgrainne had died because her heart had turned to stone, suspicion would fall upon me. For I have, I am ashamed to say, dabbled in magic in the past. The events are too shameful— no I cannot recount them for you, do not make me—but Hortall had managed to learn of them. So I was forced to cooperate."

He spread his hands out beseechingly, and I could not help but feel a little pity for the man. Pity, but also disgust, that he had helped such a villain.

"When I conducted Morgrainne Deerling's autopsy, I did as he asked. I removed her stone heart and kept it safe, locked in my office. I falsified my report, but I could not lie outright. I had to say *something*. So I said the heart was missing—which was not a complete falsehood."

"Did you know it was the woodwolves who took it?" Clarkia asked. Her voice was hard and brittle, hot and dry like a desert before a thunderstorm.

"I guessed as much," Narriott said. "Hortall had explained how they were the enemies of the Deerlings, and responsible for the fate of Morgrainne's family."

Felpz pursed his lips at this, but said nothing. Instead, it was Gandlyn who pressed forward and spoke, his voice hard with restraint.

"You spoke of magic going sour," he said. "Remember also that I am responsible for the magic of this place, and I have felt nothing. Explain to me what Hortall told you."

"Oh," said Dr Narriott, gazing despairingly at the ceiling. "I could not say now. It was something about two opposing forces—the wild beasts and the deer—and the one contaminating the other. He said . . . wait, I remember! He said the magic of the deer—his people—was what kept the moor safe for humans. Without them it would be overrun by wolves and we would all become their prey. That is why . . . when he was attacked, I acted so swiftly . . . " the doctor trailed off, his eyes glazing over. Raising his shaking hands he covered his mouth and shuddered.

"Oh," he moaned through them. "Oh . . . what have I *done?* It is as though I was *enchanted.*"

"You most assuredly were," said Felpz, his voice carefully neutral. Turning to Gandlyn and Clarkia he went on, briskly. "I think we have learned all we can here. Unless you have outstanding questions, either of you?"

Clarkia and Gandlyn shook their heads, a little numbly, and we followed Felpz out of the interrogation room, leaving the broken old man still shuddering in his seat.

"Perhaps it is my foreign obtuseness," Clarkia said to me, while we stood outside the police station and waited for Felpz and Gandlyn to finish talking with Sergeant Lecreux. "But the magic of the moor does not strike me as being contaminated."

"You probably have a better nose for this than either of us," Milky said, reassuringly. "Though p'raps it seems normal to you since you've never known it otherwise."

I had repeated the interview for Milky's benefit, and now the three of us loitered on the steps together. Around us Greenwitch was bustling happily into its midday, the very picture of prosperity, and I wondered how deep the enchantment Hortall had woven over Dr Narriott had been.

Clarkia turned the corners of her mouth down in a way that was becoming familiar. She was still grimacing sourly, her hands plunged deep into the pockets of her coat, when the two other magicians appeared.

"What did he mean about the magic of the moor?" she said at once, making a little pouncing motion towards Felpz.

"Something that I have long suspected," Felpz said with a shrug. "Come, let us discuss this as we walk. I think it time we drafted a plan of action, and I do not wish to do that here."

"Did you ever wonder why Riddlemoor *remains* a moor?" he said, once we were out of Greenwitch and passing through the rolling, barren hills. It was an open, sunny day, verging on hot, and the grass was glimmering under the sun. It was beautiful as anything, but at the same time I was struck once again by its austerity—how naked the hills appeared.

"The climate is conducive to reforestation," Felpz went on, his long legs striding swiftly over the road. "To the north and in Cairdra, there is the New Forest, which sprang up almost immediately once people stopped chopping down trees. Why has it not spread here? Why are the only trees the ones that are guarded so carefully by the wolves?"

"You mean the Deerling Grove?" Clarkia asked.

"I mean the last remnant of the Riddlewood," said Felpz. "Which, to be fair, does house your distant cousins in their arboreal forms, but they were not the first trees to put down roots there. I had a good look at it when I was a wolf—though the other wolves mistrusted me, understandably, and so I did not get a chance to go *inside*—and there are trees within that are older than the moor. Yet they remain corralled there, restricted from spreading their seeds, and not for lack of trying by the birds and other creatures who venture inside for their fruits and nuts. I even tried planting a tree outside its borders, and commanding it to grow by magic. But I might as well have been commanding a stone."

He paused, and we all stopped, gathering around him on the road. Above us the blue sky had birthed thin wisps of white clouds that trailed across it like fish in an endless sea. The wind was blowing fitfully, tugging at our clothes and hair, and I could not help but notice that it seemed to be pushing us away from Greenwitch, in the direction of Deerling Hall. I said nothing, however, but waited patiently with the others until Felpz began to speak again.

"I do believe there is a conflict," Felpz said, and began to walk again, "between the magic of the wood—here represented by their wolves—and the magic of the deer—in the form of the Deerling magicians."

"You mean to say that the *Deerlings* have been keeping the wood at bay, all these years?" Gandlyn said, his voice grave.

"I mean to suggest," said Felpz, giving him an arch look, "that, in trying to maintain an ordered balance in the magic of the moor, they have in fact been rendering it inhospitable to its native inhabitants. Whether they meant to or not."

"But Morgrainne forged an alliance with them, or tried to," Clarkia pointed out.

"Yes," sighed Felpz. "And though I do not know what its exact terms were, I fancy it had something to do with removing the magic that is inhibiting the wood. Which would explain why Hortall struck out against Morgrainne as he did."

"What?" said Clarkia, alarmed and confused. "How?"

"It has to do with the nature of magic and how it relates to humans," Gandlyn said in his flat, grave way. "Magic is power, and magic of this sort, when it is entwined with a piece of land, gives an incredible amount of power to the person who wields it. The magic of the Deerlings was—is—not just in their natural talents, but in the power they receive from the land it governs. This is how Morgrainne explained it to me. Do you not feel it to be so?"

Clarkia chewed on her lower lip for a while, frowning at the road as it passed by under our feet. "I can't say I do," she admitted eventually. "It's a bit like getting on a new horse: its got all these hidden ticks and tricks that I don't know. Not saying we couldn't make a good team in the future, but now?" She laughed bitterly. "I do not think it trusts me."

"That is interesting," said Felpz. "I wonder if Hortall feels the same way. In any case, the way these things work is: the magic of the land feeds the magic of the individual. If you detach the land-magic from the land—to *raise* it, as we used to say—you would allow for other magics to flow in and take root. At the same time, however, you would also lose the stream of power that the land supplied you."

"Because your magic isn't in it anymore?" Clarkia guessed.

"*Your* magic, technically speaking," Felpz said. "But yes, that is the principle."

"So probably Morgrainne was trying to figure out a way to let the wood back in without completely losing her . . . what? Power over the moor?"

"That is what I think," said Felpz.

"And Hortall killed her . . . because he's a Deerling and her power should have been *his* power and oh! What an absolute *crappanape!*" Clarkia stomped her foot down on that last word, which I assumed to be a Beranican expression.

"Quite so," said Felpz, serenely.

"I wonder where he is hiding," Clarkia said darkly. She seemed about to say more, but just then Milky let out a warning shout and pointed ahead, to where Tida Hammin's cart had appeared on the horizon.

It was not only Tida the cart brought, but Roke as well, who stood up as they approached and leaned towards us as far as he could and began shouting.

His words were lost in a gust of wind and the rattle of the cart, and Tida pulled him back in by his belt as she reined her horse to a halt.

"Look alive, men," she cried. "While you have been holding court with Dr Narriott, our villain as not been idle. Yes, you may tell him, Roke," she allowed, as the young man fairly flung himself out of the cart.

"I cannot believe it. It was *Jaria*," he wailed. "Jaria came to the front door this morning, and I know I shouldn't have gone to see her—but it was *Jaria*, you understand?"

"What happened?" snapped Gandlyn, speaking for all of us.

It came out, between bursts of sobbing, that Jaria had delivered a letter, supposedly for Clarkia, and then left. Mrs Wreath had then taken it upon herself to open said letter—"Since we didn't trust Hortall not to send you something awful! And . . . well, it *was* something awful!"—and had to drop it immediately as her hand began to turn to stone. Within the hour it had fallen off, and if it hadn't been for Hewlith's quick work she might have bled to death. Darby Connally had come over from Mothwitch to help, but by that point Hewlith had begun to feel a stiffening in his fingers, so when Tida had shown up in her cart Roke had taken the chance to come looking for us.

"Are you affected?" Felpz asked immediately, and when the young man shook his head Felpz *tsked* and insisted on looking him over.

"Magic such as this is easier to *prevent* than it is to counter— ah, *here*," he said, and pressed two fingers sharply into Roke's shoulder. The man cried out, but mostly in surprise, and wrung his arm experimentally. "That should hold you," Felpz said. "And now, to the Hall—and quickly!"

Taking me by the hand, he grasped Clarkia's arm in his other, and began running down the road. I felt Milky grab my hand just in time, but Gandlyn must have summoned Kierel, for they passed us overhead not long after. Felpz's folding magic proved more efficient, however, and we were the first to arrive at Deerling Hall.

We were greeted by the sight of Darby Connally standing by the front doors arguing with Dr Verdemeister, who was wearing a spiky black dress that fluttered around her shoulders like feathers. She had her hands on her hips and was leaning forward to shout at the farmer when we arrived, at which she spun around and fairly launched herself at Felpz.

"The wolves, they are furious!" she began. "That man has attacked their wood—"

"In due time," said Felpz, putting her gently aside. "I was remiss—I did not think what danger the staff would be in. Please allow me to put this right."

Darby Connally narrowed his eyes at Felpz, but at a word from Clarkia he stood aside, and we tumbled into the hall behind Felpz.

Mrs Wreath was laid out on a sofa in the sitting room, the bandaged stump of her right arm propped up on bloodied pillows, while next to her sat Hewlith del Garren, very white in the face and holding his left hand gingerly in his lap.

"You first," said Felpz, pulling the older man to his feet and bending over his hand. Looking around, he spotted Gandlyn standing in the doorway, his auburn hair blown into a wild mane around his face. "See what you can do for her hand, friend," he said. "And I beg, hold nothing back, *enhaur!*"

Gandlyn pursed his lips at the honorific, but swept forward and knelt by Mrs Wreath's side. I heard him ask after the stone hand, and Darby Connally went to fetch it. Dr Verdemeister hovered nearby, pouring a torrent of Elgan into Felpz's ear.

I retreated to a corner, where I stood beside Milky and watched the proceedings unhappily. It appeared Jaria was indeed on her father's side, and I felt a sudden pang as I realized just how much danger Clarkia had been in that day on the moor.

And to think, we had been *relieved* to see Hortall then. Why, if the wolves had not come . . . I shuddered at the thought.

Darby Connally returned, and Gandlyn took Mrs Wreath's stone hand in his and glared at it.

"There is nothing I can do, not while he keeps feeding the spell's power," the *enhauron* said bitterly.

"I have managed to stop its spread," Felpz announced. "But it appears he is bent on forcing our hand. Dr Verdemeister tells me that the ravens have seen him at Deerling Grove—it seems we must confront him there."

He stood up and looked around. "I regret to say, but Clarkia must come with us . . . " he trailed off, looking around the room.

It was then I realized, with a lurch, that though the room was filled with people—Mrs Wreath upon the sofa, Hewlith sitting beside her, Felpz, Gandlyn, Connally, Dr Verdemeister, not to mention Milky and myself—Clarkia Aldeer was nowhere to be seen.

Felpz stood up, even as Gandlyn crumpled to the floor with a soft moan.

"Did anyone see where she went?" Felpz asked, his voice like a spike of ice.

I could only cover my mouth in horror as I realized what must have happened.

"I am so sorry, my friend," I whispered.

It was obvious to me that Clarkia, with her hot, decisive nature, had grown tired of trailing after the two magicians, and had taken matters into her own hands.

"She has gone," said Gandlyn, hollowly, from the floor. He frowned, and dragged a hand through his hair. "She has gone to the moor, but where I cannot say. She has been . . . shielded somehow."

"I can guess," said Felpz, and made an involuntary jerk, as if he wished to leap into motion but was holding himself still. He looked around the room, his face twisted in frustration.

Milky stepped forward and bobbed his head.

"I'll see things right here, vicar," he said. "You go catch that bastard."

Felpz nodded in relief and made for the door, followed by Gandlyn. I hesitated a moment, caught by a sense of some momentous choice, and not knowing which answer was right. Then I thought of Clarkia, and her strong, fiery heart, and the fate that had befallen her predecessor. The vision of a stone heart and a chest with an ugly wound swam into my mind, and the next moment I was sprinting out of the hall, calling to Felpz to wait for me.

Gandlyn was already astride Kierel, who was mantling her wings in the courtyard, when I arrived. He gave me a curt nod before they took off, the eagle's wingbeats clapping like thunder as they climbed into the sky.

"You wish to come, Corianne?" Felpz asked, sounding both worried and pleased.

"I cannot help but feel responsible for her," I admitted. "You have often said I am of help in times like this—let me help you now!"

Felpz gave me a small smile. "Then by all means," he said. "But there is no time for walking now—you shall have to ride."

"Ride?" I asked, surprised. "Ride what?"

I needn't have asked. Already Felpz was changing, his dark coat ruffling and expanding, his hair becoming a shaggy mane, and in a moment it was not Felpz, but a brown-and-purple wolf that stood before me: larger than ever he had appeared before, this time he was almost the size of a pony, and had to drop one foreleg so I could scramble onto his back.

"Have no care for my pelt," he growled up at me, his voice strangely guttural coming from the wolf's throat. "Hold fast!"

Taking him at his word I dug my hands into the fur between his shoulders, and clamped my knees to his sides.

"Good," he said, and took off, hurtling through the gates and onto the moor.

If the hunt had been a thrilling ride, it was nothing compared to the ride Felpz gave me then, tearing across the moor and leaping clear over valleys and dells. At times I felt weightless, and I believe we flew for short periods. The land blurred around us, but the sky remained clear, and in it I saw the wispy clouds had solidified into stark bands. These all curved down towards a place near the horizon, as though some invisible force was pulling them in, but more than that I could not see. The world became a blur, and the wind stung my eyes.

Once, the sky was marred with the black bodies of ravens, as they swirled, croaking, around us, and Felpz howled in response. Then the birds retreated, and Felpz, if possible, ran even faster.

Just as my muscles were beginning to burn and my hands to ache, Felpz dug his hindquarters in and came to a stop, whereupon I tumbled over his shoulder and landed in the grass at his feet.

He had changed his form and was man-shaped once more—his hair only a little ruffled from the journey—but he was red in the face and breathing heavily. He was staring beyond me, not bothering to help me rise or even confirm that I was unhurt, and when I rolled myself over I saw why.

We stood at the top of the ridge separating Deerling Grove from the strange valley with the stone trees that Clarkia and I had discovered on the day of the hunt. But while I could see the grove below and behind me, before us, where the valley of stone trees should have been, there was an angry veil of wind, like a whirlpool viewed from under water. It produced a faint roaring sound, and completely encircled the bottom of the caldera.

"What in Heaven's name is that?" I whispered, finding my voice at last.

Felpz glanced down at me, his face grim and his shoulders set, and shook his head.

"Of all the foolish things to do," he murmured, then seemed to realize the question I had put him.

"It is a vortex," he said, and pointed at the sky, to where the sharp, white clouds were twining together above us. "I should have guessed immediately, but I did not wish to think . . . I have the horrible feeling that I have failed our client utterly."

"Never, Felpz," I said, getting to my feet. "Explain what is going on!"

Felpz drew in a deep breath, as if he needed to muster his strength just to do so.

"Someone—and I assume it is Hortall—has created a vortex of the moor magic, blending it with his own, so as to isolate that patch of land within from all comers."

"Even yourself?" I asked.

"*Especially* me," Felpz said bitterly, grinding his teeth. "It is the nature of a magical vortex to absorb any magic that is fed into it—even now I feel its pull—and if I were to try to enter it . . . no, that would make things infinitely *worse.*"

"What of the people inside, then?" I asked. "What of Hortall?"

"If he remains within the center, he will be unaffected," Felpz said. "It is like the eye of a storm: all is calm in the middle. That is where he waits. Unfortunately that is where Magician Aldeer is as well."

I felt despair sink heavy in my stomach, but I had to ask: "How are you sure?"

"The ravens told me so," said Felpz.

Then my friend sat down upon the grassy slope, crossed his arms over his knees, and rested his chin on them. I had never before seen him look so defeated, and the sight shook me.

"Is there nothing we can do?" I asked, helplessly.

"We can wait for Gandlyn," said Felpz. "He may be able to do things that I cannot."

When Gandlyn arrived, however, it was with a flurry of desperate flapping as Kierel struggled, and only barely succeeded, in not being sucked into the vortex herself. She landed in a heap of white wings, and fairly dragged herself over the ground towards us, keeping her head low. Gandlyn slid off her neck, and immediately stumbled down the hill towards the vortex, catching himself just in time on a clump of heather.

"It affects you too, my friend," said Felpz wanly.

Gandlyn glared at us, but the fury in his face seemed distant, and I realized we were not the intended targets.

"She is within!" he cried fiercely, crawling over to us, his hands fisting in the short grass. "She is within, and I cannot reach her! That devil, if I had a clear shot at him now, I'd—"

"You would do something unbefitting an *enhauron*," Felpz said smoothly, cutting the other man off.

Gandlyn came up next to us, still hunching low over the earth, while Kierel retreated further, disappearing behind the crest of the ridge.

"What we need," he said through gritted teeth, "is a *dragon.*"

"A dragon could destroy the vortex," Felpz said, nodding. "But it would likely take most of the moor with it. No, I think our best course of action is to starve the thing. Not the ideal solution, I'll grant you, but if you can seal off the grove I believe I can—"

He stopped abruptly, staring down at the whirling wall of wind and magic—which I now saw created a circle in the center of the valley. At its closest border, where the whipping air met the grass of the hillside, a dark figure had appeared, apparently having fought its way out of the maelstrom. We all watched as it dropped to its knees and crawled the last few feet, before collapsing upon its face, half out of the vortex.

Even from this distance I recognized the flyaway dark hair and supple figure of Jaria Hortall, and even after all her father had done I felt a strong chord of pity for her.

"Great gods," whispered Felpz, his eyes gone wide in horror.

"Is she entirely stripped?" Gandlyn asked. "I cannot go any nearer."

"I think . . . yes . . . but I believe she lives," Felpz said, and paced back and forth along the hillside.

Both magicians, I realized, could not approach the vortex for fear of their magic—and by extension, themselves—being sucked into it.

Well, I thought to myself, I have no worries in that regard. And I trussed up my skirts and scrambled down the hill towards the figure of Jaria Hortall.

Approaching the vortex I felt nothing much of anything save a slight, pungent breeze. Yet when I reached out to pluck at her shirt my hand temporarily dipped within the wall of wind, and it was like thrusting it into a torrent of cold water. I had to pull back immediately, and take Jaria by the shoulders in order to drag her clear.

Once she was free of the vortex I felt her stir beneath my hands, and she moaned faintly. Thus encouraged I placed one of her arms over my neck and began to drag her slowly up the hill.

It was a good thing she was such a slight young person, for I might not have made it otherwise. Felpz and Gandlyn were perfectly helpless, though once I got level with them they both rushed over and crowded around Jaria.

"Are you unharmed?" Felpz asked, which confused me, since the girl was unconscious. Then I realized he was asking *me*.

"Perfectly," I said. "What about *her*?"

"She has been nearly completely stripped," Gandlyn said, laying the young woman out on her back and carefully tilting her head so she might breathe more easily. "What she needs is to be away from this place. Better yet, somewhere with strong ambient magics."

"If you can get her to the grove, that would probably be best," Felpz said. "It has kept itself apart from the vortex, somehow. We must take a chance with the wolves, I'm afraid, but I don't think Jaria was entirely supportive of her father's schemes, otherwise he would not have allowed this to happen to her. We must hope that will be enough."

Gandlyn nodded shortly, and carefully picked up Jaria's limp body and retreated with it over the ridge.

"Do you mean to say she has been stripped of her magic?" I asked, once they had gone.

"Very nearly," said Felpz. "It has taken a great deal of her life with it. And that is why, Corianne, neither myself or Gandlyn can dare even to approach that thing."

He spoke bitterly, resentfully, and I realized then how truly hopeless our situation was. In my desperation I cast about for something—anything—that we might do, and to my surprise a solution presented itself immediately. Something so obvious I was surprised Felpz had not mentioned it.

"Felpz," I said, cautiously, not quite believing it would be so simple. "You say the vortex sucks in magic—your magic, Gandlyn's magic, the magic of the moor . . . "

Felpz nodded.

"Well," I went on. "I haven't got any magic, save the reverse-magic stuff you seem convinced I have. Couldn't *I* go into the vortex?"

Felpz looked at me and nodded sadly, and I realized that he *had* thought of this, probably from the moment he had set eyes on the vortex, and yet he had said nothing.

Had said nothing, because suggesting it would mean sending me, alone and unguarded, into an unknown situation of great peril. I was deeply touched that he should consider it unacceptable to place such a burden upon my shoulders, but this made me all the more determined to take it up myself.

"Then I shall go," I said, getting to my feet before the momentary swell of courage deserted me.

"Corianne," my friend said quietly. "You have already done so much. I cannot ask you to do this."

"I do not believe you have, friend," I replied shortly, knowing the longer I stood there the more likely I would be to lose my resolve. "I do this for Clarkia, and my friends at Deerling Hall."

Felpz looked at me, seeming then to be older than I had ever seen him. He nodded once, jerkily, and I turned from him and walked down the hill.

I had to crouch by the vortex for some minutes, working up the courage to go inside. Poking my arm into the current I found it was not overpowering, but still I entered on my hands and knees, my face turned away from the wind so I had some hope of breathing.

But it was not exactly wind, I found. It tugged on my blood and bones in a way that tickled unpleasantly, but fortunately I was able to breathe without trouble. After a while of crawling, when nothing came out of the air to strike me, and I grew accustomed to the constant pressure, I stood up and tried looking around.

Everything was dim and cloaked in grey, as if a heavy mist hung over the land. At the same time the air was streaked with the not-winds of the vortex, making it even more difficult to see. Nevertheless, I was able to make out the rough shapes of the stone trees looming all around me.

The wind of magic grew stronger the further I progressed, and I was forced to a crawl once again, and then to drag myself on my belly, and finally I had to stop. The pressure here was too great, and I feared that whatever force was controlling the wind would suck me in—as it had already done to Jaria's magic.

Then something remarkable happened.

The wind stopped.

That is not to say that it *ceased*. Simply that the current was forced to a standstill, and as a result, chaos erupted in the air all around me. It swirled and curled, like water does in a bowl that has been stirred into a whirl, when the direction of that stirring is reversed. Sparks of light like dancing butterflies blossomed, flapped, and went out. There was an ominous screeching sound, and then the wind began to pick up again.

Only this time it was going in the opposite direction, and the feeling of being sucked *in* had been replaced with the feeling of being cast *out,* and I realized if I was to make it to the eye of the storm it was now or never, before the winds became too strong.

I picked myself up and ran, as best I could, through the stone forest. My feet quickly disappeared into a thick sea of pink and yellow flowers, and I knew I was nearing the center of the valley. The wind strengthened, and still I forged on, through the white haze that was solidifying around me.

I fought through it like a madwoman, forcing each step to follow another, and finally one of them took me out of the storm, and I stumbled forward into a drift of flowers.

I surfaced, spitting petals, to find the sun shining down on my face and the air thick with the smell of flowers. Around me the wall of wind whirled silently, circling an area of land near the center of the valley, but whose far border I could not see because of the thick forest of stone trees that lay between us. Above me, arching into the sky, the funnel of the vortex widened, and beyond that it looked like steam was belching into the sky.

Much of this I registered later, for immediately I found my attention grabbed by a nearby cluster of stone trees, against one of which was slumped the form of Clarkia Aldeer. She was leaning with her back against the grey trunk, her legs bracing herself there, but her head was hanging forward so her chin rested on her breast, her eyes shut.

"Clarkia," I called to her, walking over a little wobbly.

She looked up at my approach, and though her brown face was drawn and tired, there was a triumphant light in her eyes.

"What has happened?" I asked as I drew near. "Are you hurt?"

Clarkia shook her head vigorously, but she did not stand. "Just tired," she said, and laughed. "Hortall will have fits when he sees you; he was so certain no one could reach us here."

"I very nearly didn't," I said. "Were it not for the break in the wind—where *is* Hortall?" I asked, looking about nervously.

"Around," said Clarkia. "The moor doesn't like us being together, which is the only reason I was able do what I did. He's *strong*, Corianne. I should have listened to Felpz."

I nodded, but only with half my mind. "What *have* you done?" I asked. "Was it you that reversed the wind?"

Clarkia's grin spread wider. "Not just the wind," said she; "the whole gods-damned *vortex*. He had it set up to suck the magic *in*, and put a lot of his own power into it—but mostly Jaria's. Corianne, if she's still alive, you must forgive her. None of this is her fault, and she did fight him, at the last."

I nodded. "She made it out; Gandlyn is taking her to the grove."

Clarkia smiled at this. "That's as good a place as any. Probably a better place to do what I did than this . . . but you work with what you've got."

"Clarkia," I said, for I had looked up then at the sky and noticed the huge, billowing piles of steam streaming into the air. "What is happening?"

"I told you," said Clarkia. "I *reversed* his vortex! Set it spinning *out*, instead of *in*. And I pushed all the human magic—the stuff that's been laid on this land like chains—into it. It's all draining out now, all the power of the Deerlings. I'm casting it free—let the wolves decide what to do with it. I am done with this place, Corianne. It is not my home, and I see now it never will be."

She sighed and leaned back against the stone tree.

Almost as soon as she had done so her eyes snapped open and she jerked herself upright. "Oh *hell*," she muttered. "Behind me, Corianne—I hoped the moor would keep him away a little longer, but when have my hopes counted for anything?"

Turning, I saw Erren Hortall had appeared from behind a large stone trunk, and was striding through the flowers towards us.

Gone was the bandage from his arm, and gone too was any sign of congeniality or good nature. His face was twisted in rage, and he left a black trail through the flowers in which tiny insects, like flies, were buzzing.

I did not like to hide, but I knew I had no choice. I backed away, taking myself out of the line of fire, my whole body tense.

That was all Clarkia seemed to be waiting for. Pushing herself off the stone she ran at Hortall, who had a moment of surprise break his fiery glare, and then he was running too.

I shouted at them to stop, knowing it was futile, and could only watch as the two magicians met, grappling with each other like ruffians in a brawl, and then suddenly the wind rose up all around us. It lifted us in a storm of petals, rising up into the sky.

But while the magicians continued to rise, borne away by the wind, I immediately began to fall. I had a moment of supreme fear, and then I felt myself caught by large, cool, furry bodies, and I felt vines twining around my arms to hold me in place. I glimpsed an amber, triangular ear, and beyond it a swarm of woodwolves, all streaming through the air.

Above us I saw the bottom of the vortex, still rising into the sky, dispersing clouds of mist and magic, but no sign did I see of Clarkia or Hortall—they were lost in that churning maelstrom.

The wolves brought me down to earth and left me sitting against a stone tree—which had been covered by a thick layer of springy green moss dotted with flowers—before they streamed away onto the moor, leaving a blanket of flowers in their wake.

This time, however, in addition to the flowers, young shoots and saplings emerged, growing to chest height in a few moments, putting out strong green leaves as they went, before their growth slowed to a more normal speed.

I sat there, my heart pounding, gulping in the thick, sweet air, until my head settled. Even then I found I was too tired to move, and it was there, among the moss-covered stones and the supple young trees, half covered in flowers myself, that Felpz and Gandlyn eventually found me.

Chapter 9:
Theories Regarding the Disappearance of Clarkia Aldeer

THE WOLVES, I LATER LEARNED, did not stop at the valley of the stone trees, but quickly spread to every corner of the moor. They were seen streaming north by Dr Verdemeister and her ravens, and by Tida Hammin in the south. They were glimpsed by the staff at Merrybriar, and though they gave Mothwitch Farm a wide berth, their howling could be heard all around.

They also passed over Gandlyn's house, but Deerling Hall they surrounded, and waited patiently outside its gates until Milky, showing the good sense that got him into such a position of trust from Felpz, came out to talk to them.

I was never quite clear on *how* they spoke, but they made Milky understand they were there to undo the magic of someone they called the Bad Deer, by whom Milky assumed they meant Erren Hortall. So he let them in, and not only did they cure Hewlith, but they also restored and returned Mrs Wreath's hand. Then they left, leaving the hall adrift in flowers, with several new saplings starting up in the front courtyard.

In the course of that afternoon the whole moor went through a similar transformation, and its inhabitants looked around in awe at the vibrant sea of flowers that now carpeted the hills, and the small, slender trees that were erupting everywhere.

These grew to the size of young trees in under an hour, whence they appeared to stabilize—with only small bursts of visible growth every few hours thereafter. Dr Verdemeister took it upon herself to document the change, and it was thanks to her that we had reliable records of the event.

For I fear the testimonies of the four people who were closest to the vortex were all in some way compromised.

Jaria, once she came around, had little memory of recent events, though she seemed aware of her father's betrayal. The magic of the grove had saved her life, but she was a worn shadow of the young woman I had first met, the fire that had sustained her reduced to the faintest of embers.

Gandlyn was so angry he could barely see straight, much less talk coherently. The fact that he, an *enhauron,* had been stopped in his tracks by the work of a mere wizard was both shameful and humbling to him. Moreso, I think he was aching over the loss of Clarkia, as indeed we all were, but I came to realize that the bond they had forged was stronger than any of us had imagined, and for many weeks afterwards he was cast into a deep depression.

Felpz was quiet and still, and of our number the only one who seemed able to string the events together. In this way what he said was perfectly clear, but also too incredible for anyone who had not been there to believe.

Hortall had created a vortex, he explained (first to me, and then to a string of other people). It was the type of vortex which sucked in magic from the surrounding land and used it to feed upon itself. Hortall had gotten it started by using his daughter's magic, and formed it around himself and Clarkia, so that they would be effectively isolated from any possible means of interference. Not even Felpz could approach for fear of being sucked in, thereby making it even stronger.

But Hortall had reckoned without the magic of the land itself; the magic which lay beneath the magic of the Deerlings and even the magic of the wood, which was the cause of the peculiar spatial irregularities that characterized both the moor and the ancient wood. It had not taken kindly to the presence of the vortex, and contrived to prevent him confronting Clarkia long enough for her to reverse the direction of the vortex, so that instead of feeding the magic into Hortall, as he had intended, it cast the magic up and *out*. In doing so she stripped the moor of the magic of the Deerlings, which had lain heavy upon it for centuries.

With this interfering magic gone, the wood was able to send out its envoys in the form of the wolves to retake its old territory. It was a good thing too. Hortall, Clarkia and myself had been caught up in the tail end of the vortex, and I might have come to harm had the wolves not intercepted me.

But what of Clarkia and Hortall? For that we had only my garbled account of seeing them swept off into the sky, which Felpz interpreted as Clarkia using the last of the vortex to cast themselves out of the world, along with the Deerling magic.

This was a distressing prospect, but one that became more and more likely as time went by, and no sign was seen of either Clarkia Aldeer or Erren Hortall.

As for myself, I could only tell people what I had seen. Which, though it corroborated Felpz's story, was equally incredible. And it wasn't until weeks later, after we had exhausted our search of the moor, that I remembered the sentiment Clarkia had expressed while the magic of the Deerlings was being siphoned off.

I am done with this place, Corianne. It is not my home, and never will be.

When I relayed these words to Felpz his face fell, but then he smiled sadly and shook his head.

"Well do I know the feeling of being finished with the world," he said. "She would probably have left anyway, even had Hortall not attacked her." He sighed. "And to her credit, she did an admirable job. The wolves have thoroughly retaken the moor, and in their wake the old forest is reseeding itself. Dr Verdemeister's *Zaubergezeitenändern* has come. And with less bloodshed than we feared. The humans will have to adapt, but then, what are humans *but* adaptable?"

"But what will become of her? Of Clarkia?"

Felpz looked unhappily out the window, to where a warm summer rain was making the sea of flowers dance. We were in my room at Deerling Hall, which had served as our base of operations, but was now bare as I packed my belongings in anticipation of our journey home the next day.

"I cannot say," he said in a small voice. "There are many paths for a magician to take, once they are out of this world. What will become of Hortall, too, I wonder? Their fight is probably not over, and they may settle their score where no one—not even you—may reach them."

"How thoroughly unsatisfactory," I said, as I put the last of my effects into my steamer trunk.

"Indeed," said Felpz, his mouth a grim line. "Unsatisfactory indeed."

We were not the only ones to think so. Gandlyn met us at the gate when we went to depart, and strode beside Tida Hammin's cart as she drove us into Greenwitch. He had jettisoned the neat, green suit, and now walked briskly along the road in robes of flowing emerald, with a cloak like moss thrown over one shoulder. Though they looked out of place next to Felpz's frock coat and myself and Tida's sensible dresses, I thought they suited him much better. He'd let his auburn hair down as well, and in his hand he carried his staff, its end thudding into the road with every stride. In the skies above us Kierel was soaring lazily, her wings occasionally eclipsing the sun like a feathery cloud.

"I have spoken with Jaria Hortall," Gandlyn told us in his direct way. "She readily confirmed that Hortall had been perfecting his stone spell for decades—though she had no idea what it was for until Morgrainne died. She told me he got the idea from the stone forest near Deerling grove—which, it appears, dates back to the coming of humans to Riddlewood."

Felpz gave a short nod. "That is as I thought."

Jaria, I must say, had been treated most fairly by all the inhabitants of Riddlemoor. When it became clear that she had only aided her father under duress, Sergeant Lecreux dropped all charges and gave her the option of moving into Greenwitch to live with her mother's family. Jaria had only spent a week in their charge, however, before she returned to Deerling Hall, where the incomparable Mrs Wreath, now fully recovered from her temporary loss of a hand, oversaw the young woman's recovery. The last I heard of her, Jaria had felt well enough to take light exercise, and was expressing an interest in taking Scarlatta for a ride.

I should mention that both Bangle and Snowflake were eventually recovered, and though they were missed for several days they came out of their escapade with no permanent damage.

"It still does not explain what the magic was that afflicted Morgrainne's family," Gandlyn continued. "They, and their old servants, are still trees. Healthy trees, if that counts for anything. But still . . . the wolves were quite ready to restore del Garren and Mrs Wreath. It leads me to believe that the attack on her family thirty years ago was something else altogether."

"Yes," sighed Felpz. "I admit, I have no concrete ideas on that point. It may have to remain a mystery . . . unless, of course, Clarkia and Hortall return to tell *their* tale."

Gandlyn pursed his lips, and his staff stabbed into the wet earth of the road even more fiercely.

"That man," he practically snarled. "That *man* . . . the more I learn of him from his daughter, the more I wish I had a chance— just a *chance*—to face him. Clarkia *is* an extraordinary magician, and I trust her above anyone, but . . . " he broke off and had to look away. I was reminded then, not for the first time, how young he looked, and how fierce young love could be.

"It is the most difficult thing," I said, to no one in particular. "When someone you care about a great deal goes someplace you cannot follow. It is like being stranded on a bleak shore, and though you trust that they can navigate the stormy sea, you don't know when, if ever, they will find their way back to you."

The two mages on either side of me were silent after this, and Tida Hammin gave me a curious look.

"You speak from personal experience," she said at last.

I nodded. Gandlyn must have caught the motion out of the corner of his eye, for his head snapped around to look at us.

"Yes," he said, sounding a little stunned. "Yes, it is *exactly* like that. But also worse, I think. Because I am not bound to any shore. I *could* follow, if only I knew where."

Felpz turned in his seat at that, and regarded the young mage gravely.

"I beg," he said quietly. "Do not do anything rash. There will come a time when you must leave this world—if only temporarily—but it is *my* experience best not to take that leap until the right time comes."

"I shall take that under advisement," said Gandlyn, his voice steeped in bitterness. But he looked up and gave me a brief smile. "Your words as well." Then he gestured to Kierel, and the huge eagle swooped down to land a safe distance from the cart, Gandlyn leaving the road to trudge through the grass and flowers towards her. Craning my head back I saw him mount, and then the giant bird leapt into the air, her wings blazing in the sun, Gandlyn's robe a streak of green streaming behind her. She circled once, to gain height, and then they were off, gliding south towards Wizard's House.

"She may yet reappear in this world," Tida remarked as she saw us off at the train station. "And you can be sure, the minute she does, I will know of it."

We thanked her, and though the sun shone on our departure, I couldn't shake the feeling of wan, grey disappointment that hung heavy above us.

Tida Hammin was as good as her word, and continued to investigate Clarkia's disappearance with her trademark vivaciousness. It was to no avail, however, and I was not particularly surprised when, a fortnight after our return to Redling, Felpz put his head into my room to tell me that Gandlyn had resigned his post as parish wizard and left Riddlemoor.

"Supposedly he has returned to Delpheon," Felpz said with a wry smile. "But I believe he has gone somewhere altogether more distant."

"Do you think he will find her?" I asked.

Felpz shrugged. "I can hope," he said. "It is a small chance, I must admit. But I find it soothing that Clarkia has someone like that searching for her."

Yet I do not think it soothed Felpz sufficiently, for in the months—and, subsequently, years—that followed, he would sometimes go missing for weeks at a time. No reason nor explanation would he give, and he always returned worn out and defeated. And though I told myself that these journeys must be related to the ongoing cases he continued to take, in my heart I knew that he could not let the matter rest any more than Gandlyn, and that Clarkia must in fact have *two* magicians searching for her.

And while that did not entirely assuage my own worries, I was anchored firmly in the material world, and could do nothing but wait and hope.

I had gotten this far in my original treatment of this story, which I wrote during the following winter, when I ran into difficulty putting an ending onto it. I battered myself against several different closings, all of which I found singularly unsatisfactory, until I realized the problem was that the story I was telling did not *have* a satisfying ending—yet. Perhaps some writers would have been comfortable letting the story out such as it was, but I could not suffer the thought of inflicting such an aggravating conclusion upon my readers. An ending which is no ending, I think, is the worst sort of trick to play upon a reader—who rightfully expects some form of closure at the end of a book.

So I put the whole thing aside, telling myself that it wasn't worth publishing without a pleasurable conclusion, but if such an ending ever presented itself then I could pull it out again and finish it properly.

Well, it has been almost eleven years—half the time, I must say, that I had to wait for Felpz—and now at last I can give you, dear reader, the closure you no doubt desire.

In the end it was not Gandlyn, nor Felpz, nor even Tida Hammin—who had since moved away from Riddlemoor—who discovered what had become of Clarkia Aldeer. Indeed, we might never have known what her fate was, had she not taken the trouble to come and tell us herself.

Yes, true to her independent nature, it was Clarkia Aldeer who found her own self and brought it home.

Home, that is, to *Beranica,* where she lived the reclusive life of a hermit for a few years, before remembering what an abrupt departure she had made from her adopted country, and deciding to drop in and see how everyone was getting on.

I was well settled into my house in Stanton Leaning by this time, and had been enjoying the peace and quiet of the country immensely, when I tottered out into my kitchen one morning to discover a pot of tea steeping on the table and a lean, brown-skinned woman with wild black hair reclining on a chair behind it.

I am ashamed to say I almost didn't recognize her after all the years that had passed. My eyesight had declined since I moved away from Felpz, and I had to fumble for my glasses and peer at her through them for several moments.

When recognition hit, however, it was like a load of falling bricks, and Clarkia threw back her head and laughed at my expression.

"Yes, Corianne, it's me!" she said, her voice at least unchanged. "And I'm happy to see you, too. Sorry for letting myself in, but the time difference from Terangahela is such that I've been keeping odd hours, and I arrived in the middle of the night! But look, I've made you tea, so please sit down and enjoy a cup."

"My dear!" I cried, gasping for breath a little. "Tea is the last thing on my mind! Look at you! Live as a spring bird, in my kitchen, after all this time! Blast the tea, tell me where you have *been* all these years! Are you well? Whatever happened between you and Hortall? Have you been back to Riddlemoor yet? Have you seen Gandlyn? Terangahela, you say? What strange world is that?"

Clarkia chuckled, and I saw how her skin had gone wrinkled and dry around her mouth and brow. She was no longer a young woman at all, but her eyes had not lost their brightness.

Indeed, they blazed with a kind of intensity I had only ever seen in Felpz—and possibly Gandlyn as well.

"Where to begin?" she said, still smiling. "Perhaps *I'll* need the tea before the morning is out. Well, first, Terangahela is no strange world—it's a really nice country on the east coast of South Beranica. I've been making it my home for the last two years—had always meant to get out there, but then I was called north to my great inheritance and . . . well . . . you know how *that* ended."

"Oh, but I do *not*," I insisted. "The last I saw, you were swept off into the sky with that devil, Hortall! We have all been worried sick over you—Gandlyn especially."

Clarkia's eyes dimmed at that, and something like guilt settled over her face. The lines were not all wrinkles I saw now, as the light from the window strengthened with the rising sun. There was a faint latticework of pale lines, fine as a spider's web, that decorated her left cheek. But whether they were scars or some intentional decoration I could not say. She was wearing clothes similar to the ones in which I had first seen her: a rusty-brown cotton shirt tucked into heavy beige dungarees, and around her neck hung an assortment of bead necklaces and pendants on leather thongs. Her hair had been pulled back into a ponytail, but still contrived to frizz out into a dark halo around her head.

"I'm sorry about that," she said. "Gods, I have a lot of apologies to make, don't I? But I can start by explaining everything to you, can't I? You will see the story shared, so I won't have to repeat myself a thousand times."

"That will do *admirably,* and yes," I said, pulling up a chair and reaching for my notebook. "You can count on me. Please explain, and then we shall both have a good breakfast before facing the rest of your old friends."

Clarkia smiled at that. "Well, to take your questions in order: I've been in a great many places in the years since I left you. Which, it turns out, were more years for me than for you. I make it to be roughly twenty, but that's only an estimate. Some of the places I went time doesn't flow properly. Anyway, that's not so important. I am well—and that *is*. Better than I ever was, in fact. What happened with Hortall? Hmm, that's a heavier matter. Give me a moment; it *has* been a while for me.

"Let me think . . . last you saw we were being swept up into the sky? Ah, that takes me back. Well, firstly nothing was *sweeping* us anywhere. I knew I was going to have to settle with him, and I preferred not to do it where we might hurt unwitting observers. So I took us up and out. If you got tumbled up in it, I'm really sorry. I tried not to include you. That was kind of the point. But things got out of control there, and I could only do my best. Anyway, I wasn't sure exactly where we went—all I knew is I needed to get *away*. Out. And with the vortex still lending me strength, well, I was able to pull us clean out of . . . what you would call the *world*. Or at least one level of it."

I nodded. "I am familiar with the multiplicity of our world," I said, smiling a little. "It's like a house with many stories, and spaces in between. I didn't live most my life with Bouragner Felpz for nothing."

Clarkia nodded. "I never thought of it that way, but it's a good analogy. Anyway, I got us safely onto a different, er, *floor,* I guess you'd say. And then we had . . . well, we had a good, proper fight." She folded her hands over her stomach, and made an involuntary motion as if she meant to swing her legs up onto the table. She caught herself, however, and went on.

"You might not find the details so interesting, but I suppose Felpz'll want to know. Fact is, it was a close one. Hortall was older than me, had more practice, and was just as strong—in a hard, gnarled way. He knew tricks I had no idea how to counter—but then again, *so did I.* We were neither of us pure Deerling, for all that's what got us into that mess. He had his Rani heritage, and I . . . well, I'm a product of the Beranican melting pot. Got a bit of everything in me, including some Maroké—and *they* have as strong a tie to the magic of the Beranican plains as the Deerlings had to the moor. It's not a magic Hortall had ever seen before, and it gave me enough of an edge that, with the help of some lucky breaks, I was able to defeat him.

"He was such a sore sport, though. He really wanted me *dead,* and that shocked me. I told him there was no possible chance of him inheriting the Deerling title, since you and Felpz and Gandlyn and the rest all knew the truth—and besides, I'd pulled their magic out of the moor. It wouldn't *mean anything* even if he did inherit. That just made him more angry. But he said things, because he was so mad, that he might not otherwise. That's how I learned that he was the one who enchanted Morgrainne's family."

"You mean the original plague?" I asked.

"Yeah," said Clarkia. "The one that turned her father, brother, daughter and grandson to trees. Only that hadn't been the point, he said. He'd wanted them to *die.* But apparently the wolves got wind of it, and managed to subvert the spell so the people just got turned into trees, and they moved them all into the grove so they could keep them safe. They also fixed Morgrainne and her mother up, I guess, because after that Hortall's spell didn't affect them. I guess that's when he started work on the stone spell, to get around the magic of the wolves."

I nodded, as the final piece of the puzzle fell into place.

"Dare I ask," said I, "what became of him?"

Clarkia shrugged. "He won't be coming back. Ever. I didn't kill him—I thought it was important, after everything, that *I* not kill anyone—but there are people out there in the wider realms who . . . well. I guess they're sort of like this world's natural defense against bad apples like Hortall. I got one to take him on as their *gardener,* of all things! Hortall was furious, of course, but there was nothing he could do. They took the rest of his magic away, and besides, most of the folks you meet in the wider realm—they're a lot more magical than us."

I did not share Clarkia's certainty, until I remembered the dream lord, Badgrave, and the royal dragon, Kasarvo—not to mention the Queen of Dreams herself. They were certainly the kind of folk you would meet in the wider realms, and I had to admit, even Erren Hortall paled in comparison to them.

"What happened then?" I asked. "Why did you not return to Kyreland?"

Clarkia colored, and looked down at the floor. "To be honest?" she said. "I got lost. That was why I had to foist Hortall off onto one of the dream folk—by rights I should have brought him back to stand trial, but in our fight we'd chased each other through so many different worlds that by the time I caught him I was totally turned around. It took me a long time just to find my way back to an area that I recognized, and once there, I realized what an amazing opportunity it was for me to travel. I'm ashamed to say I got carried away in my explorations. I found this amazing inn which traveled around all the worlds, and I stayed there for a long time—each day going out and exploring a different place. I saw so many places, it felt like centuries—and it felt like no time at all. I met a dragon, and they let me walk with them through the Dragon Lands, which are something else, believe me! By the end of that I began to feel homesick, but I couldn't face going back to Kyreland . . . so I went home. My old home. First to Mackanaw, where it came as a shock that I'd been gone almost a decade *and* that I had doubled in physical age. So I moved out to Terangahela, which is mostly mountains. I'd missed mountains, with their steep valleys and fast rivers, and I pretty much buried myself in them for two years, until I got the nagging feeling that I couldn't get on with my life until I'd made sure things were settled back in Kyreland. Besides, I'd left all my old stuff here, and I wanted it back. And I realized, with all the things I'd learned from traveling between worlds, it's not such a hard thing to do to get from one end of the globe to the other—if you don't mind taking some funny paths.

"First thing I did was drop in at Deerling Grove and check on my relatives there. The wood's been getting on nicely, though the Deerlings are as treeish as ever. I don't think there's any hope of turning them back, and really, if I were them, I wouldn't want to. Losing time—any which way—isn't a pleasant feeling, and being a tree doesn't seem so bad. I might try it myself, one day.

"Anyway, after that I went over to the hall. Have you been back recently? Maybe you heard, but Mrs Wreath and Roke have moved on. Wreath is at Merrybriar now, and Roke at Mothwitch. But Hewlith's still there, and would you believe it, so is Jaria! Yes! And Scarlatta—though she's not as spry as she once was. I guess Jaria's been keeping an eye on the new magic, and helping folks out what need helping. Pretty much what Morgrainne used to do, only less officially. She was given stewardship of Deerling Hall, you know, being the last remaining relation, and nearly fell over herself to give it back to me. I insisted she keep it, of course. She has it set up as a halfway house for troubled young mages, and it seemed a shame to mess all that up.

"She's changed her name, too. Going by Brewdin, which was her mother's name. Don't think she's any prouder of her Deerling heritage than I am. But I'm glad she came out of it all right. When I last saw her . . . well, you probably figured out Hortall used *her* magic to seed the vortex. I saw the end of it and . . . well, if the moor hadn't separated us I might have killed him in the heat of the moment.

"One last thing: I had them move Morgrainne's body. She's got a nice grave in Deerling Grove now, next to her own mother, so that family is back together at least.

"I'd intended to make peace with Gandlyn too, but he wasn't at Riddlemoor, and no one I asked knew what had become of him. So my next stop, I figured, would be to see Felpz about that. Then I discovered you were living here, and I thought I'd visit *you* first, since you were so supportive of me back in the day. I really can't thank you enough."

Clarkia looked at me earnestly from across the table, the morning sun now shining in through the rosebush that half blocked the kitchen window. Its dappled light caught the frizzy ends of her hair a brilliant copper, and she almost seemed to glow.

"My dear," I began, and found my throat had closed itself off with emotion. I spent a moment getting it unstuck, during which time Clarkia leaned forward and poured us both cups of tea out of self defense.

"I am so happy you thought of me," I continued when I could speak again. "I have to say, it has gnawed on me for years what became of you—and it was worse for Gandlyn. I don't know where he is either, but I can say he left this world searching for *you*. You should definitely see Felpz, and lose no time—it's an agony to think of you here, practically where you left him, and he off in some unimaginably distant world."

Yet Clarkia was strangely reticent when it came to finding her old amour. I was partially sympathetic, understanding the great amount of time that had elapsed and the changes that could wreak upon a person. Clarkia was not the tender young thing she had been, and I hazarded that Gandlyn had also been altered in the intervening years. Still, it was the final thread that needed tying off, and so I bundled her onto a train that afternoon, and we showed up on Felpz's doorstep without bothering to warn him.

Not that it mattered. Felpz must have sensed us coming, and came down to greet us. He was as intrigued by Clarkia's story as I had been, and asked her a great many questions unrelated to the case of Riddlemoor. Clarkia answered them bemusedly, and it was up to me to broach the topic of Gandlyn's whereabouts.

Felpz practically glowed at this, and sent Clarkia off with a list of instructions and a request that she notify him immediately as soon as the *enhauron* was found.

We had a message the very next day. It was short, but came in two parts—each written in a different hand. The first paragraph was from Clarkia, saying that she had found Gandlyn, and that the two of them would continue to travel, but together this time. Below that was a single line, printed in Delpheonian script, which Felpz translated for me.

"It says, simply, *thank you,*" he said, looking fondly at the little slip of paper. "He remains as terse as ever. But it's not a bad outcome, don't you think?"

"Not bad at all," I said, smiling back at my friend. "Quite satisfactory, in fact."

Epilogue

IF YOU VISIT RIDDLEMOOR TODAY the first thing you will notice is that it is not really a moor any longer. There are trees, young and slender, growing everywhere. The strange magic that distorts space is still omnipresent, and makes travel difficult, but I understand it has become a popular holiday destination, famous for the thick beds of pink, yellow, and white flowers that bloom in profusion every summer.

The inhabitants remain largely unaffected, though there were some complaints regarding the *invasion of the trees* at first. Even now, eleven years after the change, people still insist on referring to the resurgent forest as an invader. When I told Felpz this, he rolled his eyes heavenward.

"What did I tell you, Corianne?" he said. "What *did* I tell you?"

But then he laughed, and I could not help chuckling along with him.

Bouragner Felpz will return in
"The Hand of Rishké"

Escape Velocity

Apsis Fiction 5.2: Aphelion 2017 will appear in July 2017. In it you can look forward to:

"Davebot"
"Out of Space"
and
"The Hand of Rishké"

Find the entire library of *Apsis Fiction* issues at
heliopauseweb.com/fiction/apsis-fiction

Apsis Fiction is a Heliopause Production; written, illustrated, edited and designed by Goldeen Ogawa.

More from Heliopause

heliopauseweb.com

About the Author

Goldeen Ogawa is a self-taught writer, illustrator and cartoonist. She has penned and illustrated dozens of short stories and novellas, three webcomics, and has exhibited her original art in shows all over the world. Outside of Heliopause Productions, she can be found online at *goldeenogawa.com*.

She lives in Bend, Oregon, where she enjoys biking, running, swimming, yoga, and the plethora of excellent restaurants.

About the Text and Design

The body of this book was typeset in Elysium using LaTeX. Cover art and design by the author.